PRAISE FOR BARBARA FREETHY'S
BLOCKBUSTER ROMANTIC SUSPENSE

"POWERFUL AND MOVING."—Karen Robards

"A PAGE-TURNER."—Diane Chamberlain

"ABSORBING...AN EXPLOSIVE CONCLUSION."
—Carla Neggers

"POIGNANT, ROMANTIC, AND
SUSPENSEFUL...THE PERFECT READ."
—Susan Wiggs

"[A] FABULOUS PAGE-TURNING
COMBINATION OF ROMANCE
AND INTRIGUE."—Kristin Hannah

Taken

"Romance sizzles . . . in this riveting page-turner, which boasts a cast of well-drawn, memorable characters, including a fascinating, diabolical villain." —*Library Journal*

"Terrific and twisty intrigue makes this novel choice reading. . . . An amazingly gripping, fascinating mystery."
—*Romantic Times* (4½ stars)

Don't Say a Word

"Barbara Freethy at her best! An absorbing story of two people determined to unravel the secrets, betrayals and questions about their past. The story builds to an explosive conclusion that will leave readers eagerly awaiting Barbara Freethy's next book." —Carla Neggers, author of *Dark Sky*

"*Don't Say a Word* has made me a Barbara Freethy fan for life!" —Diane Chamberlain, author of *The Bay at Midnight*

"Dark, hidden secrets and stunning betrayal . . . potent and moving suspense. Freethy's storytelling ability is top-notch." —*Romantic Times* (4½ stars)

All She Ever Wanted

"A haunting mystery . . . I couldn't put it down."
—Luanne Rice

"A suitably eerie atmosphere." —*Publishers Weekly*

"A gripping tale of romantic suspense. . . . Barbara Freethy is a master storyteller. A fascinating blend of romance, mystery, and suspense. Don't miss it!"
—Romance Reviews Today

"Sizzling. . . . Freethy's expertly penned novel is a true page-turner." —*Romantic Times*

"Fabulous . . . the perfect story to curl up in front of a fire with." —RomanceJunkies.com

continued . . .

Golden Lies

"An absolute treasure, a fabulous, page-turning combination of romance and intrigue. Fans of Nora Roberts and Elizabeth Lowell will love *Golden Lies*." —Kristin Hannah

"Freethy's smooth prose, spirited storytelling, and engaging characters are sure to send readers on a treasure hunt for the author's backlist books." —*Publishers Weekly*

"Multidimensional characters at all levels (especially the strong-willed hero and heroine), realistic and sometimes funny dialog, and a well-constructed plot that Freethy unwraps with such consummate skill that the conclusion is at once a surprising and totally logical result in a rich and compelling tale." —*Library Journal*

Summer Secrets

"Barbara Freethy writes with bright assurance, exploring the bonds of sisterhood and the excitement of blue-water sailing. *Summer Secrets* is a lovely novel." —Luanne Rice

"Freethy skillfully keeps the reader on the hook, and her tantalizing and believable tale has it all—romance, adventure, and mystery." —*Booklist* (starred review)

"An intriguing, multithreaded plot, this is an emotionally involving story . . . sure to please Freethy's growing fan base. . . . Like Kristin Hannah's novels, [it] neatly bridges the gap between romance and traditional women's fiction." —*Library Journal*

"Freethy's zesty storytelling will keep readers hooked." —*Publishers Weekly*

"Freethy is at the top of her form." —*Contra Costa Times*

OTHER BOOKS BY BARBARA FREETHY

Companion book to *Played*:
Taken

Don't Say a Word
All She Ever Wanted
Golden Lies
Summer Secrets

PLAYED

Barbara Freethy

A SIGNET BOOK

SIGNET
Published by New American Library, a division of
Penguin Group (USA) Inc., 375 Hudson Street,
New York, New York 10014, USA
Penguin Group (Canada), 90 Eglinton Avenue East, Suite 700, Toronto,
Ontario M4P 2Y3, Canada (a division of Pearson Penguin Canada Inc.)
Penguin Books Ltd., 80 Strand, London WC2R 0RL, England
Penguin Ireland, 25 St. Stephen's Green, Dublin 2,
Ireland (a division of Penguin Books Ltd.)
Penguin Group (Australia), 250 Camberwell Road, Camberwell, Victoria 3124,
Australia (a division of Pearson Australia Group Pty. Ltd.)
Penguin Books India Pvt. Ltd., 11 Community Centre, Panchsheel Park,
New Delhi - 110 017, India
Penguin Group (NZ), cnr Airborne and Rosedale Roads, Albany,
Auckland 1310, New Zealand (a division of Pearson New Zealand Ltd.)
Penguin Books (South Africa) (Pty.) Ltd., 24 Sturdee Avenue,
Rosebank, Johannesburg 2196, South Africa

Penguin Books Ltd., Registered Offices:
80 Strand, London WC2R 0RL, England

First published by Signet, an imprint of New American Library,
a division of Penguin Group (USA) Inc.

First Printing, October 2006
10 9 8 7 6 5 4 3 2 1

To my brainstorming pals, Candice, Carol, Diana, Barbara Mc., Lynn, and Kate—thanks for all the fabulous ideas and delicious chocolate!

Prologue

He moved like a cat through the dark, narrow tunnels running under the city of San Francisco. The air was damp, filled with odors of dead, rotting animals and standing water. Cobwebs brushed his face at every turn. Rats ran over his feet, disturbed by his presence in a world that belonged solely to them—until now. The secret tunnels had been built during Prohibition to run liquor under the hills of San Francisco and later had been used as escape routes for a band of criminals in the forties and fifties. Few people knew how to navigate the maze of passageways. There were too many stops and starts, too many blocked exits and detours. Fortunately, he had a map that showed him exactly what to do.

Pausing, he turned his flashlight on the yellowed piece of paper in his hand. The lines and directions had been scrawled more than seventy-five years earlier, and it had taken a long and complicated scheme to get his hands on this very important piece of paper. He hoped it had been worth the effort. It was possible that part of the tunnels had collapsed with the development of the city or perhaps due to one of the earthquakes that rumbled through the area every few years, but if his luck held, this path would provide him direct access to the object of his desire.

Redirecting his light on the tunnel in front of him, he continued, confident that he would get what he wanted, as he always did. Many men and a few women had tried to stop him over the years. No one had succeeded. He was quite simply invincible.

He felt a surge of adrenaline as the stream of light bounced off a series of spikes set into the wall in front of him. He stopped, running his finger over one of the ladder steps. Then he threw back his head and looked up. A trapdoor was just above him. He'd found his way in—and his way out.

He thought about the activity going on in the building above him at the Barclay Auction House. They were preparing for the evening's glamorous preview party of Renaissance art and jewelry, including the Benedetti diamond, expected to sell for millions of dollars.

Unless, of course, something happened to the diamond before then . . .

He smiled to himself. At this very moment, the Barclay security team was meeting with the Italian security team, which had accompanied the collection from Florence. They would convince themselves that their security was impenetrable, that no one could steal their precious diamond. But they would be wrong.

Pulling out the ID from his pocket, he gazed at the name that was not his own, at the photo of the face that he had skillfully reconstructed with makeup, contact lenses, tanning spray and hair color. He now knew this man inside and out, his history, his friends, and his relationship to the important people at Barclay's, namely Christina Alberti. She would not suspect that he was not who he appeared to be—until it was too late. The plan was set.

Retracing his steps through the dark tunnel, he exited several blocks away from the auction house, then unzipped his baggy coveralls and tossed them into a nearby Dumpster. He straightened the tie of his black tuxedo. Let the party begin.

1

Flashbulbs popped in her face, one bright, blinding light after another. Christina Alberti paused at the entrance as the cameras continued to snap. She felt like a celebrity, but in truth the photographers were not interested in her, but in the spectacular ninety-seven-carat yellow diamond pendant that she wore on a simple chain around her neck.

While Christina had wanted to display the necklace on black velvet in a secure glass case, the Benedetti family had insisted that a model would bring the diamond to life at this very exclusive preview party. Since the directors of Barclay's hadn't wanted to entrust the valuable diamond to someone outside the auction house, Christina, with her Italian heritage, dark hair, light green eyes, and olive skin, was the perfect choice. They'd dressed her in a black strapless evening gown designed to set off the necklace. They'd sent stylists to do her hair up in cascading curls and make up her face to look like an exotic Italian beauty. When they were finished, Christina had barely recognized herself in the mirror.

She was an art historian, a gemologist, an academic, a woman who spent most of her days poring over books or studying fine gems for flaws and cuts. She wasn't a party girl. Working a room didn't come naturally to her, but it was too late to back out. The party had begun and she was the centerpiece.

The auction house itself was a massive three-story stone building that had originally been used as a bank. Tonight the main gallery on the second floor had been transformed into Renaissance Italy. Beautiful art adorned the walls, and glass cases were filled with collectibles, everything from crucifixes to swords, coins and jewelry. Violin music flowed in the background. Everyone who was anyone was present, the cream of San Francisco society as well as important art dealers and collectors from around the country, who they hoped would bid generously at the upcoming auction to be held in two days, on Friday at noon.

"Christina, you look beautiful," Michael Torrance said smoothly. But the jewelry collector's eyes were on the jewel, not on her face.

Christina tried not to blush. She wasn't used to men looking so openly at her chest, and she was certainly showing more than the usual cleavage. Her practical mind told her that the man now drooling over that cleavage was not at all interested in her breasts. The sparkling yellow diamond had his full attention. She couldn't blame him. It was spectacular, and Michael Torrance had been collecting diamonds for twenty years.

"I trust you'll be bidding," she said, when his gaze finally returned to her face.

"Of course. You know I can't let a diamond such as this go without a fight."

"And you came in person; I'm impressed." She'd handled all of Michael's previous bids over the telephone. He usually preferred to remain anonymous.

"I'm impressed, too," he murmured, his gaze moving back to the stone. The smile in his dark blue eyes was filled with covetous greed. He was a handsome, sophisticated man, in his early to mid-forties, dressed in a charcoal gray pinstripe suit. She didn't know what it was, but there was something about him that made her a little uneasy. She had no idea where he got his money, but he never seemed to have trouble coming up with the right amount of cash at the right time. Although she suspected that this particular diamond would test the depth of anyone's pocket.

"Keep moving," her boss, Alexis Kensington, murmured quietly in her ear.

Alexis, a tall, stunning blonde in her late forties dressed in a floor-length teal blue Vera Wang gown set off with some rather spectacular diamonds of her own, flashed Michael a smile. "I don't believe we've met. I'm Alexis Kensington."

"Ah, the illustrious owner of Barclay's," Michael replied. "It's a pleasure to meet you."

"And you," Alexis returned.

"I'll speak to you later, Michael," Christina interjected, as Alexis drew Michael into conversation. She had no doubt that within five minutes Alexis would have Michael chomping at the bit to own that diamond. Alexis was passionate about Barclay's. Since she'd married Jeremy Kensington, the owner and founder of Barclay's, five years earlier, she'd made it her personal mission to take Barclay's to the next level, where they could compete with Sotheby's and Christie's and the other big players. Friday's auction of the Benedetti diamond would solidify Barclay's place in that market.

In some ways Christina was surprised that they'd won the consignment. Barclay's had been in existence for only twenty years. They didn't have nearly the cachet or the reputation of the other houses, but sometimes it came down to a great salesperson and a little bit of luck. Whatever the reason, Christina was thrilled to have an opportunity to help auction off such a valuable diamond. It would definitely add to her reputation as well. Maybe then she would finally be able to outrun her past.

As she moved across the room, she was acutely aware of the security guard who followed a discreet distance behind her. Two other guards were posted at the door and another two downstairs by the main entrance to the building. Fortunately, there was only one way into the gallery, so it was a well-contained area. The guards were dressed in tuxedos designed to blend in with the party atmosphere. Champagne was flowing, and a gourmet buffet had been set up at the far end of the gallery. Small candlelit tables offered guests a place to sit and converse or study their preview catalogs.

Christina paused for a moment to say hello to several of the guests she had personally invited to the auction. She'd been working as a jewelry specialist at Barclay's for almost three years and was building a solid network of dealers and clients, who trusted her to let them know when it was time to buy. She enjoyed that part of her job, finding the perfect item for the enthusiastic collector.

She tried not to fidget as three women surrounded her. The diamond was making her skin feel hot and tingly. The stone seemed to grow heavier the longer she wore it. It was the strangest sensation. She almost felt as if the jewel were coming alive, awakening from a long, deep sleep. She couldn't help wondering where it had been the last hundred years. Its history was shrouded in mystery. The Benedettis had given little information about the stone that they claimed had been in their family for generations.

Since the entire collection had arrived only a few hours earlier, Christina had not had an opportunity to study the diamond under her gem scope. Tomorrow she planned to conduct an in-depth appraisal. An associate in Barclay's European office had done an initial review at the Benedettis' home in Florence, Italy, but Christina wanted to study the diamond herself before it was auctioned off. It was rare to find a diamond of this size without any substantial history behind it, which made her very curious. Their European appraiser had assured her that the family had the proper papers of provenance, and they were not in danger of selling off stolen property. She certainly hoped that was true. She couldn't afford another scandal in her life.

Slipping away from the women, she was careful not to let anyone monopolize her for too long. Most people were respectful of the diamond and kept their distance, which was why she was more than a little surprised when a man's hand came down hard on her arm. She whirled around, her muscles tensing as she looked into a pair of irritated brown eyes. The man in front of her was big, muscular, filled with barely suppressed energy. His light brown hair was short and spiked. His skin was tan, as if he spent more time outdoors than in, and his athletic stance seemed out of place in a room full of sophisticated art collectors.

"Why the hell haven't you called me back?" he demanded.

She started at the harsh tone. "Excuse me? Who are you?"

"J. T. McIntyre. I've called you a dozen times over the past three days. I'm with the FBI. Does that ring a bell?"

She swallowed hard, remembering all those pink slips with his name on them. "I told my assistant to forward your calls to our security department."

"I spoke to them, but I want to talk to you."

Her stomach began to churn as memories of the past flashed through her head, the men in suits knocking on their front door, her father talking to them in a hushed voice, and later that night she and her father suddenly departing from yet another house, another city, another state. The FBI had wanted to talk to her then, too, but her father had protected her—as she would protect him. "I really don't have anything to do with security," she said.

"Since you're wearing that diamond, you should know that someone intends to steal it."

Her heart skipped a beat. "Are you talking about someone specific?" She held her breath as she waited for his answer.

"Yes. His name is Evan Chadwick, and I'm convinced you're his next target."

Her mind raced to follow his words. He was talking about someone she didn't know, thank God. Evan Chadwick. She'd never heard of him. "Why?" she asked finally. "Why would I be his target?"

"Other than the fact that you're wearing the diamond?"

"I doubt he could steal it in this roomful of people, security at every door."

"You'd be surprised what Evan can do. You're one of the few people with complete access to the diamond. That means you're on his list of people to use. He's here somewhere, waiting for his opportunity. You need to know what he looks like, how he operates, everything about him."

"Security already ran down a list of known jewel thieves with me. I've memorized names and faces, but I don't recall an Evan Chadwick."

"Because he's not a known jewel thief. But he is a career criminal, a con man, a sociopath—in other words, a very dangerous man. I've been following him for five years, and I'm convinced he intends to steal that diamond you're wearing around your neck."

"That doesn't mean he'll succeed." She lowered her voice, realizing their conversation was drawing the wrong kind of attention. "I can't talk to you right now. I have to show off the diamond. And this is a party. I don't want our guests to think there is anything wrong."

He stayed close to her side as she took another pass through the room. "Has anyone new come to work for you lately, become your friend, asked you out on a date, bought you a drink?"

"No," she said, uncomfortable with his questions.

"You're absolutely certain you haven't met anyone new this past week?"

"Well, not absolutely certain. There are a lot of people working on this exhibit, and I speak to new dealers and collectors all the time."

"He's tall, blond, blue eyes, very charming, big smile. Most women fall for him in about ten seconds," J.T. added tersely.

"You sound like you're jealous," she murmured. Not that he had anything to be jealous about. With his broad shoulders and his tanned, sculpted features, he was the most ruggedly attractive man she'd seen in a long time.

"I'm just stating the facts."

"I haven't met anyone like that," she said.

"Sometimes he wears disguises. That's why you and I need to have a conversation about everyone you've spoken to since you started work on this exhibit."

"That won't happen tonight," she said shortly. "And that scowl of yours is scaring the customers. Call me tomorrow."

"Will you answer?"

"Why don't you try me and find out?"

His frown deepened as his gaze raked her face. "Most people return calls from the FBI. Why don't you? Are you hiding something, Ms. Alberti?"

"Not in this dress," she said lightly, sorry for her words when his gaze dropped from her face to her breasts. She had the distinct feeling that this man was more interested in her cleavage than the diamond. She walked away, sensing his gaze follow her across the room. The last thing she needed was an eager FBI agent sticking his nose in her business.

She paused as a tall, older gentleman stepped in front of her. He had a crop of pepper gray hair that was badly in need of styling and thick-rimmed glasses on a long nose. His skin was blemished and weathered. The only cheery thing about him was the bright red bow tie he wore around his neck.

"Christina Alberti," he murmured with a tip of his head. "It has been so many years since I saw you. You were just a little girl when we spoke last."

His lilting British accent was vaguely familiar. And there was something about his eyes that reminded her of someone. . . . "I'm sorry. I don't . . ."

"Remember me," he finished with an understanding nod. "Let me introduce myself. I'm Howard Keaton, an old friend of your father's. We worked together a long time ago at UCLA, a summer program on the Italian Renaissance."

"Of course, Professor Keaton." She relaxed and gave him a smile. "It's been a while."

"Yes, it has. You're all grown-up now, and quite . . . beautiful. You look like a princess."

"It's the diamond. It has that effect. So, are you still teaching?"

"Not for a few years now. I'm working at a museum in Vancouver. I'm surprised your father didn't tell you that. Is Marcus here?" He glanced around the room in search of her father.

"No, he's traveling," she said.

"Lucky man." Howard's gaze turned to the diamond, and his jaw hardened. "May I?"

She nodded as he moved closer. He put out his hand, his fingers reverently teasing the surface of the stone.

"It is exquisite," he said. "Such cut, such clarity, a rare gem. I'm surprised you're not worried about wearing it."

"There's plenty of security around."

"I wasn't talking about the guards, or the value of the diamond. I was referring to the curse."

Her heart skipped a beat. "Curse?"

"You don't know about the curse? I wondered why there was no mention of it in the sale catalog, but then I thought perhaps you were afraid it would affect the selling price."

"There's no curse attached to this stone. You must be thinking of some other diamond."

She could see that he was not convinced, and there was something in his intense gaze that made her very uneasy. Her skin began to tingle. She felt hot and a little dizzy. She really should have eaten something earlier in the day. She reached up to touch the necklace, to adjust the chain, and was shocked when the weight of the stone suddenly slipped away.

She gasped as Howard caught the diamond necklace with a deft hand. Their eyes met.

"It's a sign," he murmured. "Be careful, Christina. Be very careful."

Out of the corner of her eye she saw the security guard walking quickly in her direction, and she realized that she needed to reclaim the necklace. "May I have it back, please?"

"Of course."

As the professor handed the diamond back to her, a scream rang through the room, followed by shouts of "Fire!" She closed her fingers tightly around the stone as thick gray smoke poured into the room.

The crowd immediately swarmed toward the gallery doors, knocking over tables and chairs and sweeping Christina along in the chaos. Her eyes began to water, and her chest tightened as she struggled to breathe. She clutched the diamond in her hand, praying that she wouldn't lose it, but no one seemed interested in the jewel anymore. Even Professor Keaton had disappeared. She had once been the center of attention, but now the crowd's focus was on escape.

The panic in the room increased with each passing moment, and she could understand why. The smoke and the screams were disorienting. She couldn't see two feet in front of her. Out of nowhere J. T. McIntyre suddenly appeared at her side, his hand on her arm. "Give me the diamond," he said sharply.

She hesitated, reluctant to let the stone out of her hand. She didn't know this man. He could be anyone. He could be a jewel thief impersonating an FBI agent. It wasn't just her job on the line; it was her reputation, the new life she had built for herself. She couldn't— wouldn't—let it all come tumbling down. "I don't think so. I don't know you."

"We don't have time to argue. You can trust me."

"How can I do that? You could be that thief you were telling me about, the one who wears disguises." She coughed again, tears streaming down her face.

To make matters worse the sprinklers went off,

soaking them with water. Within seconds her evening gown clung to her body like a second skin.

"I'm here to protect you and that diamond," J.T. shouted.

"I'm hanging on to it just the same," she said with determination.

"Then hold on tight, because we're getting out of here."

J.T. didn't let go of her arm until they reached the doors. Halfway down the stairs, several firemen passed them on their way up to the gallery. Christina hoped they could stop the fire before the collection was lost. The glass cases offered some protection, and as soon as the smoke alarms went off the wall coverings had moved into place to guard the paintings from any water or smoke damage. But if the building went up in flames, nothing anyone could do would save the collection.

Russell Kenner, Barclay's head of security, and Luigi Murano, his Italian counterpart who had traveled from Italy to watch over the Benedetti collection, met them by the front door along with a half dozen security guards, who immediately surrounded Christina and ushered her away from the mass of people exiting the building.

They moved into the empty showroom on the ground floor, and Christina took a breath of blessed relief. Kenner, an ex-marine who still wore his short brown hair in a military cut, barked orders into a transmitter in his hand. Murano, a stocky, volatile Italian, waved his hands in the air, proclaiming the evening a disaster.

"Shouldn't we be getting out of the building?" Christina asked.

"The smoke appears to be confined to the main gallery," Russell replied. "Initial reports indicate that smoke bombs were set off in the heating and air-conditioning vents."

"What? You mean there's no fire?" Her stomach began to churn. If someone had set the smoke bombs, there had to be a reason why. Maybe it was a good thing the clasp had slipped. If the necklace had still been around her neck when the alarms went off, it would have been easier for someone to yank it off her.

"We're still assessing the situation," Russell continued. "I'll take the diamond from you now."

Christina hesitated and then told herself she was being ridiculous. She knew and trusted Russell Kenner. Still, she was relieved to see Alexis and Jeremy Kensington enter the salesroom. Barclay's was their company. It was their call what to do with the diamond.

"Is the diamond all right?" Alexis asked immediately.

Christina tried not to take offense that Alexis's concern was only for the stone and not for Christina's personal safety. The diamond was worth a lot more to Barclay's than Christina was.

"Yes, it's fine." Christina opened her palm, showing them the glittering yellow diamond. She could hear the collective gasp of relief. "I'll take it," Alexis said. "The firemen would like us to clear the building. Why don't you wait outside, Christina? As soon as we know more, I'll come and get you."

Christina handed over the diamond, not unhappy to get rid of it. The responsibility of keeping it safe had weighed her down. She felt much lighter now. She moved toward the door, pausing to take a quick look behind her, and was happy to see J. T. McIntyre in deep conversation with Russell. She'd rather have the FBI talking to security than to her.

As she exited the building, she saw three fire trucks lined up out front, their red strobe lights flashing across the people clustered in groups across the street.

"Christina. I thought you might want this," Kelly Huang said.

Christina turned at the sound of her coworker's voice. Kelly, a beautiful Asian woman who had recently joined Barclay's as a junior specialist in Asian art, handed Christina her purse.

"My bag," Christina said. "How did you get this?"

"I was in my office when the alarms went off. I saw your purse on your desk and thought I'd better grab it. There's no telling when we'll be allowed back into the building. Goodness, you're soaking wet."

"The sprinklers went off in the gallery."

"You should go home and change. You don't want to get sick. I'll let Alexis know where you are."

The idea was tempting. While she wanted to stay in touch with what was happening, she really needed to dry off. "All right." She dug into her purse, relieved to find her keys and her cell phone. "Call me if anything comes up before I get back."

"Will do," Kelly promised.

Christina paused as a news truck pulled up in front of the building. The press had arrived. She hoped the adage "there is no such thing as bad publicity" held true. She saw Sylvia Davis, Barclay's head of public relations, moving quickly toward the truck. The crowd also turned its attention to the cameras. Was the person who had set the smoke bombs standing among them, watching his handiwork, enjoying the scene? Or perhaps he was inside the building. Maybe it was the man the FBI agent had warned her about, someone in disguise, someone they thought they knew and trusted. It was difficult to imagine that any of her coworkers were out to destroy Barclay's. Then again, she knew firsthand that taking anyone at face value was a mistake. Everyone had secrets.

As she started down the steps, she saw a man walking quickly away from the far side of the building, near the receiving dock. He was too far away for her to see him clearly, but he had a long dark coat and moved with a familiar loping, lanky gait. Her heart came to a crashing halt as her brain took her to a place she didn't want to go.

No, he couldn't have done this. He wouldn't have done this. He knew the Barclay Auction House was her life, not just her job, and that she had spent the past three years trying to start over. There was no way he would try to destroy the life she'd built. Would he?

He disappeared around the corner of the building. She told herself that she was wrong, that it wasn't him, but a niggling doubt remained. She had to make sure. She jogged down the stairs, her high heels clattering against the stone steps. He was getting into a car, a dark Mercedes sedan. It shot past her, the man behind the wheel nothing but a blur. She told herself to forget about him, go home, change clothes, but all the way to her car she knew she would have to make one stop first—just to be sure.

* * *

J.T. wanted to talk to Christina Alberti, but by the time he left the building she was halfway across the parking lot. He hesitated, torn between the need to stay on top of the smoke bomb investigation and the desire to follow up with Christina. Since Barclay's security team and the local cops were flexing their protective turf muscles, he decided he might as well work another angle—Christina.

She wasn't what he'd expected. On paper she'd appeared nondescript, a twenty-nine-year-old art historian with a couple of degrees from various colleges and a certificate in gemology—in other words, a boring intellectual. He'd figured she'd be serious and smart. Stunningly beautiful had come as a surprise. When she'd first entered the gallery, she'd literally taken his breath away with her mysterious green eyes, honey-colored skin, gorgeous dark hair, and incredibly hot body. With that diamond around her neck, she'd looked like some sort of Italian goddess.

All that was beside the point, he reminded himself as he moved toward the parking lot. He was here to catch a thief, and he had to stay focused on that goal. Now that he had seen Christina, he was even more convinced that Evan Chadwick would not want to miss the opportunity to work with her. Not only did she have complete and total access to the Benedetti diamond, but she was also a gorgeous woman—two factors that would definitely be of interest to Evan, who enjoyed women almost as much as a good con.

The bureau had a file three inches thick on Evan and the many crimes he'd committed during the past decade. He was a brilliant criminal, responsible for ru-

ining the lives of dozens of people, and J.T. knew firsthand just what devastation Evan left in his wake. He
would never forget that Evan was responsible for destroying his family, and he would not rest until the bastard was sitting in jail for the rest of his miserable life.

But first he had to catch him, and he would. He'd
come close to getting Evan off the street a week earlier, but he had slipped through the hands of the local
police and escaped. However, he'd left behind a tantalizing clue—a newspaper article on Barclay's upcoming auction of Renaissance jewelry and art. Once J.T.
had realized that a spectacular and priceless diamond
was in the collection, he'd known that Evan intended
to steal it. Now that he'd seen Christina up close and
personal, he was convinced that she would play some
role in the game—the question was, what role?

He didn't like the fact that the diamond necklace
had come off Christina's neck, and that it had been in
her hand at the moment the smoke bombs went off. A
surge of adrenaline swept through his body as he
jogged to his car. Why was Christina in such a hurry to
get away from Barclay's? Was she working with Evan?
Was she going to meet him now?

He got into his rental car just as Christina pulled out
of the parking lot in her light blue Hyundai. She
seemed to be in a hurry, her tires squealing as she
turned onto the road. Was she just wet, cold, scared?
Or did she have another reason for leaving quickly?

He slid behind the wheel of his Chevy Cavalier and
took off after her, happy to see she wasn't driving a
particularly fast sports car. He managed to catch up at
a red light and stayed close on her tail as she drove

across town. A mile or two later he became convinced that she was not going home. He hadn't had time to do more than some basic fact checking on the key players at Barclay's Auction House, but he distinctly remembered Christina Alberti's residence being an apartment on Telegraph Hill. She was heading toward the opposite side of town.

His pulse began to race as she turned down a street of family homes in the Lake District. The houses were upscale but not as opulent as those a few blocks away in Pacific Heights. She pulled up in front of a two-story Victorian and parked by the curb. He continued down the street, pulled into a parking spot at the corner, then made his way back on foot. When he neared the property, he saw her standing on the porch. She rang the bell, tapped her foot impatiently on the ground, and turned her head.

J.T. ducked out of sight behind a tree. When he took another look, Christina was walking around the side of the house. Careful to be quiet, he moved across the yard, wondering if she had gone into the house through a side door. He peeked around the corner and was surprised to see Christina ditching her high heels. What on earth was she doing?

A moment later she pulled up the skirt of her long evening gown and knotted the ends around her knees, then put one bare foot on the trunk of the tree, searching for a toehold. She grabbed a lower branch and to his amazement began to climb up the tree. It didn't take her long to scale the gnarled oak, whose upper branches reached a second-floor balcony. Christina swung herself over the railing and landed with a graceful jump.

She opened the sliding glass door and disappeared into the house.

Well, this was getting more interesting by the moment. Was she robbing the place, or looking for something—or perhaps someone? If there was any chance she could lead him to Evan, he would take it.

Since the tree seemed to be the only way in, J.T. followed Christina's lead. He didn't make the climb nearly as gracefully or as quickly as she had done, but he managed to get to the balcony. He found the sliding glass door unlocked. Inside, the bedroom was empty. He didn't take time to look around; he was more interested in where Christina had gone. He heard some movement on the first floor, so he crept down the stairs. When he entered what appeared to be a den, he found Christina standing in front of an open safe in the wall. She whirled around, her face a picture of shock and guilt.

"You!" She gasped, putting a hand to her heart. "What are you doing here?"

2

"I was going to ask you the same question," J.T. replied.

Christina's mouth opened, but no words came out. He could see her searching for an answer. He'd interrogated many people in his career, and she definitely had the look of someone who was about to try to sell him a story. She bit down on her bottom lip, and he could see a nervous flicker in her green eyes as her gaze darted around the room, seeking an escape route. But she was cornered, caught like a rat in a trap. Only she was a lot prettier than a rat.

Even barefoot in a soggy evening gown, her face streaked with makeup, her brown hair falling in a wet, tangled mess around her shoulders, Christina was a beautiful woman. He especially liked the way the damp silk of her dress clung to her breasts, hips, and legs. His body tightened, and he drew in a breath, reminding himself to keep it professional.

"I'm waiting." He crossed his arms over his chest.

Christina tucked a strand of her hair behind one ear.

"You haven't answered my question yet. What are you doing here?" she asked.

"Whose house is this?" he countered, glancing around the room. A large mahogany desk was in front of a bay window. Floor-to-ceiling shelves were filled with books. Oil paintings adorned the walls. Dark brown leather couches were arranged on Oriental rugs. The room was spotless, the decor sophisticated. But the room didn't appear lived-in. There weren't any magazines lying around, no coffee mug on the desk or even a pile of loose papers, nothing to give any clue as to the owner. There was a dusty, dry scent to the house, as if it had been closed up for a while.

"Why did you follow me?" Christina asked.

It was clear she had no intention of answering his questions, but she had no idea how persistent he could be. She was about to find out. "Because I want to talk to you, and I'm not leaving until that happens. Stop stalling."

"I told you to call me tomorrow. And I don't have to answer your questions."

"Actually you do." He gave his words a chance to sink in, seeing the nervousness behind her bravado. "In case you're wondering, I saw you climb the tree and break into this house. The open safe behind you implies you're looking for something. Or perhaps you're hiding something?" He took a step forward, wondering if he'd find the spectacular diamond she'd been wearing earlier.

She suddenly slammed the safe closed, a guilty gesture if he'd ever seen one.

"It's none of your business what I'm doing," she

said forcefully. "This is my house. I forgot my key; that's why I broke in."

He shook his head. "I did some preliminary checking. You live in an apartment on Telegraph Hill. Try again."

"You checked where I live?" she asked in surprise.

"Yes, and I'm just getting started." He saw discomfort flit through her eyes. "It would be better if you tell me the truth. Otherwise I might start digging in areas you'd rather I didn't get into."

"That sounds like a threat."

"It's a simple fact."

"Fine, you're right—this isn't my place; it belongs to my father, Marcus Alberti," she said with a wave of her hand. "He's out of town at the moment. And I did forget my key. Are you satisfied?"

"I can easily check your story." He took a step forward. She moved back, but there was nowhere to go. The air between them sizzled with tension. Looking into her eyes, he saw fear and something else, something he couldn't define, and it bothered him.

"So check. You'll figure out I'm telling the truth," she said.

"Then why are you so nervous? Why did you close the safe so quickly? What didn't you want me to see?"

"If I seem nervous, it's because it's been a crazy night."

"I'll grant you that," he conceded. "What about the rest?"

"I was putting some papers in the safe. That's all. They're personal. And I'm not telling you anything else. I don't know you. I don't even know if you're really an FBI agent. I haven't seen any ID."

J.T. reached into his pocket and pulled out his identification. "Does this clear things up?"

Christina took a good look at his badge. "It could be fake."

"It's not." He took another step forward, stopping just inches away from her. He could hear her breath quicken, see the rise and fall of her breasts, her beautiful, distracting breasts. . . . He forced his gaze to her face. "What happened back at the auction house to make you run here?"

"I told you, I wanted to put some papers in the safe."

"You didn't have one single piece of paper in your hand when you climbed that tree. Try again." He put his hands on the wall behind her, trapping her in between the wall and him.

"What are you doing?" she asked, an odd catch in her voice.

When he was standing this close to her, it took him a minute to remember what he was doing. She smelled like flowers, and her mouth was trembling, her full lips slightly parted, as if she were waiting for something . . . waiting for him. He had the sudden urge to put his hands in her hair, crush those soft lips to his mouth.

"You need to move," she said.

That wasn't all that he needed. His intent had been to intimidate her, to make her uneasy enough to blurt out the truth. But she was having a strange effect on him. He couldn't seem to move backward or forward or even remember exactly what he wanted to happen next. His body had its own ideas, and his brain was having trouble keeping up.

Then Christina gave him a hard shove and darted

out from under him, putting at least six feet between
them. It was a good thing. With distance, his brain
started working again, reminding him that he had to
stay focused on his goal: catching Evan. He couldn't
let himself get caught up in Christina.

There was a fire burning in her eyes now. "You
might work for the FBI, but you don't have the right to
come in here and harass me. I could report you."

He went back on the offensive. "That might involve
an explanation of why you broke into this house that
definitely does not belong to you, why you were in
such a hurry to put away some mysterious and obviously invisible papers that you couldn't take time to
stop at home, put on dry clothes, or fix your hair or
your face—something so urgent you climbed a tree in
bare feet and an evening gown, something—"

"Stop," she said, putting up her hand, a frown on her
face. "You've made your point. I've heard enough."

"I haven't heard nearly enough from you. Let's review. Tonight, while you were wearing a diamond
worth millions of dollars, it slipped off your neck.
Some guy caught it in his hand. Who was that man?"

She stared at him for a moment and then said, "Professor Howard Keaton. He used to work at UCLA. He
mentioned that he's now at a museum in Vancouver."

"Do you know him?"

"Yes, but it's been a while since I've seen him."

"How long a while?"

She shrugged "Not since I was a child. Why?"

"Just wondering. It's odd how the necklace came
loose at just the moment the professor was looking at
it. I saw him touch it. Did he pull on it?"

"I didn't feel a tug. It just fell. It's possible the clasp opened or broke. Professor Keaton handed the jewel back to me almost immediately."

"*Almost* being the key word."

His words seemed to surprise her. "What do you mean?"

"You don't think he could have made a switch, do you—traded a fake diamond for the real thing?" It was an idea that had been running through his brain since he'd left the auction house.

Her eyes widened. "No, no, of course not. It was just out of my control for a few seconds."

He watched her carefully, but she showed nothing but amazement at the suggestion. Still, she could be a good actress. He'd originally wanted to make contact with her because he thought she might be a target for Evan, that she was someone who could help him catch his old enemy. But her behavior tonight had raised his suspicions about her. He wouldn't make the mistake of trusting her too soon.

"Are you sure?" he asked. "Sometimes the hand is quicker than the eye."

"You were watching. What did you see?"

"Just what you described," he admitted. "But I was farther away; I didn't have a particularly good view. If you took a look at the diamond now, would you be able to tell if it was a copy?"

"Absolutely. It's very difficult to copy a diamond of that size, especially with the chain. Everything would have to be an exact replica."

"But it could be done?" he queried. "It's not impossible."

"Not impossible but extremely difficult, especially because this particular diamond necklace has not been in circulation. It hasn't been on display or worn in the last hundred years, according to the Benedettis. It's been locked in a vault at their estate. Someone would have had to see the diamond to be able to copy it."

She made a good argument, but he was keeping an open mind. In his experience there was no such thing as coincidence, and the timing between the smoke bombs and the fall of the necklace was too perfect.

"I'll examine the diamond as soon as I can," she continued, "but I think you're imagining things."

"I didn't imagine those smoke bombs. Someone deliberately created a distraction."

"Yes, and it's a good thing I had the diamond in my hand. In all that commotion it would have been easier to snatch it off my neck. The smoke might have been a blessing in disguise."

"True." It was possible that the theft had been aborted, but his instincts told him that Evan had a far more complicated plan in mind than a simple grab in a smoky room.

"Look, I'm cold and I'm wet, and I need to change out of this dress," Christina said, gripping the soggy material. "You look like you could use some dry clothes as well. Why don't we call it a night?"

He'd taken off his jacket, but his pants were uncomfortably damp. Still, he didn't intend to let Christina out of his sight. "You're awfully eager to get rid of me. What are you hiding?"

"Nothing." She blew out a breath in obvious frustration. "Don't you have anyone else to interrogate besides me? In fact, why aren't you back at Barclay's talking to the police and Russell and everyone else involved in protecting the diamond? Isn't that your job?"

"My job is to catch a thief."

"Well, there isn't one here. Nor has there been a theft."

He pulled a photograph out of his pocket and walked over to show it to her. "Have you seen this man?"

She took the picture from his hand and studied it. "This is the man you were telling me about?"

"Yes, his name is Evan Chadwick."

"This looks like a wedding photograph."

"It is. The woman in the photo, Kayla Sheridan, had no idea she was marrying a con man. Evan disappeared on their honeymoon night. She thought he was in love with her, but she was just the means to an end."

"I haven't seen this man. I'm sorry; I can't help you."

"Take a good look at him, the shape of his face, the jawline, the nose, the expression, the things that can't be disguised easily."

She slowly shook her head. "Nothing seems familiar. He's an attractive man with that blond hair and blue eyes. If I'd seen him, I'd remember him."

"Well, keep him in your head, just in case. He goes by the name Evan Chadwick when he's not using someone else's identity, which is rare. So he could be using any name. His hair could be brown. His eyes could be disguised by colored contact lenses. In other words, he's very good at being whoever he wants to be. I've seen him convince parents that he's their long-lost son, or a woman that he's her supposedly dead brother."

"How could anyone be that convincing?" she murmured, a note of doubt in her voice.

"People see what they want to see. Evan is a chameleon. He can fit in anywhere. And no one knows he's been there until it's too late." J.T. paused for a moment. "The one constant in almost every con Evan pulls is a woman, usually a beautiful woman. He finds out what she wants, what she needs, and he gives it to her. In return he takes something that she might not even realize she's giving away. Something that advances his goal."

Christina met his gaze head-on. "And you think this man intends to use me in some way to get to the diamond?"

"Yes, I do."

"I'm not easily fooled," she said with a dismissive shake of her head. "And I'm not a trusting sort of person."

"Neither am I."

"I can see that, and I don't understand why you're so suspicious of me. I don't want anything to happen to the Benedetti diamond. It's very important to me and to everyone at Barclay's to have a successful auction on Friday. If I sold a fake diamond, my career would be over. My reputation could never be repaired. I wouldn't take that chance."

He could hear the passion in her voice, but still he wondered . . . "Not even for a cut of fifteen million dollars? Isn't that what you're hoping to get for the diamond? You wouldn't need a job with that kind of money."

"You're crazy, and you're wrong. This conversation is over."

He saw the defiance and anger in her eyes. Before he could respond, the tension between them was broken by the sound of the front door closing.

Someone else was in the house.

Christina swiveled around, yelling, "Dad, it's just me. I'm here with a friend."

A crash followed her words. Christina rushed into the hallway; J.T. was right behind her. A vase that had probably been on the entry table lay in shattered pieces on the floor. The front door stood wide open. Whoever had come in was gone.

J.T. moved quickly through the door and onto the porch. A black Mercedes shot down the street. The night was too dark, and the car was too far away to get a license plate. He turned to see Christina standing in the doorway. Mixed emotions crossed her face, and he remembered her quick words: *"Dad, it's just me. I'm here with a friend."*

"You warned him." He saw the guilt flash through her eyes. "Why?"

"I just said I was here so he wouldn't be alarmed that someone was in the house. That's all."

"You said you were here with a friend, and he left. You didn't want me to see him or him to see me." She could deny it all she wanted; he knew he was right. What he didn't know was why she'd done it.

She cleared her throat. "Maybe that wasn't my father. That wasn't his car."

"Whoever came in had a key."

"It could have been one of his friends."

"You can do better than that, Christina."

"Actually, I can't. I have to go. I have to get back to Barclay's."

"And you're not curious as to who came in the house, broke the vase, and ran off, leaving the door open."

She licked her lips. "I'm curious, but there's nothing I can do at the moment. They didn't take anything, and they had a key, so I'm sure it was someone my father knows."

"Or quite simply your father."

"Possibly. Look, I'm going home. You do whatever you have to do." She pulled the door to the house shut behind her, retrieved her shoes from the side yard, and then headed down the path to her car. J.T. watched her every move. He let her go for one reason—he was intensely curious as to what she would do next.

J. T. McIntyre had made no attempt to hide the fact that he was following her to her apartment. Nor did he even bother to park out of sight. Christina knew he would wait for her to come back downstairs and return to Barclay's. She mentally kicked herself for leading an FBI agent straight to her father's house. She'd never anticipated that J.T. would follow her. She'd thought he was wrapped up in the investigation at the auction house. Actually, she hadn't been thinking at all. She'd been operating on instinct. As soon as she'd heard that the smoke bombs had been deliberately set at Barclay's, she'd known that someone was after the diamond. When she'd seen a familiar face in the crowd, she'd leaped to a horrible conclusion. And she'd made a huge mistake running to her dad's house. She would have to find a way to make it right, but first things first. She couldn't afford to give J. T. McIntyre any more reason to doubt her.

After turning on her coffeemaker, she went into the

bedroom and changed clothes, putting on a pair of comfortable jeans and a heavy gray sweater. She dried her hair, pulling it up into a ponytail, reapplied her makeup, and realized that her Cinderella moment was over. She no longer looked like a goddess dripping in diamonds; she was just an ordinary woman. That was the image she wanted J.T. to see. She had to convince him that she was so normal she was completely boring and not worthy of his attention.

Returning to the kitchen, she poured coffee into two driving mugs, grabbed a towel from the bathroom, and headed downstairs. J.T. was sitting in his car, talking on his cell phone. She hoped he wasn't conducting a more in-depth background check on her or her father. She tapped on the window. He seemed surprised to see her standing there. After a moment he lowered the window.

She handed him a mug. "I thought you could use some coffee. Strong and black; I took a guess."

"You were right. Thanks."

"I also brought a towel, just in case you need to dry off."

He raised an eyebrow and gave her a suspicious look. "Why are you being so nice to me?"

"Because I'm a nice person." She forced a casual smile. "You just don't know it yet."

"You're certainly an interesting person," he conceded.

She'd settle for that. She turned to leave.

"Christina."

She paused, giving him a wary glance. "What?"

"No one has ever called me nice."

"What have they called you?"

"You don't want to know." A grin flashed across his

face, a glitter of humor in his dark eyes. When he wasn't scowling, he was quite attractive. Actually, even in a bad mood, he was a good-looking guy, strong, sexy, a man's man, with a lot of rough edges that she suspected many women had tried to smooth out. But not her; J. T. McIntyre wasn't her type, she told herself firmly. He was far too dangerous in more ways than she could count.

"I'm going back to Barclay's now, just in case we're separated," she said. "I wouldn't want you to get lost."

"Wouldn't you?"

"We're on the same side, Mr. McIntyre. You seem to have forgotten that."

"And you seem to have just remembered," he pointed out. "You're a lot more chatty now than you were at your father's house."

She could see the speculation in his eyes and knew he was still very curious about her actions. She wished she could explain, but that was impossible. If he knew she had any doubts about her dad, he would zero in on her father as a suspect, and she couldn't have that. Deciding it was best to end the conversation quickly, she walked away and got into her car.

The drive to Barclay's took only a few moments. When she pulled into the parking lot, she noticed that the fire trucks were gone. There were a few cars left, probably belonging to employees. It was obvious most of the guests had left for home. She just hoped they hadn't been scared away forever and would come back on Friday for the auction.

J.T. parked his car next to hers, and they walked to the front of the building together. The security guard checked their identification and then allowed them into the building. He told Christina that Mrs. Kensington was holding a meeting in the third-floor conference room and wanted her to go there as soon as she arrived.

"Let's check out the gallery first," J.T. said, heading up the stairs.

Christina was also curious to see the extent of the damage. The thick scent of smoke still hung in the air. The gallery doors were open and the collection had been moved out of that room and presumably returned to the storage vaults in the basement. The catering service was cleaning the floor, folding up the chairs and tables. Christina was thankful there was no sign of any permanent destruction to the room.

"It looks all right," she murmured.

"The smoke bombs were meant to be a distraction," J.T. said.

"You mentioned that before, but whoever set the bombs didn't get the diamond, so the plan didn't work."

"Maybe that wasn't the plan. Even with the smoke and the chaos, it would have been difficult to rip that diamond from your neck and get through that panicky crowd. I know you would have screamed bloody murder if anyone tried to take it from you."

"That's true. So what would be the point of the smoke bombs?"

"The fire alarm sent everyone rushing to the door, leaving other areas of the building wide open. The person who set the bombs might have wanted access to areas he would otherwise be unable to get into," J.T. explained.

"Like the vaults where we keep the diamond and the

other valuable items," she added. J.T. made a good point. Had the person simply wanted to find a way in or set up a plan to steal the diamond at a later date? "All those areas are on twenty-four-hour surveillance. I doubt anyone could walk around unnoticed by the cameras."

"It wouldn't be that difficult to dismantle a security camera, not for someone who was capable of planting smoke bombs in the air-conditioning system. They obviously knew how to get around the building without anyone seeing or suspecting them."

Which implied again that it was an inside job. She hated to think there was a thief among them. "I should get upstairs. I'm sure there's a crisis plan about to be set in motion."

"I'll go with you."

They walked up to the third floor, where the administrative offices were located. The conference room was the first door on the right. Through the glass windows, Christina could see that the room was packed with Barclay's employees. Alexis and Jeremy Kensington were in deep discussion with Sylvia Davis, head of PR; Karen Richardson, the art specialist; Keith Holmes, the auctioneer; and several other department heads. At the other end of the table, Russell Kenner was conversing with Luigi Murano, the head of the Italian security team, and another man Christina did not recognize. As she entered the room, Alexis looked up and motioned her over with a wave of her hand.

Christina was happy to see J.T. make his way to the security side of the conference room. She needed to get refocused on her job and what would happen next. "How is everything?"

"Better than expected," Alexis replied, but there was a worry in her eyes that belied her statement. "We didn't lose any of our auction items, so that's good news. You'll need to get on the phone tomorrow, Christina, and personally call every interested buyer and reassure them that the diamond and all other items are intact. This is the biggest auction in Barclay history," Alexis continued. "It will proceed without further incident. Is that clear?" She gazed around the group, and as expected no one dared to deny her confident words.

Alexis demanded absolute loyalty from her employees and did not encourage any opinions outside of her own. She knew what she wanted and she went after it one hundred percent. If anyone got in her way, they were history. Christina certainly intended to stay on Alexis's good side.

"Do we have an official explanation for what happened tonight?" Christina asked.

"I'm working on that," Sylvia interjected. "I'll give you one before you make your calls tomorrow."

"All right," Christina said, turning back to Alexis. "I'd like to check on the diamond. I'm concerned about the clasp and why it suddenly gave way when I was wearing it."

"Yes, what happened exactly?" Alexis asked, her brows drawn together in a frown. "Russell told me it came off your neck."

"The clasp opened or broke. Luckily, the man I was talking to caught it and handed it right back to me. It might have been a blessing in disguise. Once the alarms went off, it would have been much easier for someone to grab the necklace if it were still around my neck instead of clenched in my hand."

Alexis's gaze lingered on Christina for a moment, as if she was judging the story. Christina tried not to feel uneasy. She had told the truth. It had happened exactly as she'd described.

"You should have checked that clasp before you put the necklace on," Alexis said.

"You're right. Unfortunately, I didn't have a chance to look at it closely before the party. I would like to examine it now."

"We're reviewing all of our security measures and resetting our cameras at the moment," Alexis replied. She glanced down at her watch. "It's almost eleven. It would probably be best if you did it tomorrow."

Christina nodded. She hated to wait until morning, but she didn't want to suggest that anything was wrong with the diamond. In fact, she didn't know that anything *was* wrong. It was J.T. who had put crazy ideas in her head about a switch. She'd gone through every moment of the night and she didn't think there was any time at which a switch could have been made. The diamond had been out of her control for only a few seconds.

Nothing was wrong, she told herself firmly. She was simply tired, seeing problems where there weren't any.

"Don't forget we have that reporter from the *Tribune* coming at ten in the morning," Sylvia said. "He wants a photograph of the diamond to go with his story. The exposure will help reassure everyone that tonight's incident was nothing terrible."

"Got it." Christina walked out the door as they moved on to planning the rest of the auction. Her office was at the other end of the hallway, where it was quiet and dark. She often worked late and usually enjoyed the solitude, but tonight she felt tense, isolated from the others, which was odd, considering she'd spent most of the evening trying to get J. T. McIntyre off her tail. It was just her nerves. She was jittery after everything that had happened. It was to be expected. She drew in a deep breath and slowly let it out. She had to think about what to do next.

Despite her earlier denials to J.T., she was worried that someone had come into her father's house and taken off just as quickly. It had to have been her dad. J.T. was right: She had warned him away. It was old habit, a protective instinct honed since childhood. She'd used a code they'd developed years ago. And it had worked. So where was her father now? And more important, what was he up to?

The door suddenly opened behind her. She jumped in surprise and whirled around. She expected to see J.T., but the man standing in the doorway was the stranger from the conference room. His dark brown hair was long, thick, and wavy, his eyes a deep, somber black. His sideburns were long, his skin brown, his expression one of anxiety and irritation. He was obviously upset about something.

She cleared her throat, feeling uneasy, but told herself to calm down. The man had just been talking to Barclay's head of security. He was obviously not a threat.

"May I have a few moments, Signorina Alberti?" he asked, an Italian accent marking his formal English. "I am Stefano Benedetti."

Her pulse quickened. She'd read a bit about the

Benedettis and knew that Stefano, in his late thirties, was one of three sons born to Vittorio and Isabella Benedetti. Isabella had died many years earlier, and Vittorio was now in ill health, a condition that had prompted the family to sell part of their historic collection.

"I'm so happy to meet you." She moved across the room to shake his hand. "I didn't realize you were coming to the auction."

"I wasn't sure I could clear my schedule until recently. I'm very concerned, however, about the incident that took place earlier this evening, as is my father. We could have chosen any auction house, and we certainly hope we will not regret our decision to bring the collection to Barclay's."

"You won't," she said quickly, giving him a reassuring smile. She wasn't sure why he wasn't making his point to Alexis, but perhaps he wanted to make it clear to everyone at Barclay's that if they wanted this auction to take place, there could be no further trouble.

"I hope not. I understand you will be examining the diamond in the morning. I would like to be there, to reassure myself that all is well."

"Of course. Why don't you come at nine o'clock? We'll be previewing the jewels and other items to the press at ten."

He nodded. "Nine o'clock it is."

She thought they were finished, but he made no attempt to leave. Instead, he stared at her with a speculative gleam in his eyes. "Is there something else?" she asked.

"If I might ask, signorina, have you spoken to your father lately?"

Every nerve ending in her body suddenly went on full alert. "Do you know my father?"

"Marcus Alberti has spent a great deal of time in Florence," Stefano replied. "He is well-known in the art world."

"That's true. My father's father, my grandfather, was born in Florence—Nicholas Alberti was his name."

"Yes. That's what I understand, and apparently it's one of the reasons my father chose to send the collection here, to you, signorina."

Now she was truly shocked. She'd had no idea that her family's origins had played any part in the matter.

"I must admit that I asked him to reconsider in light of, shall we say, your father's rather unsavory reputation." Stefano's gaze darkened and his mouth curled in distaste as he continued, "But I was persuaded that the sins of the father should not be passed on to the daughter."

She swallowed hard at the word *sins.* "My father has never been convicted of anything."

"Lack of conviction does not necessarily prove innocence."

"It doesn't prove guilt either," she retorted. "You have nothing to worry about, Mr. Benedetti. Barclay's will do a fabulous job selling your collection, and I think you'll be very pleased with the results."

"I hope so," he said, not appearing all that convinced. "However, we are not off to a good start. I will see you in the morning."

"Wait," she said, calling him back. "Someone told me earlier tonight that they believed the diamond carried a curse. The paperwork I received indicated that the diamond has been in your family for over a hundred years and there was no particular history or legend attached to it."

"A curse?" Stefano echoed, a smile playing across his lips. "How fascinating. What exactly is this supposed curse?"

"I don't have any details."

"But you believe in curses?"

"I keep an open mind," she said. "Legends of powerful stones have been told for centuries. I don't discount them."

"Are you worried that because you wore the diamond tonight, you are now cursed?"

"No, not really." Even as she said the words, she remembered the tingly, warm sensation that had swept through her body when the diamond rested against her skin. She'd had the odd feeling that it was coming alive. Was she just being fanciful? God, she hoped so. She had enough problems without adding a curse.

"I am sorry to disappoint, but I know of no such curse, and even if I did, I wouldn't believe in it. However, please feel free to use it if you think it will make the diamond more valuable."

She realized then that the man standing in front of her had absolutely no reverence for the beauty of the stone his family had possessed for so long, nor any interest in its history. He simply wanted to reap the financial benefits of selling it to the highest bidder. With gems there were always two kinds of buyers: those who wanted to look rich, and those who wanted to enrich their lives with a piece of history. She was glad he was selling it. Maybe whoever bought it would care more about where the diamond had come from and the story behind it.

She let out a sigh as the door closed behind Stefano. She didn't like that he'd brought up her father. It had been almost five years since the last scandal, and she'd hoped most people had forgotten about him.

How ironic that she'd spent the early part of her life living in her father's shadow and the last few years trying desperately to escape it. The fact that the Benedettis not only knew about her dad but also had chosen to send the collection to her was disturbing, because it wasn't logical. If they were worried about her father's reputation, why would they send the collection to Barclay's? Could her father answer that question? Was there some connection between his sudden return to San Francisco and the Benedetti diamond?

She walked over to her desk, and then stopped abruptly, a slash of color catching her eye. A tie was draped over the back of her chair, a stark red bow tie. Her heart stopped. She'd seen that tie before—earlier tonight at the party. Professor Keaton had worn one just like it. She picked it up, her mind whirling with the implications.

The door to her office opened again, and her heart skipped a beat. She wasn't sure whether to be relieved or alarmed that it was J.T. He was sure to have more questions—questions she couldn't answer.

"What's that?" he asked.

She dropped the tie, feeling as if she'd once again been caught doing something wrong. The tie landed on the desktop between them. J.T. stared at it for a long moment before turning his gaze to hers. "Who does that tie belong to, Christina?"

"The man I was speaking to at the party was wearing it, Professor Howard Keaton."

Recognition flared in his eyes, and she knew that his quick mind was already one step ahead of her.

"The same man who caught the necklace when it fell?" he asked.

"Yes."

"What was he doing here in your office?"

"I don't know. I haven't been here since before the party."

"But he was here." J.T. picked up the bow tie and studied it. "Somehow in the midst of the chaos and confusion, Professor Howard Keaton found his way to your office."

"What are you saying?"

"I think I know who Evan Chadwick is impersonating."

Evan? He thought Professor Keaton was the thief he was after? She let out a breath of relief. Maybe he was right. Maybe Professor Keaton was Evan Chadwick. And her father had nothing to do with any of this.

"So what will you do now?" she asked.

"Not me—we," he corrected. "I need to know everything you know about Professor Keaton."

"I don't know much, but I'm happy to talk to you about him."

He gave her a suspicious look. "That's a switch."

"I told you. I want to protect the diamond as much as you do."

"Good, but in case you were wondering—you're not off the hook yet."

"Why not? You think you know who this Evan Chadwick is impersonating, and it doesn't have anything to do with me."

"It has everything to do with you. He left his tie in your office." J.T.'s gaze burned into hers. "That either makes you a target or an accomplice. Which do you want to be?"

"I think I'd like another choice."

"Sorry, that's all I've got so far." He twirled the tie around his fingers. "This was left here for a reason. You're going to help me figure out what that reason is." He paused. "We'll need more coffee."

She suspected he was right. Making a sudden decision, she said, "There's a coffee shop a few blocks from here. It's open all night. But there's something you should know, Mr. McIntyre—"

"You can call me J.T. I think we're going to be working very closely together."

"Not if you don't change your attitude. I'm offering you my help because this auction is important to Barclay's and to me. But if you're going to make ridiculous accusations, this conversation ends right now. So what's it going to be?"

He held her gaze for a long moment, as if weighing her sincerity and her courage. Finally he tipped his head. "All right. We'll play it your way—for now."

3

Sam's Coffee Shop was an all-night diner serving breakfast twenty-four hours a day, located a few blocks from the auction house. The tables were filled mainly with swing-shift workers from the nearby hospital—every now and then an ambulance went by, sirens blaring. It wasn't the kind of place J.T. would have expected a woman like Christina to frequent. But then, he hadn't quite figured her out yet. Earlier tonight she'd looked like every man's fantasy, mysterious, seductive, sophisticated. Now she appeared more like the girl next door, freshly scrubbed, with natural beauty and innocence in her eyes. He wondered if her choice of clothes had been deliberate, if everything she said and did was designed to throw him off the scent. He couldn't make the mistake of underestimating her, especially now that he'd found Professor Keaton's tie in her office.

Taking another sip of coffee, he sat back in his chair, watching as Christina dug into her vegetable omelet with enthusiasm. She was either starving or avoiding the moment when she had to begin answering his questions. Either way, she was one bite away from the start of their discussion. Finally she finished, washing down the last of her omelet with a swig of ice water.

"You were hungry," he commented, noting her absolutely spotless plate.

"I didn't eat all day. I was too busy." She cleared her throat. "So, why don't you tell me more about this thief you're chasing? Evan, right? You said you've been following him for a long time, but you haven't been able to catch him."

J.T. didn't like the implied dig, but he gave Christina credit for going on the offensive and trying to get him off balance first. It was a smart move. He would have done the same in her shoes. "No, I haven't caught him, but I will."

She seemed disappointed by his calm response. "It must be frustrating with all the powers of the FBI behind you that you can't catch one little con man."

"That's how good he is. Anything else you want to know?"

"Actually, there's a lot I'd like to know. If this Evan Chadwick is trying to steal the diamond, maybe you should tell me more about him beyond just the basics of his appearance, which you suspect he has changed anyway. What kinds of crimes has he committed? Where does he live? How well do you know him?"

"Evan and I actually go way back," J.T. replied. "Long before I joined the bureau. We were roommates in college at Cal. We shared an apartment my junior year."

"Really?" she said, surprised. "So you know him very well?"

"Better than most, which isn't saying much. The only thing I know for sure about Evan is that he can be whoever he wants to be. Who he really is—I have no idea. I was certainly fooled when I first met him. I thought he was a friend, a good guy, but it turned out he was neither."

"What do you mean?"

"Evan was and is a scam artist. When we were in college he ran various fraudulent cons out of our apartment, maids that were in fact hookers, pyramid schemes, fixed card games, stolen tests. . . . You name it; he played it. Nick, one of the other guys in the apartment, caught on first, mainly because Evan had started dating Nick's sister, Jenny, and he was being a protective big brother. Nick convinced me to help him expose Evan. To make a long story short, Nick and I took Evan down. Evan was eventually expelled, arrested, did jail time, and swore revenge against both Nick and me."

"Did he get his revenge?"

"He took his revenge on Nick last month. While Nick was out of the country on business Evan broke into Nick's apartment, hacked into his computer, and basically stole everything from him, including his identity. While Evan was masquerading as Nick, he seduced a woman and convinced her to marry him."

"That's quite a story," Christina murmured, her expression thoughtful. "What about you? You said that Evan swore revenge on both of you. Did he do anything to you?"

J.T cleared his throat, sorry now that he'd allowed the conversation to veer off into personal territory.

"Yes, he got his revenge on me. Now it's my turn." He picked up his water glass and drained it down to the last drop.

"Aren't you going to explain?" Christina asked.

"It's personal."

She made a little face at that. "Really? It's personal?" she echoed sarcastically. "Fine, I'll take that response, as long as I can use it when you ask me questions I don't want to answer."

He saw the challenge in her eyes and knew she had him by the balls. If he wanted her to talk, he would have to tell her at least some of what she wanted to know. He could do this. He could say it out loud. Couldn't he?

His brain said yes, but his heart said no. The words didn't want to come.

Christina leaned forward, resting her elbows on the table. She waited for him to continue. She looked like she had every intention of sitting there for the rest of the night if she had to.

"Evan waited until I'd forgotten about him," he said finally. "I'd finished college, graduated, moved on with my life—Evan wasn't remotely on my radar screen. But I was on his." J.T. took a long breath, drawing strength from down deep. If Christina weren't someone who could help him catch Evan, he wouldn't be telling her a thing, but maybe if he could get her on his side, she'd be more willing to help. It wasn't as if talking about it would make it worse. It couldn't be any worse. What was done was done.

"My dad was a gambler," J.T. continued. "He couldn't pass up a bet on a card game, a sporting event, or the ponies. Evan played on my father's weakness and hustled him out of his life savings with an investment scheme that promised riches too good to be true. My father was devastated when he realized that he was completely ruined. My mother was so furious she left him and moved to her sister's house. And I . . . I said some . . ." He shook his head and stared down at the table. "Terrible things," he finished, knowing he could never, ever say those words aloud again. "A week later my father shot himself with a hunting rifle. My mother and I weren't talking to him, so he was dead two days before anyone found him."

"Oh, my God." Christina gasped, putting a hand to her mouth, horror in her eyes. "I'm so sorry. I didn't know . . . I didn't imagine it was that bad. I wouldn't have asked you to explain if I'd known."

"Evan might as well have pulled the trigger," he said, still tasting the bitter fury that had been with him since the moment he'd gone to his father's house to check on him because his mother had finally gotten worried. He blamed himself for what had happened as much as he blamed Evan. He should have seen it coming. He should have done something. Instead of acting out of pride and anger, instead of being judgmental and critical, he should have found a way to understand his father's pain, his desperation at having lost everything and everyone in his life.

"You don't have to say any more," Christina said, compassion in her voice. "I shouldn't have forced you to tell me. I don't usually pry into people's lives. You just annoyed me and I wanted to get even. I'm sorry."

"It's better you know the kind of man you're dealing

with." He took a breath. Now that he'd started, he needed to finish it. "The day of the funeral Evan sent me a condolence card to let me know he was behind it all. He also sent flowers to the grave."

"That's sick."

"That's Evan." He held her gaze for a long moment. "Make no mistake, Christina; Evan Chadwick is a sociopath. On the outside he's charming, good-looking, friendly. He knows how to get people to trust him. Then he destroys them. Evan got his payback and I'll get mine. I will put him away for the rest of his life. You can bank on that."

"I'm sure you will. I can understand why you're so determined to catch him. I wish I could help."

"That's why we're here, so you can help."

She sighed. "I stepped right into that one, didn't I?"

"Yes, and I didn't spill my guts for nothing. Now it's your turn. I was reviewing what happened at the party tonight. You spoke to a man when you first entered the room. It was one of your longer conversations. Who was that?"

She thought for a moment. "Michael Torrance. He's a collector. I've worked with him over the past few years."

"So you know him well? You've had a relationship with him?"

"A phone relationship. Tonight was the first night we met in person. I usually do his bidding for him by phone—as I do for a number of other customers. It's common in my business."

J.T.'s nerves tightened. He didn't want to jump too fast to the wrong conclusion. Evan could be impersonating anyone. He needed to keep an open mind. But if Christina had never met Michael Torrance in person before tonight, then he should be checked out. "Let's move on to Professor Keaton."

"I don't know much about him except that he was a professor of art history at UCLA some years back. He told me that he now works at a museum in Vancouver. He didn't give me the name."

"That shouldn't be too hard to track down. What else did he say to you?"

"He asked me if I was nervous wearing the diamond because of the curse."

"Huh?" He hadn't heard that one before. "The diamond is cursed?"

Christina shrugged as if she didn't know how to answer the question. "He's the only one who seems to think so. I asked Stefano Benedetti about it. He said he'd never heard of a curse. I have to admit that the diamond's history is a bit fuzzy. Usually for a stone of this size there is a fairly lengthy declaration of ownership attached to it. The Benedettis have said next to nothing about it, except that it's been in their family for a hundred years and basically has been kept hidden away in a vault."

Reading between the lines of her statements, he could see that she was unsettled by something. "What aren't you telling me? You have an odd expression on your face."

"I don't know more than what I've said. But I am curious as to why Professor Keaton thinks there's a curse and the Benedettis don't know anything about it."

"Sounds like we need to talk to Professor Keaton for several reasons."

"Like why he was in my office," she said, meeting his gaze. "Even in the thick smoke, there wouldn't have been any reason for him to go upstairs rather than down. But he's an older man. I can't believe he was agile enough to set smoke bombs off in an intricate venting system."

"True, but he could have been working with someone. Or he could have been Evan in disguise, dressed up like an old, distinguished professor. Evan is thirty-two years old and extremely fit." Pausing, he said, "Putting that aside for the moment, why was Keaton at the party? How did he get on the guest list?"

"If he buys for a museum, he would be on the guest list."

"That's not something you compiled?"

"It was a joint effort," she replied. "Every department sent out invitations. We're not just auctioning off jewelry tomorrow, but also the rest of the collection, which includes paintings and other items. Professor Keaton wasn't on my list, but that doesn't mean he wasn't on someone else's list."

"If Keaton is from out of town, he's no doubt staying at a hotel. I'll track him down. We need to know if he is who he says he is. Because if Keaton is Evan, and he was in your office, then you're involved."

Christina frowned at his analysis. "You're starting to scare me."

"I hope I am. Evan has hurt a lot of people. I don't want you to get hurt, too."

"Does that mean you're no longer suspicious of me? That you don't think I'm working with him?"

He didn't answer right away, and when he saw the

nervous flicker in her eyes, he reminded himself that her actions all evening had been extremely suspicious. He couldn't forget that. "I think you're hiding something, Christina," he said. "And I believe you're the kind of woman who thinks she can handle everything on her own. But this whole situation is bigger than you realize. You might need help—my help."

"So that's a no?" she asked, a sharp bite to her tone.

He could see she didn't like his answer. "I'm not closing the door on anything or anyone. I've known you only a few hours, and so far I've seen you climb a tree, break into a house, slam the door to an open safe in my face, and warn someone off. Not exactly typical, ordinary kinds of actions, wouldn't you agree? As far as I'm concerned, no one is above suspicion, including you."

"I guess I know where I stand then."

"There's something else I'm curious about," he continued.

"There seems to be no end to your curiosity."

"Why Barclay's? Why not one of the other bigger auction houses? Why did the Benedettis choose your house for their collection? I've seen your security, and it could be better."

"You can take that up with Russell Kenner. Security is not my area. As for why us . . . Barclay's may be smaller and not as old or as well-known, but we're very well respected in the industry. We have an office in Europe, and one of our specialists there was able to win the consignment from the Benedettis. There are all kinds of deals in terms of money and percentages. I'm not privy to that particular information. You would have to discuss the details with Alexis or Jeremy Kensington, the owners of Barclay's."

He nodded. It was interesting how she had so much more to say when she wasn't being asked a personal question. "I'll keep that in mind. Since you're not in charge of security or pricing, what exactly do you do?"

"I'm the department specialist for jewelry, not just diamonds, but any kind of jewelry that we sell. I have a background in art history and I'm a certified gemologist."

"In other words, you're a smart girl," he mused. Christina was not just smart; she was also beautiful, a dangerous combination.

"You could say that."

"Do you have a boyfriend?" Where had that question come from?

Her jaw dropped, her eyes widening with surprise. "What does that have to do with anything?"

He searched his brain for a good reason. "Just wondering how vulnerable you would be to a seductive con man."

She bristled at that. "As you said, I'm a smart girl. I don't fall for phony lines."

"You didn't answer my question, Christina."

She crossed her arms in front of her as she sat back in her chair. "Not that it's your business, but, no, I don't have a boyfriend at the moment. I'm too busy with my job. What about you? Do you have a girlfriend?"

"No," he said shortly, regretting having opened up this line of questioning. Fortunately, she seemed as eager to ditch it as he was.

"So, are we done?" she asked. "It's been a long night. I'd like to go home."

"Not so fast. We never finished our conversation about your father."

She let out a sigh. "I'll tell you this. My father is an incredible man. He raised me on his own from the time I was an infant. My mother left me, but my father didn't. It was just the two of us. He was my whole world. I thought he was the smartest man alive."

J.T. picked up the nuance in her voice and wondered where it came from. "But you don't think that now?"

"Of course I do," she said quickly.

He wasn't sure he believed her. There was something going on between her and her father. "Are you still close?"

"Not like we used to be. My father is retired, and he travels a lot. We don't see each other much."

"Sounds like he has a good life. Did he ever remarry?"

"My father said he could never love anyone but my mother. He's a romantic," she added with a weary smile.

"Like his daughter?"

"No," she said with a definitive shake of her head. "I had to be the practical one or we never would have survived. My father would get caught up in his research and lose track of time. He had that absent-minded professor bit down pretty well. But I took care of him, and he took care of me. We traveled a lot. It worked." She stopped abruptly, the sound of her cell phone interrupting their conversation. She pulled out her phone and said, "Hello." She stiffened, her face turning pale. "Yes, all right," she said, then ended the call.

Christina tried to act nonchalant as she returned her phone to her purse, but J.T. could see that she was rattled. "Who was that?" he queried.

"One of my coworkers."

"So it was business?"

"Sure."

"Interesting, because your face turned white when you said hello."

"I'm just tired."

"No, you're just lying—again. I wish you could trust me, Christina. If Evan is using you in some way, if he has some hold over you, tell me. I can help." It occurred to him that Evan might have some hold over her father. From what he knew of Christina so far, her weakness seemed to be her dad, and J.T. knew better than most that when it came to fathers, Evan knew just how to strike.

For a split second Christina seemed to waver; then she straightened her shoulders and threw back her head. "Everything is fine. If I need your help, I'll ask. But for now, I'm going home."

Half an hour later, J.T. walked into his hotel room at the downtown Holiday Inn, feeling both tired and wired. He shouldn't have had that third cup of coffee. But caffeine aside, he knew he wouldn't be able to sleep; he had too much on his mind. And it wasn't just Evan's mocking smile that played through his head; it was Christina's image, her mysterious green eyes, her soft, lying lips.

His gut tightened as he remembered the way she'd avoided his questions. She was protecting someone—was it Evan? Or was it her father, who seemed a more likely possibility? If Evan was blackmailing her, she might feel compelled to go along. She certainly seemed to be protective of her dad. He couldn't blame her for that.

He should have been so protective when it came to his own father. If he'd been more attentive, more thoughtful, his family would still be together. His father would be alive. His mother wouldn't be wasting away with grief. And he . . . well, he'd probably be living a much different life right now. Everything had changed after Evan, every single last thing. But he couldn't think about any of that now. He had to focus on the present, not the past. What was done was done.

Throwing his keys down on the dresser, J.T. took out his laptop computer and sat on the bed. While waiting for the computer to boot up, he flipped on the television. He ran through the channels, pausing at one of the sports talk shows. They were interviewing a guy he'd played with in college. Henry Redeker, a star running back at Cal, had gone on to play for the New York Jets and had just announced his retirement from the game after eleven years.

Eleven years! J.T. shook his head. It was hard to believe so much time had passed since they'd graduated. Henry had had the life that J.T. was supposed to have had, the one his father had wanted for him with every breath he took.

J.T. thought back to all those years, all those practices, all those late nights at the park when it had been just him and his dad throwing passes until it was too dark to see.

In the beginning it was a shared dream; then it had become an obsession—at least for his father. They'd had so many heated arguments about what he should want for himself, what he should do, how he should act. He'd disappointed his father on so many occasions, never being quite good enough, even when it seemed he was being as good as he could possibly be. But his father had always shaken his head and told him he could do better. At times there had been nothing but hate between them. Unfortunately, it was the other times that brought him the pain now.

J.T. let out a breath, wishing he could find a way to keep those memories out of his head. He needed to catch Evan, if for no other reason than to lock the door on his past. Once Evan was in jail, he would never, ever have to revisit those days again.

He turned the channel, relieved to find a late-night comedy show. Stupid jokes about the day's events were just what he needed now. He was used to cold, impersonal hotel rooms, late and lonely nights on the road. Most of the time he didn't care. It was part of the job, and he had no one in Los Angeles who was waiting for him to come home or wondering where he was, so his life worked. But for some reason tonight he felt restless and frustrated.

He hated when things didn't add up, when he couldn't figure something or someone out, and Christina fit that bill. She'd told him just enough to tease him into wanting to know more. Her actions over the past eight hours intrigued him. She'd gotten his attention. And he wasn't just interested; he was attracted to her, a complication he did not need.

He hadn't wanted to say good night to her, and if he were honest with himself, he'd wanted to do more than question her; he'd wanted to kiss her, to explore the softness of her mouth with his tongue and trace the lush curves of her body with his hands. He ruthlessly reminded himself that she might be beautiful and smart, but she was also a liar. He should have his head examined for even considering going down that road. He was obviously in desperate need of a social life, something else he'd put on hold the last few years.

He couldn't let himself get personally involved with Christina. If he did, he'd no doubt play right into Evan's game. It would be just like Evan to use a woman, someone who could get to him and distract him. The last thing he needed was a distraction.

Turning his attention to his computer, he pulled up his old pal Nick's file. He'd compiled a chronological record of events since Evan had taken over Nick's identity several months earlier, keeping a thorough, detailed account of everything that had transpired. As he reviewed his notes, he strained to see some clue he was missing, to find a pattern or a loophole. Nothing seemed to be related to or connected between what Evan had been doing with Nick and Kayla and what he was doing now. Yet, J.T. felt certain there was some link between that job and this one. Evan's usual mode of operation was to disappear after a con. He never stayed in the same city. It was too risky, and probably too boring, J.T. suspected. So Evan moved on—but not this time. This time he had left behind a clue— deliberately. He'd wanted J.T. to stay close on the trail. So what was he up to now?

The question ran around and around in J.T.'s brain, making him crazy. What was the connection?

His gaze fixed on one word that continued to pop up in his notes—*Italian.* Evan's last job had focused on several Italian families, the Riccis, the Carmellos, the Damons, and the Blandinos. Now Evan was interested in an auction featuring a diamond from yet another Italian family—the Benedettis. The Benedettis lived in Florence, as far as J.T. knew, and it was certainly a leap to think there was any connection among the families, but he hated to discount the possibility. His instincts told him there was something there, but what exactly he couldn't say.

His nerves tightened at the sound of someone coming down the hall. The heavy footsteps paused outside his door. He swung his legs off the bed, grabbed his gun, and got to his feet. He saw a piece of paper lying on the floor. Obviously someone had slipped it under the door. Ignoring that for the moment, he looked through the peephole. The hall was empty. He opened the door to check. No one was there. Closing the door, he picked up the paper and turned it over. There was a color photograph of Christina from the party, posed at the entrance to the gallery in her black dress, the yellow diamond gleaming against her skin. The caption read, *She's pretty, and she's mine. You know you can't stop me. Why do you even try?*

J.T. blew out a breath of frustration. He'd seen enough notes from Evan to recognize his handwriting and his taunts. Evan loved to make sure J.T. was paying attention. And it was clear Evan intended to use Christina. Did she know it? Was she a willing partner? Was she working to set him up? Anger raced through J.T.'s body. If she was involved, she was going to be very, very sorry.

Debating for one long minute whether he wanted to get Christina on the phone, he decided to go another route. He pulled out his cell phone and dialed the home number of his assistant, Tracy Delgado. Tracy had been with him for four years and knew almost as much about Evan as he did. She was probably asleep and would give him hell for waking her up, but it wasn't the first time, and it wouldn't be the last.

As expected, Tracy answered the phone in an annoyed voice. "This had better be important, Mac."

"It is. I need you to find out everything you can about Christina Alberti. Oh, and while you're at it, check out her father. I think his name is Marcus Alberti."

"Christina, got it. She's the chick at the auction house?"

"That's right."

"Is tomorrow good enough?" she asked. "I'm kind of busy at the moment."

He heard a man's voice in the background and suspected he'd caught Tracy at a very bad time. Sometimes he forgot that other people had actual lives. "Tomorrow is fine. Oh, and I also need you to track down a Professor Howard Keaton. He works at a museum in Vancouver. He's probably staying at a hotel in San Francisco."

"That's all you know?"

"For now. Call me tomorrow—as soon as you can. Evan's plan is already in motion, and I don't want to be the last one to find out what it is."

*   *   *

When Christina arrived at the small lab on the first floor of Barclay's Auction House where they conducted their jewelry appraisals, she was shocked to find her part-time assistant, David Padlinsky, looking through the gem scope at the Benedetti diamond. David, a grad student from Berkeley, had joined Barclay's a month earlier. Somewhere in his late twenties, he looked more like a rock star than a historian, with a diamond earring in one ear and long dark hair that today was swept back in a ponytail. A thick beard and mustache covered the lower half of his face. But it wasn't his appearance that upset Christina; it was his actions.

"What are you doing?" she asked shortly.

"Setting up the scope for you." He straightened up, giving her a curious look. "Is something wrong?"

She hesitated, realizing there were more people in the room than usual. Normally she did her work in the lab on her own or with David, but today Alexis and Stefano Benedetti were also present, as well as J.T., who was currently following every word of the conversation between her and David. "No, nothing is wrong," she said.

"What's with the audience?" David murmured, as she joined him by the worktable.

She shrugged. "Everyone wants to make sure the diamond is all right."

"Why wouldn't it be?"

"No reason."

David sent her an odd look, but she didn't want to explain any of J.T.'s suspicious theories to him. She pulled up a tall stool and sat down, adjusting the scope so she could examine the diamond. David opened a file on the adjacent computer screen that showed a digital drawing of the diamond from several angles. She would compare her findings to the initial appraisal conducted by their associate in Florence.

First, she wanted to look at the clasp on the chain. She moved the necklace under the eye of the scope. The clasp was very old and ornate but didn't appear to be broken or loose. Perhaps it just hadn't been attached properly the night before. She tried to remember who had closed the clasp. There had been so many people around her, Alexis, Jeremy, Sylvia—wait, Sylvia. Christina distinctly remembered the head of public relations taking the necklace from Alexis and fastening it around her neck. Sylvia must not have snapped it all the way closed. She probably wouldn't admit to that, though. She was tight with Alexis, and very ambitious. She wouldn't want to be blamed for the necklace falling off of Christina's neck.

"Well?" J.T. demanded in an impatient voice. "What do you see?"

"The clasp looks good," she murmured.

"So why did it break?" he asked, stepping forward.

She wished she could tell him to move back. His nearness was distracting. She could smell the musky scent of his cologne and feel the heat of his breath on the back of her neck. She didn't know why he had to be so close. She forced herself to concentrate on the task at hand. "The clasp must not have been hooked properly."

"You would have thought someone would have made sure it was," J.T. replied.

She moved the stone under the scope. She would normally conduct a lengthy examination, but today she didn't have time for more than the basics. They had a reporter and photographer coming for a photo shoot at ten. As she looked at the stone, she reviewed the diamond's culet and girdle thickness along with polish and symmetry, also checking for indicators of diamond treatments or synthetics, then compared them to the statistics listed on the initial report. She reviewed the diamond's brightness, fire, sparkle and pattern, weight ratio and durability as well.

Everything seemed to match . . . but something bothered her.

"May I, signorina?" Stefano asked.

She looked up and saw the eagerness in his eyes. Just behind him, Alexis gave a nod of approval, so Christina stepped aside. No one spoke as Stefano studied the stone. She grew uneasy as his review went on for several minutes. Was something wrong? He seemed to be taking a long time to reassure himself that everything was fine. And while he might not be interested in the stone's history, he appeared to be educated enough to know how to study a gem for evaluation purposes.

Finally, he nodded and stepped away. *"Grazie."* He turned to Alexis. "I'd like to run through the rest of the collection now."

"It's in the other room," Alexis said with a relieved smile. "I'll take you." She paused at the door. "Christina, I'll see you in the gallery for the photo shoot."

As Alexis and Stefano left the room, Christina turned to David. "You can go, too. I'll just finish up my notes."

David appeared disappointed. "Are you sure you don't need my help?"

"I'm fine. Thanks." When David left the lab, she was alone with J.T. "Don't you have something else to do? Weren't you going to track down Michael Torrance or Professor Keaton?"

"I'm working on that."

"Really? How are you working on that if you're standing here with me?"

He smiled. "Don't worry about it. And stop trying to get rid of me. I might start to wonder why you want to be in this room alone with the diamond."

"There are two guards outside the door, and no other escape routes."

"I noticed."

She sighed. "Fine, if you want to stand there and watch, go ahead. I must say I thought FBI agents led more exciting lives."

"Sarcasm will not get rid of me. I have a very thick skin. So is this diamond really worth fifteen million dollars?" J.T. asked.

"It's worth whatever anyone will pay for it."

"But you expect to get something in that range?"

"Yes. There are only a limited number of colored diamonds in existence, especially of this size. It's one of a kind."

"And it's been sitting in some family vault for a hundred years?"

"That's as much as I know."

"Seems you'd want to know more before you sold it. Isn't there some danger that the claims of ownership are fraudulent?"

"Not in this case. The Benedettis provided ample proof of ownership." She met his gaze head-on. "There have been a few scandals over the years, but not at Barclay's. Our house has an impeccable reputation, and it's going to stay that way." She took another look through the scope. She wanted to get rid of any lingering doubts about the diamond's authenticity. If the diamond was a copy, it was excellent, a perfect match, right down to the flaws. Or was it? Her heart began to race.

She wanted to read through the report again. She wanted to move back and forth between the scope and the computer screen, but she didn't want to raise J.T.'s suspicions. If she implied that there was anything wrong with the diamond, he would be all over her. He'd suggest that she'd switched it with the professor. After all, Professor Keaton's tie had been in her office. And J.T. already thought she was being conned by Evan. She had to think. She had to buy herself some time.

Maybe she was wrong. It was possible. Stefano Benedetti hadn't seen anything out of the ordinary. Sometimes flaws could be detected only under particular lighting conditions, especially small mineral inclusions.

She could take a few minutes to think. There were only a few people in the world who had the ability to copy a diamond of this magnitude. Who would know how to find those people? One man came to mind. And she knew just how to find him. He'd already told her where he would be when he'd called her the night before. But first she had to get through the next hour without J.T. suspecting anything was wrong.

"Everything all right?" J.T. asked.

"Perfect," she lied. "Everything is perfect."

4

He'd asked her to meet him at the San Francisco Zoo by the lion's cage at noon. Christina knew the clandestine meeting appealed to her father's sense of drama. They'd played out many such meetings in the past. Marcus Alberti loved action, excitement, suspense, and intrigue. She suspected that in his own head he was more James Bond than academic historian. He had spent his life researching the past, but over the past two decades his desire to become more of an active participant than an observer had changed him. It hadn't been enough for him to read about great adventurers; he'd wanted to be one.

She hadn't realized just how far he would take this desire until it was too late. It had all started out so innocently, with such a sense of justice. Her father had become obsessed with setting right the wrongs that had been done in the art world. He believed that works of art that had been stolen during times of war or other turbulence should be returned to their rightful owners. It was a laudable goal. Until his arrogance got in the way. Until he started bending the rules, stealing back items from those who believed themselves to be the legal owners. At some point her father had lost track of what was right and what was wrong, and she'd found herself in that same hazy gray area with him.

She'd been his partner in crime; only she hadn't realized it until it was too late, until the ties that bound them together began to unravel. She had never thought they would be as estranged as they were now. She had never thought there would come a day when she would never want to see him again, not want him to be part of her life, but that day had arrived. That day was now.

Why had he returned to San Francisco? He'd promised he would stay away from her, play his games elsewhere. What had changed? She had to find out.

Christina paused by the entrance to the zoo to take a look behind her. She hoped no one, specifically J.T., had followed her. When she'd left Barclay's, J.T. had been reviewing videotape from the security cameras to see if they could figure out who had set the smoke bombs. She'd told David that if J.T. asked, to let him know she had gone to lunch and would be back around two o'clock. Hopefully that would buy her enough time to meet her father and figure out whether or not he was in any way involved with the diamond.

The street behind her held no familiar faces, so she entered the zoo and bought a ticket. A large number of schoolchildren milled around the entrance, and a tram was loading up for its next trip around the park. Off in the distance was the carousel she'd ridden so many times with her father. The familiar music made her feel a little sad that those happy, carefree days were gone. One thing about her dad—he'd made her childhood fun. A born teacher, he'd wanted to expose her to everything. He'd encouraged her to learn as much as she could, to be curious, to ask questions.

Now she was curious about him, what he was up to, and how it could affect her. She walked through the zoo, barely glancing at the tall giraffes, enormous elephants, squealing birds, and howling monkeys. She was too worried about what was coming next. She'd worked so hard to build a life for herself after losing everything five years earlier. She didn't want to have to start over again.

She stood by the railing looking at the expansive cage that housed the lions. It was the middle of the day, when sometimes the big cats were sleeping. Finally, she saw one lion deep in the brush. He raised his head, as if wondering what had disturbed him; then he settled back down, but not all the way down, his eyes still open, his body positioned to spring or flee at any second. His instincts were on full alert. That was exactly the way she felt whenever her father was around, as if she couldn't let down her guard for one second.

Not that this lion had much to fear in a controlled zoo environment.

It seemed wrong to have such noble creatures behind bars. Wouldn't they be much happier running free in the wild? Wasn't that where they really belonged?

She smiled to herself. Maybe she wasn't as different from her father as she liked to think. Freeing the lions was something Marcus Alberti had always wanted to do. It was just another example of his romantic, impractical mind-set.

The hairs on the back of her neck began to tingle. A

shadow fell across the pavement next to her. She turned her head. A man stood beside her, a fishing hat on his head, dark glasses hiding his expression, a beige windbreaker over his tan slacks. He looked like any other tourist, but when he turned to gaze at her, she caught her breath at the familiar grin.

Marcus pulled off his glasses so she could see his dark brown eyes. He'd always had ridiculously long eyelashes, of which she'd been extremely jealous. There was no doubt that her father was a handsome man, one who smiled with his eyes as well as his mouth. His sideburns showed streaks of gray, and there were a few more lines on his face, but that was to be expected; he was in his early sixties, after all. Not that he ever seemed to age. In his own head she doubted he ever felt older than twenty-five. He was still reckless, still optimistic, still filled with dreams of what he could achieve. Was that laudable or stupidly unrealistic?

"How's my sweetheart?" He opened his arms, and for a moment she wanted to move into his embrace, hug him tight, the way she had so many times before. But she held back, and his eyes filled with disappointment. His hands dropped to his sides and he dug them into his pockets. "You are not happy to see me," he said heavily.

"Should I be? What's going on, Dad? Why the mystery meeting?"

"I'm worried about you, Christina." His expression was somber, concerned.

"How could you be worried about me? I haven't seen you in over a year or talked to you in the last three months. You don't know what's going on in my life, do you?"

"I stayed away because that's what you wanted, wasn't it?" he challenged.

"Yes, that's what I wanted," she admitted. "And it bothers me that you've chosen to come back now, when Barclay's is about to auction off a very valuable diamond."

"That is why I've come back," he admitted.

His candor shocked and disappointed her. "Oh, Dad."

"It's not what you think. I came to warn you, Christina. The diamond is dangerous. It is cursed."

His words echoed her conversation with the professor. Were they working together? "I heard that yesterday from an old friend of yours, Professor Keaton. Do you remember him? He was at the preview party last night."

"Yes, of course, I remember Howard. He told you about the curse of the diamond?"

"Not in any detail. But when I asked Mr. Benedetti to confirm the story, he said it wasn't true."

Her father's lips formed a taut line. "He's lying. Vittorio Benedetti wants to get rid of the diamond and the curse. That's why he's selling the stone, why he wants it out of his family."

His words made her uneasy, but she tried to dismiss his worry. "Even if there is a curse, it has nothing to do with me. I'm not going to buy the diamond."

"But you've touched it, worn it. I am afraid for you, Christina, afraid of what curse you may have unleashed upon yourself. I don't want you to touch it again."

"You're going to have to tell me more if you want me to understand."

"Good versus evil, two sides of the same stone, Christina. In its rightful place the diamond bestows great luck. Taken from that place, it devours with evil all those who covet it."

Despite her resolve to remain skeptical, his words sent a chill down her spine. Her father certainly had a dramatic flair.

"Don't touch the diamond again," he continued. "Call in sick. Let someone else handle the auction. Stay away from Barclay's until the diamond is gone."

"You know I can't do that. It's my job."

He shook his head in frustration. "I don't understand how you can work at an auction house, how you can sell priceless works of art as if they were merchandise like shoes or toilet paper. I taught you to respect the past, not to make a profit from it. That diamond belongs in Italy."

"That diamond belongs to the Benedettis, who are free to sell it to whomever they please. I'm not cheapening the past. I'm part of a company that allows ordinary people to touch extraordinary things. I don't understand why you can't see that." His criticism stung, not just because he was insulting her job, but also because he was making her doubt herself. Sometimes the commercialism of her business did irritate her. Sometimes she cringed to see a beautiful vase or painting pass into the hands of someone who wanted to have it because they were rich, not because they appreciated it. But who was she to judge other people's motives? That was definitely not in her job description. "I have to go back to work."

"Vittorio Benedetti stole that diamond, Christina." Passion filled his voice; determination was written in his eyes.

She wanted to believe him, but how could she? "You always think everything is stolen."

"I know him. I met Vittorio many years ago."

"I would need a lot more than your word. Do you have any proof?"

"My word should be enough for you—my daughter."

"That's why it isn't, Dad." The gaze she gave him was direct and honest. "I'm not a little girl anymore whom you can fool with your games. I know who you are, what you're capable of doing."

"I don't think you do, and it makes me sad."

"Well, you've certainly given me some sad days, too. Where was your protective instinct when I lost my job at the museum? You want to know why I work for an auction house? Because no museum would hire me, and it took me almost two years before Barclay's would take me on. All because of you and your ridiculous obsessions."

He let out a heavy sigh. "I am sorry about that incident. But it was not as it appeared."

"It never is." She paused, knowing she had to ask him the question that had been burning through her brain for the past two hours. "There is something I want to know. Who would have the ability to copy a diamond like the Benedetti?"

His eyes narrowed. "Why do you ask? Do you think the stone is a fake?"

"When I looked at the diamond this morning, the specifications didn't exactly match those on the appraisal report done last month in Florence. That report mentioned a small mineral inclusion in the shape of a heart. I couldn't see it."

"Mineral inclusions are not always visible from various angles."

"I'm aware of that. What I want you to tell me is if I have a copy of the diamond or the real thing. And if I have a copy, who made it, who put it there, and who has the real stone?"

"That's a lot of questions, Christina."

"Last night someone set off smoke bombs at Barclay's, causing a huge commotion. I was wearing the diamond, and it slipped off my neck for a split second." She paused. "I was talking to Professor Keaton at the time, your old friend. Is he working with you? Did he somehow switch the diamond, bring you the real thing?"

"Is that why you went to my house last night?" he asked.

"Yes, I wanted to see if the diamond was in the safe," she admitted. "And I thought I saw you leaving Barclay's. Were you there?"

"You weren't alone at my house," he said, not addressing the second part of her question.

"No, I wasn't."

"Who was with you?"

"Oh, just a special agent with the FBI named J. T. McIntyre, who, by the way, now happens to be extremely suspicious of me and will no doubt have run a full background check on both of us by the end of the day. You have to leave, Dad, go away—far away. But before you do, you need to give me back the real diamond if you have it."

"Did it ever occur to you that the diamond could have been switched at any time, perhaps by the

Benedetti family? Think about it, Christina. They
show your appraiser the real thing, and then they ship
a fake to Barclay's. You said yourself that you can't be
sure if the diamond is real or fake."

"No, I'm not sure. But why would the Benedettis try
to sell a fake diamond?"

"It would be difficult to trace it to them. If anyone
found out, it would be blamed on Barclay's."

"On me," she muttered. Was she being set up? Was
that what this was about?

"Or the other alternative is that the appraiser in Florence made a mistake in his report. It would be difficult to copy an entire necklace, especially one that
hasn't been in the public eye. The only person who
could do that would be someone who had a great deal
of time to study the diamond and the chain."

It was the same point she'd made to J.T. Maybe her father was right. She would check with the appraiser in
Florence, discuss the flaws, the mineral inclusion. Perhaps one of them had simply made a mistake. It wasn't
as if she'd had a great deal of time to study the stone, not
with J.T. looking over her shoulder. Perhaps all of his
talk about thieves and con men had clouded her brain.

"If there is some possibility that the diamond you
have is a copy, then it's even more reason for you to
distance yourself from it, Christina," her father said.
"Learn from my mistakes. Don't get so close that it
looks like you're involved."

"At the museum it didn't just look like you were involved, Dad. You *were* involved."

He gave a dismissive wave of his hand. "That's all
in the past. What's important is that I love you, and I'm

worried about you. Call in sick. Stay home. Make up an excuse."

"I can't do that. I have to figure out if the diamond is a fake, and if it is, I can't let Barclay's sell a false stone. It would ruin the company, and it would ruin me."

He frowned in dissatisfaction, stroking his jaw with one hand. "All right. Maybe I can help. I have some . . . contacts. I can see if anyone knows anything about a copy being made. Can you give me a little time?"

She hesitated, not sure she wanted his help, but what choice did she have? "The auction is tomorrow at noon. I have to make a decision early in the morning."

"You can call it off right up to the last minute," he told her.

"I'd have to give a reason why I didn't call it off today."

"You weren't sure. You had to take another look, which is the truth. I know you're big on the truth," he said with a half smile. "I guess I did something right raising you."

She felt herself weaken at his fond smile. He always did this to her. He always made her forget that she had every reason to be seriously angry with him. In many ways he was like a little kid who never had to answer to authority, a regular Peter Pan, who considered life one big game, the world one enormous playground. "I have to get back to work," she said.

"I understand. I'll be in touch," he said. "Stay away from that FBI guy."

"Believe me, I'd like to, but he appears to be permanently attached to me. Fortunately, he seems to think someone named Evan Chadwick is trying to steal the diamond. I don't suppose you've heard of him."

He shook his head. "Can't say that I have, but I don't know every thief in the world."

"Just most of them," she finished.

"You give me too much credit." He paused, an odd look coming into his brown eyes. "I didn't realize how much you've grown up. You're so beautiful. You look . . . just like your mother," he said, his voice growing husky.

Her breath caught in her throat. "I do?" He had never said that before.

He nodded slowly. "Yes, and you know that I'd do anything to protect you, don't you?"

"Are you trying to tell me something?"

Smiling, he leaned forward and kissed her on the cheek. Then he slipped on his dark glasses and walked away.

She put her hands on the railing in front of her and let out a breath of air. She was relieved in some ways, but disturbed in others. Her father had made a point of saying he'd do anything to protect her, as if he thought she was in some kind of danger. Why? Was he really just concerned about a curse? Or was there something more he wasn't telling her? She wondered if she'd made a mistake confiding in him her concerns about the diamond. He certainly hadn't managed to allay them; instead he'd given her more to worry about.

Evan Chadwick moved through the hallways of Barclay's Auction House as if he owned the place. His disguise was so good no one gave him a second glance. He had their trust. And soon he would have their diamond. As he walked down the hall he saw J.T. in the conference room talking on his cell phone. He couldn't help but smile. He loved it when J.T. was close and yet so far away. They'd actually spoken earlier. J.T had looked right at him and seen a stranger. He had no idea who he really was. It amused him to see J.T. spinning his wheels. It also amused him that J.T. thought Christina was Evan's pawn. Well, she was, but not in the way J.T. thought. He had plans for Christina Alberti, big plans, and nothing J.T. could do would stop them.

He breezed past the conference room and strolled down the stairs to the first floor. When he left the building, he saw the limo parked a block away. She had no idea how to be discreet, he thought with annoyance. He deliberately walked past the white stretch limo, past the chauffeur who had stepped out of the car to open the door for him. He saw the surprised look on the man's face, but he kept walking. They were too close to Barclay's for this meeting.

Evan continued on around the corner, down the block, blending in with tourists and locals taking their lunch break. A block later the limo pulled up next to the curb and double-parked. He opened the door and got in. He sat back against the plush leather seat, not bothering to look at her.

"Damn you, Evan," she hissed. "How dare you dismiss me like that?"

"I said I would call when I needed to talk to you."

"Well, I needed to speak to you," she said. "Look at me."

He was tempted not to, just because he loved to push

her buttons, but for the moment he would let her believe that she was still in control. This scheme might have been her idea, but it was now his job. And he would handle it.

He took his time turning his gaze to hers. When he finally looked at her face, he could see the anger in the taut pull of skin over her cheekbones. She was very thin and appeared to be in her forties, maybe older. It was impossible to tell. She'd had at least three plastic surgeries. Nothing about her was real, from her enlarged breasts to her full lips to her straight nose. She was as fake as he was, and there was the same wild look in her eyes that his mother had had right before she'd gone crazy and tried to kill him. He'd learned then how to survive. Kill or be killed. He hoped she wouldn't make the same mistakes his mother had made.

"There's a dinner party tonight," she said. "You'll be there."

"Of course. I've already arranged it."

"I want you to get rid of that FBI agent."

"Why?"

"Why? Because he's a fed and he's going to ruin everything."

"He tried before."

"And he had you in jail," she reminded him.

"But not for long."

"Get your revenge on your friends on your own time. I want him out of it."

Evan shrugged. "When it's time for him to go, he'll go."

She shook her head, annoyance adding lines to her

face. "That's not good enough. I can't take the chance of losing everything now. We're so close. I want it done."

He loved her desperation. Desperate people believed what they wanted to believe and saw what they wanted to see—the perfect mark. She thought she was in charge. She was so wrong. "Tomorrow it will be over."

Her eyes hardened. "If I don't get what I want, you will be of no further use to me."

He didn't bother to tell her that her usefulness to him would come to an end far sooner than that.

"Where have you been?" J.T. asked, following Christina into her office. He didn't like the way she avoided his gaze. She'd taken a very long lunch, and he was still damning himself for letting her leave the building without him. She'd certainly made no mention of her intentions when he'd left her talking to the press a few hours earlier.

"I've been at lunch," she replied, sitting down behind her desk. "I have some calls to make; do you mind?"

"Not curious as to whether or not I've learned anything about who set the smoke bombs?" he asked, taking a seat in the chair across from her.

"Did you?"

"That question is a little late in coming."

"I told you before, my job is not security. As long as the diamond is safe now, I'll leave it to you and the others to worry about who set off the smoke bombs last night."

She busied herself shuffling the stack of papers on her desk. He could see that she wanted him to leave.

Tough. He knew a bit more about her now than he had the night before. His assistant, Tracy, had come through, as she always did.

The silence was getting to Christina. Finally she looked up at him. "Is there something else you want?"

"Yes. I want to know where your father is right now and where he was last night."

"I told you that he's traveling. I don't know where he is."

"You're lying." He leaned back and kicked his feet up on her desk, knowing it would piss her off.

"Do you mind?"

"Hey, I'm just getting comfortable. Looks like we're going to be here awhile if you continue to stall."

"I don't know what you want me to say."

"How about starting with the fact that your father is a thief?"

She swallowed hard and licked her lips. "That's never been proven."

"But you're not denying it." He swung his feet back to the floor. Resting his arms on her desk, he gave her a hard stare.

"There have been a lot of rumors about my father over the years, but deep down he's a good person, and he would never hurt me by stealing something I'm supposed to protect."

"Unless you're working together, as you did before," J.T. suggested. "As I understand it, you were employed at the same museum and resigned about the same time he did—just after some very important artifacts went missing. I find that curious."

"Really? You find that curious? My father gets accused of stealing, and it surprises you that I might be painted with the same brush? Isn't that exactly what you're doing?" She challenged, a fire in her eyes. "You're using previous accusations against my father to suggest that I'm up to something now, along with him—a man you've never met."

"If you were innocent of any wrongdoing at the museum, you would have fought for your job," he said. "You seem to have enough guts to stick up for yourself."

"I've grown a stronger backbone since then. I resigned because I didn't like the way they treated my father or me. It was better for me to move on."

"And your fiancé didn't beg you to stay?"

She sat up in surprise, a frown knitting her brows. "How do you know about Paul?"

"I made some calls. I spoke to a few people at the museum. They told me you were engaged to the assistant curator, Paul Michaels, until he turned your father in."

"If you know everything already, why are you asking me?"

"I thought you might want to give me your version."

"I don't have a version. I was engaged. We broke up. That's the end of it."

"Paul told me that you would do anything for your father—that he was the only man you could ever love."

Shadows filled her eyes at his harsh words. He felt a twinge of remorse at having spoken so bluntly. But he needed to get to the truth, find a way to break through the guard Christina had put up.

"I'm sorry Paul feels that way," she said quietly. "He didn't understand me then, and he doesn't understand me now."

"Or maybe he does. Maybe he's right."

She shrugged. "You can think what you want. You weren't there. You don't know me. You don't know any of us."

"What I want to know is where your father is."

"You have a better chance of finding him than I do. You seem to have plenty of resources to work with."

"Oh, I'll find him. I just thought you might want to help clear his name before I dig any deeper."

"Clear his name of what?" she challenged. "My father hasn't done anything."

"How would you know that—if you haven't seen him or talked to him recently?"

She fumbled for an answer. "I just know what I know."

"Well, that convinces me," he drawled.

"I don't care if it convinces you or not. I have to work. Get out of my office."

He smiled at her demand. Even when she was trying to be rude, there was a veneer of politeness to her words. He was surprised she hadn't added *please* at the end. She might be a liar and perhaps even a thief, but she did have good manners. He decided to change the subject. "Before I go, you might be interested to know that I spoke to Michael Torrance."

Her posture relaxed slightly at his words. She obviously didn't have a vested interest in protecting Michael Torrance from him.

"I take it he's not the guy you're looking for?" she asked.

"He doesn't appear to be. I sat not three feet from him. I don't think Evan could fool me if we were face-to-face. He also spoke extensively about his art collections and, quite frankly, bored the shit out of me. The paintings on his wall looked like something a five-year-old had drawn."

She smiled at that. "Michael has eclectic taste, and he's very passionate about his art. He also has an extensive collection of diamonds."

"Yeah, he told me about that, too. He said a diamond is a great chick magnet."

"I doubt he said it like that. He's much more refined."

"That was the gist of it. You don't really buy his polished-sophistication act, do you? That guy is a tool. I can't believe he never tried to pick you up."

"He flirted a bit on the phone, but we hadn't met in person until yesterday."

"Well, I'd keep your eye out for him. He thinks you're hot."

A rush of warm color spread across her cheeks. She seemed embarrassed and even a little surprised by his comment. "You don't know you're hot?" he asked, the words coming out before he could stop them.

"I don't think about it," she said, fidgeting with her papers once again.

Her modesty was disarming. Most of the women he knew spent so much time looking in the mirror they knew exactly how attractive they were. But Christina wasn't like most of the women he knew. That was becoming more obvious with each passing moment. "There's one more thing," he said. "Professor Keaton didn't sleep at any hotel in the city last night. And he's on an official leave of absence from the museum in Vancouver where he works, which I find more than a little suspicious. If he's on leave, why was he here last night? And where is he staying?"

"Maybe with friends or a hotel across the bay," she suggested.

"My assistant is checking, but there's something odd about that guy. If he resurfaces, contacts you in any way, you need to let me know."

"Of course. Now, I really have to get back to work." She punched the intercom button on her phone. She frowned when it went unanswered. "I wonder where David is. I could use his help."

"Your assistant? The dude with the earring?"

"Have you seen him?"

J.T. nodded. "Yeah. Some reporter arrived after you'd gone to lunch, and David stepped in and showed her the diamond."

"He did what? Why would he do that?" she asked, obviously upset by the information.

"He said he always subs for you. Is there a problem?" J.T. could see quite clearly that there was, but he doubted Christina would admit it, which raised more questions in his mind. Why didn't she want David looking at the diamond?

"I just didn't want the stone to be exposed again," she prevaricated, not meeting his gaze. "The more time it's out of the vault, the more chance someone has to steal it. I can't believe Alexis allowed it. Or Russell."

"We were all there to watch," J.T. replied. "Everything was fine. David was very knowledgeable. He examined it just like you did, although I think he was a little starstruck. When he picked up the stone, he looked like a virgin about to have sex for the first time." He paused, seeing that his words drew tight lines around her eyes. "Okay, what's the deal, Christina? I thought you said you trusted everyone here at Barclay's. Is there something about David Padlinsky I should know?"

She hesitated and then shook her head. "I guess not. He has handled the press previews before. I just wish he had called me before he took it upon himself to show the diamond."

"He said he couldn't reach you."

"My cell phone was on."

"How long has David worked here?" he asked.

"About a month. He's part-time, a grad student at Berkeley." She paused, taking a breath. "He didn't do anything wrong, and I shouldn't have implied that he did. He's a good guy, just a little too ambitious at times."

"He's on your heels, huh?"

"I'm not worried about him stealing my job. He has a long way to go to get the credentials I have. Although I must admit he's very good at schmoozing the right people. He seems to have Alexis eating out of his hand. I guess she likes that rock-star look of his."

He smiled to himself. Christina might say David didn't bother her, but it was obvious that she was feeling the pressure of staying one step ahead of her assistant. "Will David be at Mrs. Kensington's party tonight?"

"No, of course not."

"Too bad. I'd like to talk to him a bit more."

"You're not going to Alexis's dinner party," she said with a definite shake of her head. "It's for the top people at Barclay's only, and some key buyers for to-morrow's auction. The diamond will not be there."

"But the players will be. If Evan is here, working among you, then he'll be at the party, and so will I."

"Alexis won't give you an invitation."

"She already has," he said with a lazy grin, loving the way Christina's brows knit into a frown when she was irritated. She also seemed surprised by his state-ment. "What? I can be charming when I want to be."

"You could have fooled me."

"Well, you haven't seen me at my best—yet." He stood up and sauntered toward the door. "I'll pick you up tonight. We'll go together. Wear something sexy. I like that Italian-goddess look you had going last night."

Her jaw dropped. "You don't get to tell me what to wear. Nor am I going to the party with you. I don't even like you."

"I don't care if you like me, but we are going together."

"You're crazy."

"I'm not, but Evan is." His smile slipped away as he added, "Last night a piece of paper was slipped under the door of my hotel room. Do you want to know what was on it?" He didn't wait for her reply. "It was a pic-ture of you from the party, and the words, 'She's pretty, and she's mine,' signed, 'Evan.' "

Shock flashed in her eyes. "That can't be true."

"It is true." He let the words sink in, and his tone was completely serious when he added, "Evan wants something from you, Christina, but he's not going to get it, not on my watch. I'll pick you up at seven."

5

Evan watched Jenny Granville through the glass window of her beauty salon in Noe Valley, a middle-class neighborhood at the southern end of San Francisco filled with bookstores, bistros, and clothing shops. Jenny was blow-drying a young woman's long blond hair. She worked too hard. He could see how tired she was by the droop in her shoulders, the strands of brown hair that fell loose from her ponytail. She looked thin, worn out, older than her twenty-eight years. But that would change soon. He had big plans for Jenny. Soon she would realize that he was her destiny, her soul mate, the man she was supposed to be with forever.

She'd had a dozen years to find someone else—if she'd wanted to. But it was obvious that she hadn't wanted to. He was the only man for her. She'd told him that when they'd first met in college, and she would tell him that again—soon. They would have the child they were supposed to have had. They would live in a big house. She would wear his ring and call him her husband. She would never have to work again, because he would take care of her, protect her. And she would adore him, cherish him, look at him with admiration, pride. He smiled at the thought.

Jenny looked up and saw him through the glass. She froze in midmotion, the round brush slipping from her fingers. The woman in her chair must have said something, because Jenny suddenly came back to life, pulling a new brush out of a drawer, continuing on with the blow-dry. But he could see from her now jerky movements that she was rattled. Good. He needed to shake her out of the boring rut she'd put herself into. This wasn't the life she was supposed to have. Soon he would make her realize that.

He moved a few steps away and leaned against the wall, adjusting the black ski cap on his head. He didn't want to draw questions about what he'd done with his hair. Without the makeup and contact lenses he was almost his old self, close enough anyway, especially in the shadows illuminated only by the dim streetlights. He'd change out of his jeans and sweatshirt after they spoke. He had a party to go to.

Lighting up a cigarette, he took several long drags as he waited. She would come outside—if only to see if he was gone.

Ten minutes later the door to the salon opened. The blonde walked out, running her fingers through her hair as she passed him.

He dropped the stub of his cigarette to the ground. The door opened again. Jenny stepped out. Wearing a pair of jeans ripped at the knee and a pink T-shirt, she was quite simply the most beautiful woman he'd ever seen. But he wanted to see her in an evening gown, jewels dripping from her ears, stiletto heels on her feet, those gorgeous legs revealed by a sexy slit. She would be his—all his.

She moved down the sidewalk, sending him a wary look. "I thought you left town."

"Without saying good-bye? I would never do that. You and I have unfinished business."

"We don't. You hurt my brother. I can't forgive you for that."

He waved off her concerns. "I don't want to talk about Nick. I want to talk about us."

"Evan, please—"

"You and I are meant to be together, sweet Jenny, and we will be soon. I will give you everything you ever wanted and more."

"I want you to leave me alone," she said, putting up a hand as if she could stop him from moving back into her life with that one small gesture. "That's all I want. Don't come by. Don't call me. Just stay away. Live your life. Let me live mine."

"You don't mean that, Jenny," he said with a smile. "I know you're afraid, but I'll take care of you. I'll give you a better life."

"Evan, you need to get some help. There's something seriously wrong with you."

Her words burned through him, lighting the fire of fury in his blood. Not his Jenny, too. She couldn't criticize him. He couldn't stand it. Her face blurred in his mind, her image replaced with that of another woman, a woman who wouldn't stop telling him what a rotten piece of shit he was. He couldn't listen to her. She had to stop talking. He grabbed Jenny's arm and gave her a hard shake. "Don't ever say that again. Do you hear me? Don't ever say that again."

She stiffened and tried to pull away. "Let me go. You're hurting me. Evan, stop."

Her voice cut through the roar in his head. He looked down at his hand on her arm and slowly released his grip. When he met her gaze, he saw the fear in her eyes. He had scared her. "I'm sorry. I didn't mean to hurt you."

"Just everyone else that I care about. I defended you, Evan, for a long time. I believed in you, but I'm done. It's over. Go away. Start your life over somewhere else."

"You're worried for me," he said, feeling pleasure at the thought. "I knew you loved me."

She shook her head in frustration. "Why are you still here in San Francisco? Don't you know the police and the FBI are looking for you? What are you doing?"

"I'm finishing what I started, and I'm taking care of our future. You don't know how good I am at what I do, Jenny, but you'll see. I can be whomever you want me to be. I can give you the world on a silver platter— make that a diamond platter." He glanced down at his watch. "I have to go, but I'll be back."

"I'm going to tell J.T. you were here."

He tilted up her chin with his hand, gazing deep into her eyes. He'd taken her virginity a long time ago. Soon he would have her heart. Because what he wanted, he got. It was as simple as that. "I *want* you to tell J.T. I want him to know that I'm not done ruining his life. The game is not over."

*   *   *

J.T grabbed his coat off the passenger seat of his car and shrugged it on, wishing this job assignment didn't involve so many parties. He was much more comfortable wearing jeans and his favorite brown leather jacket. As he stepped out of the car, he double-checked the parking brake. Christina's apartment building was at the top of Telegraph Hill on a street so steep that had to park sideways to prevent runaway vehi

The neighborhood was quiet, not much this Thursday evening. He made his way building and buzzed her apartment. She and for a moment he wondered if she'd He wouldn't put it past her. But she was too to realize it would be only a temporary delay. He where she was going. He rang the bell again. A m ment later the front door buzzed, and he let himself in.

Her apartment was on the third floor. He took the stairs, relishing the small amount of exercise. He hadn't had a chance to run or work out the last few days, and he missed the sweat, the rush of endorphins, and the release of tension. In his job he usually needed that release on a daily basis, especially when he was on Evan's case.

He knocked on Christina's door, suspecting she was enjoying the fact that she could make him wait. She was certainly taking her time getting to him. Finally she opened the door.

Her gorgeous smile and short red dress with spaghetti straps knocked the wind right out of him. In his head he could hear the referee counting down the seconds until his breath came back into his chest. While he was searching for a way to speak, he let his gaze drift across her face, her not just beautiful but also interesting face, her shadowy green eyes, the thick, dark hair that fell in soft curls around her shoulders, and the luscious red lipstick that matched her dress. There was no diamond necklace around her neck tonight, but she didn't need one. In fact, he found the bare expanse of skin leading down to her cleavage far more tantalizing without the heavy yellow stone. He couldn't take his eyes off her. And she knew it. He saw the gleam of triumph in her eyes. Hell, she deserved it.

"Well?" she prodded.

"You look . . . nice," he said, finally finding his voice.

"That was a pretty long stare for *nice*," she replied, a smile playing across her lips.

He tipped his head in acknowledgment. "You surprised me. I thought you'd be wearing sweats just to pay me back for telling you to wear something sexy."

"I didn't wear this for you."

"Sure you did." He captured her gaze and held it for a long moment. The battle between them was suddenly being played on more than one level. He had the feeling it was very important that he keep his wits about him. He couldn't let her get under his skin, although the thought of having her under him in any way at all was damned appealing.

She shrugged and looked away, breaking the connection. "It's my party dress; that's all. By the way— you're early."

"I didn't want to give you a reason to take off."

"I have no reason to run from you."

"Then why do you keep doing it?" Without waiting

for a reply, he moved past her, curious to see where she lived.

Her apartment was small but beautifully decorated. Everything was coordinated. The rose-colored walls complemented the deep burgundy sofa and love seat. An Oriental rug on the hardwood floor enhanced the color scheme. Oil paintings and watercolors adorned the walls, the kind of art that was old and expensive. There were other small, interesting items on the end tables, and even a curio cabinet filled with crystal and vases. The apartment wasn't as formally decorated as her father's house, but it was obvious she'd put some thought into her surroundings. It was a sophisticated, intelligent room, and she could probably tell him the history of every piece of art on the walls. A smart girl, he reminded himself. He couldn't risk underestimating her.

"Well, what do you think of my apartment?" she asked.

"Oh. It's . . . nice."

"Kind of a long stare for *nice*," she repeated with a small smile.

He grinned back at her. "I'm a man of few adjectives; what can I say? Did you get all of this stuff from Barclay's?"

"Some of it. Other pieces I picked up on my travels. My father used to take me on his research trips when I was a little girl. He made me realize that things are not just things. They're pieces of history. Everything we use today will teach future children about the way we lived, what we valued, how creative we were."

"They're going to learn all that from our disposable garbage?"

She made a face. "Unfortunately, yes, that will be part of our history, but there are still great artists today, singers, writers, sculptors, painters. We have a rich culture." Her voice drifted off, and she looked embarrassed. "More than you wanted to know, right?"

"Not at all." He realized that this was the first conversation between them that wasn't adversarial, and he found himself liking it, wanting to learn more about her. Most of the women he knew were not particularly deep. They read *Cosmopolitan* and *People* magazines and could rattle off the name of Jennifer Aniston's latest boyfriend. He didn't usually care about the limited range of topics, because he wasn't that big on conversation with beautiful women; he could think of far more interesting things to do with his mouth, but he had to admit that Christina's brain intrigued him along with her beauty. She had the whole package going on.

Except for the fact that there was a good chance she was a thief, he reminded himself—a not so minor detail. "So how long have you lived here?" he asked, figuring that might be one more question she was willing to answer.

"A couple of years. I like the neighborhood. I'm close to North Beach, which has the best Italian food this side of Italy. I can see the Wharf, Alcatraz, and the Golden Gate Bridge from my windows, and it's a quiet building. I can't complain."

"Have you seen any of the infamous wild parrots since you've lived here?"

Her smile widened. "You know about the parrots?"

"I went to college at Cal. I had a friend whose parents lived here. Every afternoon the parrots would fly around their deck and land on the railings as if they were coming home. He used to name them. Then there got to be too many. I forget where they come from."

"The cherry-headed conure comes from the west side of the Andes in southern Ecuador as well as the extreme north of Peru," she said. "It's believed that the birds were originally imported from South America, but they were so noisy and disliked captivity so intensely that many of them were released by their owners or they escaped." She stopped abruptly. "Boy, I am rambling tonight, aren't I? Sometimes I forget that most people just want simple answers to simple questions."

"I'm pleased you're talking at all. You're certainly a fountain of information when it comes to educational matters. I'm surprised you didn't become a teacher. You seem to have a natural bent for it."

"I thought about it. I do teach some classes through Barclay's educational program, which gives me a chance to spout off fairly useless trivia. Most people don't care about wild parrots or history, but it's fun for me."

He liked her self-deprecating smile, the fact that she didn't take herself too seriously, even though she was at heart a serious woman.

"Do you live here in San Francisco?" she asked. "You said you went to college at Cal."

"No, I live in LA. I followed Evan here a few weeks ago. I'm staying at a hotel on Van Ness until I catch him. Then I'll go home."

"They don't have agents in San Francisco who can catch him?"

"Evan is mine," J.T. said firmly. "The office here will assist me if I need help."

"So you're kind of the Lone Ranger at the moment."

"If you want to call it that. I can request whatever backup I need at a moment's notice." That wasn't completely true. In actuality, his boss had wanted to pull him off Evan, saying it was time to bring in someone new, someone with perspective and a fresh eye. J.T. had to prove that he could catch Evan, that he could close the deal, not just for his own personal reasons but also for his professional future. "Are you ready to go?"

Christina cocked her head to one side, her gaze speculative. "Not yet. I have a question for you."

"Now look who's the curious one. What's the question?"

"What does J.T. stand for?"

He smiled. "I'm afraid I don't know you well enough to share that information."

She raised an eyebrow. "Really? How well would I need to know you to get the answer to that question?"

He closed the gap between them. "Do you want me to tell you?"

The air between them sizzled with tension. Blood roared through his veins. He felt as if they were on the brink of . . . something. . . .

Then Christina moved away—in retreat. It was a smart move, but disappointing all the same.

"I don't actually care that much," she said with a breezy wave of her hand.

Her words were casual, but he noticed she took care not to look at him. She always did that when she was lying, he realized. She glanced away, and she fidgeted with her hair, tucking one strand behind her ear. She couldn't stand still, gaze into his eyes, and tell a lie. He filed that information away, figuring he'd need it—probably sooner than later.

When he didn't say anything else, Christina walked over to the table and picked up her purse, a small red piece of leather no bigger than his wallet. "We should go. Alexis hates it when people are late, especially her employees."

"I guess we're changing the subject."

"I guess we are," she said.

"Fine." He followed her to the door. "Tell me more about Alexis. Is she a tough boss?"

"Very demanding. But I respect her drive and her intense desire to make Barclay's as good as it can be." Christina locked the door behind them. "Are you driving or am I?"

"Me," he said.

"Figures. You hate to give up control, don't you?"

"When it comes to driving, yes," he admitted.

"When it comes to everything," she muttered.

"I heard that."

"You were supposed to." She flashed him a smile. "Stairs or elevator? Wait, let me guess. Stairs. Then you can go as fast as you want. You have complete and total control over the situation."

"Are you calling me a control freak?" he asked as they walked out to his car.

"If the shoe fits."

"You seem to enjoy being in charge as well," he commented as he unlocked her car door.

"But I don't have to be in control; hence I can sit in the passenger seat and not complain."

"You can sit in the passenger seat," he agreed. "The not-complaining part I'll reserve judgment on. And who says 'hence' anymore?"

"People who read a lot," she answered as he slid behind the wheel. "Those people say 'hence.'"

He smiled to himself as he started the car. He liked the fire in her eyes, her quick wit, her sharp tongue. He also loved the way she smelled, like wildflowers on a summer breeze. In the quiet intimacy of the car he was acutely aware of her presence, every move that she made, even the sound of her breathing. He cracked the window slightly. The evening air cooled off the heat building in his body. Catching Evan would be difficult enough. He didn't need to complicate matters by getting tangled up with Christina, and man, did he want to get tangled up with her. He'd like to slide his hands up her slender, bare legs, feel her smooth skin beneath his fingers, watch her eyes widen with desire and her lips part with anticipation.

He rolled the window all the way down.

"Are you hot?" Christina asked.

That was a loaded question. A lot of answers came to mind, none of them appropriate, so he simply rolled up the window and said, "Sorry. So tell me again who will be at this shindig?"

"First of all, I wouldn't call it a 'shindig' in front of Alexis. She may have blue-collar roots, but she considers herself San Francisco blue blood these days."

"Blue-collar roots?" he queried.

"Alexis was working as a clerk in an antiques store

when Jeremy Kensington came in one day and asked her out. They had a whirlwind romance, and eventually the shopgirl became the wife of one of San Francisco's most prominent businessmen. It was quite a Cinderella story. Jeremy's father founded Barclay's. Jeremy ran it himself for a while, but was actually thinking of selling the business until he met Alexis. I believe he gave her Barclay's as a wedding present. She took over and has never looked back. In fact, Jeremy rarely comes into Barclay's anymore, with the exception of this exhibit. He runs an investment company as well, and I think that usually takes up most of his attention."

"Why would this exhibit encourage Jeremy to spend more time at Barclay's?"

"Probably because of the diamond and the overall value of the auction. There has also been a lot of media interest, and both Jeremy and Alexis like good press. They're very public people. The success of this particular auction will definitely move Barclay's into the big leagues."

"So Alexis and Jeremy have a lot at stake. Especially Alexis, because Barclay's is her baby."

"I'm sure she'd like to impress Jeremy and his family as well as the rest of the world. As I recall, there was some controversy within the Kensington family when he put her in charge of the company. Not everyone was happy that the family business was going to be run by a newcomer."

"Interesting."

"Why is that interesting?" She turned sideways in her seat, a curious look in her eyes. "You make it sound as if I just gave you an important clue of some kind."

"I'm not sure yet why it's interesting, but I like to know who has the most to lose and who has the most to gain in any situation. That usually takes me to the heart of the matter." He paused. "For instance, you have a reputation to lose, one you've tried very hard to rebuild after you and your father left the museum in disgrace." He shot her a quick look, but except for the frown spreading across her face, she gave away nothing. "You love your father. He raised you on his own. You want to protect him. And you're worried that he's back in town and interested in the diamond. That makes you vulnerable, and interesting. How am I doing so far?"

"I thought we were discussing Alexis and what she had to lose."

"I'm right, aren't I?"

"In that I'm worried about the diamond like the rest of the staff at Barclay's? Yes. We'll all breathe a lot easier when it's sold tomorrow and off the premises."

"A very diplomatic answer."

"My personal life has nothing to do with my job, J.T. I keep the two separate, as I'm sure you do in your job."

"I don't have a personal life, so that makes it easy."

"Why don't you?" she asked.

The curious tone in her voice made him regret opening that door. "My job can be twenty-four/seven. No time to make a relationship work," he said shortly.

"No time or no desire?"

"Getting back to the diamond, I certainly hope nothing happens to it tonight while you're all toasting the success of tomorrow's auction."

"You don't want to talk about your pathetic love life?" she challenged, amusement clearly evident in her eyes.

"It's not pathetic. I'm happy with my choices."

"Sure. That's what everyone says."

"Do you really want to get into this conversation, Christina? Because I have a file on you, and it says that the last man you dated for more than a month was your ex-fiancé, and that was five years ago."

His challenging words turned off her smile. "Okay, you win. We'll keep our love lives out of the conversation. But getting back to the diamond, as you said earlier—why aren't you at the auction house guarding it? Wouldn't that be a more productive use of your time?"

"I plan to check on it later, but Russell Kenner and that Italian guy, Luigi Murano, assured me that they have doubled their guards for the night, rechecked their cameras, and that there is no possible way anyone is getting near that vault."

Christina's gaze narrowed on his face. "You don't sound confident."

That was because he wasn't confident. "I'm just hoping that Evan hasn't maneuvered himself into the security ranks," he said. "If he's managed to snag himself a guard uniform and a fake ID, we could be in big trouble."

"I'm sure everyone has been cleared."

"Oh, they have," he agreed. "I double-checked many of them myself. But Evan is a slippery snake. He slithers in and strikes you before you know he's there."

"I almost want to meet him just so I can see who you're talking about," Christina replied.

"I'm betting you already have met him, Christina. He had a photo taken of you at the party. I'm sure he was there. Has there been anyone in your life lately who makes you feel uncomfortable? I think you have good instincts. Maybe someone has made you uneasy, but you dismissed it for no good reason."

She pondered that for a moment. "David, my assistant. He makes me nervous. It could just be his ambition, or maybe his eyes. He has this way of looking at me, as if he knows something I don't."

"I talked to David earlier." J.T. reviewed the brief conversation in his head. "He's about the right height. But I think I would have seen Evan in him somewhere. I was standing two feet away from him. Anyone else?"

"I don't know," she said with a weary shrug. "Everyone seems to make me nervous lately. Even Russell Kenner has me on edge. I don't think he trusts me. Nor does Luigi Murano. When the diamond came off my neck last night, they both looked like they wanted to accuse me of something." She paused, meeting his gaze. "But the person who makes me the most uncomfortable is you. Maybe you're Evan."

"I'm not. And we both know why I make you nervous. We're attracted to each other."

She drew in a sharp breath at his blunt words. It might be a mistake, but he thought it was important that they put all the cards on the table so they could deal with them.

"I . . . I . . . that's not true," she stammered.

"It is true. It should make our plan tonight a lot easier."

"What plan?"

"Alexis didn't want me to attend as an FBI agent. She thought it would make her guests uncomfortable, at least those guests who are not Barclay's employees. Apparently there are going to be several key buyers present tonight, as well as some press. She asked me to come as your date." He smiled as her jaw dropped. "Good idea, don't you think?"

"Are you out of your mind? I'm not going as your date."

"Well, you do have another choice."

"Good, what is it?"

"When we arrive, you can tell Alexis that you don't want to be my date and let everyone know I'm at the party to figure out if any of them is planning to steal the diamond."

"Very funny," she said sarcastically. "You know I can't do that. Alexis would have my head."

"Guess you're stuck then." He pulled up in front of a stately two-story mansion in Pacific Heights and turned off the engine. "I think we're here. Nice digs."

"The Kensingtons are old money," she murmured.

"I've never cared whether the money was old or new, as long as it was green." He noticed she didn't comment; nor did she seem to be in any particular hurry to get out of the car. "Relax, it won't be so bad, Christina. I promise not to pick my teeth, use the wrong fork, or exit the bathroom with toilet paper attached to my shoe."

"Great. You're a comedian as well as an FBI agent. How did I get so lucky?" she drawled.

"You must be living right," he said with a grin.

"This isn't going to work. Everyone at Barclay's knows you're an agent. Someone will say something."

"Alexis assured me that they wouldn't."

"Fine." She got out of the car and slammed the door shut. "Let's get this over with."

"Smile. You're not going to the dentist. It's a party." He escorted her up to the front door and paused. "Before we go in, Christina, tell me something."

"What now?"

"Do you kiss on the first date? Because in case you were wondering—I do."

She swallowed hard. "I wasn't wondering." She reached past him to ring the bell, her gaze fixed on the front door as if it were the entrance to the Magic Kingdom.

"Did you know that you never look at me when you're lying? I find that interesting."

"You find everything interesting," she muttered.

He smiled to himself. She still wasn't looking at him. She was one beautiful liar, and for tonight, anyway, she was his date.

6

Christina was relieved when the door to the Kensingtons' house opened. She needed to put some distance between herself and J.T. so she could catch her breath. J.T.'s mix of arrogance and charm was dangerously appealing, and when he looked at her like he wanted to kiss her, it was difficult to remember that he was an FBI agent and not her friend or her date, no matter how much he flirted with her. She couldn't believe he'd come right out and said they were attracted to each other.

She told herself it was just a ploy to keep her off balance, trip her up, get her to say something incriminating about herself or her father. It wasn't going to work. She would not let him get to her—even if she was attracted to him. Unfortunately, he was right about the inconvenient chemistry between them.

It was his fault. He was too damn sexy. Even in a black suit, clean-shaven, with his hair slicked back, there was no mistaking his rugged physical appeal. He was all male and, for the moment, all hers.

That thought sent a reckless shiver down her spine.
Not that she was going to do anything about it. But she
had to admit that when he put a hand on her back to
usher her into the living room, she felt a delicious heat
sweep through her. She wanted to fight the feeling. She
told herself to push him away, but a little voice inside
her head wondered why she had to battle every little
thing.

The last few days had been incredibly stressful. She
was on pins and needles waiting for her father to contact her about the necklace. She wasn't sure if the diamond at Barclay's was a fake or the real thing, and in
less than twenty-four hours it would go on the auction
block with her name attached to the appraisal. If she
made the wrong decision, she could be completely ruined. But what was the right decision? The diamond
had already been verified by their European office and
she had seen only one tiny discrepancy, which might
mean nothing. Her doubts had no basis in fact. She was
just worried because her father was back in town. If
she called off the auction and it turned out the diamond
was real, Barclay's would lose a huge commission. If
she let the necklace be sold and someone discovered it
was a fake, she could go to jail. She had to pray that it
was all in her imagination, that the diamond was real,
and that nothing would happen to it before the bidding
began at noon tomorrow.

She definitely had worse things to worry about than
J.T.'s hand on her back. In fact, it felt pretty good to
walk beside someone, to feel as if she were part of a
couple. J.T. was right: She hadn't dated anyone seriously in five years. She'd been gun-shy after her

breakup with Paul. She'd given her heart to him, and he'd stomped all over it. So she'd put her love life on the back burner, and there it had stayed.

And there it *would* stay, she reminded herself. J.T. was not her boyfriend. He was an agent on a job, and after tomorrow she'd probably never see him again.

They mingled for the next few minutes, speaking to several of Barclay's most avid collectors. She was somewhat surprised that J.T. could converse so easily with people he had nothing in common with. He didn't know much about art or jewelry, but he knew how to ask intelligent questions and draw other people out. He could be very disarming when he wanted to be. And she appreciated the way he redirected the conversation every time someone wanted to ask her about the fire at the auction house. Apparently, rumors were flying over whether or not the fire was a cover-up for an attempted robbery. The incident had actually increased interest in the auction, not just the diamond but the entire collection.

The excitement in the room made Christina feel more optimistic. Or maybe it was the champagne. Either way, she started to relax. J.T.'s dire warnings about Evan Chadwick had encouraged her to believe the worst, but maybe the worst wouldn't happen. Maybe the auction would go as planned. She really hoped it would.

"Who's that?" J.T. asked.

She followed his gaze to a sexy, bosomy blonde in a very short black cocktail dress, who was carrying what looked like a fur ball in her arms, but on second thought was no doubt the infamous Harry, a six-pound

Pomeranian dog with a thick white ruff around his neck, sharp dark eyes, and a feathery tail. "That's Nicole Prescott," Christina answered. "She's the society columnist for the *Tribune* and can make or break a reputation. If you want to get a mention on her page, it's important to be nice to her."

"What's she carrying?"

"Her dog, Harry. She talks about him in her column all the time."

"That's not a dog," J.T. said with a disapproving shake of his head. "Dogs are big and slobbery. They run, bark, jump up and down, chase balls and cats."

She smiled. "Small dogs that can almost fit in your handbag are the latest rage."

"At formal dinner parties?"

Christina nodded. "Absolutely. I think it's cute."

"Must be a girl thing," he grumbled. He paused, his eyes narrowing as Nicole and Alexis embarked on what appeared to be a very heated conversation. They had moved toward the large stone fireplace in the living room, their voices hushed, but their body language made it clear they were disagreeing about something. "Alexis doesn't appear to be sucking up," he commented.

"No, she doesn't." Christina wondered what they were discussing. It wasn't like Alexis to let her emotions get away from her, especially with a member of the press.

Jeremy joined the two women a moment later. A short, stocky man, Jeremy was at least a few inches shorter than his tall, willowy wife. He was a plain man with a square face and a receding hairline. There was nothing warm or friendly about him. Christina had spent very little time in his company, but she'd always come away feeling chilled. If the man had a personality, she hadn't seen it. Perhaps he reserved his attention for family and friends as opposed to employees.

Alexis certainly seemed to care about him. She had her hand on his arm now and gave him a long, passionate kiss on his lips. Either she didn't care that Nicole was standing there or it was a deliberate move to make some sort of point. A moment later Jeremy led Alexis away. If Christina hadn't been watching so closely she might have missed the look of contempt that flashed across Nicole's face. There was no love lost between the two women; that much was clear.

"That was interesting," J.T. murmured.

She couldn't help but smile at his choice of words. "This time I agree with you."

"We're making progress." He flashed her that boyish grin that was quickly becoming her favorite smile.

Concentrate, she told herself. "I don't know why Alexis would risk annoying a member of the press the night before the auction. Who knows what Nicole will say in the morning paper? Alexis hates bad press. I'd sure like to know what they were talking about."

"Maybe we can find out. Let's go talk to Nicole."

"I don't know her at all," Christina protested.

"So, it's a party. We'll introduce ourselves."

J.T. was a lot more outgoing than she was, Christina realized, especially when it came to cocktail-party conversation. "Maybe you should go on your own."

"Not without my date." He gave her a gentle push. "Come on; maybe we'll get your name in the paper."

"That's the last thing I want," she murmured, wishing she could find a way to disappear, but it was too late. Nicole was right in front of them.

"Ms. Prescott," J.T. said, flagging her down. "I hope you don't mind the interruption, but I wanted to tell you that I'm your biggest fan."

Nicole preened at J.T.'s flattery. "Really. And you are . . . ?"

"J. T. McIntyre. And this is Christina Alberti. She's the jewelry specialist for Barclay's."

"How nice," Nicole muttered, not taking her eyes off J.T. She put out a hand and pretended to straighten his lapel. "I don't usually have such handsome readers."

"I'm sure you do," he said.

"That's lovely of you to say."

"Your dog is . . . uh, very small," J.T. said. "I've always wanted one of those. What are they called?"

"Pomeranians."

Christina wanted to roll her eyes at J.T.'s phony interest in Nicole's dog. For a man who had accused her of lying, he seemed to have no problem doing exactly the same thing. He would do anything to get what he wanted. She would have to remember that.

She shifted her feet uncomfortably, feeling very much like a third wheel as the conversation between J.T. and Nicole grew more flirtatious. J.T. wasn't getting information about Nicole's conversation with Alexis, but he definitely had Nicole wrapped around his little finger—make that his bicep. Nicole caressed his arm as she leaned into him, saying, "What a charming man you are. I hope we can get better acquainted later tonight."

Christina felt a surge of anger at the woman's blatant suggestion. Was she invisible? Couldn't Nicole see that she was standing right there? And J.T. was just as bad, smiling at Nicole as if he'd like to lap her up.

"Honey," Christina said, deliberately interrupting them, "I think they're about to serve dinner. Why don't we say hello to Alexis before we sit down? You remember Alexis, don't you?"

He met her pointed look with a smile. "Of course I do, sweetheart." He turned back to Nicole. "You know Alexis, don't you?"

Nicole's gaze sharpened into a hard point. "Far too well. I don't think you'll find her nearly as fascinating as me."

"I'm sure that would be impossible," J.T. agreed. "But since Alexis is Christina's boss, I'll have to ask you to excuse us."

"If I must," Nicole said reluctantly. "Perhaps we can share a drink after dinner."

"I'd like that," J.T. replied. "By the way, will you be attending the auction tomorrow?"

"I might stop by. I haven't had a chance to see the diamond yet. By the time I arrived at the party last night, there were fire engines blocking the entrance. It was very disappointing." She glanced over at Christina for the first time. "I wonder if you might arrange a private showing for me before the auction, just for a few moments."

Christina was surprised by the request. She didn't want to offend Nicole, but she also didn't want anyone else looking at the diamond until she knew what she was dealing with. "I would have to ask Alexis," she prevaricated. "I'm not sure exactly what the schedule is for tomorrow. I can let you know."

"Please do."

Christina took J.T.'s hand and gave it a seriously painful squeeze as she led him away from Nicole. She pulled him into the foyer outside the living room.

"Ouch," he said, yanking his hand away from her. "What was that for?"

"For blowing our cover," she said angrily.

"Our cover?"

"You told people you were my date. My dates don't usually flirt with other women while I'm standing right there." He grinned, and she didn't like the look in his eyes.

"You're jealous," he said with a knowing smile.

"Don't be an ass. I'm not jealous. I'm concerned about our cover story."

"Nicole wanted me, and you didn't like it," he observed.

"I don't care who wants you. I just care about my own reputation, all right? I don't want to be seen as some pathetic woman whose date won't even look at her."

"Well, I can fix that."

His mouth came down on hers before she could reply. His kiss was hot, potent, his touch releasing some sort of delicious drug that swept through her body, making every nerve tingle with pleasure.

"What was that for?" she asked breathlessly.

"Our cover story," he replied.

"Oh. Okay. Right." She drew in a breath and let it out, feeling an odd disappointment at his words.

He stared back at her, not smiling anymore. "I lied. That kiss was for me. And I'd like to do it again."

Christina was torn between wanting another kiss and wanting to run away as fast and as far as possible. The decision was taken out of her hands when the caterer called them to dinner. She started, realizing that anyone at the party could have walked by and seen them kissing in the foyer. What would Alexis think? Everyone else might believe that J.T. was her date, but her boss knew that he was an FBI agent, and it was definitely inappropriate for her to be kissing him. Wasn't it?

The line between right and wrong seemed to blur more with each passing day.

J.T. put his hand on her back to urge her toward the dining room. "Time to eat."

"Don't touch me," she said sharply.

His hand dropped away abruptly. "Sorry."

"You shouldn't have done that. You shouldn't have kissed me."

"You shouldn't have kissed me back."

He had a point. Deciding there was no way to win this battle, she turned on her heel and walked quickly toward the dining room. They were the last to arrive. Their seats were at the far end of a massive table, which seated twenty-four—Alexis's version of the cheap seats, no doubt. Christina didn't mind the location. She'd rather sit across from Sylvia Davis, the head of public relations, who knew that she and J.T. were not a couple, than to have to pretend to be enamored with him throughout soup, salad, and another three courses. However, the man sitting next to Sylvia was another matter. It was David Padlinsky, who greeted her with a satisfied smile.

"I didn't realize you were coming, David," Christina said with a frown. "In fact, I spent half the afternoon looking for you. Where were you?"

"I had a meeting at the university," he replied. "I thought I told you that. As for the party, Alexis was kind enough to invite me when I expressed an interest in seeing her beautiful home."

His words were so polite, so formal, so odd, she thought. She couldn't figure out who David really was—wannabe rock star, earnest grad student, self-absorbed ambitious social climber . . . ? He didn't seem to fit into any clear category. Which made her wonder if she knew him at all. J.T. was convinced that if someone was going to steal the diamond, they would do it from the inside. Was David part of some scheme?

"I understand you gave a press demonstration when I was at lunch," Christina continued.

David cast J.T. a quick look. "Yes, I did. Your . . . date was standing right there."

"So he said," Christina murmured. "You should have called me."

"I tried your cell phone, but you didn't answer."

"I didn't get any missed calls," she replied.

David shrugged. "It must have been one of those odd cell phone problems."

Christina didn't buy that for a second. David hadn't called her. He'd wanted to do that demonstration on his own. Why? So he had a reason to examine the diamond again? Out of the corner of her eye she noted Sylvia's curious gaze on her. Sylvia was obviously following their conversation and would no doubt report every word back to Alexis. Sylvia and Alexis worked quite closely together. They were both in their late forties and shared the same vision and determination for success. Sylvia often acted as Alexis's eyes and ears throughout the company. Christina wished now that she'd kept her mouth shut, but it was too late to drop the question.

"I asked David to show the diamond," Sylvia interjected. "A reporter from the *Sacramento Bee* arrived while you were at lunch, and I didn't want to miss the opportunity to get additional press coverage. I didn't realize that would be a problem. Alexis approved it, and David did an excellent job discussing how you both analyze a stone. It was fascinating. The reporter was thrilled to have a chance to look through the gem scope at what David was describing."

Christina drew in a quick, sharp breath. She'd hoped that the gem scope hadn't been part of the demonstration. Christina silently prayed that David hadn't seen anything wrong with the diamond when he'd conducted his review. She told herself that he wasn't as experienced as she was in looking at diamonds. He didn't have as good an eye—at least, she didn't think he did.

It was also possible that there was nothing wrong with the diamond. She would have liked to check it again, but to do so would have raised too many questions. She would wait until tomorrow to take another look. It would be expected then and not at all out of the ordinary.

"Is something wrong?" David asked quizzically.

"No, everything is fine," she said, realizing Sylvia and David were both sending her speculative looks. The last thing she needed was to raise any more suspicion. She picked up her water glass and took a long drink as two waiters began to serve the salad. She was grateful for the distraction. Sylvia began conversing with the gentleman on the other side of her, and David excused himself, presumably to use the restroom.

"What was that all about?" J.T. asked quietly.

"I don't know what you mean."

"You're pissed that David did that presentation without you. What's the big deal?"

"There's no deal. Forget I said anything."

J.T. sent her a curious look. "You don't trust him, do you?"

"I'm just surprised he's here. He's a part-time assistant. This party is only for the department specialists, potential buyers, and selected members of the press."

"That sounds like professional jealousy."

Maybe J.T. was right and she was a little jealous. David was moving ahead in the company far more quickly than she had. She certainly hadn't been invited to Alexis's house until she'd worked at Barclay's for over two years.

"Do you think David saw something in the diamond that you didn't?" J.T. asked. "Is that why you're so nervous?"

"I'm not nervous."

It wasn't until he put his hand on her thigh that she realized she'd been tapping her foot against the floor in a restless beat. His warm hand burned through the silk of her dress, which did little to calm her nerves. She placed her hand over his and moved it off her leg. He smiled. "Sorry; did that bother you?"

"I think you'll need that hand for your salad."

"I'm right-handed." He picked up his fork with his right hand while moving the left hand back to her leg. "I can do two things at once. And you seem to need someone to anchor this leg down. Why are you so jumpy, Christina?"

"Because I am, and I'd really prefer you keep your hands to yourself." She took his hand and moved it off her leg again, unwilling to admit, even to herself, that she missed his warmth.

They didn't speak again until they had finished their salads. David returned to his seat, engaging Sylvia in conversation. Then the waiters arrived with the next course, steak and lobster. It was a fancy meal for a fancy party. Christina certainly couldn't complain about the food. She gazed down the long table, now wishing they'd been seated in the middle, where they could have listened in on more conversations. She almost felt more like the hired help than a guest.

She shook off the thought, knowing deep down that her feelings came from long years of being the odd girl out. It had been difficult growing up without a mother. She'd always felt different from the other kids, especially since her father had never been an ordinary dad. It had been easier when it was just the two of them. When they tried to mix in with the rest of the world, they didn't quite fit. Even now, without her father in her life, she still struggled to feel a part of the group. It was her own insecurity, she reminded herself. Alexis and Jeremy had been perfect hosts, and she really couldn't complain about anything.

"Sylvia, I was wondering if you were the one responsible for getting the media here tonight," J.T. asked, breaking the silence at their end of the table that had begun to grow uncomfortable.

Sylvia nodded, appearing pleased by the question. "Absolutely. That's my job."

J.T. leaned forward, flashing Sylvia his charming smile. The man should have a patent on it, Christina thought. It was lethal, and Sylvia was obviously not immune. A blush as red as her strawberry-blond hair colored her cheeks, and she sat up a bit straighter, making a subtle movement that thrust her well-endowed breasts toward J.T. Christina couldn't believe the woman was flirting with him. She was married, for God's sake. Although her husband wasn't here tonight, so apparently that made a difference.

"You do it very well," J.T. continued. "I was wondering what you know about Nicole Prescott. She seems like a fascinating woman."

Sylvia shot a quick look down the length of the table to make sure she couldn't be overheard, which wasn't possible, since Nicole was seated next to Jeremy at the far end. Sylvia dropped her voice down a notch. "She's beautiful, rich, and has had more men than anyone can count. She wields tremendous power on the society pages. She can make you a star or turn you into a social leper. Everyone is afraid of her poison pen, but it is just that poison that brings the readers back for more. Controversy always sells more papers."

"She doesn't seem to get along very well with Alexis," J.T. continued. "I saw them arguing earlier tonight."

Sylvia hesitated. Christina wasn't surprised. Sylvia was used to guarding Alexis's privacy, but she seemed torn between wanting to talk more to J.T. and revealing how much of an insider she really was. In the end J.T.'s encouraging smile won out.

"I don't think Nicole will go after Alexis in print," Sylvia said. "They are family, after all."

"Family?" Christina questioned. "Really?"

"They're cousins. I don't think their parents got along well. I'm not sure exactly what caused the rift between them. Nicole loves to remind Alexis that she can destroy her in the press at any time," Sylvia added. "Believe me, I have had to tread very carefully between the two of them over the past year. Fortunately, Alexis and Jeremy are so well-known for their philanthropy as well as Barclay's success that it's easy to get them good press. I think that for the most part Nicole and Alexis respect each other's territory." Sylvia paused as Jeremy rose to his feet and the chatter at the table quieted.

Jeremy cleared his throat, and his dark gaze roamed the table as he waited for the last lingering conversations to end. "I'd like to thank you all for coming," he said. "Tomorrow Barclay's will celebrate one of its most important auctions. I would like to thank Mr. Stefano Benedetti for entrusting us with his family's valuable collection. We are very proud and honored to be of service to your family." He raised his champagne glass in Stefano's direction.

Stefano tipped his head in acknowledgment and lifted his own glass.

"To tomorrow's success," Jeremy continued. "*Salut.*"

"*Salut,*" the rest of the crowd echoed.

As Jeremy sat down, Nicole whispered something in his ear and then left the table. Alexis got up a few moments later. Christina wondered if it was a coincidence that the two women both needed to leave the table at the same time. David surprised her by excusing himself as well. The table was emptying quickly. She pushed back her chair. "Don't eat my dessert," she told J.T.

"I make no promises."

As she left the dining room, she ran into a maid, who told her there was a restroom across the foyer and down the hall. Christina took her time getting there, curious to see more of Alexis's beautiful rooms. Antiques were the order of the day. It was clear that Alexis's passion for art extended to her house. But while the place was fabulous, rich and sophisticated, it didn't feel at all like a home. Christina wondered where Alexis and Jeremy relaxed, read the newspaper, or shared meals, where they talked, laughed, made love. Perhaps the upstairs had a warmer feel. She would have liked to venture up the staircase, but she wasn't that brave. She didn't want to run into Alexis and have her boss accuse her of snooping.

As she approached the end of the hall, she heard voices coming from a nearby room. Pausing by the door, she tried to figure out who was talking. It sounded like David and perhaps Alexis, although the voices were somewhat hushed. Taking a quick look behind her to make sure she was alone, Christina crept closer to the half-open door, shocked to hear her name.

"You need to speak to Christina," David said in a voice that sounded far too authoritative for a subordinate to use to his boss. "This could be a disaster."

"I'll take care of it," Alexis said.

"There's something else."

"I can't do this right now. I have to get back to my guests, David."

"What's going on?" J.T. whispered in Christina's ear.

She jumped, startled to be caught eavesdropping. She'd thought she was alone in the hallway. At least it was J.T. She clapped a hand over his mouth and tipped her head toward the adjacent room. Unfortunately, it now appeared that Alexis and David had finished their conversation and were heading toward the door. Christina did not want to be caught listening.

Grabbing J.T.'s arm, she pulled him across the hall and opened the first door she could find. It was a coat closet. The voices were getting louder, so she shoved J.T. inside, following him in, and pulled the door almost all the way shut. She could hear Alexis and David talking as they walked down the hall.

"This can't wait, Alexis. I've already been too patient. I should have said something earlier," David said.

"I'll take care of it," Alexis said. "Trust me."

Take care of what? Christina wondered. What on earth was going on between David and Alexis, and what did it have to do with her?

"If you wanted to get me alone, all you had to do was ask," J.T. murmured.

She suddenly became acutely aware that she was pressed up against J.T.'s chest. The closet was dark and smelled like leather, or maybe that was J.T. Her senses began to sing. Her breasts began to tingle. She licked her lips. "I didn't want Alexis to catch me eavesdropping."

"What did you find out?"

"They were talking about me. I didn't hear enough to learn why I was the subject of their conversation, but it didn't sound good."

She could feel his gaze on her face, his hand on her waist, his legs tangling with hers. She needed to move, but her body quite simply did not want to go anywhere. The memory of his earlier kiss lingered in her mind. Had it really been as good as she remembered? Did she want to find out? "We should go," she said.

"Yeah, we should," he echoed, but his hands tightened on her waist as if he had no intention of ever letting her go.

She didn't know who moved first. Maybe it was him. Maybe it was her. When their lips met, nothing else mattered. She put her arms around his neck, drawing his head down. She slid her tongue into his mouth, tasting the dessert he'd eaten earlier. Chocolate and J.T.—it was a heady mix. She felt dizzy, hot, needy, until a door slammed nearby, jolting her back to reality.

She pulled away, her breath coming in ragged gasps. Her heart pounded against her chest.

"It's okay," J.T. murmured. He pressed his lips against her forehead.

She closed her eyes, trying to catch her breath and her sanity. What they were doing wasn't okay; it was very, very wrong. She was making out in her boss's closet with an FBI agent, a man who was more likely to become her worst enemy than her lover. What the hell was she thinking? She was completely out of her mind.

"Let me go," she said.

"It was just a kiss." He stroked her hair, no doubt meant to be a comforting gesture, but his hands anywhere on her only made her feel more tense.

Maybe it was just a kiss to him. He was a guy, after all. But to her it had felt like the start of something—a fact she did not intend to share with him. It was bad enough she was so attracted to him that she couldn't think straight half the time. If he knew she was feeling anything more, he could try to use it to his advantage. She had to be careful. It wasn't just a matter of risking her heart. She could be risking her father, her reputation, the life she'd so carefully built during the past few years.

She reached for the door handle.

"Wait. Make sure the coast is clear," J.T. said.

She pushed the door open another inch. It was a good thing she hadn't gone barreling out of the closet, because several people were walking down the hall. They paused just outside the closet door. Christina held her breath as panic raced through her once again. Were they coming to get their coats? How on earth could she explain the fact that she and J.T. were in there?

"It was a perfect evening, Jeremy," Nicole said. "You must be so pleased and proud of yourself. Tomorrow you'll be the talk of the town. I'll make sure of that."

"It was all Alexis's doing," Jeremy declared.

"You give her too much credit," Nicole said. "You always do."

"Because you don't give her enough," Jeremy said, a bite to his tone. "It was a pleasure to have you here this evening, Mr. Benedetti. I'm sure you're looking forward to tomorrow. I believe your family will be very pleased with the results."

"I hope it all goes smoothly," Stefano replied.

"It will. I just checked with Russell Kenner. He said it has been extremely quiet tonight, nothing at all unusual."

"Wonderful," Stefano said. "My father chose Barclay's for its reputation, but I must admit I was worried when I learned that Christina Alberti was the jewelry specialist. Her father has quite an unsavory reputation."

Christina let out a small gasp. J.T. quickly put a hand over her mouth.

"Christina is a very loyal and honorable woman," Jeremy replied. "You need have no doubts about her ability or her integrity."

"I am happy to hear you have so much faith in her," Stefano said. "I will see you in the morning. Thank you for a wonderful dinner."

"You're very welcome," Jeremy said.

"I'll walk out with you," Nicole said. "I'd love to hear more about Florence."

Christina's ears were still burning after the three of them continued down the hall.

"You certainly are popular tonight," J.T. murmured. "The topic of every conversation."

"I can't believe Stefano brought up my father's reputation in front of Nicole. God, what if she puts something in the paper about me and my father?"

"What could she possibly print? Nothing has happened, has it?"

"No, but still." She pushed open the door another inch. The hall was empty. She stepped out of the closet, straightened her dress, and patted down her hair. Then she reached over and ran her finger across the corner of J.T.'s mouth. He tensed, and his eyes glittered with the desire that had not been extinguished. "Lipstick," she said quickly, not wanting him to get the wrong idea. "You had lipstick on your mouth."

"Maybe I wanted it there," he teased.

"Well, I didn't."

"Afraid someone might think you want me?" he challenged.

She looked away from his penetrating gaze, worried he would see far too much in her own expression. "I don't want to talk about it."

"There's a big surprise."

"J.T., please, not here."

He nodded. "Fine. Then tell me this. Were you aware that Benedetti knew about your father? Because you don't seem surprised, just annoyed that he mentioned it in front of Nicole."

"He said something to me last night," she admitted. "He came by my office. He said his family knew of my father."

"That's interesting. If they already knew about your father before they sent their collection to Barclay's, why would they suddenly be worried now? This new concern must have something to do with the smoke bombs that went off last night."

"Which my father had nothing to do with."

"I hope not," J.T. said. "But the fact that you ran straight to your father's house after it happened still sticks in my brain."

She didn't know how to reply. She had run to her father's house because she'd thought she'd seen him outside Barclay's, because she'd sensed he was involved. But he'd told her he wasn't. Hadn't he? Or had he just sidestepped the question, as he was so good at doing? She needed to think, and she couldn't do that with J.T. standing so close to her. When he was around, her brain went to mush.

"You can't deny it, can you?" J.T. asked.

"We need to get back to the party." She started walking, hoping to avoid any more questions.

"If your father is involved, Christina, you're going to need me."

"I don't think so."

"Then think again, because as far as I can see I'm the only ally you have. If anything happens to that diamond, you're going down, and fast. Barclay's will be looking for a scapegoat. And, honey, you'll be it. Make no mistake about that."

His words chilled her to the bone, because they were honest and true. She put a hand on his arm, drawing his gaze to hers. "If something happens to that diamond, can you stand here and tell me that you'll still be my ally? That you won't try to put me in jail?" He hesitated a second too long. She had her answer. "That's what I thought. Excuse me. I'm going to say my good-byes to Alexis and Jeremy. Then we can leave."

7

J.T. let Christina go. He knew she was pissed because he hadn't answered her question. What was he supposed to do—lie? *Yes*, a voice inside him answered.

He should have assured her that he was her friend and that she could count on him. He wanted her to trust him, to confide in him, to help him catch Evan. While everyone else might be worried about Christina's father, J.T. was more concerned about Evan. He knew Evan was involved. Evan had left him a note telling him so.

It was possible that Christina's father was also a player in the game, but J.T. had no doubt that Evan was calling the shots. Or was it possible that Evan had some competition, that there were other thieves eyeing the diamond? He needed to think more about that possibility. It would be interesting if another thief foiled Evan's plans. Evan's arrogance might work against him.

"What are you thinking?" Christina asked, rejoining him in the foyer. "You have a funny look on your face."

"Nothing. Did you say good-bye for me, too?"

"I spoke to Alexis. I don't know where Jeremy went. Are you ready to leave?"

He waved her toward the front door. "After you."

"The party seems to have emptied out pretty quick," she commented as they walked out of the house and down to the car.

"It sure did. By the way, you never told me exactly what you overheard earlier."

"David said he wanted Alexis to talk to me about something. That it was important. There was a sense of urgency in his voice."

"And that sent you into a panic? Why? Does David have something on you?" His gaze narrowed as she glanced away from him. "You didn't like it that he examined the diamond earlier. Is that what this sudden worry is about? Did David see something in that diamond you didn't want him to see?"

"No," she said quickly. "Of course he didn't. The diamond is fine. And David is just a jerk. He probably asked Alexis to talk to me about giving him more responsibility or more money or something. Forget I mentioned it."

J.T. unlocked the car door for Christina and then paused. He tipped his head toward the man walking across the street. "There's your boy now." They watched as David got into a silver Mercedes with a convertible top. "He has good taste in cars; I'll say that for him."

"Expensive taste for a grad student," Christina murmured. "He certainly didn't buy that car with what Barclay's pays him."

"Maybe he comes from money. He seemed to fit in well tonight with the Kensington crowd."

"Too well. I still don't know how he got himself invited. Maybe there is some connection between him and the Kensingtons that I don't know about."

"He's worth checking out," J.T. said. There were too many things about David Padlinsky that did not add up. He needed more information about who he was, where he came from, what kind of money he had.

"You don't think he's Evan, do you?" Christina asked.

J.T. shook his head. "There's no way. Evan couldn't sit across from me all night and fool me."

She sent him a skeptical look. "You've been telling me all along that Evan is a regular Houdini, but he couldn't fool you? Are you that confident?"

"It's extremely doubtful," he amended. "But it's certainly possible Evan is using David in some way. David had access to the diamond today." Now that J.T. thought about it, he wondered if David could have pulled a switch during his preview with the reporter. Who would have known? Christina, who had the most knowledge about the diamond, hadn't been present. "Let's see where he's going," he said. He opened Christina's door and hurried around to his side. He had a feeling David's Mercedes could outrun his Chevy. Fortunately, David didn't seem to be in a hurry, and they were able to stay close as he drove across town. It was after midnight, and traffic on the city streets was thin.

"I think he's heading to Barclay's," Christina said as David made another turn. "Why would he be going there so late at night?"

"Only one way to find out," J.T. replied. "There's a notepad in the glove compartment. Write down his license plate number for me, and I'll run it through the computer later."

"You can do that? Run anyone's license plate?" She retrieved the pen and paper. "I guess Big Brother really is watching."

"I only run plates on people who act suspiciously, and David fits that category."

As they turned down the street where Barclay's was located, J.T. slowed down and pulled over by the corner, cutting the lights. David continued down the road, parking across from Barclay's. He made no immediate move to get out of the car.

"What's he doing?" Christina asked.

"I think he's on the phone."

"What should we do?"

"Wait and watch."

The minutes ticked slowly by. David was certainly having a long conversation. The fact that he'd parked directly across the street from the auction house suggested that he wasn't worried about being seen. But J.T. couldn't think what business David could possibly have at Barclay's after midnight. The street was quiet. They hadn't seen another car in the past five minutes. The commercial neighborhood was completely deserted. It would be different tomorrow morning. The auction house would be filled to overflowing with people wanting to get a look at the diamond.

Christina put a hand on J.T.'s arm. "Look. I think he's getting out."

Sure enough, the light went on in the car as David

stepped out. He closed the door and adjusted his coat. Then he started across the street.

"David is going into Barclay's," Christina said with excitement. "Should we follow him?"

Before J.T. could answer, a pair of headlights at the far end of the block suddenly came to life. David froze in the street, seemingly blinded by the unexpected bright light. The car's engine roared.

J.T. realized what was about to happen a second too late. He had his hand on the door handle when the car hit David head-on, flinging his body like a limp rag doll halfway to the next intersection.

Christina screamed in horror.

J.T. jumped out, trying to catch a glimpse of the car that had just hit David, but it sped past them, moving too fast for him to read the license plate. The night was too dark. He couldn't make out the model or the driver. He ran down the street to David, worried that it was too late. Christina was right behind him. She collided with him when he stopped abruptly.

He grabbed her arms. "You don't want to look."

"He could be alive. He could need our help," she said, her eyes wild and scared. "Let me go."

He did as she asked. David's crumpled body lay in a heap in the middle of the street, a pool of blood under his head, one leg twisted beneath him, a bone sticking through his pant leg.

"Oh, God." Christina gasped, putting a hand to her mouth.

J.T. knelt down and put his finger on David's neck in search of a pulse, but there was none. He turned to Christina. "I'm sorry."

"He's dead?" she asked in disbelief. "How is that possible? He was alive a second ago. I think I'm going to be sick."

"Take a deep breath," he advised.

"We watched it happen. We just sat there and watched it happen," she said. "We should have gotten out of the car. We should have screamed or said something. Warned him. If we had, we could have saved him." Her voice grew more agitated with each note. J.T. stood up and put his arms around her, pulling her into his embrace.

"It's not your fault, Christina. We were down the street. It happened too fast. We had no chance of warning him."

She shook her head. "It's so wrong. This can't be happening."

"It is happening, and I need to call for help." He took out his cell phone, keeping one arm around her as he dialed 911 to report the accident. After he hung up, he looked down the street. No one had emerged from any of the buildings. If they hadn't been following David, there would have been no witnesses to the accident. Only he didn't think it was an accident. The car had not attempted to slow down or stop. Someone had been waiting for David to get out of his vehicle.

J.T. let go of Christina and bent over David's body. He didn't want to disturb the scene, but he knew that once the cops arrived, they would take over the case, and it might be days before he could get the answer to a simple question. He slipped his hand into David's coat pocket.

"What are you doing?" Christina asked, keeping

her distance. She had both arms wrapped around her waist now.

"Looking for David's cell phone." He found the phone and pulled it out, flipped it open, and pressed redial. A number flashed on the screen and began to ring. A moment later the call went to voice mail. "This is Alexis. Leave me a message."

Alexis Kensington? His heart sped up. Why would David, a part-time assistant, be talking to Alexis after midnight, after a party during which they had shared a private conversation? Christina was right: Something had been going on between David and Alexis. Had she known he was coming here? Had someone else known as well? Someone who had wanted to stop David from entering Barclay's?

He heard the distant sound of sirens and got to his feet. Christina suddenly moved. "I don't want to be here. I can't talk to the police. They'll ask why we were here, what we saw. Everyone at Barclay's will wonder if I did something."

"They won't wonder. I'll tell them we were coming to check on the diamond."

She shook her head. "It's no good. I'll be a suspect again. I can't have everyone looking at me with suspicion. I can't do it again."

He could see the panic setting in. He knew Christina was completely innocent of any wrongdoing, but she was right; she would be part of the investigation, as would he. She took off before he could tell her that he would protect her.

"Christina," he called. "Wait."

She ignored him, pausing only long enough to pull

off her high heels. With her shoes in one hand, she ran through the parking lot next to Barclay's and disappeared around the corner. It was after midnight, and she had no car and perhaps no money. He wanted to go after her, but the paramedics and cops were turning down the street. He reluctantly watched her go, praying she would make it home safely.

J.T. had just finished giving his statement to the police when Russell Kenner came out of Barclay's. He walked over to J.T. "What happened?" he asked.

"David Padlinsky was run down a few minutes ago."

"What?" Russell asked in surprise. He glanced over at the paramedics loading David's body into the ambulance. "That's David?"

"Yeah, I think he was on his way into the building when he was hit by a car."

"Who hit him?"

"I don't know. They didn't stop," J.T. replied.

Russell's lips drew into a taut, worried line. "What was Padlinsky doing here so late? What are *you* doing here so late?"

"Following David," J.T. said. "He was at the Kensingtons' party. I thought he was acting odd, so I followed him. Unfortunately, I wasn't close enough to protect him from what happened."

"How was he acting odd?" Russell queried. "Did it have something to do with the diamond?"

"I just had a gut instinct that he was up to something." J.T. didn't know Russell Kenner well enough to confide in him. In fact, he found himself searching the man's face for any sign of Evan. It didn't make sense that Russell was Evan, since Russell had been Barclay's head of security for over a year. But J.T. hated to discount any possibility. Some of Evan's games lasted longer than others, and he knew Evan had been in and around San Francisco for the past several months. "How have things been around here?" he asked.

"Until now, quiet. When I heard the sirens I thought someone was setting up another distraction. I double-checked our security before coming out here."

J.T. had wondered the same thing, except that murder was a big and very messy distraction even for Evan. "Why don't I go inside with you, just to make sure nothing is off?"

Russell frowned. "Fine, but I can assure you that I have everything under control. I think that guy you're worried about has probably given up."

J.T. doubted that was even close to being true.

Evan could hear the sirens, the rumble of cars overhead. A spatter of loose dirt fell in front of him as the tunnel narrowed and turned. The front of Barclay's was swarming with police, firemen, and paramedics. They'd cordoned off the street with yellow crime tape. He had no doubt that the guards inside of Barclay's were on high alert, not sure where the danger would come from. He smiled to himself as he considered what would happen next, how surprised everyone would be, how shocked and how ruined.

He directed his flashlight on the path ahead of him, taking one last turn, then ending at the ladder set in spikes along the wall. He climbed up the steps and turned his attention to the trapdoor overhead. He loosened the nuts and bolts and opened the door, wincing as it made a small protesting clatter. He climbed through the hole and onto the basement floor of Barclay's. He paused for a long moment to make sure no one was around, but all was quiet. He was at the far end of the basement, away from the secure access areas. This was where they kept the garbage. There were no cameras, no guards, no one waiting to pounce on him.

He brushed the dirt off his slacks as he got to his feet, then headed for the back stairs. He had no interest in stealing the diamond tonight. It would give him no pleasure to lift the stone in the shadow of darkness. That was for amateurs. He had a much bolder plan in mind. He would take it when they least expected it. And then they would know who he really was.

J.T. would realize once again that he had been outwitted. He had been chasing the wrong person. And Christina Alberti would discover just what he had planned for her.

He made his way up the back stairs. He'd already studied the cameras a dozen times, knew exactly when and where to move to avoid detection. Fortunately, the area where he wanted to go was not under intense surveillance. There was nothing to steal on the third floor. All the valuables were in the basement.

Tonight he wasn't here to take anything, but rather to leave a few clues behind.

His first stop was Christina's office. It was child's play to open the lock on her door. Her office was neat, organized, a place for everything and everything in its place. She worked so hard to maintain her illusion of complete control. Too bad it wouldn't last beyond tomorrow. Her past had given him the ideal avenue for distraction. He turned on her computer and hacked into her e-mail program, leaving her a little present. If she didn't come back to her office tomorrow, someone else would find it. Either way, she would become a target. All eyes would be on her and her father.

He left Christina's office and moved silently through the dark building. Some guards were talking in the distance. Through one of the windows police lights flashed. The officers were still conducting their investigation into the hit-and-run accident—a poor Barclay's employee struck down and killed in seconds. It was so tragic, so sad; it would add even more color to tomorrow's event. The employees would be discussing the victim. They would be distracted—again.

It was amazing how easy it was to convince people to look the other way.

Evan returned to the basement. He slipped through the trapdoor, pulling it closed behind him. Once he was out of the tunnels, he moved quickly to the car he'd left parked a few blocks away. He had one more stop to make before dawn.

Christina's teeth were chattering and her body was still shaking as she ran back downstairs to pay the cab driver. She knew she would have to explain when J.T. returned, and she had no doubt that he would be back with even more questions about why she'd run away from a criminal investigation.

God! What had she done, she asked herself again as she returned to her apartment. She couldn't seem to stop drawing suspicion to herself. She'd heard those sirens and panicked. She could imagine all the questions about why she was there, the nature of her relationship to David. . . . It would thrust her into the spotlight—the last place she wanted to be.

She knew she could have stayed with J.T. He would have told the cops that they were together when it happened. He was a federal agent. They would have believed him. She hadn't needed to run. It was an old habit. How many times had her father told her, *"You hear sirens, you run."* It was an instruction right up there with *"Wash your hands before you eat"* and *"Say your prayers before you go to bed."*

But she wasn't a criminal, and she shouldn't have left. Because this time it wasn't about her—it was about David.

She sank down on her sofa and let out a sigh. David was dead. She couldn't believe it. One minute he was alive, and the next he was gone. Had he known in that split second when he saw the car bearing down on him that it would be the last breath he would take? Had he felt the impact? Had he screamed? She knew that she had screamed. Her throat was still raw.

Had it been an accident? It seemed unlikely. The car hadn't even tried to slow down. Why?

It had to have something to do with Barclay's. Why had David gone there so late at night? Was he after the diamond? He certainly had the credentials to gain access to the restricted areas. His presence in the building after midnight, however, would have alerted the guards and Russell. David would have had better luck stealing the diamond in the middle of the day, when everyone was milling around—if that was his intent.

Getting up from the couch, she walked into her bedroom and changed into sweats and a T-shirt. She didn't even think about getting into bed. She suspected she would not be alone for long. She had to think about what to do next before J.T. came looking for her.

Picking up the phone, she dialed her father's number. As she'd expected, he didn't answer. "Dad," she said, still hearing the panicked note in her voice, "I really need to talk to you about that diamond. My assistant looked at it earlier, and tonight he was killed in a hit-and-run accident. I'm worried about you, about the diamond, about everything. Please call me, or find a way to get in touch with me. I might not be alone, though, so whatever you do, be careful. I've got the FBI breathing down my neck." She hung up the phone and drew in another deep breath. She had to calm down, think rationally.

It was after one o'clock in the morning. In less than twelve hours they would be auctioning off the diamond. How could she let that happen without being positive it was authentic? On the flip side, how could she prove it wasn't? On the original report the appraiser had seen a mineral inclusion in the shape of a heart, but in different kinds of light, it was possible that the inclusion couldn't be seen. Could she really stop everything based on a gut instinct that something that small was off?

Her conscience screamed, *Yes!* Deep in her heart she knew she should share her concerns with Alexis and Jeremy and let them make the final decision. But as soon as she said one word, they would look at her and wonder if she was involved in something dishonest, trying to pull a fast one . . . just like her father. She'd made a new life for herself. She couldn't destroy that life without more information.

She'd decide tomorrow. Hopefully, her dad would get in touch with her by then and confirm that no copies of the necklace had been made and that he wasn't going to do anything to try to stop the auction or steal the diamond.

A knock on the door gave her a little jolt, even though she'd been expecting it. For a split second she thought that it might be her father, but it was J.T. standing in the hallway. He strode into her apartment without waiting for an invitation, his expression a mix of anger and worry. He shoved her purse into her hands, then grabbed her by the shoulders. "Are you all right?"

She felt a surge of pleasure that his first words were filled with concern and not accusation. "I'm fine."

"Good. Now what the hell were you thinking—taking off like that?"

"I wasn't thinking. I'm sorry. I don't know why I ran. I've never seen anyone killed right in front of me, especially someone I know, someone I was talking to a few hours earlier. I was in shock."

"That's not why you ran. You ran because you were scared that you would be implicated in the accident. You didn't want to talk to the cops. You didn't want anyone at Barclay's to know you were there—did you?"

He gave her shoulders a little shake.

"You're hurting me."

His grip eased slightly, but he didn't let go, his

eyes filled with stubborn determination. "Answer the question."

"Okay, you're right. I panicked—for a lot of reasons. I know we didn't do anything wrong. I just didn't want to explain why we were following David." She paused. "What did you say to the police?"

"Not much. I told them what happened. David started to cross the street. A car came racing around the corner and hit him without slowing down or stopping. I also told them I couldn't ID the car." His gaze narrowed on her face. "You didn't recognize it, did you?"

"No, it was too dark. The lights were too bright. They were in my face. I saw David freeze and I heard the engine roar. The next thing I knew he was flying through the air." She put a hand to her mouth, feeling another wave of nausea at the memory. "I can't believe he's dead, J.T. What happened? Was it an accident? Was it deliberate? Who could do such a thing?"

He stared at her for a long moment, as if assessing the sincerity of her questions. Finally he let out a sigh and gave a weary shake of his head. "I don't know anything for sure, except that it wasn't an accident. Someone ran David down on purpose. It had to have something to do with why he went to Barclay's after the party. While I was talking to the cops, Russell Kenner came outside. He was concerned that the accident was a diversion."

"Oh, my God. I never thought of that. Please don't tell me David was killed as a distraction."

"Kenner and I checked on the diamond. It's still secure in the vault, and I don't think Kenner will be leaving it alone for the rest of the night." J.T. ran his hands up and down her arms. "You're trembling."

"I'm cold."

"And scared." He looked at her with compassion. "I know you're mixed up in something, Christina. You need to trust me. People are dying."

She wanted to trust him. She really did. She wanted to lean on him. His shoulders were broad and strong. But how could she do either of those things? J.T. might be willing to protect her, but what about her father? Would J.T. be willing to protect him, too?

It was too big a risk to take. She could wait a few more hours. It would all be over tomorrow. As soon as the diamond was sold, her life would go back to normal. She could get through a few more hours, couldn't she?

She set her purse down on a nearby table. "I don't know what you want me to say." She saw the disappointment in his eyes and felt as if she'd let him down. She didn't know why his opinion was important to her. They were more adversaries than friends. Still, she had to admit that she liked him. His humor, his intelligence, his determination were very appealing, and his beautiful body had a way of getting her all hot and bothered.

It had been a long time since a man had gotten under her skin the way J.T. had. He seemed to know what was in her head even before she did. That was what scared her the most, that he would discover her secrets before she was ready to share them.

"I'm not the bad guy," J.T. said quietly. "And I'm not going to jump to conclusions about you or your father."

"You already have. That's why you're interrogating me right now. You're suspicious of me. You think I'm going to help someone steal the diamond. That's why you keep showing up wherever I am."

"I wish that were the sole reason why I came here tonight, but it's not, Christina. It's you. I can't stop thinking about you," he confessed.

She caught her breath at the husky note in his voice, the look of desire in his eyes. "Because you're suspicious of me, that's why."

"Because you're beautiful, and I want you."

"You're just trying to get information out of me," she argued. "You want me to tell you my secrets. You want me to confide in you. Trust you."

"I do want all that," he admitted. "But right now, all I want is you."

"You're lying."

"No, I'm not. On the drive over here, I told myself I would just check on you, make sure you got home safely, confirm that you weren't in trouble. But as soon as I saw your face . . . your beautiful mouth . . ." His gaze dropped to her lips. "I knew I came for one reason and one reason only—you."

She swallowed hard at the purposeful note in his voice. She wanted to fight him, but her body was already on his side. She was tired of fighting herself, tired of worrying and feeling scared and alone. As he lifted his questioning gaze to hers, she told herself to say no, to play it safe, to keep him at a distance. That would be the smart thing to do, and as he'd said earlier, she was a smart girl—at least most of the time, just not tonight.

"This is crazy," she murmured. "You, me, we're on different sides. We want different things."

"Do we?" His devastating smile played across his lips. "I think at this moment we want exactly the same thing." He pulled her up hard against him, her hands pressed against his strong, broad chest. "Yes . . . or no?"

She wanted to say no, but she knew she'd made her choice the moment she'd opened the door. "Yes."

"Yes," he agreed, sliding his tongue into her mouth. He grabbed her head with his hands, tangling his fingers in her hair as he deepened the kiss, tasting, exploring, savoring each sweet second.

She slid her arms around his waist as the sparks that had been smoldering between them jumped and crackled. She'd never felt such passion, such need, such demanding desire to be with a man. Her heart raced; her stomach clenched with every kiss, every touch. She felt as if she were standing on the edge of a cliff and she very much wanted to jump. She wanted to release herself from the bonds of trying to do the right thing, be the good girl, follow the rules, play it safe.

Running her hands up under his coat, she massaged the taut, powerful muscles in his back. It wasn't enough. She tugged at his shirt, pulling it out of his belt, undoing his buttons as fast as she could. She had a desperate need to get her hands on his bare skin. When his shirt was open, she pulled it off him along with his jacket, then ran her fingers across his broad chest, through the light smattering of dark hair.

J.T. grabbed the hem of her T-shirt and yanked it over her head. She wasn't wearing a bra, and his hands came down on her breasts as his mouth slid down her throat. She threw back her head and moaned with pleasure as his tongue swirled along her collarbone, dipping down to her breasts, finally replacing his hands with his mouth.

She ran her fingers through his hair and closed her eyes as a jolt of desire threatened to knock her off her feet. She told herself they should slow down, but in truth she wanted to go even faster. J.T. must have read her mind. He straightened, grabbed her hand, and pulled her into the bedroom.

The room was dark. Moonlight danced in shadows along the wall. She pushed down her sweats along with her panties and stepped out of them, standing naked before him. She was grateful for the darkness. She didn't want to be reminded of who he was—who she was. J.T. reached for the light switch. She caught his arm with her hand.

"No," she said. "No lights. No questions. No confessions."

"I want to see you," he muttered.

"Not tonight," she whispered. "Tonight . . . just use your hands."

He did as she asked, his thumbs grazing her nipples, teasing them into sharp, aching points. She reached for his belt buckle. She unhooked it and helped him slide off his slacks so that he was as naked as she was.

J.T. pulled her into his arms, his flesh heating hers from the tips of her toes to the top of her head. She loved the feel of the hair on his legs, his chest, his arms, the shadow of whiskers that scraped her cheek and her breasts as he ran his mouth up and down her body.

She pulled him down on the bed, suddenly impatient to have him inside her, but he wouldn't be hurried. He took his time to explore every inch of her, first with his hands, then with his mouth, loving her ruthlessly until she was hot and tingling all over. When he moved away, she wanted to scream.

"What are you doing?" she asked breathlessly.

He grabbed his wallet from his pants pocket and pulled out a condom.

"Oh," she whispered. "I almost forgot." It worried her that she had forgotten, that J.T. had driven every last responsible thought out of her head. But when he straddled her body, finding the soft place between her thighs and sliding into her eager and impatient body, she didn't even consider thinking. She gave herself up to the passion and the pleasure.

In the shadows of the night, her secrets didn't seem nearly as important as the man making love to her.

8

J.T. awoke to sunlight streaming through the half-open curtains in Christina's bedroom. She was gone. He stared in bemusement at the empty side of the bed. He didn't remember letting her go. In fact, he didn't remember falling asleep. But it was morning and she was gone.

Those were the facts—shitty facts, but facts all the same. He touched the pillow that had cradled her head. In his mind he could still see her dark hair spread across it, her soft face lit up with desire as they moved together in perfect harmony. Making love to her had been incredible. She might be selfish with sharing her private thoughts, but she was more than generous with her body. *Damn.* He wished he'd woken up before her. He'd wanted to see her in the light.

Rolling onto his side, he glanced at the digital clock on the table. It was seven thirty. They still had plenty of time to get to Barclay's. The auction wouldn't begin until noon. In a few hours it would all be over. That thought was disturbing—in more ways than one. He knew the day would not pass easily. Evan had not given up. He would attempt to steal the diamond, and J.T. would have to stop him. He truly hoped that Christina would not get caught in the middle.

He got out of bed and pulled on his pants and shoes. He heard Christina moving around in the living room, and was relieved she hadn't left without him. They needed to talk, figure out a plan for the day. He had to try once more to get her to confide in him. Of course, he'd had several chances the night before, but he hadn't wanted to ruin anything. She'd laid out the terms—no lights, no questions, no confessions—and he'd agreed to the deal. Now he had to get her to listen to his terms. He hoped she'd be more willing to trust him now that they had become intimately involved. She'd be ready to talk.

The sound of the front door closing cut into his confidence. He raced into the living room. "Christina?" No answer.

He grabbed his shirt, coat, and car keys and dashed down the stairs, hoping she'd opted for the slower elevator. She hadn't. Her car was just pulling out of the garage when he reached the sidewalk. He called her name again, but she didn't stop. He didn't know if she hadn't seen him or was ignoring him.

The closeness he felt to her was suddenly replaced by massive doubt.

Jumping into his sedan, he drove after her. When she turned away from Barclay's, his worries increased. Where was she going? And why hadn't she woken him up to say good-bye?

He'd been a fool to think she trusted him and an

even bigger fool to trust her. What did he really know about her? Very little. Maybe she'd slept with him to throw him off the track, to distract him, to stop him from questioning her.

If that was her plan, it had definitely worked. He hadn't used his brain at all in the last few hours. Now he suspected he was going to pay a price for that lapse in judgment.

His cell phone rang and he answered it quickly. "McIntyre," he said, hoping it was Christina.

"J.T., it's Jenny."

Jenny? His stomach turned over. This couldn't be good. "What's up, Jen?"

"Evan," she said wearily. "He came by my shop last night. He's acting really crazy, J.T. He was talking about us being together and how he was going to give me the world on a diamond platter, and he really scared me. I was looking right at him, and I didn't recognize him anymore. It's like the Evan I knew had disappeared. There was a stranger in his eyes. I don't think he's completely sane."

"He never was."

"Then he's even less so now."

"I'm glad you called, Jen. I've been trying to find him. You said you didn't recognize him, but I take it you didn't mean he was in disguise?"

"No, he looked the way he always did."

"His hair was still blond? Eyes still blue?"

"Well, he had on a ski cap, and it was dark, so I couldn't see him clearly. His eyes were the same. It was his personality that was different."

J.T. thought about that for a moment. Evan had

probably changed his hair color, and if he wore contact
lenses, those were easy enough to remove. The fact
that he'd worn a ski cap confirmed his suspicion that
Evan was wearing a disguise, but it had to be a disguise that was easy to modify. It made sense that Evan
would not have wanted to upset Jenny by showing up
on her doorstep as someone else.

"What is he up to, J.T.? Do you know?" Jenny asked.

"I think he's planning to steal a very rare and valuable yellow diamond from Barclay's Auction House
today."

"How can he do that? Isn't it heavily guarded?"

"Yes, but I still think that's his intent, and it goes
with what he told you about giving you the world on a
diamond platter."

"I guess."

"Did he say anything else?"

"He said to tell you that he's not done ruining your
life. He knew I would talk to you. He wasn't worried."

J.T. felt a jolt of anger at the arrogant statement, and
his resolve to put Evan behind bars for the rest of his
life doubled—again. "Thanks for the call, Jenny. Look,
I don't want you to talk to Evan anymore."

"Believe me, I don't intend to."

"What happened to the guard your brother hired to
watch you?"

"I let him go last week. I thought it was over."

"Hire him back, and don't go anywhere alone. If
Evan is not done with me, he sure as hell isn't done
with you."

"I can't believe I once loved him," Jenny said, with
a deep, raw pain in her voice. "I was a fool to believe

his lies. I should have been smarter. I should have seen through him. How could I be so stupid?"

"You weren't stupid. You were in love."

"Same thing," she said with a sigh. "Good-bye, J.T., and good luck. I really want you to catch Evan before anyone else gets hurt."

As J.T. closed his phone, he saw Christina drive into a parking lot across from Pier 39. What the hell was she doing? Where was she going?

He slowed down, not wanting her to see him just yet. She was going to lead him to someone important—her father, or maybe Evan? Right now, he'd take either one.

Christina glanced down at the handwritten note on her passenger seat. She'd found it by her front door when she'd gone out to get the newspaper. It said, *Meet me at the Pier 39 Fun House, 8:00.* There was no signature, but she knew. The note was from her father. She was glad he hadn't knocked or rung the bell. He would not have been happy to find her sleeping with the FBI.

She could hardly believe she'd spent the night making love to J.T. She'd never done anything so impulsive, so reckless, or so incredibly wonderful. In J.T.'s arms she'd felt like another woman, a woman she quite liked, a woman she wouldn't mind being again. But where they went from here she had no idea. It could all be over in a few hours. J.T. didn't live in San Francisco. His job was in LA or wherever his next case took him. He could be gone by the evening. She might never see him again.

She felt a rush of sadness at the thought. Yet she had no right to want more. J.T. had made no promises to her. He hadn't pretended that they were having a relationship or that he was in love with her. He'd just wanted her, and she'd wanted him. It had been good. Now it was probably over. She had to be okay with that. She couldn't let herself have regrets. She *wouldn't* let herself have regrets.

As she parked her car in the lot, she thought about calling J.T. and letting him know that she'd meet him at Barclay's, but she knew an endless list of questions would follow. That was why she'd left the apartment while he was still asleep. She hadn't wanted to lie to him again. Nor had she wanted him to follow her. She needed to keep him away from her father. She just hoped to God her father would tell her what she wanted to hear.

Christina got out of her car and crossed the street to Pier 39, a tourist destination filled with dozens of shops, restaurants, and a carousel. With the exception of a coffee hut, most of the shops were still closed, and there was no one around. It was a cold, foggy morning in San Francisco, and no doubt the tourists would arrive later with the sun. She walked down the length of the pier, pausing to look at the dozens of sea lions that had taken up residence on wooden floats in the harbor. They barked and squealed as they jostled for position, the smaller lions ending up in the water more often than not.

She walked around the far end of the pier that faced Alcatraz, the infamous island prison that also offered a gorgeous view of the Golden Gate Bridge. As she approached the fun house, she noticed a large construction sign. Apparently the funhouse was being remodeled and wouldn't reopen for another month.

Not sure what to do, she hesitated. Her father was nowhere in sight, but his note had been very specific. She tried the door to the building and found it unlocked. Reminding herself that her father loved a good clandestine location, she opened the door and stepped into the entry, pausing to let her eyes adjust to the darkness. She was standing in a small room with dark wood paneling and a podium that had been pushed against one wall. An aluminum ladder leaned against the same wall, a toolbox next to it. A line of small windows set just below the ceiling sent dim light into the room.

"Dad," she called. Her voice bounced off the walls, a slight echo behind it. She waited another moment, tempted to leave. Her nerves were on edge, and this odd place was not helping. But if her dad had information about the diamond, she really wanted to get it.

Across the room she saw another door. It was ajar. She heard a rumbling sound and then a voice.

"Dad," she called again. "Are you there?"

"Christina," he said, his voice distant and muffled.

Relief surged through her. He was in the building. "Where are you?"

"Christina," he repeated.

She followed his voice to the open door and moved through it. She found herself in a long, narrow hallway. There were doors every few feet, and she had no idea which one to open. "Dad, where are you?" she called again.

"Christina."

Why did he keep saying her name and nothing else? She opened the door where she thought she'd heard the voice coming from and took a step forward. It was so dark she couldn't see where she was going.

Her foot came down on a slippery surface. She floundered, trying to grab hold of something, catch her balance, but her hands found only air. A second later she was on her butt. Her body bounced up against hard metal. It took her a minute to realize she was on a twisting, slick slide descending through a pitch-black hole in the ground.

As her speed increased, so did her scream. It seemed like an eternity before she hit the bottom of the slide and her body went airborne. Finally she landed with a hard thud on some sort of mattress. She was still trying to catch her breath when a body came hurtling down the slide after her, a large, hard, male body that slammed against hers. He was all over her, solid muscles and heavy hands. She screamed again, trying to push him off.

"Christina, it's me, dammit. Stop hitting me."

Shocked by his voice, she squinted in the darkness, trying to make out his face. "J.T.?"

"Yes. It's me," he said with annoyance.

"What . . . what are you doing here?"

"I followed you. Now why don't you tell me what you're doing here?"

His breath was in her face, his mouth just inches from hers, his hard hips reminding her of the way he moved when he came inside her. She squirmed beneath him. "You need to get off me. I can't breathe," she added with a gasp.

"I'm trying."

"Try harder." She put a hand against his chest and pushed, feeling a desperate need to take in some air.

J.T. moved off to one side, kneeling on the mattress. He extended his hand and pulled her into a sitting position. After drawing in several gulping breaths of air, she took a look around. They were in a small square room, about eight feet across. There was no other furniture besides the thick mattress and the end of the slide from which they'd just descended. A line of small, dim lights around the baseboard made it possible to see, but it was still dark.

"That was a hell of a ride," J.T. commented, running a hand through his hair. "There's never a dull moment with you, Christina."

"You might not believe it, but I actually lead a very quiet life."

"You're right. I don't believe it." His gaze met hers. "What are you doing here? Why did you sneak out on me this morning without a good-bye? Didn't I deserve at least that?"

She swallowed hard, not knowing how to answer. There was an intimacy between them now that made it more difficult to keep her secrets. "I had someone to meet. I didn't want to wake you. You were sleeping so peacefully."

"That's not the reason," he said with a scowl. "You didn't want me to know who you were meeting, did you? Is it your father? Or is it Evan? So help me, Christina, you'd better tell me the truth."

"It's certainly not Evan," she said, surprised he could even think that. "I told you before, I'm not involved with him. Why can't you believe me?"

"Oh, I don't know. Maybe it has something to do with the fact that you keep lying to me, sneaking around, running out on me when I'm not looking," he said sarcastically.

She wished she could refute his statement, but what could she say? She had done all those things. But she hadn't betrayed him with Evan. "I found a note slipped under my apartment door this morning. It was from my father. He asked me to meet him here." She drew in a deep breath. "I would never lie to you about Evan, J.T. Maybe you can't believe me, but that is the truth." She could see by the expression on his face that he still had doubts.

"You're right. I can't believe you," he said shortly. "You've been lying to me since we met. Hell, maybe last night was just another part of the lie, a way for you to seduce me into trusting you."

His cold words cut her to the quick. "That's not the way it was, and as I recall, you did as much seducing as I did. Maybe you wanted to get me into bed so I'd say something to incriminate myself."

"Is there something you could say that would incriminate you?" he asked sharply.

Damn. She'd stepped right into that one. "No, but you didn't know that. You could have been thinking that—"

"I wasn't thinking at all," he said, cutting her off. "I didn't have an ulterior motive last night."

His words took a weight off her heart. "Neither did I." She looked him straight in the eye so that he could see she wasn't trying to hide anything, at least not where their personal relationship was concerned. "As far as Evan goes," she continued, "I have told you nothing but the truth. I don't know who he is or where he is or what he's doing. If I did, I would tell you, because I know that what Evan did to your family was horrific. I wouldn't try to stop you from finding him."

"What if he was blackmailing you? Holding your father hostage?" J.T. challenged. "Would you still tell me the truth then? Because from where I sit you'd do just about anything to protect your old man."

She'd never considered either of those possibilities, and a chill ran down her spine. "Why would you suggest that Evan has my father under his control?"

"It's a possibility. There has to be a reason why you're keeping secrets."

"Well, it's not—" Her words were cut off by the sound of her father's voice, louder now.

"Christina," her father said.

She frowned, wondering where he was. He seemed to be calling her from the other side of the wall. That was when she realized there was a door hidden in the shadows. She jumped to her feet. "He must be in there," she said, rushing to the door. "I don't know why he keeps saying my name like that. It's creepy."

"Everything about this place is creepy. I think you're being set up, Christina."

"Why would you say that?"

"Because the location is too perfect—a building under construction, a woman alone . . ."

"My father wouldn't set me up," she countered, moving across the room.

"Let me go first," J.T. said.

She supposed she should have argued that she was a

capable, independent woman, but in truth she preferred having his big, strong body in front of hers. "Be careful," she whispered. "I can hardly see a thing."

As he opened the door, a bright light blinded them. J.T. took a step forward and she went with him. She didn't realize they were in a tunnel until the walls began to turn around them. With the light in her eyes and the walls spinning, she could hardly stand up straight.

"Hold on to me," J.T. said.

He didn't have to ask twice. She had a death grip on his arm. He wasn't going anywhere without her. She tried to concentrate on his back instead of on the white walls going around and around. She'd never been good at spins. She'd even thrown up once on the merry-go-round at the park. Why had her father asked her to meet him here? Why was he putting her through this? He knew she wouldn't find it fun.

J.T. moved relentlessly forward. She had no idea how he was doing it, but she was more than a little grateful to have him leading the way. Finally he reached another door and shoved it open. They walked into a room filled with mirrors. Oh, God, more horrors, only the horror was her. Everywhere she looked she saw her body distorted into grotesque shapes and sizes, made worse by the fluorescent light hanging on the ceiling. At least it was better than the spinning tunnel. That was something.

The voice came again, louder this time. "Christina."

"Where are you?" she shouted.

J.T. reached for something on a table. He held up a cassette player just as the voice came again: "Christina."

She gulped back a knot of fear as the truth sank in. Her father wasn't in this building. It was a setup. What the hell was going on?

"What is this—another signal?" J.T. asked. "Some game the two of you play? Because if it is, you are both seriously twisted."

"No." She gave a worried shake of her head. "My father wouldn't bring me into a place like this and scare the crap out of me."

"Really? Then why did he ask you to meet him in an abandoned building? And why did you come without question? You had to believe he was here."

"I did, because it's not the first time," she muttered.

"What do you mean?"

"It's not the first time," she repeated more loudly. "Okay, yes, we've met in strange places before. Over the years, whenever my father is in trouble, he has asked me to meet him in clandestine spots. Since he left the museum five years ago, he thinks people are watching him. Maybe he's right. Maybe he is under surveillance. I don't know what he's been doing. To be honest, I haven't wanted to know."

"Until he showed up at the same time as the Benedetti diamond," J.T. said, a perceptive gleam in his eyes.

"You're right. I hadn't heard from him in months until I thought I saw him outside Barclay's Wednesday night. That's why I went to his house. He called me later that night when you and I were at the coffee shop, and he asked me to meet him at the zoo the next day."

"The zoo?"

"He likes crowded public places or deserted, abandoned buildings—places where he can hide in a crowd or we can be completely alone. He loves drama. It's part of his charm, I guess you could say."

"I think I'll reserve judgment on his charm," J.T. said with a sigh. "So far he's pissing me off. What he did tell you when you met yesterday at the zoo?"

Christina hesitated, wondering how much information would be too much.

"You still don't trust me?" J.T. asked in amazement.

"It's not a matter of trust. You're an FBI agent. You're sworn to uphold the law."

"And you think your father is breaking it?"

"If he was, I sure wouldn't want to tell you. He's the only family I have, J.T. And I love him. I don't want to lose him."

J.T. stared at her for a long moment. "I respect your loyalty, Christina. I do. I even admire it. Maybe if I had worried about my own father more, he'd be alive today." His voice hardened. "But I'm concerned that your loyalty will take you into the middle of a very dangerous situation. If Evan wants the diamond and your father wants the diamond, they're either working together, or they're about to clash. Either way there's going to be trouble. Maybe I can help."

"I want to tell you. I'm just afraid that . . ." She didn't know how to say it.

"I'll put your father behind bars? Perhaps, if you trust me, I can prevent that from happening. As far as I'm concerned he hasn't committed a crime yet."

"Okay, but don't make me regret this," she warned. She drew in a deep breath, not even sure where to start.

"Yesterday when I met with my father he told me to call in sick today, that something could go wrong with the diamond."

"Because he was going to try to steal it?"

"No, because the diamond is cursed. He's worried about me."

He shook his head, his expression skeptical. "Oh, come on, Christina. There's no curse. That's just his cover story. He doesn't want you to be around when he tries to steal the diamond. That way you can't be blamed."

She wanted to deny it, but how could she? "I begged my father to go away, to leave it alone. He knows how much Barclay's means to me. He knows how hard I've worked to put my life back together. At least, I thought he did. I had to remind him yesterday that the reason I work in an auction house now is because no one at a museum would hire me. He ruined my name along with his own. I asked him to leave me in peace."

"Then why did you come running to meet him today?"

She debated telling him the rest, but the situation was unraveling so fast, she wasn't sure she had another choice. Her father wasn't here; that much was clear. She didn't know if he'd left when he'd realized J.T. had followed her, or if he had never been here at all. "I came because when I looked at the diamond through the gem scope, I noticed a discrepancy between what I was seeing and the appraisal report. There was a very small flaw that was noted by the original appraiser in Italy that I couldn't see."

"What kind of flaw?"

"A naturally occurring mineral inclusion in the shape of a heart."

"Which means what?"

"I don't know. It just bothered me that the stone didn't exactly match the specs in the original report."

His gaze sharpened. "Let me get this straight. The diamond you looked at yesterday is a fake?"

"It's a very slim possibility. It's also possible that I couldn't see the flaw in the light I had and with the scope that I was using. It was such a small variant. And when I looked at the chain and the clasp, I couldn't believe that anyone could duplicate an entire necklace so perfectly. That's why I didn't say anything to anyone— except my father. I asked him if he'd heard about someone trying to copy the diamond."

"Because you had doubts."

"With my father around, I always have doubts," she admitted. "He actually suggested that the Benedettis might have made the switch in Italy—that they're trying to sell off a fake stone and have set me and Barclay's up to take the fall."

J.T. rubbed his chin. "That's a different spin."

"I thought so. At any rate, my father said he would ask around. He has contacts in the jewelry world. That's the last I heard. I told him I needed to know this morning so I could make a decision about what to do. I don't want to sell a fake necklace. I also don't want to cause a big crisis if I'm wrong. That's it. That's the whole story. And that's why I came here today, because I was expecting to meet with him."

"Thank you." J.T. leaned forward and surprised her with a kiss.

It was a brief caress, but the touch of their lips immediately took her back to the night before and the passion they had shared.

"I know that wasn't easy for you to do," J.T. said. "I appreciate the vote of confidence."

"Don't let me down."

"I'll try not to," he promised.

It was not the definitive answer she would have liked, but it was clearly all she was going to get for now.

"We need to leave," J.T. said. "Whatever plan is in motion, it's happening at the auction house, not here."

"Do we have to go back through that spinning tunnel?" She looked around the mirrored room for another exit, but couldn't find any.

"I don't see any other way out." J.T. walked back to the door through which they'd entered. It was closed.

She didn't remember shutting it behind her. Her pulse began to speed up as J.T. wrestled with the knob. Had someone come up behind them and closed the door? She hadn't heard anything, but she'd been caught up in J.T.'s questions and the tape recorder.

"It's locked," J.T. said, confirming her fears.

"Oh, my God!" Panic swept through her body. "We can't be trapped in here."

"I'd say that's exactly what we are—trapped," J.T. replied, a grim note in his voice. "I told you this was a setup. Your father wanted to make sure you weren't at the auction house this morning."

She immediately shook her head. "My father would not set me up like this. He wouldn't trap me in this house of horrors."

"He wanted you to call in sick and you refused. So he took matters into his own hands."

"That can't be the explanation."

"All right. Then I'll give you another one," he said, surprising her.

"What?"

"Evan. He wanted you out of the way—maybe both of us. He knew I'd follow you, that I'd want to protect you."

This was her fault, she realized. She'd acted far too impulsively. She'd led them both into a bad situation. A sudden grinding sound, followed by quiet, drew her attention to the door. The tunnel in the next room had stopped, she realized. Maybe someone was coming to rescue them. "Hello," she yelled. "Anyone there?" She pounded on the door. "We're locked in here. Let us out."

A burst of laughter came from the other side of the door. Christina stiffened. That wicked, evil laugh did not belong to anyone she knew.

"Who's out there?" she called. She looked at J.T., seeing the truth in his eyes.

"It's Evan," he confirmed.

9

"What does he want?"

"You know I can hear you, Christina," Evan said with amusement. "Why don't you just ask *me* what I want—what I'm doing here?"

"How do you know me?" she asked instead. "I've never met you."

"Of course you have. You just didn't realize it. We've actually spent some quality time together."

J.T. grabbed hold of the doorknob and yanked as hard as he could. Unfortunately, the knob came off in his hand and the laughter grew louder. Obviously Evan had loosened the screws, but the lock was intact. J.T. squatted down to look through the hole. He could see the edge of a suit coat but nothing else. "Dammit, Evan, what the fuck are you up to?"

"I thought we'd have a little fun today in the fun house. It was just going to be Christina and me. I didn't know you were coming to play, too, J.T. Well, the more the merrier, I always say."

His voice sounded weird, disembodied, as if he was

talking through a speaker or under water. He was trying to disguise his voice, J.T. realized. Why? Was he afraid they would recognize him as someone they'd spoken to in the last few days?

"What do you want?" J.T. asked. "I'm sure you have some plan in mind."

"Of course I do, but that's for me to know and you to find out."

"Don't play games."

"Why not? I love games. You used to love them too, J.T. You were the big man on campus—the football star. You couldn't be beaten, except by someone better than you—someone like me. You never see me coming, do you?"

J.T. hated the smug tone in Evan's voice, the reminder that Evan had eluded him for so many years. His hands clenched into fists. He wanted to smash Evan in the face. He wanted to hit him until he was bloody and dead. He'd never felt so much rage for any other person in his life. But he wouldn't give Evan the satisfaction of reacting.

"It's almost too easy," Evan continued. "You've slowed down, J.T. Your father would be so unhappy with your performance these days—so disappointed in your inability to come through when it counts. You've choked, J.T. We both know that. You're no longer a clutch player. You can't win anymore. You're a loser."

"I'm going to put you away," J.T. said. "You'll see who wins in the end."

"I don't think so." Evan laughed again. "I'd love to stay and chat, but I have things to do. It's a very important day, you know."

"Wait," Christina interrupted. "How did you get my father's voice on the recorder? How did you imitate his handwriting? What have you done with him? Where is he?"

"Ah, your father—Marcus Alberti, a very interesting man—some might say a man after my own heart. It's a pity really."

"What's a pity?" she asked, fear in her voice and in her eyes.

J.T. shook his head at her. He didn't want her to give Evan any more power, and there was nothing Evan enjoyed more than knowing someone was afraid of him.

"What's a pity?" she repeated desperately.

Silence greeted her words. Evan was gone.

J.T. slammed his fist against the door. The impact sent a massive pain from his wrist to his shoulder, but it released some of the tension in his body.

"He's gone," Christina said, terrified. "He left us here."

Her face was pale, and she was trembling. J.T. hauled her into his arms. She was stiff and cold. "It's okay," he said soothingly. "We're going to be all right."

She shook her head. "I don't think so. He set all this up so perfectly. God! What do you think he did to my dad?"

"Probably nothing," he said, wanting to reassure her.

"It didn't sound like nothing. He had my father's voice on tape. He copied my father's handwriting. I was completely convinced that note was from him."

"Evan is extremely clever. But just because he taped him and copied his handwriting doesn't mean he hurt him."

"If he didn't, where is he? Where does he think I am?" Christina pulled out of J.T.'s arms and began to pace in small, agitated circles. "We have to get out of here." She stopped abruptly. "My cell phone," she said, reaching for her purse. She frowned as she tried to dial. "No signal."

"I figured," he said. "Evan probably checked that out ahead of time."

"What are we going to do?"

He wished he had an answer. She was looking to him to save her and her father, and he very much wanted to do both. Restless, he roamed the room, running his hands along the sides of each mirror, wondering if any one of them might cover up another door or some sort of secret passageway. Was there really only one way in and out of this room?

"What are you doing?" Christina asked.

"Searching for another way out."

"I'll help. It's better than just standing here." She followed his lead, checking the opposite wall.

They didn't speak for almost ten minutes. By then they had covered every inch of the small room. They met in the middle. J.T. took her hands in his and gazed into her eyes. "I'm sorry, Christina, but I think we're going to be here until someone comes to find us."

"Which could be a long time from now. Who knows when the construction crews will be back?"

She let go of his hands and put her arms around his neck, pressing her face into the curve of his shoulder. He gave her a tight hug, knowing it wasn't nearly enough.

"At least we're together," she murmured. "If you

hadn't followed me, I'd be all alone in here. I guess your nosiness paid off."

He smiled as he stroked her hair. She was already bouncing back. She certainly wasn't a woman who stayed down for long. He liked her spirit. "Following you is always interesting."

She stepped out of his embrace and sat down on the floor by the door, leaning her back against the only bit of wall space that wasn't covered by a mirror. He sat down next to her, suddenly tired. They hadn't slept more than an hour or two the night before. Not that he was complaining. He put his hand on her knee. She was wearing a tan business suit with a short skirt. He moved his fingers up her thigh. She swatted his hand away.

"What are you doing?" she asked.

"Just passing the time," he said with a small smile.

She rolled her eyes. "How can you even think about that—now?"

"It's dark, we're alone . . . the mirrors are a little kinky."

"The mirrors are grotesque. If I see myself naked in one of those mirrors, I will probably never take off my clothes again."

"Well, we can't have that," he said.

"Then keep your hands to yourself."

J.T. picked up the doorknob that had fallen to the floor. "Look at this: The screws are missing. I'm guessing Evan jimmied with this when he set up the cassette tape." Getting to his feet, he slid his fingers into the hole where the doorknob had fit and tried to pull the door open. It didn't work. He took a few steps back and ran at the door, hitting it hard with his right shoulder. The door shook, but didn't open.

"You're going to hurt yourself," Christina commented.

"I can't just sit here and do nothing." He tackled the door again and again, groaning with the effort. His swearing grew louder and more colorful with each frustrated attempt. Unfortunately, he had nothing but bruises to show for his exertion.

Finally he gave up. He looked at Christina. She patted the floor next to her. Reluctantly he sat down.

"Feel better?" she asked.

"Not really." He scanned the room. There had to be something in here he could use to pry the door open. Maybe he could take apart one of the mirrors. But they were sheer glass with a fine aluminum frame around the edges. That wouldn't get him anywhere.

"I keep wondering what's going on at Barclay's," Christina muttered. "People will be looking for me. There's so much I do before an auction. Alexis will probably fire me for this."

"Alexis may have more pressing matters on her mind. I'm sure the police will be questioning her about David's death."

Christina started. "Oh, my God, I almost forgot about that. David is dead. So much has happened in the past twenty-four hours I can't keep up. Do you think Evan is the one who ran David down?"

"I can't rule him out, but I think there are other, more likely suspects."

She shot him a curious look. "Who?"

"Jeremy or Alexis. Didn't I tell you that David spoke to Alexis on the phone before he was killed?"

"No, you didn't tell me that. I remember you looking at his cell phone, but you never said who you called."

"Didn't I? I guess you ran off before I could."

"Don't remind me," she said with a sigh. "It wasn't my finest hour. So tell me the rest. Is there some relationship between David and Alexis?"

"I don't know. They obviously spoke right before he was killed. I haven't had time to do any further research. I gave the police the cell phone, so I'm sure they'll be talking to Alexis, if they haven't already."

"If Alexis and David had a personal relationship, it would explain why David was at the party," Christina said slowly.

"Maybe she was having an affair with David," J.T. said.

"It's hard to believe she would do that to Jeremy."

"Is it? Jeremy and Alexis strike me as kind of an odd couple. I take that back. She's beautiful. He has money. It's not like we haven't seen that combination before," J.T. said dryly.

"They could still love each other," Christina said. "Even if they didn't, I can't see Jeremy mowing someone down with his car."

"He didn't have to do it himself. He's a rich man. He can pay people to do his dirty work."

"I guess. It's weird how it's all happening at once—David dying, the diamond going up for auction." She turned to him with a puzzled look. "Do you think the car accident is related to the diamond? Or is it just a coincidence that it happened the night before the auction?"

J.T. considered her question. "I don't see the connection yet, but that doesn't mean there isn't one."

"It's more likely that Evan ran David down," Christina said. "He sounded so spooky. I wish I could see him, get a handle on what he looks like. I didn't recognize his voice."

"I think he was speaking into a microphone, something that distorted the tone," J.T. agreed. "He must have been afraid we would connect his voice to whoever he has been impersonating."

She nodded. "That's why he sounded so strange. What was the reference to the game playing about?"

"Football." J.T. drew circles with his fingers on the dusty floor, the word *football* making his stomach turn over. It had once been his passion, but it had become his nightmare.

"Go on," Christina urged.

"I don't want to talk about it."

"Come on, J.T. If Evan knows about it, why can't I?"

"Fine. I went to Cal on a football scholarship. I was the quarterback. I actually got drafted after college by the New York Jets."

"Really? You were that good?"

"Don't sound so surprised."

"Sorry. So how on earth did you get from the football field to the FBI?"

"It's a long story," he said, rolling his head around on his shoulders.

"Apparently we've got time." She settled herself more comfortably against the wall.

He had a feeling she was prepared to wait him out. What was the big deal? That part of his life was long gone. "All right. Here's the short version. My second year in the pros, I got hit and tore up my knee. I had to have surgery. It was a long recovery. When I eventually got better, I tried to play, but I quickly realized that I didn't have the will or the heart. Things got bad and then they got worse. So I quit." He paused, remembering those odd days of nothingness after he'd walked away from the game. He'd been focused on football for so much of his life he'd felt completely lost when it was gone. And yet strangely relieved.

"So you went into the FBI?" Christina asked. "Seems like an odd leap."

"I didn't do anything right away. I was exploring my options and dealing with my father's disappointment. It was his dream for me to be a pro football player. He groomed me to be a quarterback since I was six years old. He used to take me out every day after school, and I would practice throwing spirals to him. He was my coach all through the peewee leagues. He was at every game I ever played in high school and in college he never missed a home game. I thought I was living my dream, but when I got hurt, I realized it had been his dream. I'd just gotten tangled up in it. I hadn't wanted to disappoint him. The best times we ever spent together were on the football field. Those were some of the worst times, too."

He drew another breath, wondering why it was so

easy to talk to Christina. He hadn't spilled his guts about his relationship with his father to anyone—not even his ex-wife, not that she'd been eager to talk about anything that didn't concern her.

Christina gave him a nod of encouragement. "Go on."

"My father didn't understand how I could walk away from the game while I still had so much promise, so much unrealized potential. We had a love/hate relationship even before Evan came between us." He gazed into Christina's eyes. "I think that's why Evan went after my dad. He knew my father was the one person who could get to me."

"Your father was your Achilles' heel," Christina said. "I'm so sorry, J.T."

"It's not your fault."

"I'm still sorry. You had unfinished business with your dad. You never had a chance to tell him how you felt about any of this, did you?"

He shook his head. "We said a lot in anger. I don't think either of us was even listening to the other most of the time. Anyway, that's it."

"Not quite. You still haven't told me how you went from football to the FBI."

"That was Evan. When he took my father down, he gave me a strong motive to go into law enforcement. Fortunately, that degree in prelaw I'd earned at Cal gave me an entrée into the bureau. Once I became an agent, I specialized in fraud and started to track Evan. I've been on his trail ever since. Other cases come and go. I've caught lots of bad guys, but not him, not yet."

"You will," she said confidently.

"I will," he agreed. "I don't have one doubt about that. I'll stay on him as long as it takes."

"It sounds like everything worked out then, making the change from football player to special agent."

He tipped his head. "Not quite," he muttered. "My wife didn't like my change of job any more than my father did."

"Your wife?" she squealed, her jaw dropping in surprise. "You didn't tell me you had a wife."

"Relax. I meant my ex-wife. We met in college. Cheryl wanted to be married to a pro football player. When I quit the game, she quit me. It wasn't meant to be. We were young and stupid when we got married. We didn't know what the hell we were doing."

"I'm surprised she got you down the aisle at such a young age. You don't seem like the marrying type."

"That's because I've been married," he said pointedly. "It's not all it's cracked up to be."

"I wouldn't know. Paul dumped me at the first sign of trouble. I know it was probably better for me to find out sooner than later that his devotion could only go so far. When things got rough, he bailed."

"If he was that big a coward, you're better off without him."

"And you're better off without your ex-wife, who doesn't sound very nice, by the way, although I'm betting she was hot."

He grinned back at her. "I was the quarterback, Christina."

"And could get any girl you wanted. I suspect you still feel that way."

"Are you implying I have a big ego?"

"Absolutely," she said with a laugh.

"Hey, I'm not that bad. I have grown up a little since college."

"Don't worry, J.T. Your arrogance is part of your charm."

"That's a backhanded compliment if I ever heard one."

She gave a little shrug. "Thanks for telling me your story."

"No problem. I know you can keep a secret."

She made a little face at him. "Very funny." She cocked her head to one side as she studied him. "Don't you worry at all that you're too personally involved with Evan? That you won't be able to see him as clearly as you should?"

"No, I don't worry about that. I know him better than anyone, and he's mine. I had him in jail a couple of weeks ago, you know. I thought it was over. Unfortunately, I left him at the jail and he managed to trick an incompetent cop out of his uniform and his badge."

"How did he do that?"

"He asked for a cup of coffee. When the cop came close, he grabbed him around the neck, hitting two key pressure points, and the guy went down without a whimper. I won't leave Evan alone again. I won't take my eyes off him until he's locked up for good."

"You're awfully cocky for a man trapped in a room of mirrors," she pointed out. "That ego we were talking about."

"You're the reason we're trapped," he grumbled. "It was my personal involvement with you that clouded my judgment, not my relationship with Evan. I followed you in here to protect you. If you'd trusted me enough to tell me where you were going, neither one of us would be here."

"I know that. I'm sorry," she added guiltily.

"Me, too."

"Just about being trapped, or about last night?"

He leaned forward, pulling her hair away from her ear so he could whisper, "Not for a second." He slid his tongue around the edge of her earlobe. He heard her soft intake of breath, felt her heart quicken along with his own. She put her hand on his shoulder. He wasn't sure if she wanted to pull him closer or push him away. Unfortunately, she didn't have time to make a choice as a voice called out, "Hello? Is someone in there?"

J.T. jumped to his feet. "We're locked in here," he yelled. He grabbed Christina and pulled her to her feet.

"What happened to the knob?" the man asked.

"It came off," J.T. replied.

"Stand back."

A moment later a construction worker pried open the door with a crowbar. "How did you two get in here? This building is supposed to be locked up."

"The door was open," Christina said. "We just thought we'd take a peek inside."

"Didn't you see the sign? We're closed for remodeling."

"How did you know we were here?" J.T. asked, sure he already knew the answer.

"Some dude called my boss and said he thought he saw someone come in here."

"We're really sorry," Christina said. "We didn't mean to get trapped. I opened one door and suddenly I was on a slide."

"Yeah, well, don't do it again," he said gruffly. "Next time I'll call the cops."

J.T. didn't bother to flash his badge or explain. He didn't want to delay getting out of the building. The construction worker escorted them all the way up to the front door and out to the pier. J.T. was happy to be back outside with the wind on his face and a chance to regain control of the game.

Christina checked her watch. "It's almost eleven thirty. I think we can just make it to Barclay's before the diamond goes up for bid."

"I'm sure we'll make it. In fact, I think we're right on schedule."

"What does that mean?"

"Evan called that guy to let us out. He didn't want us to be trapped forever, just long enough to set his plan into motion. Now he wants us at the auction house."

"Why?"

"Only one reason I can think of," he said grimly. "So we can see him steal the diamond."

Evan walked into the showroom at Barclay's. The auction had begun thirty minutes earlier, and every seat in the room was taken. Clusters of bidders stood in the back, paddles in one hand, catalogs in the other. At the front of the room the auctioneer stood at a raised podium with the Barclay's insignia on the front. Behind the auctioneer was an electronic board that continually updated the latest bid, be it on the phone, the Internet, or in the room. The individual lots were brought into the room via a wood-paneled revolving door next to the podium. With each turn of that door, the energy and excitement in the room grew more palpable. They were getting close to the big-ticket items, the ones everyone had come here to see or to buy.

Evan loved these moments right before the kill. His heart was beginning to speed up. Adrenaline surged through his bloodstream. He felt completely and utterly alive. For the first time since he'd begun this game, he had difficulty keeping his face composed, dispassionate, his stance calm and relaxed, but he'd always had complete and utter control over his body, his expressions, and his voice. Today was no different. He would not slip up. He would not make a mistake. He would keep to the plan.

As the auctioneer rattled off bids rapid-fire, his mind drifted to Jenny. He could imagine how she would react when he showed her the fruit of his labors. Her beautiful hazel eyes would widen with amazement. She would finally understand that he was doing this one for her, just for her. He'd waited a long time to have her.

Jenny didn't know how difficult it had been to walk away from her all those years ago. She didn't understand the sacrifice he had made to let her have her life. He'd never been noble or generous, except with her. But it had become clear to him in recent months that Jenny had no life without him. She'd never married, never had children. She'd been waiting for him to come back. She just hadn't had the courage to tell him. Now he knew the truth. And he would have her. They would be together. He would dress her in designer clothes, adorn her with exquisite and expensive diamonds. He would take her around the world and show her everything she had never seen. He would no longer be alone in his adventures; he would have Jenny by his side. It was almost time.

He started as the door opened behind him. Alexis Kensington entered the room. She looked tired, as if she'd been up half the night. He suspected that was exactly what had happened. He knew she'd spent most of the morning answering questions about the tragic death of David Padlinsky. Evan smiled to himself. The police had helped him out this morning, keeping everyone at Barclay's busy with the investigation into the hit-and-run accident. It seemed that David and Alexis had had a relationship. Who knew? Certainly not the employees, who'd also spent most of the morning huddling around cubicles and hallways, gossiping about the latest events instead of doing their jobs.

God, he loved distractions. It was remarkably easy to turn someone's head in a different direction. So many people thought that things happened by chance, that fate stepped in and took what it desired. It was never fate or chance. It was usually him—or someone like him—someone who moved in the shadows, who manipulated the game of life without anyone even knowing they were playing—like Christina Alberti.

He figured that J.T. had told her about their history. Christina had been warned to look out for him, to keep her wits about her, which, of course, she hadn't done when she'd followed an anonymous note to a deserted location. He could still hear the panic in her voice when she'd realized that her father wasn't coming, that she'd been trapped in the room of mirrors. He'd always enjoyed irony, and he loved the thought of J.T. seeing his powerless, impotent image in the mirror every time he turned around. J.T. wouldn't be able to escape his own ineptness. Ah, life was sweet sometimes. If only he'd had more time, he would have stuck around to enjoy their quandary.

But he would have the pleasure of their company again—soon. He had made sure of that. It would be amusing to show his real face to Christina, to reveal his true nature. She would be shocked to know that they had stood face-to-face and spoken to each other. She would swear to J.T. that she had had no idea, that she had been completely fooled. That would be the truth. She had been so busy chasing her father, she hadn't seen what was right in front of her.

His phone vibrated in his pocket. He ignored it, knowing who was calling. He would let her sweat it out. She should have more faith in him. He never failed, and today would be no exception. In a few hours they would both get what they wanted—not that she would be able to keep the diamond. He had other plans.

Folding his arms across his chest, he leaned against the wall, watching and waiting.

"And now we move on to Lot Sixty-four," the auctioneer said. "A painting by Biagio d'Antonio, entitled *Madonna and Child in a Landscape*, on the turntable now." He paused as the panel slowly turned to reveal the painting on an easel. "This is a beautiful example of the Florentine Renaissance style and reveals the strong influence of Pesellino and Fra Filippo Lippi," he continued. "Let's open the floor at fifty thousand.

Who will start us off?" He pointed to a gentleman at the front. "Fifty thousand on my left. Do I hear fifty-five? Yes, we have fifty-five in the room. Sixty on the phone," he continued, calling out the escalating bids. He looked to the room, then to the bank of employees working the phones and the two women monitoring the Internet bids. Finally the bidding began to slow down. "All done then?" he asked. "Fair warning—I'm selling now to the lady on my left for ninety-two thousand."

A smattering of polite applause followed his words. Then he moved on to the next lot.

Evan checked the catalog in hand—six more items and then the diamond. It was time to make his move. He walked out of the showroom and turned down a long hallway. The door at the end was marked PRIVATE. He didn't hesitate to open it, and not one of the people he passed gave him a second look.

10

Christina tapped out the number for Barclay's on her cell phone as J.T. drove them across town. They'd left her car at the pier, figuring it would be faster to go together. Unfortunately, the midday traffic was slow and heavy, making her painfully aware of the passing seconds. "Answer," she muttered.

"Put it on speaker," J.T. said. "I want to hear what's going on."

She punched the speaker button just as Kelly Huang answered the phone.

"It's Christina," she said.

"Oh, my God, where are you?" Kelly asked. "Alexis is going crazy. We've been calling you for hours."

"I know. I got stuck somewhere. It's a long story, but I couldn't get to my phone."

"Are you all right? When you didn't show up this morning, we all wondered if something had happened to you. Did you hear about David? He was killed last night—right in front of the auction house. A hit-and-run. The police have been here half the morning. There are so many rumors about what happened I can't keep up with them all."

"Like what?"

"Like maybe David was having an affair with Alexis. Can you believe that? Oh, and I also heard that David was trying to steal the diamond and someone ran him down so he couldn't do it. I don't know what's going on. When are you getting here?"

"Hopefully in the next ten minutes. How is the auction going?"

"Very well. It's standing room only. I have to go."

"Wait. The diamond hasn't come up yet, has it?"

"Not yet. I think there are about six lots to go. I hope you can get here by then."

"Me, too," Christina said, ending the call. She glanced at J.T. "Lots of rumors, huh?"

"Makes me wonder who is starting them," J.T. said. "If Evan is working at Barclay's, he could be stirring the pot, using David's accident to his advantage."

"Or Evan might have been the one who ran David down." Now that she'd heard Evan's evil laugh and had a taste of his madness, it was easier to believe that he was capable of murder.

"I'm not discounting anything," J.T. said tersely. "I just want to get to the damn auction house before Evan takes off with the diamond." He slammed his hand down on the steering wheel as he hit another red light.

J.T. was all business now, grim, determined, and annoyed—with her as well as himself, she suspected. If he hadn't followed her to the fun house, he wouldn't have gotten caught in Evan's trap. She'd been so sure the meeting at the fun house had been another one of her father's dramatic, clandestine meetings that she'd been stupid enough to go into an abandoned building. Now she was in danger of being fired. She had to get to Barclay's before the diamond went up for bid so that she could . . . Well, what would she do? Did she let the diamond go up for auction? It seemed the easiest course at this point. And the fact that Evan had trapped them in the fun house implied that the diamond at Barclay's was the real thing. She felt marginally better at that thought. She still had big problems. If the diamond was real and Evan intended to steal it, how were they going to stop him? Evan had a huge head start and obviously a detailed plan in mind.

"Who do you think Evan is impersonating?" she asked J.T. "If you had to guess. If it's someone at the auction house, who would it be?"

"Evan told you that he's spoken to you at work. Does that ring any bells?"

"I talk to a lot of people at Barclay's every day—the security guards, the department specialists and their assistants, the auctioneer and his staff, the front-desk staff, the guys in shipping and receiving who unload the trucks, who package items to be shipped. . . ." Her voice trailed off as she became overwhelmed with possibilities. "It could be any one of those people."

J.T. hit the gas as the light turned green. "Something else worries me. Your father."

"What about my father?"

"If you see him at Barclay's, Christina, you have to tell me. You can't keep it to yourself, can't try to get him out of the way, or hustle him out the door without anyone knowing. Promise me. If he's working with

Evan, he's not going to be any use to Evan after he has the diamond. Don't think that letting your dad go is a good idea."

Christina hesitated. What he said made sense, but she had to protect her father, didn't she?

"Promise me," J.T. ordered, a ruthless note in his voice.

"Will you promise me you won't arrest him?" she countered.

"As long as he doesn't have the diamond in his possession, I have nothing against him."

He'd thrown her a bone, and she'd take it. "Okay, then I'll tell you if I see him. But I don't think he'll be there."

"I hope you're right." J.T. pulled the car into a parking spot a block away from Barclay's. "It will be faster to walk from here. Everything looks packed up ahead."

They got out of the car and ran, not walked, down the street. When they entered the building, they found the lobby area as well as the adjacent exhibit room packed with people. She grabbed J.T.'s hand and pulled him into the showroom, desperate to see what lot they were on. The electronic board told them there were three more lots to go before the diamond. "We're in time," she said thankfully.

J.T. glanced around the room, his sharp eye searching for anyone or anything out of the ordinary. She followed his gaze, almost afraid to look at the male faces, terrified she would see her father in the crowd. Unfortunately, it was difficult to identify anyone. There were too many people in the room. One thing was clear, however: No one appeared worried or stressed, at least not here on the main floor. There was an air of excitement and anticipation, but nothing else. She needed to get behind the scenes.

"Let's go around the back," she said.

As they left the showroom, Christina led J.T. down a long, narrow hallway and through a door marked PRIVATE. She had taken no more than three steps into the room when she came face-to-face with Alexis. The older woman's face was pinched and pale and downright furious when her gaze locked on Christina.

"Where have you been?" Alexis demanded. "I've left you a half dozen messages. I had to reassign all your duties. This is completely unacceptable, Christina."

"I know and I'm sorry. It's a long story, but I couldn't get to my phone. Is everything all right?"

"No, it's not all right. And why is your father calling me? You assured me when I hired you that your father was out of the country and would never in any way be connected to your work here."

"My father called you?" Christina asked in astonishment. "What did he say?"

"He left me a message on my voice mail, something cryptic about putting things back where they belong. So help me, Christina, if your father tries to mess with this auction, I will have both your heads."

Before Christina could reply, Sylvia Davis interrupted them. "Alexis, I need you. Christina, you finally showed up, huh? We really had to scramble without you."

Christina would have offered another apology but the two women were already moving away. She had intended to tell Alexis about Evan, but the news of a phone call from her father had completely thrown her offtrack. Why would her father call Alexis? And what had he meant? That he was planning to steal the diamond? Why would he warn her in advance?

"Christina." J.T.'s sharp voice brought her back to the present. "Focus."

"Why would my dad call Alexis?"

"Maybe he didn't. Maybe it was Evan, giving Alexis one more distraction."

"That makes more sense than my father trying to warn someone," she muttered, hoping J.T. was right. It still bothered her that Evan had been able to get her father's voice on tape and leave voice mails on her boss's phone. He really was clever. Was there any way they could stop him?

"Where's the diamond right now?" J.T. asked, his impatient gaze roaming the room.

She looked around and saw a huddle of important men in one corner. "I'm guessing it's right there."

As they approached, Russell Kenner stepped forward, giving them a tense nod.

"Everything still all right?" J.T. asked.

"So far," Russell replied.

Christina muttered hello to the three other men guarding the diamond, Luigi Murano, Stefano Benedetti, and Jeremy Kensington. Apparently no one was leaving anything to chance. She stepped forward to look at the diamond, which was protected in a glass case on the table. The yellow stone glittered in the light. For an odd moment she almost felt as if it were winking at her.

She straightened and looked around the rest of the

room, wondering if Evan was one of the employees standing just a few feet away, dealing with the items that had already been sold, finishing up paperwork, and preparing for packaging and delivery. She thought she knew everyone, but certainly not that well.

She stepped back from the group, studying the television monitor that was mounted from the ceiling in front of them on which she could see the action in the main showroom. They were getting closer to the diamond—just a few minutes to go. She glanced back at J.T. He'd made a pass through the room, pausing to talk to one of the workers nearby. She made her way over to him as he finished his conversation. "Do you see Evan?" she whispered.

"No. I don't like the fact that there are so many people back here. Too much opportunity for distraction."

"Perhaps all these people will make it impossible for Evan to steal the diamond," she said, feeling more confident by the minute. What could happen in this crowded room with so much security?

"I doubt it. He'll make an attempt; I'm sure of it."

She wished J.T. didn't sound so skeptical. "Well, it's almost over," she said, watching the electronic board on this side of the wall. It showed the next lot up—the Benedetti diamond.

"So what happens?" J.T. asked. "Someone puts the diamond on the revolving door and then it goes into the showroom?"

"Right."

"And the guards are all back here?"

"There are guards at the showroom door and also the front door," she said, wondering why he was still so tense. "It's impossible, J.T. There is no way Evan can grab that diamond and walk out of here with it." She paused. "You don't think he's going to pull out a gun and take the diamond by force, do you? I don't want anyone to get hurt."

"No. Too risky and too messy," J.T. said.

Christina looked up as the light flashed for the next lot. Russell opened the glass case and lifted out the necklace. "May I?" Stefano Benedetti asked as he stepped forward.

Russell nodded and handed Stefano the necklace. Christina held her breath as Stefano examined the diamond. He held it up to the light and then slowly gave a nod of approval. He stepped up to the revolving door, waiting patiently as someone removed the previous lot. An assistant placed a black velvet oval display form on the turntable. Stefano attached the necklace to the display. It looked stunning and magnificent. The crowd would go crazy when they saw it.

Christina glanced up at the television screen. The auctioneer called for the grand finale, the lady of the evening, the spectacular Benedetti diamond. Stefano hit the button to send the diamond into the showroom.

Christina looked back at the screen. She could hear the murmurs of the crowd over the audio, but it wasn't until the gasps of shock were followed by loud cries that she realized what they were seeing. The diamond was no longer on the display form. In its place was a candy necklace.

"What the hell?" J.T. swore.

Stefano and Russell rushed toward the revolving door, their hands coming down together on the button that would bring the turntable back into the workroom. Moments later the candy necklace was in Stefano's hand.

Russell barked into his radio transmitter to lock down the building, not to let anyone in or out until further notice. Christina was jostled as people rushed around the room in a mad, chaotic, and purposeless frenzy. She didn't know what to do. The diamond was gone. It had disappeared right in front of them. Who could have taken it? How had they done it?

As she looked around, she realized that Stefano, Russell, Luigi, and Jeremy had left the room. Even J.T. was gone. Where the hell did he go? Did he know something she didn't? Had he finally figured out who Evan was?

She headed out the door, down the long hallway, and back to the showroom. Pandemonium greeted her. Several buyers flagged her down, demanding to know what had happened to the diamond and why they couldn't leave. Some of them had just authorized purchases worth thousands of dollars. They were furious and insulted, and she couldn't blame them. But she also had absolutely no authority to let anyone out of the building. She placated them with useless promises that everything would be resolved shortly, when in fact she had no idea what was going to happen next.

She ran into Kelly at the bottom of the stairs.

"Did you see what happened?" Kelly asked, her eyes lit up with excitement.

"I was in the back room when the necklace was put on the turntable," Christina said. "I saw it go into the showroom with my own eyes. How could it disappear like that?"

"I have no idea. I was in the showroom. It seemed to take forever for the door to turn, slower than usual, I thought. In fact, I wondered if we were trying to build excitement by slowing down the speed of the turntable."

Had it been slower? Christina wondered. There was a small space between the two rooms where the revolving door turned, but she couldn't imagine it was big enough for a human being to stand in. She'd let the others figure that out. She had to concentrate on her end, which involved keeping her job and making sure her father wasn't on the premises. "Have you talked to Alexis?" she asked Kelly. "What are we supposed to do now?"

"I'm trying to find her. I think she and Sylvia went upstairs. I know Russell has the building in lockdown. No one is getting out of here with that diamond."

If they weren't already gone, Christina thought. She headed up the stairs, checking the gallery for her father or J.T., who wasn't anywhere to be seen either. She really hoped he had a lead on Evan.

Next, she ran up the stairs to the third floor. The hallway was fairly empty, so she was more than a little surprised to hear voices coming from her office. She paused outside the door, wondering who was inside.

"It's clear that Christina's involved," Alexis said. "Look at this."

Christina's heart came to a thudding stop. Involved? What was going on?

"I thought her father was out of the picture," Jeremy replied.

"Obviously not," Alexis said. "She must have been

working with him to steal the diamond. He called me earlier, left a message on my voice mail that he was going to put it back where it belonged. You know how he thinks he's some Robin Hood, rescuing artifacts from their greedy owners. That has to be what this is about."

"We need to isolate Christina until we know exactly how she's involved," a third man interrupted. "She was in the workroom when the diamond disappeared."

It was Russell, Christina realized. And they were talking about her as if she'd had something to do with taking the diamond. Why would they think that? She'd been standing in full view of Russell and Jeremy. In fact, she'd been the one farthest away from the diamond. So where was the suspicion coming from? Was it just the supposed phone call from her father? What were they doing in her office? What else were they looking at? Had her father left something in her office, a note, a message?

Realizing they could walk out at any second, she ran down the hall as quickly and as quietly as she could. It suddenly hit her that she was in very big trouble, and if she wasn't careful, she was going to be railroaded straight to prison. She had to stay free long enough to find her father and the diamond.

J.T. looked at every single face he passed as he strode through the auction house, the old, the young, the men, and even the women. Evan was here. He had somehow, in some sleight of hand, managed to steal that necklace. J.T. still didn't know how he'd done it. Maybe there was a way to get in between the panels, so that when the turntable rotated, a switch could be made. He returned to the showroom and went over to study the door. He pushed the button and it slowly revolved. As the door moved, he checked the space in between. It seemed impossibly narrow for anyone to get in there.

How could the diamond have disappeared in the minute it took for the panel to turn?

Had someone been standing near the panel inside the showroom? A man, he recalled, wearing the same navy blue suit coat as the auctioneer. Had it been Evan? But wouldn't someone have seen him grab the necklace and run?

Racking his brain, J.T. tried to remember what he had seen on the monitor. He'd been watching the screen, as had Christina, waiting to see if anyone in the showroom would rush the diamond or if the auctioneer would make a sudden move, if someone would ask to examine the diamond up close. He'd anticipated any number of possible scenarios, but not this one.

Glancing around the room, he tried to place everyone in the spot in which they had been standing when the diamond had gone onto the display. Russell, Luigi, Jeremy, and Stefano had been together by the table, which was now empty. The diamond had been in a glass case. Two other employees, a man and a woman, had been packing up some art on the adjacent table. Christina and he had moved away after she'd checked the diamond. They'd been standing in front of the monitor, which was now off. He knew he was missing something important, but whatever it was, it was just out of reach.

He went over the four men again in his mind. Russell, Luigi, Jeremy, Stefano. A Barclay's employee had set the necklace display form on the turntable. Stefano had placed the necklace on the display form. Why him? Sure, it was his necklace technically, but why hadn't the Barclay's employee done the deed? Had it just been professional courtesy? Jeremy Kensington had been standing right there, overseeing the moment.

J.T. wasn't sure what he thought of Jeremy Kensington. The hit-and-run accident the night before, the tie-in between Alexis and David, the fact that Jeremy's wife might have been cheating on him—what did it add up to? Was Jeremy involved in some insurance scam? Was there a policy on the diamond? Was that why he'd taken it upon himself to be right there when the diamond was placed on display?

J.T. would have to ask Christina if it was common for Jeremy to be backstage. It seemed more likely that he would have been out in the showroom, overseeing the bidding.

And what about Alexis? Where was she when the diamond went missing? They'd run into her and Sylvia as they'd entered the room, but he wondered where the two women had gone after they'd left.

"J.T." Christina burst into the back room, her voice breathless, her eyes panicked. "You have to get me out of here. You're the FBI. They'll let me walk out with you. Please, we have to hurry."

She grabbed his arm, but he stopped her. "Whoa, what's going on, Christina? What's wrong?"

"I can't explain. There's no time. Someone is setting me up to take the fall for the theft. Everyone is upstairs in my office—Russell, Alexis, Jeremy, God knows who else. They'll be down here in a minute. You have to get me out of here."

For a split second J.T. wondered if she was playing him. Was this the final move in the game? Was she working with Evan? Or with her father? He hated to think so.

"You have to trust me," she said, obviously seeing the doubt in his eyes. Her agitated fingers twisted the sleeve of his coat. "I haven't done anything wrong. But someone wants to blame me for everything. I can't let that happen. Please, J.T. Help me."

She was asking him to cross a very big line. If he was wrong about her, all hell could break loose. He could ruin his career, the rest of his life. If she was telling the truth, he needed to help her. He wanted to help her. And deep down, he knew no matter how much he argued with himself, there was no way he could resist the terrified plea in her beautiful green eyes. "All right. But if you're messing with me, Christina, you will be very sorry."

"The employees' entrance is the closest," she said, taking his hand.

"Fine, but don't look so nervous. Take a breath. Calm down. Otherwise you're going to raise suspicion."

She paused a moment to draw in several deep breaths. "Okay, I'm ready. Let's go."

When they reached the employee entrance, two security guards barred their exit. Christina greeted one of them by name. "Hi, Sam. This is J. T. McIntyre. He's with the FBI. We have to go down to his office."

Sam nodded. "Sorry. Mr. Kenner said no one goes out."

"You can search us," J.T. said, "but Ms. Alberti and I have to continue with the investigation off the premises. You can call Mr. Kenner, check it out."

Sam hesitated, casting a quick look at his partner, who simply shrugged. "Okay, but we'll have to search your purse, Ms. Alberti."

Christina let Sam rifle through her purse while J.T. turned his pockets inside out for the other guard. A few minutes later they were cleared to leave. J.T. kept a hand on Christina's arm as they walked quickly back to his car. He could feel her tension as if it were his own. She looked over her shoulder every other second, as if she expected someone to come running after them. Fortunately, their parking space down the block allowed them to leave without raising any flags. They were two miles away before she let out a sigh.

"God," she murmured, "I can't believe this is happening. How did that diamond disappear right in front of us?"

"I've been trying to figure that out."

She ran a hand through her hair. "I keep seeing that turntable come around and the candy necklace on the display."

"That touch was pure Evan," he said.

"But how did he do it?"

"That's what we have to find out. First, tell me where we're going."

"Do you remember how to get to my father's house?"

"I think so. Why? Is he there? Have you heard from him?"

"I haven't heard a word, but I can't think of where

else to go. I have to find him so I can clear his name and mine. Maybe he left some clue as to where he is."

J.T. turned left at the next corner. "Let's hope so. Now start talking. Tell me what happened back at Barclay's."

"I went upstairs to my office. I heard Alexis, Jeremy, and Russell talking about how I must be working with my father, and something was obvious proof of that. Russell said I needed to be found and questioned as soon as possible." She shook her head in confusion. "I don't know what they discovered in my office, but it must have been incriminating in some way. They think I did this. They think I stole the diamond or that I helped my father steal it."

"He makes a good scapegoat. So do you," J.T. said, computing the facts. "Evan set you both up."

Christina crossed, then uncrossed her legs, fidgeting restlessly in her seat. "What I don't understand is how anyone could get out of the auction house with that diamond. The doors were locked immediately. We were searched before we left. Everyone will be searched. How could Evan get out with the diamond in his hand or his pocket, or in anything for that matter?"

He'd been wondering about that as well. If Evan was responsible for stealing the diamond, then he had an escape route. "There was a moment of indecision," he said, "before Russell called for the lockdown."

Christina sent him a doubtful look. "You think there was enough time?"

"Unlikely but not impossible." J.T. turned left as they neared her father's street. "We'd better make this quick. If Russell calls the dogs on you and your father, this will be the first place they check."

"It will just take a few minutes. We won't stay long."

"I don't suppose you brought a key this time," he said as he parked the car in her father's driveway.

"Actually, I did. I put it on my key ring yesterday just in case I had to come back here."

As they entered the house Christina called for her father several times, but no one answered. She headed straight for the study and the safe hidden behind a painting. In a few seconds she had it open. "I checked this the other night and nothing was here, but maybe he came back in between then and now." She stuck her hand into the safe and pulled out an envelope with her name on it. "This wasn't here before."

"Read it aloud," J.T. commanded.

She removed the slip of paper and read, " 'Christina—I know you're angry with me now. But I had to take the diamond. It is cursed and needs to be returned to its rightful owner. It is more important than you can imagine. I will be in touch when I have made things right, when I have put the diamond back where it belongs. Don't hate me. Love, Dad.' "

She let out a breath, biting down on her lip as she lifted her gaze to meet his. He saw pain and disappointment in her eyes. Her father had let her down bigtime.

"You were right," she said. "My father did steal the diamond. I can't believe it's true, but it's right here in black and white."

"Is it? Are you sure that note is legit? Could Evan have written this, too?"

"I don't know." A frown marred her features as she

stared back down at the paper. "I was fooled before, but this note sounds just like my dad, the way he thinks, the way he talks. It's pretty much what he said to me yesterday when I saw him at the zoo."

J.T. could see that she believed the note, which made him believe it, too. "Is there anything else in the safe?"

She looked back inside. "Oh, my God, there is." She pulled out a gray wig, letting it dangle from her fingers, as if she couldn't quite believe what it was. "What is this?"

J.T. moved next to her. He reached into the safe and pulled out a fake nose, a pair of thick glasses, and an ID for Howard Keaton, Ph.D. He let out a low whistle. "Look at this." He held up the ID so Christina could read it. "I guess we know how your father got into the auction house."

Christina's jaw dropped, surprise spreading across her face. "Professor Keaton? My father was masquerading as Professor Keaton? How can that be? I talked to him. I looked him in the face. I stood a foot away from him at the preview party. I would have recognized my own father—" She stopped abruptly.

"What did you just remember?"

"Well, now that I think about it, my father did fool me once before. He came to see me right after he left the museum and before I resigned. There was about a week in between when I was trying to fix things. He came into my office dressed as a janitor. I was talking to him for five minutes before he let me know it was him. And then there was that other time—"

"Dammit, Christina, you should have told me this

before," J.T. said, cutting her off. "The fact that your father likes disguises would have been helpful to know."

"I didn't think it was important, because I didn't want to believe he would steal the diamond from me. But I was wrong. It didn't matter that this theft would hurt me. It didn't matter to him at all." She threw the wig back into the safe along with the rest of the items and slammed it shut.

"Something is off," he muttered, as she pushed the painting back into place.

"Like what?"

"Too many thieves and not enough diamonds," he said. "Professor Keaton hasn't been at the auction house since Wednesday night, since the smoke bombs went off. He wasn't there today, not as Professor Keaton anyway." J.T.'s mind raced back to Wednesday night, the images from the party flashing through his head. Christina was talking to the professor. He reached up to touch the necklace. It slipped off her neck, landing in his hand. He handed it back to her. The smoke alarms went off. Someone shouted, "Fire!" Everyone went running.

"J.T., what are you thinking?" she asked impatiently.

He blinked, her voice bringing him back to the present. "If your father was impersonating Professor Keaton, and the last time Keaton was at the auction house was Wednesday night when the smoke bombs went off, then he took the diamond that night."

Christina's eyes lit up. "The clasp opened, and he caught the diamond. But he gave it back to me."

"Only he didn't give you the real stone. He gave you

a fake, an exact copy. So when you looked at the diamond under your scope and didn't see that flaw you were looking for—"

"It was because the diamond was a fake," she finished. "I think you're right, J.T. My father took the real diamond on Wednesday. He probably had it on him when I saw him at the zoo the next day." She drew in a quick breath. "But if that's true, then who stole the necklace today?"

"Evan."

She met his gaze head-on. "Do you think he has any idea the diamond he stole is a fake?"

"He might not know yet, but he's going to be royally pissed off when he finds out."

11

Success was sweet, Evan thought, relishing the pleasure of the moment. He loved stealing in the middle of a crowd, doing what no one else could do. There had been people standing not three feet away from him when he'd taken the diamond. In the chaos that followed no one had regarded him with suspicion, or accused him of being a thief. No, he'd made sure the clues led down a different path—to Christina and her father, Marcus Alberti. He'd put his plans into motion weeks ago, ensuring that every detail had been covered, and today it had paid off.

As Evan made his way up the elevator to the woman's thirty-fifth-floor penthouse apartment, he thought of what was to come. She believed he would hand over the diamond in return for the cash she had promised him. It had been their deal from the beginning. At the time he hadn't wanted the stone. He'd had no use for a gem that would be difficult to fence, but cash was always good—not to mention the thrill of the steal, the knowledge that he had done what no one thought could be done. It had been fun—while it lasted.

Now he had another plan in mind, another woman whom he wanted to please far more than the one waiting for him.

She answered the door, her face lit up with expectation. Twin fires blazed in her eyes, and her hand shook as she grabbed his arm and pulled him into the apartment.

"Where is it?" she demanded. "You're late. You should have been here thirty minutes ago."

"Always so impatient," he drawled. He dipped his hand into his pocket and pulled out the necklace. When she moved to take it, he held it away from her greedy hand. "Not so fast. Where's my money?"

"In the living room."

He followed her into the next room. The curtains were drawn. He had no doubt that her maid had been dismissed for the day. They were alone.

"I want to see the diamond," she said. "Give it to me."

He saw a silver case on the coffee table. He walked over and flipped open the locks. Stacks of bills greeted his eyes. "Very nice."

He handed her the diamond. She sat down on the edge of the sofa and picked up a jeweler's loupe. She looked through the magnifying glass with a skilled eye. He frowned. "What are you doing?"

"What the hell do you think I'm doing?"

"How do you know how to examine a diamond?"

"My aunt works in a jewelry store, remember?" She twisted the stone in every direction, holding it up to the light. "It's not here," she said, her voice becoming shrill. She turned on him, the fire in her eyes turning to madness. "It's not here. Where is it?"

"What are you talking about?"

"You're supposed to be able to see a heart in the stone—the heart of the Médici." She looked at the stone again and began shaking her head. "It's not here. This isn't it. This isn't the real diamond. What did you do with it?" She jumped to her feet, waving the stone in her hand. "This is a copy."

She was out of her fucking mind. "No way. I stole the stone ten seconds before they were going to auction it off."

"You switched it then."

"I didn't." His mind raced to keep up with her accusations.

"Someone did. Dammit, Evan. You screwed up. You brought me a fake, you stupid bastard."

Her insults burned into his brain. And suddenly he wasn't hearing her voice anymore, but his mother's, telling him he was a worthless piece of shit and that she wished he were dead. "Stop it!" he yelled.

She wasn't listening. She never listened. She kept talking and talking. She lifted her hand and struck him across the face.

Her slap unleashed a roar of fury. She couldn't talk to him like that. She needed to shut up. She lifted her hand again. He grabbed her arms. He shook her but she wouldn't stop talking, telling him he had failed. He couldn't listen anymore. He put his hands on her throat. She gasped for air, and the sound drove him over the edge. "Stop talking!" he yelled, squeezing tighter and tighter. Her eyes bulged out of her head as she finally realized what was happening, her breath coming in choking gasps—until she was quiet, until her eyes closed and her body slipped out of his hands, falling to the ground with a dull thud.

He stared at her for a long moment. Then he took the diamond from her hand. His heart began to slow down as reality set in.

There would have to be another change in plan. It would look like a robbery had gone bad. She had come home in the middle of the day. She had been alone. Someone had broken in.

Carefully and deliberately he did what needed to be done. Then he picked up the case of money and took one last look around, making sure that he hadn't left behind a print or any other evidence of his presence in her apartment.

After leaving her apartment building, he got into his car and put his hands on the steering wheel. He looked at his fingers for a long moment, seeing them not on the wheel, but on her neck.

She had driven him to it. He'd had no choice. She wouldn't stop talking. She'd deserved what she'd gotten.

Now he had to finish the rest. No one got the better of him. His brain whirred like a computer assessing the facts. Someone had taken the diamond before him. They'd made a switch. He could think of only two people who could have done such a thing: Christina Alberti or her father, Marcus. The knowledge burned through his gut. He would not let them win. The game wasn't over yet.

He would find the diamond and get it back. He

couldn't give his Jenny a fake. She deserved the real thing.

She would have it, and he would have her.

"Soon," he whispered. "Very soon."

Christina paced back and forth in front of the window of J.T.'s hotel room. He'd never seen her so on edge, not even when Evan had trapped them in the fun house. Her father's apparent betrayal had cut her deeply. He knew there was nothing he could say to ease the pain, so he didn't even try. She would have to work out her feelings about her father herself. In the meantime, they had bigger problems to deal with.

"Why don't you sit down? Catch your breath," he suggested.

"How can I do that? The police could come knocking on the door at any second. Everyone knows we left Barclay's together. After my father's house and my apartment, I'd say this is the next place they'll look."

"That's why we're not staying long. I just want to pick up a few things. Then I'll drop you off somewhere safe while I go back to Barclay's."

"You can't go back there," she said with alarm. "They'll ask you where I am."

"Exactly, and I need to give them an answer. I'm going to tell them that you took off, ran away when I had my back turned. After all, I didn't know you were under suspicion at the time we left, so I wasn't watching you. I'll tell them I don't know where you are now. Otherwise, I won't be able to get any information. And we need to know just what Evan planted on you."

She stared at him in amazement. "You're going to

lie for me? Why would you do that? You could get in so much trouble."

He was already in trouble, and it had as much to do with the way he was feeling about her as any rules he was about to break or had already broken. But he didn't want to discuss that now, so he simply shrugged and began to throw his clothes into an overnight bag. "Let me worry about that. Where can I take you that you'll be safe? Do you have any friends nearby?"

She thought for a moment, a frown marring her features. "Nobody I want to pull into the middle of this. I know," she said abruptly. "I'll go to the library. It's perfect, and quiet, particularly in the historical stacks. No one will think to look for me there, and I can do some research on that diamond. My father's note said he was going to put it back where it belonged. I have to figure out where that is."

"How difficult will that be?"

"I have no idea, but at least I'll be doing something productive, taking some action. I hate feeling so helpless, so out of control, at everyone else's mercy. It's the way I felt the last time, and I swore I'd never feel this way again. I really hate my father for doing this to me."

"But you love him, too. That's the worst part, isn't it?" He saw her eyes blur with tears and fought back an impulse to reach for her. If he touched her again, he might not let her go.

"Yeah, that's the worst part." She turned her back on him, gazing out the window at the city below.

He opened drawers, grabbing his clothes and throwing them into his overnight bag along with his laptop computer. In only a few minutes he was ready to go. Opening the door, he took a quick look down the hall before motioning for Christina to follow. They made it down to the underground garage without incident. So far, so good.

A few minutes later he let Christina off in front of the San Francisco Main Library. He watched her enter the building and waited to make sure no one followed her inside. Hopefully this time he was one step ahead of Evan. Maybe Evan hadn't yet discovered the diamond was a fake. In fact, he might never figure it out. He was a con artist, not a jewelry expert. But at some point, Evan would try to fence the diamond somewhere; that was when all hell would break loose.

Media trucks were parked in front of Barclay's when J.T. arrived. Field reporters were setting up for their evening newscasts. It had been two hours since he'd hustled Christina out of the building, and now the auction house was noticeably empty. A lone receptionist sat at the front desk in the lobby, sipping a cup of coffee. He'd met her before. Her name was Elizabeth. She gave him a nod and a weary smile.

"It's been quite a day," she said. "Any news on our thief?"

He shook his head. "Not on my end. Are the local police still here?"

She shook her head. "I think everyone left a while ago, except the press. They keep knocking on the door, but no one wants to talk. Apparently the Kensingtons are going to host a press conference at five o'clock. I can't imagine what they'll say. Can you?"

He saw the inquisitive look in her eyes and shook his head. She probably knew more about the Kensingtons' plans than he did. "Sorry. By the way, were you here at the desk when the word came to lock the doors?"

Elizabeth gave a vigorous nod. "I was. I couldn't believe it. We've never had that much excitement at an auction before."

"Did you happen to notice anyone leaving right before the doors were locked?"

"I didn't notice. I already told the police that. There were a lot of people in the lobby at the time. It was standing room only in the showroom, and some people were watching the auction on the monitor," she said, nodding toward the television monitor suspended from the ceiling in the far corner of the room.

"Thanks anyway. Where's Mr. Kenner?"

"In the third-floor conference room with the Kensingtons. They said they didn't want to be disturbed, but I'm sure they didn't mean you."

J.T. doubted he was high on their list, but he simply smiled and headed up the stairs.

As he approached the conference room, he saw a shell-shocked Alexis at one end of the table. Sylvia Davis sat next to her, jotting down notes on a pad of paper. Jeremy Kensington was seated at the opposite end. His face was as cold as ice and completely expressionless, but J.T. suspected that Jeremy was feeling the heat. In addition to the diamond theft, he had other problems, including David Padlinsky's death and Alexis's relationship with David. A lot had happened in the past fifteen or so hours since the Kensingtons had raised their champagne glasses to toast the success of the auction. This was supposed to be their biggest day. It was big, all right, but not the way they'd hoped.

The conversation ceased when J.T. entered the room, all eyes turning to him with one emotion—anger.

"Where the fuck have you been? And where is Christina?" Kenner demanded.

"I've been trying to find her," J.T. lied. "I didn't realize there was a problem with Christina or her father until I got your messages on my cell phone. By then we had already parted company. Rather than come back here, I decided to check her apartment and also her father's house."

"Why did you help her leave in the first place?" Alexis asked. "You heard me tell Christina that I received a phone message from her father on my voice mail. Didn't you wonder why she needed to leave the building so quickly after the theft?"

"No, I didn't, because I was standing right next to her when the diamond disappeared. We were both in complete view of everyone else in that room. Christina did not steal that diamond. And I personally watched while she was searched by the security guard before leaving the building."

"Where did you go?" Russell asked. "Why didn't you stick around to help us figure out what happened?"

"I thought I saw the man I was looking for—Evan Chadwick," he replied. "I believed he might have slipped out before we did."

"That's impossible. We locked down almost immediately."

"*Almost* being the key word. In those few moments

of chaos, the real thief could have gotten out of the building."

"No, I don't think so." Russell gave a definitive shake of his head. "The guards were on those doors right away."

"Well, if you didn't find the diamond, and everyone is gone but the four of you and the receptionist in the lobby, then someone got away with it."

"There are other people still in the building," Sylvia interjected, nervousness in her voice now.

"I hope you won't let anyone leave without searching them and their belongings." J.T. knew he was putting Russell's back up, but he could use distraction as well as Evan could.

"I know what to do," Russell snapped. "And I'm not worried about who's still here. I'm concerned with who isn't here—Christina Alberti. Where did she go after you left the building?"

"We checked the parking lot together. I thought she might be able to tell me if she recognized Evan as anyone who had been working here at Barclay's the past month or so. Unfortunately, we weren't able to find the man I saw."

"Really? How surprising," Kenner said sarcastically. "So you lose your lead and you disappear with our key suspect. Maybe you're working with her, McIntyre."

J.T. didn't waver under Kenner's accusatory stare. "Don't look at me as a way to cover your ass. You're the head of security, as you told me many times. It was your job to protect the diamond, not mine. I was just trying to help."

"Or to hinder."

J.T. shrugged. He didn't much care what Kenner thought about him. "Do you have anything else on Christina's father besides some anonymous phone message?"

"E-mails on her computer," Alexis interjected. "And David told me that—" She stopped abruptly, darting a quick look at her husband.

"Why don't you just shut up, Alexis?" Jeremy said, anger and weariness in his voice, in his posture, in the way he shoved back the chair and strode from the room without giving the rest of them another look.

"David told you what?" J.T. prodded as Alexis stared after her husband as if she were afraid he was never coming back.

Sylvia patted Alexis's hand. "If this is too much for you . . ."

"No." Alexis drew in a deep breath and then continued. "David told me that he thought Christina was acting oddly when she examined the diamond. He also said he took a call from her father one day and wondered if Marcus Alberti had his eyes on the diamond."

J.T. was surprised by her latest revelation. "David had a conversation with Christina's father?"

"Yes, and Mr. Alberti asked a lot of questions about the diamond." Her gaze filled with worry. "Do you think the car accident had something to do with what David knew? Oh, my God!" She clapped a hand over her mouth. "Do you think Christina is the one who ran him down?"

"She certainly didn't like him much," Sylvia interjected. "They were arguing at your dinner party last night, Alexis. You heard them, Mr. McIntyre."

"I wouldn't say they were arguing," he denied, not liking the way the noose was being pulled even tighter around Christina's neck. "As a matter of fact I saw the accident last night. I was just arriving when David was hit. It wasn't Christina driving the car."

"You said you didn't see the car or the driver," Russell reminded him.

"I didn't. But I took Christina home. There was no time for her to get her car and beat me back here." God help him for all the lies he was telling. "I know David called you right before the accident." He turned back to Alexis. "I found his phone. Yours was the last number he'd dialed."

"I just told you why he was calling. It was about Christina."

J.T. studied Alexis's face. She averted her gaze, as if she was afraid of what he would see. He didn't completely buy her story. There was something else going on. Her husband hadn't stormed off without good reason. "It seems odd to me that David was at your party last night. He was just a part-time assistant, a grad student, hardly in the league of your other guests."

"David was very helpful yesterday in previewing the diamond while Christina was gone. Another strange disappearance, I might add," Alexis said on a huffy note. "I thought David might be able to answer questions from the guests. And I am not the one on trial here. We need to find Christina. She has a lot of explaining to do."

"The police are checking her house and her father's house," Kenner said. He shot J.T. a speculative look. "I hope we can count on your help."

"Of course you can. But first I'd like to take a look at the security tapes from the workroom. Unlike you, I'm keeping an open mind about the identity of our diamond thief. I told you from the beginning that the man I've been following intended to steal it. I know he has been in the area. He's left me notes to that effect. Now the diamond is gone. I'm not discounting the fact that he's the one who took it and planted evidence on Christina's computer to discredit her and her father."

"You keep talking about this mysterious man," Alexis said with a frown, "but none of us knows who you're talking about."

"Because he's pretending to be someone you know, someone you trust."

"I know everyone in my company," Alexis said. "It's not possible that he's an employee."

"Maybe not. I'd still like to see the tape."

"We were just watching it," Kenner said. He hit the remote control and the monitor in the corner of the room lit up.

They studied the tape for several moments in complete silence. The scene played out exactly as J.T. remembered. The four men surrounded the diamond, Russell, Luigi, Jeremy, and Stefano. Then Stefano took the necklace and placed it on the display. He set the display on the turntable and reached to push the button that would send the turntable into the other room.

His body blocked the camera, J.T. realized. All they could see was Stefano's broad back. "Where is he?" he asked abruptly. "Where's Benedetti?"

Russell blinked. "Uh. I don't know. I haven't seen him in a while."

"I'm surprised he's not here raising holy hell," J.T. said. "In fact, where's Murano? Where's our Italian security contingent?"

"Mr. Murano was on the phone in the security office earlier," Alexis said. "Why? What are you thinking?"

"Benedetti's body blocks the camera," J.T. said again.

"So what?" Kenner asked with a frustrated wave of his hand. "Mr. Benedetti is the owner of the diamond. He wouldn't try to steal it."

J.T. felt a rush of excitement as the puzzle pieces began to click into place. "Maybe he would. There must be insurance on the diamond."

"Yes, but . . ." Alexis stopped, her jaw dropping, mixed emotions running through her eyes. "No, that is a crazy idea. Mr. Benedetti would not set us up like that. His family is very well respected in Italy. They have a reputation to maintain. They would make far more money selling the diamond than collecting the insurance."

"Not if they got the insurance money and kept the diamond," J.T. pointed out.

"They would never be able to sell it again. It would always be on the list of stolen jewels," Alexis argued. "If it was discovered in their possession, they would be in very big trouble. You're on the wrong track."

"I don't think so. Benedetti was the last one to have his hand on that diamond."

"And he's a far more respectable man than Marcus Alberti." Alexis stood up. "I need to take care of some things before the press conference. Russell, call me when you find Christina. She and her father are the

ones who stole that diamond. I'm sure of it." She gave
J.T. a pointed look, then swept from the room, Sylvia
on her heels.

J.T. glanced at Russell Kenner. "Where is Benedetti
staying?"

"The Crestmoor Hotel." He scratched his jaw. "I
have to admit I never considered that angle."

"Maybe you should. What about Murano?"

"Best Western, two blocks down."

"Thanks. We need to eliminate them from the list of
suspects."

"All right. I can do that, but frankly I think you're
just trying to turn the attention on someone else. Hell,
maybe you're in on the theft with Christina. She seems
to have you wrapped around her little finger, or maybe
it's some other part of her body. I'm warning you,
McIntyre, if you helped Christina escape with that diamond, I'll make sure you lose your job."

Kenner's threat hung in the air long after he left the
room. J.T. picked up the remote control and rewound
the tape so he could play it again.

As the turntable moved, Benedetti stepped back
with a satisfied smile. There was something about that
smile that unsettled him. The answer hit him like a
freight train.

Was it possible that Evan was Stefano?

J.T.'s heart leaped into his throat. It couldn't be.
He'd spoken to Stefano Benedetti several times. He
would have known if it was Evan in disguise, wouldn't
he? Stefano's image flashed in his head, the long, curly
dark hair, the olive skin, the deep brown eyes, the Italian accent. Jenny had said that Evan wore a ski cap on

his head when he came to see her, so he'd obviously wanted to cover his hair. He could have accomplished the rest with makeup, contact lenses, even faked the accent.

Still, if Benedetti were Evan, wouldn't the head of the Italian security team, Luigi Murano, have known he was an impostor? Wouldn't they have spoken in Italian? It didn't make sense.

But J.T.'s instincts were screaming at him to pay attention. Stefano Benedetti was the last person to touch the diamond. His back blocked the cameras. He could have taken the necklace before he stepped back with that smile on his face. The turntable was no longer in view. And everyone was watching the monitors to see the reaction of the crowd when they first saw the diamond.

When the necklace vanished, Kenner had called for a lockdown. Everyone had gone running in a dozen different directions. Where had Stefano gone?

J.T. let the tape run, but the camera had not captured Stefano's exit from the workroom. The real question was whether Stefano could have left Barclay's without being searched. He was the owner of the diamond—the victim, not the perpetrator. Or at least, that was what everyone thought.

It was a great plan. Evan had once again played a perfect game.

Make that almost perfect.

Because Christina's father had stolen the necklace two nights earlier, and Evan had stolen a fake. How ironic was that? The con man had been outconned by the man he'd set up to take the fall. J.T. had to smile.

The bottom line, though, was that the diamond was

missing and the heat was on Christina. No one at Barclay's wanted to believe in a con man they'd never met. It was far easier to blame Marcus Alberti.

J.T. turned off the monitor, feeling a renewed sense of energy and purpose. He needed to track down Benedetti and Murano. Either Murano was in on it or Evan had conned him, too. And if Evan was playing a part, where the hell was the real Stefano Benedetti?

12

Christina felt her tension dissipate the longer she sat in the library. She loved the rustling quiet in the old building, the sound of pages turning, patrons speaking in hushed voices, the occasional clatter of high heels on the uncarpeted floors. She liked the smell of the books, some fresh off the press, others dusty from years on the shelves. She loved the idea that in every volume in the library there was the potential for a grand adventure, a fantasy escape, or a chance to learn something new. Her father had first introduced her to the library. Before the age of computers he'd done most of his research in big, cavernous buildings such as this one, in every city in the world. And she'd often sat by his side, reading her own books while he lost himself in stories of the past.

Sadness swept over her as she thought about how much trouble they were both in. Would they ever recapture those carefree days when they had been father and daughter without any secrets, without any lies? Would they ever be able to be together without wearing a disguise, meeting in a secret location, worried that someone would see them, call the cops, have them arrested?

It seemed crazy that their lives had turned out like this, especially *her* life. She wasn't an adventurer like her father. In fact, she'd played it really safe for as long as she could remember. While her father's talk of adventure and drama had always appealed to her imagination, she'd felt she couldn't let loose, because one of them had to be practical, responsible, and that one had always been her. It wasn't fair. In fact, at the moment it was downright infuriating. She couldn't allow herself to forget that while she was innocent of any wrongdoing, her father was not. He had stolen that diamond. He had committed a huge crime. And no matter what his reasoning, he was wrong. But even worse than the theft was that he had lied to her. He'd put on a disguise, walked right up to her, and introduced himself as Howard Keaton, pretending to be someone he wasn't. He'd smiled and joked, knowing all the time he was putting one over on her, and he'd enjoyed every second of it. She still couldn't believe she hadn't seen through the disguise.

Maybe J.T was right. Maybe people saw only what they expected to see. She'd certainly never expected to see her father at that party. By coming to Barclay's, he'd put her job and her life in jeopardy—and for what? A diamond, a cold, hard, beautiful stone—but a stone nonetheless. She loved jewelry. She'd spent years studying it, training to be an expert. But she never would have put a diamond before her father. He was her family. They had only each other—how had he come to forget that? How had he come to value a diamond more than her?

Well, damn him. Damn him for caring more about a stone than his daughter. For loving the past more than the present, for trying to put things right from hundreds of years ago, never mind trying to right the wrongs that were happening today.

Why was she always working so hard to protect *him*, when it was becoming clearer with each passing day that he had no intention of protecting *her*?

Oh, sure, he said he'd taken the diamond to do just that—save her from some terrible curse—a curse that no one else had ever heard of, including the owner of the diamond. Was her father lying about the curse, too? Or did he believe his own fantasy? She'd worried for years that he might one day slip over the line between reality and fantasy. Was that time now? Had he completely lost his mind? It would almost be easier if he had gone crazy. Then at least there would be a clinical diagnosis for his behavior.

With a sigh, Christina sat back in her chair. She'd settled into a cubicle on the second floor and surrounded herself with books on the Italian Renaissance, and diamonds in particular. If the Benedetti diamond was cursed, then someone besides her father had to know about it. Someone had to have written about it. She just hadn't found that someone yet.

She rubbed her tired eyes. She was working on adrenaline, fear, and very little sleep. So much had happened in the past few days her head was spinning. If she could just get the world to slow down for a minute, she might be able to think. But no one was waiting for her to catch up; they were running full steam ahead with their plans, plans in which she seemed to play enough of a part to be guilty but not enough of a part to have any say in the matter.

Picking up the next book, she saw that it was about the de Médici family. A merchant and banking family, the de Médicis had practically run Florence for almost three centuries. Their power had extended to the Church and the most powerful European courts.

As Christina thought about the de Médicis, she considered the fact that the Benedettis were another powerful Florentine family in the banking industry. She wondered if their bloodline ran back to the de Médicis. It certainly wasn't impossible, and it was even more probable that a yellow diamond the size of the Benedetti stone had once belonged to someone rich and powerful like the de Médicis.

Skimming through the next chapter, she read the description of Catherine de Médici's wedding to Henry, who would later become the king of France, making Catherine his queen. The union had been set up by the pope, the marriage merging two powerful families. An enormous dowry had gone with Catherine to France. Many jewels, including diamonds, had exchanged hands on her wedding day. Several sources noted three particularly interesting pieces, the Egg of Naples, a large pear-shaped pearl encircled by rubies; the Tip of Milan, a hexagonal diamond; and the Table of Genoa, a large, flat-cut diamond. Some believed that the names of the stones represented a secret code between the pope and the king and referred to cities in Italy that the couple would receive. But in later inventories, the jewels were no longer mentioned, and there was some mystery as to what had happened to them.

Christina considered those missing jewels. None matched her yellow diamond, but it certainly gave her pause to consider the possibility that the Benedetti diamond could have been part of the magnificent wedding dowry as well.

Picking up the book again, she read through several more paragraphs. She had studied Catherine de Médici in school and was already familiar with her somewhat sad story, the fact that the French court considered her an Italian upstart with no real breeding and treated her with little respect. Her husband, Henry, had blatantly and flagrantly continued his relationship with his mistress, Diane de Poitiers, throughout the course of his marriage to Catherine. In fact, as proof of his devotion to Diane, Henry often presented her with jewels that should have gone to Catherine. Was it any wonder that the lonely and scorned Catherine had later become known as "Madame Snake," with secret hideaways for poison rings and daggers?

If the diamond had belonged to Catherine, it could very well be cursed, Christina thought. But how on earth was she going to find out? She needed more detailed information on the exact jewels that had been part of Catherine's dowry, as well as any precious stones that Henry had given to Diane throughout the years. Of course, she could be completely on the wrong track, but it made sense to her to start with the most famous Florentine family of all. Unfortunately, as much as she longed to dive into research for the next few days or weeks, she didn't have the time. There had to be a shortcut.

Perhaps if she spoke to Stefano Benedetti again, he

would tell her more about the diamond. Even as the thought came to her mind, she immediately dismissed it. Stefano would probably have her arrested before she got one question out of her mouth. Like the others, he believed she had stolen his family's diamond.

How else could she find the information? Was there something in the books her father kept at his house? He had a library full of old texts, and he had spent many summers in Florence. She might have to go back to his house again . . . maybe after she was sure the police had already checked it out.

Getting up, she made her way back down to the first floor of the library and over to the bank of computers that would take her onto the Internet. She put several words into the search engine, *Medici*, *Catherine*, *jewels*, *diamonds*, and *wedding dowry*. A bunch of sites came up. Most told her nothing new. She needed something more obscure. Tapping her fingers on the desk, she considered how best to dig into the subject.

Perhaps she was going about it the wrong way. She was starting at the beginning of the trail instead of the end. She shouldn't be searching for Catherine de Médici but for the Benedettis.

She typed in *Vittorio Benedetti* and felt a rush of excitement when his name came up. The article was about the recent death of his son, Frances Benedetti, thirty-two, who had been killed in a car accident. Frances had left behind two brothers, Stefano and Daniel, and his father, Vittorio. She checked the date on the article. Six months ago. That was sad.

A shadow fell across her screen, and she started. She was more than a little relieved when J.T. pulled up a chair next to hers. For a moment she'd thought the police had found her. She couldn't read much from J.T.'s expression. He looked tired. He was still wearing his formal suit from the evening before. She realized he'd never had time to change after spending the night at her apartment, then following her to the fun house and so on. She was almost afraid to ask what had happened at Barclay's, but she couldn't stop the question from crossing her lips. "What did you find out?"

He put his arm around the back of her chair. "Everyone thinks you and your father stole the diamond," he said in a quiet voice.

She cast a quick glance around them, but there was no one within earshot. She'd already known that everyone at Barclay's was suspicious, but it still hurt to hear him say it so bluntly. "They're half right. My father did steal the diamond. I just didn't help him do it." She paused. "Maybe if I could find him, I could convince him to give it back."

J.T. raised a skeptical eyebrow. "You think?"

She couldn't blame him for the cynical response. "He's not a bad person. He has a good heart. He can be reasonable."

"Sure. That's why he went to the trouble of concocting a disguise in someone else's name, commissioned someone to make him a fake diamond necklace, and then switched it in front of his very own daughter, knowing that every action he took could possibly destroy her life."

"Well, when you say it like that . . ."

"There's no other way to say it, Christina. I'm not trying to hurt you, but you have to face facts. Your father didn't just steal this diamond on a whim. He had a plan, a very complicated plan, which he carried out."

"I know. You're right. I get it."

"Good. Now tell me, have you made any progress here?"

"Not really. I've been trying to trace the diamond. A stone that big and that unusual probably belonged to someone rich and famous, a king or a queen, someone along those lines. The most powerful family in Italy during the Renaissance was the de Médicis. There were many precious stones that were part of Catherine de Médici's dowry, and it is believed that some of those stones disappeared." She saw the blank look on J.T.'s face and had a feeling history had not been his best subject.

"Cut to the chase," he said.

"I can't. I'm not to the chase yet. Since Catherine lived in the fifteen hundreds, information about her is not that easy to find. I thought I'd go in reverse, start with the Benedettis, another rich and famous Florentine family."

He nodded approvingly. "I'm more than a little curious about that family."

"Why?" she asked, seeing a glint of excitement in his eyes.

"When I was at Barclay's, I reviewed the security tape from the workroom, went over the sequence of events. Stefano Benedetti put the diamond on the display, but when he reached over to push the button to turn the door, his back blocked the view of the diamond."

She stared at him in confusion. "You think Stefano stole his own diamond?"

"He was the last one to touch it. When you think about it, he was the only one who could have taken it. I checked the space in between the revolving panel. A human could not fit back there. It makes sense. No one would ever look at Stefano as the thief."

"Because he doesn't have a motive. Although I guess he could have done it for the insurance money. Did you tell Alexis your theory?"

"She and Kenner dismissed it out of hand. But my gut tells me I'm onto something."

"Even if Stefano took the diamond, he couldn't have left the building without being searched," Christina said.

"At first I thought he might have done just that. But the thing is, no one ever saw him leave. I checked with all the guards. I even went over the tapes from the security cameras fixed on the entrances. There was no evidence that Stefano ever left the building."

"Maybe he's still there then."

J.T. shrugged. "I searched every floor. I didn't see him. I did, however, have a little chat with Luigi Murano. He was hired by a lawyer representing the Benedetti family to travel with the collection and ensure its safety."

"I already knew that," she said, not sure what point he was trying to make.

"There's more. Luigi said he was surprised when Stefano showed up, because it had been his understanding that none of the Benedettis would be traveling to the United States. He told me that he had never met Stefano before, and once Stefano arrived he handled all communication with the family lawyer."

"Okay, I see where you're going. You think that Stefano is really Evan. That's what you're saying, isn't it?"

He nodded. "I have to admit it's not quite jiving, because I talked to Stefano and I think I would have recognized Evan if he were in disguise."

"Maybe not. My father stood right in front of me at the preview party when he was masquerading as Professor Keaton, and I didn't see him. I'm betting I've spent more time with my father than you have with Evan. You said before that Evan's games work because people see what they expect to see."

"And I assumed that everyone else, including Luigi Murano, had met Stefano before," J.T. said. "I even asked Murano if they had spoken in Italian. He told me that Stefano only speaks English in the States. He claimed it was more courteous."

"Or he isn't fluent in Italian. So what do we do now?"

"We need to find out more about the Benedettis. Put in Stefano's name. Let's see what his background is."

Christina typed in *Stefano Benedetti*. A moment later several sites came up. The first few were actually about the auction at Barclay's. She moved farther down the list and clicked on a link. "Here's something," she murmured, skimming the article. "Stefano Benedetti broke up with supermodel Francine Galiana just after Valentine's Day. I guess that doesn't help."

"Maybe it does. Click on *'Images'* and put in Stefano's name and Francine's. Supermodels and their dates often have their photographs taken."

He was right. Sure enough, a picture of the two of them attending a film festival in Cannes appeared. Unfortunately, the photograph of Stefano was not very clear. "He looks like the man we've been talking to," she said.

J.T. rubbed his chin thoughtfully. "It does look like Stefano, sort of. The photo is grainy. Let's keep going."

She hit another link, then another. There was nothing particularly newsworthy, mostly gossip line items about Stefano's playboy ways. Apparently Stefano and his father did not get along well, and Stefano was little more than a figurehead in the family business. His youngest brother, Daniel, had recently become the CEO when their father Vittorio's health had taken a turn for the worst.

"Wait a second, go back," J.T. told her.

She automatically hit the back button, not sure what he'd seen that she hadn't. There was a photo of a racing sailboat. J.T. drew the tip of his finger along the computer screen, underlining the caption. " 'Stefano Benedetti joined the racing team for the final lap of their race around the southern tip of Africa,' " she read. "I still don't get—"

"The boat doesn't dock for two more days, Christina," J.T. said excitedly. "There's no way Stefano could be there and here."

She looked into his eyes, wanting to jump on board his bandwagon, but . . . "Wouldn't Vittorio or the other brother realize that someone was here masquerading as Stefano?"

"Maybe not," J.T. said with a wave of his hand. "Stefano arrived Wednesday night out of the blue. He came separately from the collection. He introduced himself to Luigi as Stefano Benedetti and no doubt showed him the appropriate identification and knew enough about the collection to discuss it intelligently."

"Which wouldn't be difficult to do, since every item in the collection was previewed in our spring catalog that was printed a month ago," she continued.

"Exactly. As far as the Benedettis are concerned, they sent their collection off with the trusted Luigi Murano."

"But when Luigi stopped calling the Benedettis' lawyer, wouldn't he have gotten suspicious?" Christina argued. "Wouldn't he have picked up the phone and called Mr. Murano to find out what was happening?"

"We're talking about a fairly short period of time," J.T. answered slowly. "Less than forty-eight hours. Evan probably figured exactly the amount of time needed for his ruse to work."

"Or he could have called the Benedettis' lawyer as if he were Luigi Murano," Christina said.

J.T.'s smile lit up his eyes. He grabbed her face and kissed her. "I knew you were a smart girl. I bet that's exactly what happened. It was a good disguise. No one would question the actions of the owner of the diamond. Evan, as Stefano, stood right there in front of us and slipped that diamond into his pocket just as the turntable went around. And that candy necklace was all Evan. When everyone started screaming, Stefano simply joined in the fray. No one was looking at him. He was the victim. They were looking at you and your father, the perfect scapegoats. That's it. We figured it out."

She hated to stick a pin in his happy balloon, but she had no choice. "Even if that's true, J.T., Stefano is gone and so is the diamond. From where I sit, I'm still in the hot seat and Evan is calling the shots."

"Not all the shots."

"What do you mean?"

"Your father has the real diamond, right?"

"I think so," she said slowly, hating the road he was now taking her down.

"Which means Evan has a fake, which means—"

"Evan is going to try to find the real diamond." Their eyes met. "He's going to go after my father, isn't he?"

"And so are we," J.T. finished. "Hopefully we have a head start this time, and Evan hasn't yet figured out he doesn't have the real diamond. We might need that extra time to locate your father. In the meantime, I need to keep you safe."

"Why would I be in danger—except from the police?" she asked.

"Because you're an obvious first step on the trail to finding Marcus Alberti."

"I don't know where he is," she countered.

"Evan doesn't know that," J.T. pointed out. "He may think that if he finds you, he'll find Marcus, or he'll smoke him out."

"At this point, I'm not at all certain my father would come running to my rescue," she said.

"Whether he would or not isn't the issue. Come on, Christina. Let's get out of here. This place is too quiet and stuffy. I need to breathe some air and figure out our next move."

She was almost afraid to leave the safety of the library. She had no idea what was waiting for her outside. But J.T was already heading for the entrance, and she had no choice but to follow him. Still, as they neared the door, she slowed down, fighting back an odd sense of fear.

"What's wrong?" J.T. asked impatiently.

"My life is completely out of control. I don't know who to trust, where to go, what to do."

"That's easy. You trust me, and the rest will follow."

She wished it were that simple. "My father taught me a long time ago never to trust a man with a badge."

"And at this point, you still want to listen to your father?" he asked in disbelief.

"Maybe not, but—"

"But what?" he snapped.

"There's a little voice inside me that keeps asking whether you're really on my side or if you're just using me to get to the final prize—to Evan."

Anger flared in his eyes. "Haven't we gotten past that point?" he asked with a scowl. "I put my job on the line getting you out of Barclay's. I just spent a half hour lying about where you are. And you don't trust me yet? Are you kidding me?"

She realized her words had hurt him, but it was too late to take them back. And maybe she didn't want to take them back. "So many people are not who they appear to be," she said, forcing herself to look directly at him, even though the anger emanating from his gaze made her want to flinch. "I know you're obsessed with finding Evan. You want him so badly you'd do anything to get him. You just said that if Evan wants my father, I'm going to be his first stop. Maybe I'm the lure you're using to land your big, fat fish." She wanted him to deny her words, to yell at her for even thinking such a thing, to tell her he was with her because he liked her, because he wanted to protect her, because he cared—hell, maybe because they'd slept together.

Although, at this moment, it was difficult to even remember the intimacy they'd shared the night before. There was a rapidly growing wall between them, and she'd had more than a fair hand in putting that wall up. J.T.'s silence wasn't helping. Nor was the cold, dark, furious look in his eyes making her feel at all reassured about his motives. Was he mad because she'd questioned him—or angry because she'd spoken the truth?

"You need me," J.T. said finally. "And I need you. Why don't we leave it at that?"

Why? Because it was a crappy place to leave it, that was why. He hadn't cleared anything up; he'd just confused her more. And now she wasn't merely worried and scared but angry, too.

"My car is parked out front," J.T. continued.

"What about my car?" she asked. It was still parked down at Pier 39.

"We'll pick it up later. Right now I want to keep you away from anything that could lead the police to you." He paused. "You can come or not, Christina. If you want to take your chances on your own or with the cops, go ahead. I won't try to stop you. It's your decision."

"No, you'll just follow me and stalk me, the way you've been doing since we first met," she snapped back.

"Probably true," he admitted without apology.

The tension between them deepened, but Christina knew there was really no choice to make. "Fine, I'll come with you. But I make no promises about how long I'm staying."

She made no promises about how long she was staying.

J.T. fumed all the way to the car. Who the hell did Christina think she was? Her beautiful ass would be in jail right now if it weren't for him, and she thought she could call the shots? Not that she wasn't half right about the fact that he needed her help, but he wasn't *using* her, per se. There was a distinction. As far as he was concerned it was a mutually beneficial relationship. And it annoyed the hell out of him that she didn't trust him.

They'd spent most of the night licking each other's naked bodies. She'd trusted him enough to do that. She'd given her body, but not her heart, not her emotions, not her brain. Well, that was the way he usually liked it. He should feel good that she wasn't trying to wrap the sex up with a pretty bow and call it a relationship, the way most women did.

But for some reason her attitude pissed him off— probably because he trusted her, and he had hoped the feeling was mutual. Apparently it wasn't.

"Where are we going?" she asked.

"I don't know. Do you have to ask so many questions?"

She shot him a dark look, but remained silent as he started the car and pulled into traffic. He knew he was taking his frustration out on her. It wasn't just

Christina's lack of trust that made him want to hit something; it was the knowledge that Evan had once again gotten the best of him. But it wasn't over yet. He could still win. He could still put Evan away.

As the blue waters of San Francisco Bay came into view, he made an impulsive turn and headed toward the Golden Gate Bridge. The awesome orange structure was alight in the sunshine. The fog had burned off to reveal a beautiful late-afternoon sky. It was almost four o'clock, but traffic was still relatively light. After crossing the bridge, he turned into the narrow winding streets of Sausalito and parked by the bay. He stepped out of the car and walked to the water's edge, drawing in deep gulps of air.

He heard Christina's car door open and close and a moment later she was next to him, standing a few feet away, keeping her arms wrapped around her waist. She stared out at the view, as did he, taking in the scenic beauty of San Francisco on the other side of the bay.

Putting some distance between him and the city helped. He needed to catch his breath, get some perspective, take some time to think. He'd been rushing from one crisis to another, too busy putting out fires to figure out a way to prevent those fires. In other words, he'd been dancing to Evan's tune. Not anymore. The game had changed. Christina's father was a new player, and quite possibly as good a player as Evan. Certainly, the two men both loved a drama and to dress in disguise. If it were just the two of them, he wondered who would win.

Not that it mattered, because it wasn't just the two of them. He was going to take them both down. Christina wouldn't be happy if her father went to jail. He knew he would have to deal with that issue at some point. He was a federal agent, after all; he couldn't look the other way. That was why she didn't trust him. Logically, it made sense, but it still pissed him off. Her lack of trust gave him less power over her. And his trust in her gave her more power over him. That didn't seem like the right balance. Somehow he'd have to make it work.

While he did think she could help him find Evan and her father, that wasn't the real reason he'd kept her away from the cops. He'd wanted to help her. When she'd begged him with those beautiful green eyes to get her out of Barclay's, he hadn't even considered saying no. God help him if she ever figured out how easy it would be for her to get him to do just about anything.

She cleared her throat, and from the corner of his eye he could see her looking at him.

"There's a little hotel not far from here," she said a moment later. "You could take a shower, change your clothes."

He glanced down at his wrinkled suit, realizing he'd been wearing it since the party last night, except, of course, for the few hours he'd spent naked in Christina's bed. He hadn't had time to change before following her down to the fun house or trying to get to the auction on time.

"I don't think I can use a credit card, though," she continued. "Too easy to trace, right? I don't have that much cash on me. I guess I could use an ATM, but that's easy to trace, too."

"I'll take care of it."

"Won't they be looking for you, too? They know you helped me get away."

"I told them I wasn't aware of their suspicions about you when you left the auction house. But . . . in any case I have a different credit card we can use. It won't be traceable."

Christina frowned and shook her head. He had no idea what she was thinking now.

"What did I say?" he asked.

"I just don't know how I keep ending up with guys who have fake identities and untraceable credit cards, men who can be whomever they need to be at a moment's notice. You may not believe it, but I'm a normal, law-abiding person, J.T. I don't break the rules. I don't take long lunch breaks. I don't call in sick unless I'm sick. I've never stolen anything, not even a paper clip. Whatever my father did, he did on his own, and whatever I did to help him, I did when I was too young and too stupid to know better. So tell me, how did I end up on the run?"

"You should ask your father that question, not me."

"He'd just lie and tell me that he only took things from people who didn't deserve them. He believes that exquisite art objects belong with their original owners. He was so disappointed when I went to work at the auction house. He acted like I was selling historical artifacts as if they were no more important than toilet paper or shoes. He thought I'd sold out." She blew out a long sigh. "Maybe I did sell out. But no one in the museum world would hire me after my father left in disgrace. My reputation was in tatters. Sometimes I do hate it when I see a painting or a jewel go to someone who just wants it because they're greedy, not because they appreciate the beauty or the history. I guess that sounds stupid to you. I'm sure you don't understand."

"I don't understand what historical things mean to you," he agreed, "but I do understand disappointment. I'm an expert on the subject, in fact."

She gave him a thoughtful look. "You think you let down your father, don't you?"

"I don't think it. I know it. But we're not talking about my father; we're talking about yours."

"You have to live your own life," she said, ignoring his attempt to return the subject to her father. "You can't be what someone else wants you to be. Believe me, I've tried to go that route, and it doesn't work."

"I've tried it, too," he admitted. "Those couple of years in the pros were all for my father. Not that he appreciated it."

"I'm sure he did."

"No, he didn't," J.T. denied. "My father sacrificed a lot for me. He'd come home after work and spend hours with me throwing balls until I got it right. Some years he worked two jobs so I could play on tournament teams, have special coaching. Getting me to the pros was the culmination of his life's ambition. The thing is, I could have kept doing it. It wouldn't have killed me. It wasn't a bad life. But I quit. I was selfish."

Christina walked over to him, her eyes filled with compassion. "It was selfish of your father to want you to be something you didn't want to be, J.T. Parents are supposed to support and encourage, not force their children to live out their own dreams. Your dad had his chance to be a pro football player."

"He wasn't good enough."

"That wasn't your fault."

"I let him down." He dug his hands into his pockets as he gazed out at the view, at the sun beginning to slip down over the horizon. "This was the time of day we used to play. There was a field just down the street from our house, and whenever I think of my dad I always see him at dusk, the shadows creeping over the grass, the scent of the flowers from the park, the smell of dinner cooking at the houses next door. I was usually hungry by then, too, wishing we could finish early, get back so I could eat and talk to my friends. But he always said, 'One more throw, J.T. Someday you'll thank me for making you stay out here and practice.'" J.T. let out a humorless laugh. "I should have thanked him the day I led my team to a win at the Rose Bowl. But I forgot. All those hours he spent with me, and I forgot. I was a lousy son, and I don't know why the hell I'm telling you all this."

"You must have needed to get it out," she said, her expression understanding and not at all judgmental. "Families are complicated, aren't they?"

"You can say that again." He kicked at a stone half-buried in the dirt beneath his shoe. When it came loose, he picked it up and threw it in the bay.

"I thought you said you could throw," Christina teased. "I think I can do better than that."

"Oh, yeah? Show me."

She reached down and picked up a medium-sized rock, took her arm back, and threw it with all her might. It skidded off the water, but still landed short. "Damn. I thought I could beat you."

"I wasn't even trying on that first throw."

"Yeah, yeah, that's what they all say."

"It's true. And you throw like a girl."

"That's because I am a girl."

"I'm very well aware of that fact," he said, taking a purposeful step in her direction.

She put up a hand. He grabbed it and placed it against his chest. She licked her lips "Hold on a second, J.T. I thought we were talking."

"I'm done talking."

"Well, maybe I'm not."

"Well, maybe that's too bad." He covered the rest of her protest with his mouth. Her lips were soft, warm, tender, and he loved the way she responded to him, as if she wanted to do nothing more than kiss him back for the rest of his life. She might not be able to say she trusted him, but when she put her arms around his neck and pulled him closer, he could feel it in every bone in his body.

He couldn't help but respond in kind. She made him want things he shouldn't want . . . like going back to living a life in a nice neighborhood with kids on bikes, fathers and sons throwing footballs in the park, dogs barking, dinner cooking, a mother calling her children in for dinner—family. He hadn't had a family in a long, long time. His solitary apartment, his never-ending job, seemed far away at this moment.

But even as he kissed Christina, his pragmatic conscience reminded him that she wasn't his wife or his girlfriend. She was in trouble. She was lonely, lost. She needed a protector. But what else did she need? What did she really want from him? And what the hell did he want from her? Things were moving way too fast. Kissing Christina was a mistake. A big mistake! He pulled away so abruptly she stumbled. She grabbed hold of his arms, her green eyes dazed with passion. He forced himself to look away, because while his brain wanted to call a halt, his body was definitely on a different track.

"What? What did I do?" she asked in surprise.

"Nothing. You didn't do anything." He stepped away from her. "This is crazy. I don't know what I'm thinking. We can't do this right now."

"Do what?" she challenged.

"You know what. We're in the middle of a case. We need to get a hotel room and get back to business."

"In a hotel room? You think we'll be able to get down to business in a hotel room with one bed? Because I don't know what the hell happened to you just now, but I wasn't the only one enjoying that kiss."

"It was good, but it's over." He put his hands back in his pockets so he wouldn't be tempted to do anything else with them.

"Just like that? You decide it's over and it's over?"

"We need to focus on finding your father and Evan. That's all that's important right now. So this isn't going to happen again."

"Sure, whatever you say," she said, an edge to her voice. She walked to the car, her back as stiff as an iron poker. She was even more beautiful when she was angry. He was in deep shit.

Maybe he'd get two hotel rooms.

13

Over—he thought it was over? He was crazy. She'd let him know when it was over. Christina stomped around the hotel room, annoyed that there hadn't been more than one room available, and even more irritated that J.T. had asked for two rooms. He was the one who'd kissed her first, who'd poured out his heart to her, who'd made her like him even more with that sorry tale about his father, who'd made her feel like she wasn't the only one with a crazy family. J.T. was the one who'd devoured her like a starving man went after a feast. Then when she responded, he had the nerve to stop, to say it was good, but it was over. As if he had the right to call all the shots. Well, he didn't. And she intended to tell him just that. Unfortunately, he was in the shower.

She hoped he was taking a cold shower, because if he thought she was going to sleep with him the next time he decided he wanted to start things up again, he'd better think again.

Pausing by the table, she hit the computer key to finish booting up the laptop computer he'd set up for her—so she could get back to business. The ass! Who did he think he was?

She ran her hand through her hair, glaring at the bathroom door. Was he singing? She could hear his voice over the water. And it definitely sounded like he was singing. She walked over to the door and paused, hearing some sort of garbled rock-and-roll song. So that was it? No tension for him? No restless frustration?

It wasn't fair. He was the one who'd gotten her all warmed up . . . so to speak.

A reckless idea took hold in her brain. She told herself it was foolish, probably stupid, and it certainly hadn't been her week for good ideas. Then again, could things really get any worse? Couldn't they only get better? The thought of a naked J.T. with water streaming down those beautiful muscles made her stomach clench and a delicious heat sweep through her body. It would be over between them when she said it was over.

She pulled off her suit jacket and unbuttoned her blouse with jerky fingers, making just as fast work of her bra, skirt, and panties. Second thoughts were already trying to take hold, but she pushed them ruthlessly away. She turned the knob on the bathroom door and walked in. Steam swirled around her, clouding up the mirrors. The scent of soap and the thought of J.T. completely overwhelmed her senses.

Could she really be this bold?

Well, why the hell not?

She was tired of dancing to everyone else's tune. She wanted some control over her life. And what she wanted right now was J.T. She opened the sliding glass door.

His song stopped in midnote, his eyes widened at the

sight of her nude body, and he drew in a sharp breath. She stepped into the shower with him, putting her hands on his hard but slippery biceps. "It's not over," she said.

His gaze darkened with desire. "I guess it's not."

She ran her fingers up and down his soapy arms, then took the bar of soap out of his unresisting hand and ran it across his chest. She loved the fine dark hairs that played across his skin, dipping across his flat abs, down to his groin. She followed the path with the bar of soap.

"Uh, Christina, I already got that part," J.T. said, a sly grin spreading across his lips.

"I think you missed a spot," she teased. The soap dropped from her hand as she stroked him with her fingers, feeling him harden against her.

He put his hands on her buttocks, pulling her up against him, pressing his mouth against hers, his tongue sweeping past her lips. She moaned as the pleasure of his kiss slammed through her. She'd started this game, but he was taking over, and she didn't mind a bit. His hands were roaming now, moving over her slick, wet body with a restless hunger. His mouth moved from her lips to her throat, his tongue tracing the line of her collarbone, then sweeping down to her breasts, leaving a wet path around her nipples.

He dropped to his knees. She leaned against the wall of the shower, her legs feeling weak as his tongue delved into the hot space between her thighs, tasting, exploring, making her crazy. She felt the tension knotting her muscles. She dug her hands into his hair, holding him against her as she cried out his name in blessed release. He slowly moved back up her body. Reaching behind her, he turned off the shower and helped her out of the tub.

"Wait," she said. "You—"

He cut her off with another kiss, grabbed a towel from the rack, and wrapped it around her. Then he dug into his shaving kit and took out a condom, making no mistake of his intention to have his turn.

He kissed her all the way into the bedroom. Her legs hit the side of the bed as she fell backward. J.T. came down on top of her. She wrapped her legs around his waist as he entered her. He moved inside of her with restless, driving passion. She shuddered with each powerful stroke, giving in to the moment, the pleasure, and the man in her arms, in her body, and in her heart.

Christina's heart was still beating in double time when J.T. moved off her, stretching out next to her. She rolled to her side, putting her head on his chest. She could hear his heartbeat, too, and it was just as fast. But gradually it began to slow. Their breathing started to sound normal, instead of ragged and rough. "J.T.," she murmured, lifting her head to gaze into his eyes.

"Yes?" he asked, a wary note in his voice.

"Now it's over." She smiled with satisfaction.

He grinned at her as he ran his hand down her back. "Are you kidding? No way is it over now." He pulled her head down and gave her a hard kiss. "We're just getting started."

"You always like to be in charge."

"Hey, you're the one who interrupted my shower," he reminded her.

"Because you always like to be in charge," she repeated.

"Okay, I'll tell you what. You get to pick what we

have for dinner." He grabbed the room service menu off the bedside table and handed it to her. "It's all yours, every single, solitary decision."

She made a face at him. "If you think you're going to placate me by allowing me to order you a steak, you have another think coming."

"I love steak."

"Just for that, we're getting fish."

"I like fish, too."

She blew out an exasperated breath. She had a feeling she could order sardines and he'd be perfectly happy. So he wasn't picky about his food, so what? He could still be extremely stubborn and heavy-handed and far too controlling. Of course, he was also sexy, passionate, tender, a generous lover who could do extraordinary things with his tongue. . . .

"Christina. You're not looking at the menu," he pointed out, his eyes darkening. "If you keep staring at me like that, it's going to be a while before you get to eat. However, the *decision* is completely up to you."

She scrambled off the bed, grabbing the white terry-cloth bathrobe off the back of the bathroom door. "In that case, I think I'll order dinner."

"Are you sure?" He patted the empty spot on the bed that she'd just vacated. "You could let me try to change your mind. We could test the strength of your decision-making skills."

His wicked grin and his uninhibited naked pose almost made her reverse the decision, but she decided it would look far too wishy-washy on her part to get back into bed with him. "I'm sure. As you reminded me earlier, we have work to do."

With a groan he flopped back on the mattress and closed his eyes. "I'm tired. You wore me out."

"Some food will perk you up."

He laughed and cocked one eye open. "You could perk me up."

"You are bad." She grabbed the wet towel on the bed and tossed it at him.

J.T. caught it and stood up, wrapping the towel around his waist. He paused to kiss her on the cheek before heading for the bathroom.

With a little sigh, she turned her attention to the menu, then picked up the phone. She ordered steak, potatoes, vegetables, salad, and chocolate cake for dessert. She was starving. In fact, she couldn't remember when she'd last eaten. Then she walked over to the table and sat down in front of J.T.'s computer. She needed to refocus her thoughts on her father and that damn diamond. If only the Benedettis had sent their diamond to some other auction house, then her life would still be her own. Her father would be out of the picture. Evan wouldn't be involved. And J.T. . . . well, that was the one person she didn't want to wish away. But the truth was that he was with her only because of the situation she was in. They never would have met otherwise.

They didn't have anything in common—not really. He knew next to nothing about history, art, jewelry, the things that mattered to her. He was a jock. He knew about football and sports. Okay, he was an FBI agent, too, so he was probably up on the law as well. But they led different lives—well, sort of different lives. He lived alone. So did she. His job was his life; so was hers. He understood the disappointment of family. He knew what betrayal felt like. He understood what it meant to lose a parent.

She let out a sigh, realizing she'd just blown her own argument. They did share some common bonds, but still . . . what did it matter? As soon as this case was over, they'd each go back to their own lives. Wouldn't they?

But what exactly was her own life? Would she even have a job, or would she have to start over again?

She put her elbows on the table, resting her chin in her hands, wishing she could answer just one of her own many questions.

As J.T. returned to the bedroom, he began to get dressed, throwing on jeans and a long-sleeved sweater. She hated to see him cover up that beautiful body, but they would probably get more done if they were both dressed. Not that she'd bothered to put on her business suit. The bathrobe was far more comfortable.

J.T. sat down in the chair next to hers and turned the computer so it was facing him.

"You haven't gotten far," he said.

She shrugged, the euphoria of the past hour turning to weariness. It was back to reality, a state of mind she was not particularly excited about these days.

His gaze narrowed on her face. "You okay?"

"Just not sure where to start."

"Maybe you should lie down, take a little nap. You look tired."

"A few minutes ago you said I looked beautiful."

He smiled. "You still look beautiful, just tired. I noticed before, but I wasn't interested in convincing you to take a nap at that moment."

"Ah, so the truth comes out."

"Seriously. Take a break."

"I'm okay. I know time is passing, and my father already has a big head start. It's possible we may not be able to catch him before he puts the diamond back."

"You don't think he'll just keep it somewhere, stash it away?"

She shook her head. "Absolutely not. He doesn't steal to own. He steals to retrieve items he believes belong elsewhere. He thinks of himself as the Robin Hood of missing artifacts."

"That's a romantic tag for taking what doesn't belong to you," J.T. said dryly.

"It's his definition, not mine."

"Okay, so we have to figure out where the diamond is supposed to be. I'm assuming your father doesn't believe it belongs to the Benedettis?"

"No, he said they stole it. He didn't give me any more details. I asked him to prove it. He couldn't. He said I should take his word. If you can believe that."

A sudden knock at the door sent her heart back into overdrive. For a split second she thought the police had caught up with them. J.T. was on his feet when the knock came again and a man called out, "Room service."

Christina was about to relax when she saw J.T. reach into his overnight bag and pull out a gun. She stiffened in shock. J.T. had a gun! Of course he did. He was an FBI agent. He was law enforcement. It just hadn't seemed so real before.

"I ordered dinner," she said as he headed toward the door. "It is room service."

"Let's just be sure." He took a look through the peephole, then slipped the gun into the back of his jeans, hiding it under his shirt. He opened the door and a young waiter pushed a table into the room. Christina grabbed a few dollar bills from her purse as J.T. signed for their meal. The waiter left with a smile and a thank-you.

"I didn't realize you had a gun," she said when they were alone again. Her heart was still beating too fast.

"It's part of the job," J.T. replied, returning the gun to his bag.

"I'm sure it is. I guess," she added belatedly. "Have you ever shot anyone?"

"Yes. But only because they shot at me first," he said, meeting her gaze.

"Did they hit you?"

"No. They missed. I got lucky. And I made the better shot."

"Oh." She thought about asking what had happened to the other guy but decided against it. She fell silent as J.T. walked over to the table and took the lids off their dinners. Although the steak smelled wonderful, her appetite had diminished a bit.

"This looks good," he said. "Nice decision making." He offered her a smile; then his gaze turned speculative. "The gun bothers you?"

"A little—actually, a lot. I've never seen a gun before that wasn't on television or in a locked glass case." She crossed her arms in front of her. "It's intimidating."

"Your father never had a gun?"

"Goodness, no."

"Hey, don't act so surprised. A lot of thieves carry guns. That's why I carry one—to keep up with the bad guys."

She frowned. "My father isn't a bad guy, not the way you mean. I want you to meet him. I want you to talk to him. You'll see in five seconds that he has a good heart, and while he might get mixed up about what things belong where, he would never hurt anyone."

"I think your opinion of your father is somewhat biased, Christina, but I'll reserve judgment until I meet him, which I hope will be very soon. But while your dad might be a mild-mannered guy, Evan is not. So I think I'll keep the gun handy all the same."

"Could you really shoot him—if it was just you and Evan, face-to-face? Could you pull the trigger?"

"In a heartbeat." His gaze was direct and unflinching. "But . . . I wouldn't."

She was surprised by his answer. "Why not? He killed your father. An eye for an eye. Revenge. Payback. You said you wanted justice."

"I do want justice. I took an oath to uphold the law, Christina, not take it into my own hands. I want to see Evan in prison. If he dies there, or someone else kills him, fine."

"What if he threatened you, put a gun in your face?" she asked. "Or mine?"

"Well, then I'd shoot him straight through the heart—not that he has a heart." J.T. walked over to her and put his hands on her shoulders. "The law won't get in my way if Evan tries to hurt you, Christina. I would never stand by and let that happen."

"I believe you. I'm just worried, afraid of the future. I love my father. You love your job. I want to protect my dad. You want to put Evan away. It seems like we should be on the same side, but I have a terrible feeling one of us is going to have to choose, that we won't both be able to get what we want. And the closer we are to each other, the harder that choice will be."

"Let's not borrow trouble."

"You're the one who made me realize I need to start thinking ahead. You tried to warn me that the diamond was going to be stolen and I didn't listen. I didn't see how it could possibly happen, so I dismissed it. Obviously I was wrong. I also thought I could handle my father by myself. Wrong again. I don't want to make any more mistakes."

"Just know that I'll do whatever it takes to keep you safe, and I'll try to include the people you care about," he added, gazing deep into her eyes. "Can we eat now?"

It wasn't exactly the answer she wanted, but it was close enough. "Sure, we can eat."

J.T. sat down across from her. "Looks good."

It did look good. The steaks had been broiled to juicy perfection. The potatoes were loaded with butter, sour cream, and chives. The medley of vegetables made her mouth water, and the huge piece of chocolate cake almost made her want to skip straight to dessert. She sat down at the table and picked up her knife and fork. Cutting off a piece of filet mignon, she took a bite and sighed with pleasure. "Mmm. This is incredible."

"Okay, now you're hurting my feelings," J.T. told her. "You made that exact same sound in the shower when I kissed your breast. Apparently all I needed to do was feed you."

She grinned. "I'm a simple woman with simple pleasures."

"Expensive pleasures. Filet mignon? You couldn't have picked a cheaper cut?"

"I believe you said the decision was all mine," she reminded him. "Besides, I could be one meal away from the slammer. I figure I'd better live a little—while I have the chance."

Christina was good at making lemonade out of lemons, as J.T.'s grandma used to say. Christina got knocked down. She bounced back up. J.T. had a feeling she would need to hang on to that spirit during the upcoming days. They still had an uphill battle ahead of them. They had to find her father and the diamond and catch Evan, three not-so-easy tasks. Part of him wanted to send her away somewhere safe, keep her out of it entirely, but he doubted there was anywhere she would truly be safe until Evan was behind bars.

Evan might not need Christina to find Marcus Alberti. It was certainly possible Evan already knew where her father was. But the best way to get Marcus to give up the diamond would be through Christina.

"You're staring at me," Christina said as she pushed away her now empty plate. "And from your expression it's clear you're not thinking happy thoughts. Am I going to have to cheer you up again?"

He smiled, as she'd intended him to. "Oh, so that little shower scene was about cheering me up?"

"It worked, didn't it?"

"Yes, and you looked pretty happy yourself."

She flushed a little under his gaze. She might be a sophisticate when it came to intellectual matters, but there was an appealing air of innocence about her when it came to sex. She seemed to bring more enthusiasm than experience, an eagerness to learn what he wanted, and he liked that—liked it a lot, too much, in fact. He wanted to make love to her again. He wanted to forget about everything else that was going on and just spend the next couple of days in bed with her.

"J.T.," she said on a husky note. "What are you thinking?"

"You don't want to know," he said with a teasing grin. "Believe me."

"Maybe I do."

"We need to get back to work."

She frowned. "In a minute. There's something I've been meaning to ask you. I cannot go one more second without knowing. It's too important."

He tensed at the sudden seriousness in her tone. "What is it?"

"I don't know how to ask—so I'll just say it."

"Fine, say it."

"I need to know what J.T. stands for."

The tension fled from his body at the mischievous light in her eyes. Two could play this game. With a shake of his head, he said, "I'm afraid that's classified information. If I told you, I would have to kill you."

"Hey, don't make that joke with a gun in the room." She leaned forward. "I'm not going to stop asking until you tell me."

"Why should I?"

"Because you've seen me naked. That means I get to know your entire name, not just your initials."

"One thing about deals, Christina: You have to make them before you give anything up. Otherwise, they don't work. I already got what I wanted. I have no motivation left."

"I'm sure I can think of some motivation."

He had a feeling she could, and he'd probably be willing to give up more than his name. In fact, was that her toe sliding up the inside of his jeans? He felt his whole body tighten at the gesture and saw the triumph in her eyes.

"You are so easy," she said with a little laugh.

"Where you're concerned, maybe."

"Is it really embarrassing—your name? Is that why you won't tell me?" She sat back in her chair, tilting her head upward as if she were in great thought. "I'll just guess then. Jasper Thorndike? Jedediah Thomasina? Or maybe it's kind of a girly name, like Jamie Talulah. You grew up like that boy in the song who wanted to fight everyone because his father named him Sue."

"John Timothy," he said shortly.

A disappointed frown crossed her lips. "Well, that's not even interesting, much less bad."

"Thanks."

"You know what I mean. I was expecting something a little longer. Why go by your initials? Why not just be John or Johnny or Johnny Boy?"

"Yeah, I think Johnny Boy would have made my high school years really fun," he said dryly. "The reason for the initials was simple. I was named for my father. When I was young he was Big John, and I was Little John. It always seemed more his name than mine. When I went to college, I just introduced myself as J.T. It was the beginning of the break between us. He got so pissed off during the first television interview I did, when the reporter called me J.T. instead of John McIntyre. It was like I'd cheated him out of his moment in the sun. Even my damn name was part of his dream."

She gave him an understanding look. "That was always the problem, wasn't it? You couldn't figure out where he ended and you began."

He'd never thought of it like that, but he supposed she was right. "Yeah, I guess. Anyway, I don't answer to John, so don't try it, because it won't work. I will not come running."

"Got it," she said lightly. "No John. What about 'sexy,' 'hot stuff,' 'good-looking'? Do those work for you?"

He appreciated her smile. It released the tension that knotted his stomach every time he thought of his father. "I don't know how you get me to talk about him," he said. "It's not my favorite subject. So, how about some dessert?"

She rubbed her stomach and groaned. "I think I'm too full."

"Are you serious?" he asked, exaggerating his shock and surprise. "I thought every woman, especially a stressed-out woman, was a candidate for dark, rich chocolate." He took his fork and lightly scooped a bit of chocolate icing off the cake. He held it out to her. "Are you sure you don't want a bite?"

She smiled back at him. "You are the devil."

"I can't tempt you—just one small bite? You know you want it."

"I do want it, but I'm full, and believe it or not I'm usually a very disciplined person, when you're not distracting me."

"Hey, it hasn't been all me," he protested. "You've done your share of distracting."

She took the fork out of his hand and set it down on the plate. "Later. It's time to work."

"You're right." It was past time to get down to business. Unfortunately, when he was with her, business seemed to be the last thing on his mind. He got up from the table and picked up his cell phone. "I'm going to call my assistant, Tracy. I checked in with her after I left Barclay's to ask her to track down your father. She's an expert with computers." He punched in Tracy's number. She answered almost immediately.

"About time, Mac," she said. "Where the hell are you? Cameron is all over me."

Cameron was his boss and usually stayed out of his business. "What does he want?"

"He wants you off the case, that's what he wants. Cameron said he's getting calls from everyone and their brother that you screwed up. Not only did you not prevent the theft of the diamond, you helped their key suspect get away. Are they right, J.T.?"

"I didn't know Christina was their key suspect at the time," he prevaricated. "But I do know she didn't steal the diamond; Evan did."

"That may be, but Cameron told me to tell you that he's pulling you from the case. He doesn't want you anywhere near Barclay's. In fact, he wants you back in LA for reassignment first thing tomorrow."

"No fucking way," J.T. said with quiet rage. Evan was his. He had too many years on the line. "I'll talk to Cameron."

"I don't think it will do any good, Mac—unless . . ."

"Unless what?" he asked, sure he didn't want to know.

"Unless you drop Christina Alberti at the local cop shop and let them do their job. If she's innocent, they'll figure that out."

He considered her suggestion. If he turned Christina in, he could still pursue Evan. But as his gaze drifted to the beautiful woman at the table who had told him that she was afraid one day he would have to make a choice, he knew he couldn't make that choice—yet. "I can't do that."

Tracy gave a plaintive sigh. "Do you really want to jeopardize your job for this woman? Or for Evan, for that matter? Wouldn't that just make Evan's day to see you get kicked out on your ass? You'd never be able to catch him then."

She had a point, but the thought of letting Evan walk free was impossible to contemplate. "If I bail, no one will look for him. They'll focus completely on Christina and her father, and that is exactly what Evan wants to happen. I won't do it. I can't do it."

"I understand, Mac, but I don't think Cameron will. This is business for him. For you, it's personal. And personal doesn't make a good objective agent."

"Do you have any other information for me?" he asked, changing the subject.

"Yes. I did some checking on David Padlinsky. It turns out the car he was driving was actually purchased by Alexis Kensington and registered in David's name about three months ago. I also found out that Jeremy Kensington hired a private investigator to spy on his wife about that same time."

J.T. began to pace as Tracy's information took him down a new road. "So David and Alexis were having an affair?"

"I'm betting yes. You also asked me to check into the relationship between Alexis Kensington and Nicole Prescott. They are cousins, as you mentioned. But get this—remember those Alcatraz guys you were researching a couple of weeks ago, the ones who stole the fortune in gold coins?"

"Yes," he said, his pulse quickening. He'd always suspected there was a reason Evan had stayed in San Francisco. He just hadn't been able to figure out what that reason was.

"Nicole Prescott is Nathan Carmello's niece," Tracy continued. "Nicole grew up listening to stories about her uncle's daring adventures during the fifties, when he and his gang of bandits roamed the city and later escaped from Alcatraz. She also has quite a past of her own. Despite her blue-collar roots, she managed to marry four times very well, and with each divorce she banked a fortune in settlements and alimony, thereby allowing her to move up, up, and up the social ladder. She ran into a snag with potential husband number five, Jeremy Kensington—that's right. Nicole was dating Jeremy when she made the unfortunate mistake of introducing her cousin Alexis to him. Apparently, Alexis stole Jeremy right out from under Nicole. That's what started the rift between them."

No wonder there had been so much hostility at the party. Alexis had probably invited Nicole because she couldn't afford to offend her any further, but there was obviously no love lost between them.

"You'll also like this. Nicole loves jewelry," Tracy continued. "Especially diamonds, and she has quite a collection, from all reports. And there's another link between Nicole and the Kensingtons. The private investigator Jeremy hired also spent a great deal of time on Nicole's payroll. Put the two together, and—"

"And it looks like Nicole is the one who tipped Jeremy off about her cousin's affair with David," J.T. finished.

"Hey, that was my line. I do all the work and you steal my punch line."

"Sorry." His mind raced at the picture growing clearer in his head. Nicole had a penchant for diamonds and an extreme dislike of her cousin, Alexis, who just happened to be auctioning off a very valuable diamond. Nicole had either tipped Jeremy off about Nicole and David, or Jeremy had simply come to her for help. Whatever way it had worked, there were triangles all over the place. "I need to speak to Ms. Prescott," he muttered. "She's the missing piece, especially since Nicole was tied to the people in Evan's last con. I wonder if there is a link between them as well." A rush of excitement swept through him. If Evan was working with Nicole, she might be able to help him find Evan.

"Don't get too worked up," Tracy told him. "You can't speak to Nicole. She was found dead at her penthouse apartment at two o'clock this afternoon."

His heart came to a crashing halt. He sank down on the edge of the bed. "Are you serious? She's dead? What happened?"

"I just got off the phone with one of my police contacts in San Francisco. We were talking about the diamond, and he mentioned that Alexis Kensington was going to have even more to deal with following the murder of her cousin. Of course, I put it together faster than he did. Apparently it was a botched robbery, or made to look that way. Some cash and jewelry were taken. Nicole was found in the living room. It appeared as if she came home and surprised someone."

"Cause of death?" J.T. asked.

"It looks like strangulation. We'll know more after the medical examiner finishes his review. Not bad, huh, boss?"

J.T. ran a hand through his hair. "Not bad at all. That's a shitload of information."

"I'm good. What can I say?"

"Hopefully you can say some more. I need to figure out if anyone has seen Evan and Nicole together, or if there has been some new man in her life. I'm betting Evan used her for some type of information on the setup at Barclay's. He had to have inside help."

"I'll see what I can do. But I have to warn you that you probably have me for about the next twelve hours before Cameron cuts the rope between us. And I do plan to sleep at some point."

"Duly noted. There's one more thing."

She gave a long-suffering sigh. "There's always one more thing with you, Mac. What is it?"

"See if you can find out if Marcus Alberti bought a plane, bus, or train ticket to anywhere in the past couple of days. In fact, put a trace on his credit cards. I need to find him, and fast."

"I'll do what I can. I have to warn you that Jessica Gray wants in on the action. She investigated Mr. Alberti during a museum theft a few years ago. When his name came up, she was all over Cameron to get you out of the picture. She's still kicking herself for letting Alberti walk the last time."

He understood the sentiment, and ordinarily he would have been happy to bring Jessica back in, but not when she wanted him out. There was no way he was getting out. "Thanks, Trace. You know I love you."

"Yeah, yeah, you always say that when you want something. I saw her picture, you know. Christina Alberti. She's gorgeous. You're still thinking with your brain, right, Mac?"

He scratched his head, darting a quick look at Christina, who was quite openly listening to his side of the conversation. "I hope so," he muttered. He ended the call and tossed his phone onto the bed.

"That was a long conversation," Christina commented, her expression serious and worried.

"My boss wants me off the case. I'm supposed to report for a new assignment tomorrow—in LA."

She swallowed hard and pulled the edges of her robe over her bare legs. "So you need to get a flight tonight?"

"I'm not going. I'm not walking away from Evan."

She gave him a thoughtful look. "Are you in trouble because of me? I heard you tell your assistant I wasn't guilty."

"The local cops are pissed, and Barclay's is putting pressure on them. You and your father are their only suspects. They want to pin the robbery on someone. They want it to look like they're making progress in retrieving the diamond. I'm sure the press will mention your name as a person of interest. They may run your picture in the morning paper. It will be difficult for you to hide any-where in the city, or the Bay Area, for that matter."

She got up and paced around the table. "What are you saying? That I should turn myself in? If I do that, I'll never find my father or Evan. And I'm beginning to want him as badly as you do. Evan is the one who set me up. My father may have stolen the diamond, but Evan turned the spotlight on me." She paused. "Do you think they would believe you if you told them that I was innocent, that I didn't know anything?"

He wanted to reassure her, tell her he could keep her out of jail, but he hadn't lied to her before, and he couldn't start now. "I can't promise that you won't be held for questioning."

"In the meantime Evan goes after my father. My dad could be in danger."

"Yes," he agreed. "There's something else I need to tell you. There's been another death. Nicole Prescott was murdered in her apartment earlier today."

"Nicole?" Christina said with a gasp. She put a hand to her heart. "She was killed?"

"Strangled."

Christina sat down next to him. "Oh, my God. And Alexis is Nicole's cousin. One more horrible thing for her to deal with."

"That's right," he said slowly, meeting her gaze. "It's interesting, isn't it—that two of the people we had dinner with last night are both dead and both of them had a relationship with Alexis."

Christina's eyes widened with surprise. "You surely aren't suggesting Alexis killed anyone?"

"I don't think she strangled Nicole or hit David with

her car, but she's involved. Nicole and Jeremy had a relationship before Alexis came into the picture. And Jeremy had a PI following Alexis and David the last few months, a PI that Nicole had also worked with."

"Whoa, slow down. David and Alexis were having an affair?"

"It looks that way, and if Jeremy knew about it, I'd say he's suspect number one for the hit-and-run. However, it appears there may have been a connection between Nicole and Evan. She's related to one of the people involved in Evan's last con. The loose ends are starting to come together. And someone has killed two people."

"The same someone?" she queried, clearly worried.

"Maybe. The Kensingtons, Nicole, and Evan are tangled up. We have the same key players involved with the theft of the diamond."

"Adding in my father," she said. "But I don't think he was working with any of them."

"If he wasn't, he shot the hell out of their plan," J.T. said. "That would make someone very angry—angry enough to kill to protect their own secrets."

Christina stared back at him for a long moment. "Someone like who? You think you know who the killer is, don't you?"

14

Christina waited an eternity for J.T. to answer the question. Not that she needed him to say the words. She could see the answer on his face.

"Evan," J.T. said.

"Not Jeremy? If Alexis was having an affair . . ."

"I can't discount Jeremy entirely. He obviously had secrets he wanted to keep, and passion and rage can drive a man to kill."

"David perhaps, but Nicole? That wouldn't make sense, would it?"

"She might have been blackmailing him, if she knew about Alexis."

Christina pondered that scenario. Jeremy Kensington was a distinguished, smart, sophisticated businessman. Was he really capable of running a man down with a car or strangling his wife's cousin? He didn't have a warm and fuzzy personality. But just because he wasn't emotional didn't make him a killer.

Evan was a better suspect. He was a psychopath,

from what J.T. had said. He had no conscience, no boundaries, and he seemed to be pure evil. Certainly the brief encounter she'd had with him at the fun house had sent chills down her spine.

"Tracy said Nicole had a diamond collection," J.T. continued. "You know anything about that?"

"She didn't buy any of it from Barclay's," Christina answered. "I guess she wouldn't have wanted to put any money in Alexis's pocket. It's weird how Nicole was even at the dinner party last night, with so much bad blood between them."

"I don't think it was by chance. She was there for a reason."

"I agree. Something was going on last night with all of them. What I don't understand is how I became a subject of conversation for David and Alexis."

"According to Alexis, David spoke to your father."

"What? That's impossible."

"I suspect it was simply part of the setup. It would have been easy for Evan to do it. David didn't know your father personally, just his reputation. Evan used David, figuring the guy was ambitious and had an in with Alexis. That he would tell Alexis you and your father were going to steal the diamond."

"And now David is dead," she said with a heavy heart. She'd never particularly liked David, but she hadn't wanted him killed, especially since it appeared he'd been used by Evan.

J.T. stood up and grabbed his leather jacket, then headed for the door. "I need to check on something."

"You're going out?" she asked, feeling a bit unnerved by the idea. "Why? Where?"

"I can't just sit here and speculate. I know where Stefano was staying. I want to check it out."

"He wouldn't still be there."

"He might have left something behind."

"Can I come?" She felt like a clingy female when she saw the expression on his face, but couldn't take the question back. She didn't want to stay at the hotel alone. Two people had already died, both of whom she'd had dinner with the night before.

"It's not that I don't want you to come," J.T. said, "but for the moment you need to stay hidden away. There are too many people looking for you. I'll only be gone an hour—tops. You can do some research on the diamond. The time will fly by."

"Sure," she said, lacking conviction. "It will fly by."

He took her hands in his and gazed into her eyes. "I know you're scared, Christina. I also know that you're brave and strong."

"How could you possibly think that?" she murmured. "It seems I've done nothing but run for my life since I met you. That's more cowardly than brave."

"Hey, a strategic retreat is always good in a battle." He kissed her on the lips, his mouth lingering. "When I get back we'll have dessert."

"Fine. But if you're not back in exactly two hours, I'm eating the cake by myself," she warned.

"Then I will definitely not be late," he promised. "Lock the door behind me, and don't open it for anyone. Not room service wanting to take the plates—no one. And if someone tries to get in, call the front desk immediately."

His words did nothing to ease her rapidly growing

tension. Nor did the fact that he'd slipped his gun into the pocket of his jacket. Two people were dead. She did not want to make it three. She got up, putting her hand on his arm. "Be careful, J.T. I really . . . don't want to eat that cake alone." It wasn't what she wanted to say, but he knew what she meant. She gave him a pleading kiss to come back alive, then let him go, locking the door after him.

Evan picked the lock with a quick and steady hand. A moment later he opened the door to Marcus Alberti's house and paused to get his bearings. The house was spotless, as if no one had lived there in a long time. It was the kind of family house he'd always wanted for himself. As he put his hand on the sleek wood banister of the elegant staircase, he remembered the dreams he'd had as a kid living in the backseat of a car with his drunk of a mother. He'd always imagined owning a real house with a banister you could slide down, with dinner waiting on the table at six o'clock, with a father who came home carrying a newspaper, and a mother who spent her days cooking and taking care of the kids—instead of boozing and doing drugs and beating the shit out of her offspring.

He frowned, not sure why *she* was coming into his brain so often now. He'd put his mother out of his mind years ago. He'd banished her into nonexistence, which was where she belonged. She never should have been born, and certainly never should have had children. His two sisters had been the lucky ones. They'd been taken away and sent to foster homes.

No one had wanted him. He was too old, too bruised, too wrecked—by *her.* God, he hated her. And every

woman like her. Every woman who thought she was better than him, who thought he owed her. Like Nicole. The
bitch had deserved to die. He wouldn't have killed her if
she hadn't attacked him. It was her fault she was dead. It
was his mother's fault that she was dead. The world was
better off without them. He hadn't committed murder;
he'd provided a public service.

He walked down the hall and entered the study.
There were books everywhere; it was the room of an
intellectual man. He paused by the desk, picking up a
photograph of Marcus and his precious daughter,
Christina, taken at her college graduation. She was
wearing her cap and gown and looking so damn proud
of herself. The Albertis probably thought they were
smarter than him. But they weren't.

They'd just surprised him, that was all. He hadn't anticipated that Marcus would actually steal the diamond.
When Nicole had suggested they contact Marcus and
lure him back to the city because he would make a good
scapegoat, it had seemed like the perfect plan. Nicole
had assured him that Marcus would never be an actual
threat because he wouldn't do anything to put his daughter in jeopardy again. It would go against his nature not
to protect his child. Evan had believed her. Marcus had
taken the bait. They'd been able to get his voice on tape
and a sample of his handwriting, as well as his e-mail address. Everything was going like clockwork.

Until Marcus decided to steal the diamond before
they did. So much for his paternal instincts.

Evan didn't know how Marcus had pulled it off. The
only answer was that Christina had helped him. How
ironic.

Evan had set the Albertis up to take a fall for something they hadn't done, when in fact they'd actually done it. The knowledge burned through his gut. They might have outplayed him this time, but they wouldn't possess the diamond for long. He would find Marcus and get it back. Now that he knew the kind of man he was dealing with, he would be better prepared. Having Nicole as a partner had clouded his brain, kept him from realizing there was someone else in the game. That wouldn't happen again. He worked better alone.

The only question was—where the fuck were they? Obviously not here.

With a rush of impotent rage, he began yanking books off the shelf. He would destroy this perfect little family house first, and then he would destroy them.

It was remarkably easy to get into Stefano Benedetti's room at the Crestmoor Hotel, located at the top of Nob Hill. J.T. had simply flashed his badge and his smile at the female assistant night manager, and told her he needed to make sure Stefano Benedetti was all right after the disturbing robbery earlier that day. Since the theft at Barclay's was all over the news, she was more than happy to help. She escorted him straight up to the sixth floor and knocked on the door. When there was no answer, she slipped in her master key and allowed him to enter the room. "Thanks, I'll take it from here," he told her.

She looked disappointed but nodded and shut the door behind her.

J.T. wasn't surprised that Evan hadn't checked out of the hotel. That would involve paying the bill, and no doubt there was a stolen credit card on the account, probably the real Benedetti's card. Since that man was on a boat in the middle of the ocean, he probably wasn't following his credit card statements.

J.T. walked across the room and opened the closet. Several expensive suits hung on hangers as well as dress shirts and ties on the tie rack. The rest of the room was neat. He checked the bathroom and found the usual men's cologne, toothpaste, dental floss. At least Evan was taking care of his teeth.

Returning to the bedroom, he checked the bureau. In the bottom drawer he found some curious items: a flashlight that attached to a hard hat, a large white coverall that a construction worker or janitor might wear, a screwdriver and other assorted tools. Why had Evan needed all the hardware?

He sat back on his heels, considering the situation. Evan must have used the uniform to get into Barclay's, but J.T. didn't recall seeing anyone wearing such gear. Evan had to have also used the uniform to get out of Barclay's. But how? Even in a uniform, he would have been searched for the diamond.

There had to be another way in and out of Barclay's. J.T. leaned forward, digging deeper into the drawer. His fingers curled around a piece of paper. He pulled it out and was shocked to see his name scribbled across the front. He unfolded the paper. It was yellowed and obviously old. It appeared to be a blueprint, a diagram of what looked like an underground network of tunnels under the city. The streets bordered Barclay's Auction House, he realized, and the tunnels ran right under the building. Evan must have used the tunnels to get out of Barclay's with the diamond.

Was that where Evan was hiding now?

He could check out the tunnels, but since Evan had left the map behind with his name on it, he doubted there would be anything else to find. In fact, he suspected Evan wanted to send him on a wild-goose chase. That wasn't going to happen. In the long run, it didn't matter how Evan had escaped. J.T. couldn't worry about the last play. He had to concentrate on the next one. And there would be a next move, because Evan hadn't won. He didn't have the real diamond, and until he did, the game was still on.

Christina watched the clock turn to the next number. The two hours since J.T. had left had passed with interminable slowness. She was giving him three more minutes and then she was eating the cake. The only problem was . . . she was not remotely hungry. She shifted on the bed, settling herself more comfortably on the pillows, her back against the headboard, J.T.'s computer on her lap. She'd spent the past two hours researching yellow diamonds and had come up with several stones, but none that matched the Benedetti diamond. It was as if it had never existed. Only she knew that it was real. She'd seen it, held it, worn it. She'd felt it tingle against her skin.

Reaching for her purse, she pulled out her cell phone and dialed her father's cell phone number—the one he'd given her for emergencies. She didn't expect him to answer, and he didn't. But she was desperate, and she had to try something. "Dad, it's me. I got the note you left in the safe. You have to tell me where you are, or where you're going. I'm in trouble. Everyone at

Barclay's thinks I took the diamond or helped you steal it. Please just call me." She hung up the phone and let out a sigh.

The clock flipped over another digit.

She shoved the computer off her lap and stood up, moving resolutely toward the table. She picked up a fork and eyed the enormous piece of chocolate cake. "Looks like it's you and me." She cut off a chunk of cake. It was halfway to her mouth when she heard a knock at the door, followed by J.T.'s voice.

She set the fork down, then ran over to the door and turned the dead bolt. "You're late," she said as he stepped into the room. "Where have you been? What did you find out? Did you run into Evan? Are you all right?"

He put up a hand, his smile reassuring her that at least he was fine. The other answers she could wait for.

"One question at a time," he said. "I promise I'll tell you everything." He walked over to the bed and pulled his gun out of his jacket, setting it down on the dresser.

She sat down cross-legged on the bed in the middle of the comforter, waiting for him to explain. Finally he sat down. "Here's what I figured out. Evan escaped through an old aborted transit tunnel, one of several that run under the city. A long time ago there was a master plan for an extensive subway system that went beyond the scope of the current system, but too many earthquakes put an end to that grand scheme. However, a lot of the tunnels had already been started, and one ended right under Barclay's in a basement area near the garbage, an area that was not covered by a security camera."

"That's why you never saw Stefano leave on the security tapes," she said.

"Exactly. He knew he couldn't just walk out of the auction house with the stone in his pocket. There was no way he could have pulled it off without an escape route."

"Okay, so we know how he got away. What's next?" She didn't see how the information brought them any closer to catching Evan. Unless . . . "Do you think he's hiding in those tunnels?"

"No. He's too crafty to live on the street. He could easily pickpocket someone's credit card and get himself a hotel room somewhere."

"Is that it?"

His eyes narrowed. "I take it you're not impressed."

"We still don't know where Evan is or where my father is," she said in frustration.

"Did you have any luck tracing the diamond?" he asked.

"No," she said with a sigh. "I'm completely stumped. There's no mention of the Benedetti diamond anywhere on the Internet, and I couldn't find any other stones that matched the diamond's measurements or colors or flaws or anything." She flopped backward on the bed, staring up at the ceiling. "I hope the card you're using for this hotel room has a big credit limit, because we might be here awhile."

He scooted down the bed, stretching out next to her. He moved a strand of hair away from her forehead and gazed into her eyes. "We'll get the answers we need. Don't worry."

"How can I not worry? I just saw a preview of the late-night news on TV. A reporter was standing outside of Barclay's announcing they'd have news on a suspect at eleven. What if they point the public finger at me?"

"They don't have any proof, Christina."

"I tried to check my e-mail. My account was closed."

He frowned. "That wasn't a good idea. There might be a way to trace the Internet path back to us."

"I didn't even think of that. God! I feel so out of my league."

"That's why we're in this together."

"For the moment. You're supposed to report to your office in LA tomorrow or turn me in," she reminded him. "What's going to happen if you don't do either one?"

"I'm sure I'll be suspended, put on probation, maybe fired, depending on how long it takes me to bring Evan down."

He spoke pragmatically, but she could hear the underlying concern in his voice.

"It's your job, your future, your life. Maybe you should think twice about it all, J.T."

"Are you trying to get rid of me?" he asked, tracing her cheekbone.

"I'm trying to tell you that I would understand if you said you had to go to LA tomorrow. However, I have to admit that I would prefer you leave without turning me in."

He gave her a half smile at that. "I'm not leaving you. And I have other plans for tomorrow."

She raised an eyebrow. "What plans?"

"The best way to figure out where someone is going is to look at where they've been."

She sent him a questioning look. "Are you going to explain? Because my brain is too tired for riddles."

"It seems obvious to me that if your father is taking the diamond back to where it belongs, then he's no longer in the city. And if the Benedettis had the diamond, then it's a good chance that the stone originated—"

"In Italy," she said with a rush of excitement. She sat up so abruptly, she butted him in the head.

"Ouch," he said, rubbing his temple.

"Sorry. Are you saying you want to go to Italy?"

"To Florence, yes—to visit the Benedettis. They're the only ones, besides your father and Evan, who could possibly know where that stone came from."

She couldn't believe what he was saying. "Are you serious? Can I leave the country—just like that?"

"If you do it fast," he replied with a dry smile. "Since you were standing in full view of the security cameras when the diamond was stolen, it's going to take some time to build enough of a case to get sufficient cause to bring you in—especially if they can't find you. I called the airlines. There's a flight tomorrow at nine a.m. I think we should be on it."

"Are you sure? Think about it, J.T. You're taking a huge risk by leaving the country with me. Your goal is to catch Evan, isn't it? Do you even care that much about the diamond? About finding my father? About any of it—except Evan?"

"I care about the diamond because Evan cares about it," J.T. said bluntly. "Finding that stone will lead me to him. He may not have it now, but you can bet he's looking for it."

"Unless he doesn't know he has a fake," she pointed out. "We aren't certain he does."

"You're right. We don't know that for sure. But my gut tells me that Evan probably had a buyer lined up for the stone, someone who would be able to tell if it was a fake or not. Maybe that person was Nicole Prescott. And she's dead—which is a sign of something. Either Evan was done with her, or there was an unexpected glitch in their plans."

"Like a fake diamond."

"Yes. Evan knew enough about your father to set him up. If he figures out that he has a fake, it won't take that big a leap for him to conclude that your father has the real diamond. I think the trail leads to Florence. The real question is, who is going to find your father first, Evan—or us?"

"It had better be us," she said, afraid for her father. She might be angry with him, but she didn't want anything bad to happen to him. And Evan seemed to have no qualms about committing murder.

J.T. nodded. "So are you with me?"

"I'm with you."

"Now that we have that settled, how about some dessert?"

"I must admit the chocolate cake looks really good now."

He put a hand on her shoulder and pushed her back down on the bed. "I wasn't talking about cake," he said with a wicked grin that sent a shiver of anticipation down her spine.

"You don't really think your kiss is going to make me want you instead of that chocolate cake, do you?" she teased, her heart already feeling lighter now that they had a plan of action.

"I'm going to give it one hell of a try, sweetheart."

15

Evan had known Christina would return to her apartment. It was just a matter of time. It wasn't his usual choice to spend the night in a car, but he hadn't wanted to take a chance on missing her.

She'd come in the dusky light before dawn, probably hoping to avoid notice. The police were looking for her—he'd seen several patrol cars go by in the past few hours—but she wasn't a big enough fish, nor was it a heinous enough crime to put her apartment under twenty-four-hour surveillance. She was being careful, though. So was J.T. They'd hid out somewhere the night before; he'd checked J.T.'s hotel room as well.

But they were here now. Christina parked her car in a space directly in front of her building. J.T. pulled in behind her. Evan had figured that J.T. would be with her. He loved to play the protector, the defender of justice, the pursuer of the truth, especially when a beautiful woman was watching. When they were in college J.T. had always been the big man on campus, the star quarterback, the guy with the girls. But he wasn't such a superstar now. He was in big trouble, aiding and abetting a thief, Evan thought with a smile.

He considered confronting them in Christina's apartment. He was impatient to get the diamond, to rectify his mistakes, to reestablish his superiority. But he was too smart to make an impatient blunder. Christina didn't have what he wanted—the diamond. He would have to be patient, let her lead him to it. And she would; he was convinced of that.

They emerged from the building a few minutes later. Christina had changed into jeans and a sweater and was carrying an overnight bag. They were obviously taking a trip, Evan thought with satisfaction. They were going after her father. He was sure of it.

Starting the ignition, he waited until they had turned the corner before following them. He caught sight of their car at the stop sign and maintained a discreet distance behind them. His adrenaline began to surge as they got on the freeway heading south. Twenty minutes later J.T. pulled into the parking lot of the San Francisco International Airport. Evan did the same. He retrieved his own small bag from the trunk and meandered along, keeping several people in between them at all times. J.T. looked over his shoulder more than once. So did Christina. But they didn't recognize him. He wasn't Stefano anymore; nor was he Evan Chadwick. Today he was Mitchell Holloway, a fifty-something, red-haired male, dressed in a cheap brown suit with a coat that barely covered his paunch. He was also a frequent-flyer business traveler, who was on every airline's preferred customer list.

He adjusted his dark glasses as J.T. and Christina made their way into the ticket line at the international terminal. He took a look at the departure board and smiled with pleasure. They were going to Florence, Italy. Well, why the hell not? It made perfect sense. He took out his wallet, his new credit card, and his fake passport. Mitchell Holloway would be traveling to Florence as well, and he was going first class.

It was the longest day of Christina's life. Sixteen stressful hours on a plane wondering if she'd be arrested during the long layover in Frankfurt or when they eventually landed in Florence had permanently knotted the muscles in her shoulders and neck. Luckily everything had gone uneventfully, and as they hailed a taxi just after four o'clock Sunday afternoon, an entire day later than when they had left, she finally began to breathe easier.

As the taxi pulled away from the curb, she rolled down her window, eager to get some fresh air and to catch her first glimpse of Florence. It was a beautiful sunny spring afternoon with a royal blue sky and not a hint of a cloud in sight. The road into town weaved through hillsides dotted with cypress and olive trees, and as they neared the city she saw the red-gold roofs of Florence. Her heart skipped a beat. She had been to Rome but never to Florence. Her father had always steered clear of the city in which his own grandfather had been born. She'd asked him many times to take her to the cottage in Tuscany where he used to spend his childhood summers, but Marcus had always come up with an excuse why they couldn't go. Now she was here, and she leaned forward in her seat, eager to soak in the atmosphere.

"You look like a kid in a candy store," J.T. commented, stroking her thigh.

She gave him a quick smile, feeling a renewed sense of energy now that they were finally in Italy. "I'm excited. I can't help it. I'm an art historian. For me, Italy is my candy store."

"I can't believe you've never been here."

"Me either. Florence has so much history, so many famous artists, cultural icons—Michelangelo, Donatello, Brunelleschi . . . and let's not forget Botticelli and Leonardo da Vinci," she added with a wave of her hand.

"We also can't forget that we're here to find your father and that diamond, remember?"

"I know why we're here," she said with a sigh. "But I can still enjoy the scenery, can't I? It's so beautiful. It's like another world. I almost feel as if I've escaped my life, left all my problems back home."

"Perhaps momentarily, but I don't think Evan is far behind us. In fact, he may already be here."

She shot him a disappointed look. "Can't you forget about Evan for one second and just look at where we are?" She gestured toward the view. "Tell me this doesn't get to you just a little."

Dark glasses covered J.T.'s eyes, but she could see the smile on his lips. "Okay, it's nice," he said. "What do you want from me?"

"I know you're a passionate man. Surely you can do better than 'nice,' " she teased.

"Scenery doesn't turn me on, Christina—you do." He leaned in and stole a quick, tender kiss.

Her pulse pounded at the brief but intimate contact that always left her wanting more. J.T. was fast becoming an addiction—and one that she was in no hurry to break. She'd grown accustomed to having him at her side. In fact, when he wasn't there, she felt as if some part of her were missing. She didn't know how it had happened, how he'd gotten so close to her in such a short time. She'd spent most of her life afraid to get involved with a man, knowing that there were secrets in her life she couldn't share. But J.T. knew all her secrets. That particular barrier no longer divided them. Not that they were having a relationship, she reminded herself. Whatever this was—it wasn't that. Was it?

She turned her gaze back toward the view, knowing that she had far more important things to worry about than love. But right now all she wanted to do was gaze at the red-gold roofs of the city, the winding Arno River that meandered through town under the famous Ponte Vecchio bridge.

The narrow brick streets were filled with a mix of old and new buildings. Stern, forbidding palaces and government buildings abutted boutiques, cafés, and bakeries. The Florentines loved their statues. Everywhere she turned she could see sculptures, especially in the Palazzo Vecchio, where a valiant line of heroes greeted them, including Cosimo I on horseback by Giambologna, a copy of the David by Michelangelo, and Hercules by Bandinelli. Oh, how she longed to explore the city, but first things first, she reminded herself.

The taxi pulled up in front of their hotel, located in a reconstructed sixth-century Byzantine tower and medieval church set in a small, quiet square in Florence's center. J.T. had left the hotel booking decision to her, and she hadn't been able to resist getting a room in such a historically interesting building. Someday she would have to figure out how she was going to pay for it all, but at the moment J.T. seemed content to keep charging on his government credit card.

After asking the taxi to wait, they checked into the hotel, dumped their bags, and headed back out the door. They hoped to catch up to Vittorio Benedetti before evening. They'd already called the house and had been told that Signor Benedetti was not receiving visitors, but they weren't about to let some housekeeper or personal assistant turn them away. Hopefully J.T.'s badge would convince someone to let them in.

The Benedettis' palatial home was set on a narrow street of equally forbidding cold stone mansions. A wrought-iron gate met them at the entrance. There was a definite change of mood in this part of town, one that was not at all welcoming.

Christina felt her tension return as J.T. opened the gate and stepped inside to ring the bell. She had no idea how they would be received or what the Benedettis knew about her and/or the diamond theft. Was Vittorio aware that someone had been impersonating his son Stefano? Or was he still in the dark about that? It was more than likely her name had come up, so she and J.T. had already decided that she would play the role of his assistant, Tracy Delgado, for this meeting, so as not to send Vittorio rushing to the phone to call the local police.

J.T. rang the bell again. Christina shivered. The sun was beginning to go down, and the tall buildings sent dark shadows down the street where they stood. "I don't have a good feeling about this," she muttered.

J.T.'s mouth drew into a grim line. "I don't either. But I'm not leaving until I talk to someone."

A moment later the door opened. An older woman wearing a black dress with an apron tied around her thick waist appeared in the doorway. Her hair was gray and pulled back severely from her wrinkled face. She glanced first at J.T. and said, *"Buona sera."* When she turned to Christina, her black eyes widened; her breath quickened. "Isabella," she proclaimed. She put a hand to her heart and then sank to the floor in a dead faint.

"Oh, my God!" Christina gasped, exchanging a quick look with J.T. "What happened?"

J.T. knelt next to the woman. "She's still breathing, but she's unconscious."

"What should we do? Should we call someone? We can't just leave her here."

"Shut the door. At least we're in the house," J.T. said in a matter-of-fact voice.

"We can't just wander around," she protested as she closed the door.

J.T. stood up and moved into the center of a grand rotunda with a marble floor, an enormous chandelier hanging from a twelve-foot ceiling, and a sweeping staircase leading up the stairs.

"We need to find help," he said. "Don't we?"

"Yes, but—"

"Don't worry. This is perfect. We have a great excuse for being inside." He walked over to the stairs and called out, "Hello? Anyone here?"

A moment later a young woman came running down

the stairs. She appeared to be in her midtwenties and was wearing a black dress similar to that of the woman who was on the floor. Christina thought she was probably a maid and was surprised when the woman called out, "Mama," and came flying down the rest of the stairs.

"She fainted," Christina explained. "We rang the bell, and she answered the door and then she just went down."

The younger woman knelt beside her mother and patted her gently on the cheek. The older woman began to stir. She blinked her eyes open, her expression still dazed.

"Non le e successo niente?" her daughter asked.

The woman looked at Christina and her eyes widened again. She spit out a sentence in rapid Italian. Christina caught only two words: *Isabella* and *Vittorio*.

"What did she say?" Christina asked the younger woman, hoping she spoke English.

"She said you must go now, please."

The older woman sat up with her daughter's help. She couldn't seem to take her eyes off Christina.

"Can we help?" Christina asked. "Can we get your mother a doctor?"

"She'll be all right. Please, you must leave. No one is supposed to be in the house."

Christina glanced back at the older woman. "Do you speak English?"

For a moment she thought the woman didn't understand her, but then she nodded and said, *"Si.* Yes," she amended.

"May I speak to you for a moment?"

"Help me up," the woman said to her daughter. With some effort, she got to her feet and smoothed down her apron and dress.

She looked embarrassed and worried, Christina thought. Why on earth had the woman fainted?

"We're looking for Signor Benedetti," J.T. interrupted, striding back to join them. "Is he home?"

"The signore does not have visitors," the older woman said, her voice less shaky now. "If you leave your name, I will give him a message."

"It's too important for a message," J.T. said. "I'm with the FBI. I'm here regarding the theft of an extremely valuable diamond that belonged to Signor Benedetti. I'm sure he would want to speak with me. Please let him know I'm here."

The older woman hesitated. Finally she nodded. "Very well, but only you, signore," she said in thickly accented English.

"But I'm with him," Christina protested. "We're partners."

The older woman shook her head. "You will come with me. I will make you tea. We will go into the garden. You will wait."

Christina frowned, not at all happy to be relegated to the position of having tea while J.T. met with Vittorio. Still, it seemed to be all or nothing. She glanced at J.T., who nodded, encouraging her to go with the housekeeper. Maybe it was better if they split up. She might be able to get some information from the woman. "All right," she said. "I'll have tea."

"Francesca will take you upstairs," the housekeeper told J.T., and then motioned for Christina to follow her down the hall. She led Christina through a door that opened onto a central courtyard. Christina was surprised to see a beautiful and colorful garden. The house itself was so strong and imposing, so very masculine, that this feminine oasis seemed completely out of place.

She sat down at a table while the housekeeper excused herself to make tea. As Christina waited, she couldn't help wondering why she had been barred from the meeting upstairs. She looked up, noting the pulled curtains on the upstairs windows. Who else lived in this house besides Vittorio and the two women? She knew there was another Benedetti brother besides Stefano. Did he live here as well? It was an awfully big house for so few people. A rather sad house, she thought, except for this little garden. She'd felt the coldness the minute she stepped through the front door, an air of grief perhaps. She knew one of Vittorio's sons had died a few months earlier. Or maybe the sadness was caused by something else, something more mysterious, even sinister.

Had the old woman recognized her and perhaps put in a call to the local police? Was that why the woman had fainted? Perhaps the Benedettis had been alerted that she and her father were suspected in the diamond theft—perhaps they'd been given photographs of both of them. Christina jumped to her feet, suddenly swamped with fear. Should she stay and see what was coming or run for her life?

J.T. waited in the upstairs hallway for Francesca, who had disappeared into a room a few minutes earlier. He hoped she would not come back with a negative answer. He wanted to speak to Vittorio Benedetti face-to-face. His instincts told him that it could be a very important meeting, and one that would hopefully put him on the trail to finding Marcus and Evan.

Francesca returned a moment later. "Signor Benedetti will see you," she told him, motioning him inside. "But only for a few minutes. He is ill, you know. He must rest."

The master bedroom was designed for a king with large, heavy, masculine furniture, a big chest of drawers, a thick carpet on the floor, paintings on the walls, and a sitting area in one corner of the room. Vittorio Benedetti was seated in a chair by the window. His casual clothes hung on his long, thin frame. His hair was white, and his face had the strong, angular planes of a haughty eagle. He might be sick, but he still had a commanding presence. For a moment J.T. almost felt as if he were in the presence of royalty.

Vittorio waved him forward with an impatient hand. "Francesca said you have information about the diamond."

"Yes. My name is J. T. McIntyre. I'm a special agent with the FBI." He extended his hand to Vittorio, who gave him a surprisingly strong handshake. He took a seat in the armchair across from Vittorio.

"What can you tell me about my diamond?" Vittorio asked. "That fool Murano says it was stolen right in front of his face."

"That's true," J.T. admitted. "Did Mr. Murano also tell you that someone has been impersonating your son

Stefano at the auction house? He is a well-known con artist who often goes by the name Evan Chadwick."

Vittorio's gaze sharpened. "That explains why Signor Murano kept telling me that Stefano was in San Francisco. I told him that Stefano was not in the States, but he insisted I was mistaken. He said he had seen identification, that the man he spoke to was the spitting image of my son, but it appears that Signor Murano was mistaken."

"The disguise was very good," J.T. said.

"And this con man has my diamond?"

J.T. cleared his throat. "No, actually, I don't believe he does. It's a complicated situation, but I believe the person who stole the diamond is here in Florence, and that it wasn't greed that drove the theft, but rather a desire to put the stone back where it belongs."

"Where it belongs?" Vittorio echoed in amazement, his thick brows drawing into a tight line. "It belongs to me. Who is this person of which you speak?"

J.T. hesitated, not sure he wanted to turn up the heat on Christina's father, but he didn't have time to mince words. Besides that, he suspected that Vittorio had already been completely briefed on Barclay's list of suspects. "Marcus Alberti."

Vittorio's face turned to stone, and a white fury filled his eyes, but he didn't appear surprised, just angry. "Marcus Alberti stole my diamond?"

"Yes, but you already knew that, didn't you?"

Vittorio gave him a hard look. "How did he do it? How did he steal my stone?"

"It appears he had a copy made and was able to

switch the real thing with the fake without anyone knowing."

"Not even his daughter?" Vittorio asked sharply.

J.T. would have preferred to omit Christina's involvement in the matter, but apparently that wasn't going to be possible. "Not even her. Do you know Mr. Alberti?"

"I have heard of him."

"Really? I understand he spent some time here in Florence. Do you have any idea, if he were here, where he might be?"

Vittorio stared back at him for a long, tense minute. "No."

J.T. didn't believe him. He was lying. Why? Had the Benedettis stolen the diamond themselves? Had Marcus been telling the truth when he told Christina that the Benedettis had switched the diamond before it had ever gone to Barclay's? Were they all on the wrong track?

He caught Vittorio watching him. The speculative look on the old man's face suggested he was waiting for J.T. to say something or reveal something. What?

"Can you tell me anything about who owned the diamond before it came into your family?" J.T. asked, trying to find another way to get to the heart of the matter. "Mr. Alberti said something about putting the stone back where it belongs."

"It belongs to me," Vittorio repeated, not a hint of doubt in his voice.

"Well, let's just say for argument's sake that hundreds of years ago it was taken from somewhere. It's my understanding that the diamond dates back to the fifteenth century. If that were the case, where else might it belong?"

"I cannot help you," Vittorio said.

"I'm sorry to hear that." J.T. paused. "I should warn you that I'm not the only one looking for the diamond. Besides law enforcement, the con man who originally intended to steal the stone is also after it. If there's anything you can tell me to help me get to Marcus first, it would be better for all of us. This man, Evan Chadwick, already impersonated Stefano. That means he knew enough about your family to be able to get Stefano's identification and to pass himself off as your son. He is dangerous and he is crazy. And he is not to be taken lightly."

"Are you implying that Stefano is in trouble?"

"It's possible." J.T. felt it was important for Vittorio to realize the potential danger to his family.

"No," Vittorio said with a negative shake of his head. He stared down at his clasped hands for a long moment. Then he lifted his gaze. "Is there anything else you can tell me?"

J.T. was disappointed by his cool response. "You should try to contact Stefano. Sometimes when Evan steals an identity, people end up dead." He got to his feet. "I'm staying at the Brunischelli Hotel in town. Call me if you feel inclined to talk." He turned to leave.

"Wait," Vittorio said in his imperious voice. He waved him back into the chair. "There is more I can tell you."

*   *   *

The herbal tea was delicious. Christina took a sip of the hot brew and glanced across the table at the house-keeper, who had introduced herself as Maria. Once it had become clear to Christina that Maria had not called the police and that they were simply going to have tea, she had started to relax. Perhaps she could get some information out of the housekeeper before J.T. returned. Sometimes the hired help knew more about a family than anyone.

"This is very good," she said. *"Grazie."*

Maria nodded. "What is your name?"

Christina opened her mouth to give the cover story she and J.T. had agreed upon, but the words didn't want to come out. "Christina," she said simply.

Maria lifted her teacup to her lips and took a drink.

"Have you worked for Signor Benedetti for a long time?" Christina queried.

"Si. For almost forty years."

"You must know him very well. What's he like?"

Shadows filled Maria's eyes. "The signore is a hard man. He lost his heart a long time ago. He never found it again."

Well, that was certainly a cryptic statement. Christina waited for Maria to explain, but she didn't. Christina decided to change the subject. "What happened when you answered the door, Maria? Did we startle you? You seemed surprised to see us—actually me," she corrected. "Why?"

"I . . . just felt dizzy," she said with a flutter of her fingers. "Would you like a cookie?"

"No, thank you." Christina frowned. "You said a name

right before you fainted. *Isabella.* Isn't that the name of Vittorio's wife, the one who died a long time ago?"

Maria slowly nodded. "*Si.* She died many years ago. I was her childhood nurse. I was with her from the day she was born. I came to live here after she married, to help her raise her children. When she was gone, I had to do it without her. This house has never been the same. The life went out of it." She gestured toward the garden. "This was her special place. I keep it for her— in her memory."

That explained why the beautiful garden seemed so at odds with the air of cold grief that lingered in the house. However, Maria's rambling did not explain why she had fainted when she'd seen Christina.

"What is your last name, Christina?"

Maria's abrupt question made her nerves begin to tingle. "Why do you want to know? What's going on?" Christina asked. "You wanted to talk to me alone, didn't you? That's why you sent J.T. upstairs without me."

The housekeeper's gaze didn't waver. "What is your last name?"

Christina hesitated for a long moment, then said, "Alberti."

A pulse jumped in Maria's throat. Her hand shook as she set her cup down on the saucer so hard that some of the liquid spilled over the side.

"You know my name," Christina said. "You know my father, don't you? How do you know him?"

"I knew Marcus a long time ago," Maria answered. "He was a young man then—a friend of Isabella's."

A shiver shot down Christina's spine. Her father was a friend of Isabella's, Vittorio's wife? And Vittorio

Benedetti had sent his collection to Barclay's, where Christina just happened to work? That seemed an unlikely coincidence. What was the tie between Vittorio and her father?

"I'm actually trying to find my father," she said. "I think he might have information about the diamond that Signor Benedetti sent to San Francisco to be sold at auction. Do you have any idea where my father might stay here in Florence?"

"He used to stay at his family's farmhouse, a few miles outside of town. Perhaps you would find him there." Maria let out a breath. "You don't know, do you, Christina?"

"Know what?" she asked, chilled to the core by the ominous tone in Maria's voice. "What don't I know?"

16

J.T. waited for Vittorio to continue, but the man seemed to have lost his voice. Finally he said, "I spoke to Stefano this morning after I talked to Signor Murano. I alerted him to the fact that someone has been impersonating him. He will be back in a few days, but he is alive and well."

"Good. I'm happy to hear that."

"I am confused as to why you believe this con man would be a danger to me if he doesn't have the diamond."

"He's looking for it," J.T. replied. "And you would be one step on the path to finding it. If Evan believes he can find Marcus Alberti through you, he will. It wasn't difficult for me to get into your house today. It would be even easier for him."

"I will make arrangements to correct that," Vittorio said.

J.T. nodded approvingly. "Now, will you please tell me what you know about the diamond, because I believe its history will ultimately provide the key to learning where it is now and to getting it back. I assume that's what you want."

"I don't want the diamond back," Vittorio said shortly, surprising J.T. "The stone is cursed. That's why I chose to sell it." He paused, and a grim smile crossed his lips. "I can see that you don't believe in curses. I felt the same way for most of my life, but too many accidents, too many deaths, too many unexplained diseases have made me a believer."

"I see. So you sent the cursed diamond to Barclay's to be sold to some unsuspecting buyer."

Vittorio shrugged. "What is that expression you use in America—'Let the buyer beware'?"

"Right, let the buyer beware. Only, you're not telling me the whole story." J.T. paused, thinking about what he'd learned. "You know Marcus Alberti. And you've heard of his daughter, Christina. You knew she worked at Barclay's. Was this a setup from the beginning? Did you want Marcus to steal the diamond? Was that the plan?"

"Don't be a fool. I wanted the money from the sale."

"I don't think that's all you wanted," J.T. said.

Vittorio returned his gaze "That's true. I also wanted Christina to touch the diamond before it was sold to remove the curse from my family."

"How could Christina remove the curse?"

"Her bloodline goes back to Catherine de Médici, the woman who cursed the stone. I believed that if Christina wore the diamond, since she is a descendant of Catherine's, it would remove the curse from me. Added insurance, so to speak."

"Why didn't you tell Christina the story before you sent the diamond to Barclay's?"

"I didn't want her any more involved," Vittorio said, his tone ice-cold. "She was to wear the diamond and then to sell it."

"But whoever bought the diamond would still be cursed," J.T. pointed out. "Because they wouldn't have the right blood running through their veins."

"That was not my concern," he said.

Vittorio Benedetti was a ruthless businessman. J.T. could see that plain as day. The rest of his story was a muddy mess. Clearly, J.T. was still missing something. "What aren't you telling me, Signor Benedetti? Because I suspect there's more."

"What don't I know?" Christina repeated.

Maria stared back at her. "Forgive me. It is nothing. I should not have spoken. Do you wish more tea? A cookie? I wonder what is taking your friend so long?"

"Maria, please. You asked me a question, and I need to understand why. You know something about me, about my father. You have to tell me what it is."

"He would never forgive me." Maria clasped her hands together on top of the table, twisting her fingers in agitation.

"Who? My father?"

Maria shook her head. "No, Signor Benedetti. He made me promise. And I have kept that promise for many years."

Christina searched desperately for a way to make Maria talk. She suspected that whatever secret Maria was keeping was in some way important to her and to her father. She decided to go for broke and confide in Maria, throw herself on the old woman's mercy.

"Please, Maria. My father is missing, and he's in terrible trouble. I think he stole the diamond. He told me that it didn't belong to Vittorio, that he had to take it back to where it was supposed to be. The police are after him, and me as well. If there's something you know that can help me understand any of this, I would be forever in your debt."

Maria pursed her lips together. Her gaze roamed across Christina's face. "Come with me," she said abruptly, rising to her feet.

"Where are we going?"

Maria didn't answer. She led Christina into the house, down the long hall, and through the arched doorway leading into the living room.

"If anyone asks, you came in here on your own. You found out by yourself," Maria said. "You understand?"

Christina nodded, feeling the knot of fear in her stomach grow bigger.

The housekeeper stopped in front of a large framed photograph on the wall. It was a family portrait, a man and a woman and their three sons. The Benedettis, Christina realized. But as her gaze zeroed in on the woman in the picture, her heart came to a crashing stop.

"Isabella," Maria said, pointing her finger at the woman in the photograph.

"Oh, my God!" Christina clapped a hand to her mouth to prevent herself from screaming. How could it be? The woman in the picture looked exactly like her. It was as if she were gazing into a mirror. No wonder Maria had fainted when she'd seen her. She'd thought she was Isabella come back from the dead.

"Isabella died a year after that photograph was taken," Maria said. "The boys were so young, Stefano only ten, Frances eight, and Daniel, the baby, five."

"I don't understand." Christina shook her head, trying to clear her brain, trying to make sense of what she was seeing.

"You didn't know?" Maria asked again, her gaze locking with Christina's. "Your father didn't tell you? All these years—he never said a word?"

"A word about what?"

"Your mother."

Christina immediately began shaking her head. "I don't have a mother. She left when I was a baby. And her name was Rose," she added desperately, latching on to the one fact that she had about her mother's identity.

"Isabella Rose." Maria pointed again at the woman in the picture. "She is your mother."

"No. No." Christina began backing away. "That's not true."

"They met in the library," Maria continued. "Isabella loved books and art. She was a smart girl, but she had married Vittorio when she was eighteen years old. She couldn't attend the university, as she wished. So every afternoon when the boys would attend school or take their naps, she would go to the library in town. She met him there—your father. She told me they started out sharing coffee, but their relationship quickly progressed. She was starving for love, for affection. Vittorio didn't provide either."

"No!" Christina clapped her hands over her ears, but she could still hear Maria.

"Your father was so passionate. He swept her off her

feet. Then the summer ended and he went home, to America. She didn't realize she was carrying his child until he was gone."

Christina shook her head, her eyes blurring with angry, disbelieving tears. Her mother was not Isabella Benedetti. She was not the result of her father having an affair with a married woman. It wasn't possible. It was wrong—so wrong. "No," she said again, but the word came out weak, unconvincing.

Maria gently pulled Christina's hands away from her ears. "Yes, it is true. Isabella is your mother."

"I can't listen to this," Christina said, turning on her heel. She ran to the front door and yanked it open. She pushed through the gate and tore down the street, not sure where she was going. She just knew she had to get away from the house, from the past, from the secrets, from the lies. What was true? What wasn't true? She had no idea anymore.

J.T. sprinted down the street after Christina. He couldn't believe how fast she was moving even in a pair of high-heeled sandals. She was running like the wind, as if her life was in jeopardy. What the hell had happened to her? He'd come down the stairs from Vittorio's room just in time to see the front door slam. He'd given Maria a questioning look, and she'd simply shrugged, but she'd looked guilty as hell. Had Christina learned something about her father?

"Christina!" he yelled. "Wait up."

Christina didn't slow down or even turn her head. She gave no indication that she'd heard him at all. As she reached an intersection he felt a rush of panic. A car was coming down the street, and Christina was paying no attention. A shot of adrenaline urged him forward. He grabbed her arm, yanking her out of the way just in time. She stumbled and almost fell to her knees. He caught her around the waist. He could feel the heat of the car as it blew past them just inches from their bodies. The driver gave an angry honk on his horn, then sped away.

Christina stared up at him in bewilderment, raw pain in her big green eyes. She looked as if someone had just killed her puppy, told her Santa Claus didn't exist, done something to destroy what was left of her innocence.

"What the hell happened to you?" he demanded, his hands tightening on her arms.

She couldn't seem to hear him. His words weren't registering in her brain. It was as if she'd lost herself in her own head. He gave her shoulders another little shake. "Dammit, Christina, talk. You're scaring the shit out of me."

Her eyes slowly began to clear. She blinked and her gaze came back into focus. "What . . . what happened?"

"That's what I want to know. You just ran in front of a car. You almost got yourself killed." He skimmed his hands up and down her arms, feeling the need to reassure himself that she was still in one piece. Even through her sweater he could feel the chill in her bones. Whatever she'd learned had left her ice-cold. "Let's walk," he said. "You can catch your breath. Then you'll tell me everything that happened."

He put his arm around her and they began to walk. Her gait was awkward. She leaned heavily on him, as if she wasn't sure she could make it on her own. She didn't ask where they were going, and he didn't care.

He just wanted to get her blood moving, give her a chance to walk off the panic that had sent her rushing headlong into traffic.

One block turned into another and another. They left the residential area and drew closer to the historic center of the city. He knew Christina still wasn't feeling right, because she made no comment about the beautiful architecture or the statues or anything. Her mind was somewhere else—somewhere frightening. He wanted to bring her back, but he didn't know the right words. He'd never been good at reading women's emotions. When he tried to guess, he usually guessed wrong. Not that it took much guessing to figure out that whatever Christina had learned from Maria had completely upset her world. It had to be about her father. What the hell had Marcus Alberti done now?

The streets grew more crowded as they neared some popular restaurants and bars. Christina seemed to wince at the noise, the people, so he walked her toward the river. It was quieter there. Night was falling on Florence, and the rising moon was reflected in the silver waters of the Arno. A street performer sat on the cement ledge that ran along the river, strumming love songs on his guitar.

Christina paused, the music bringing her out of her reverie. He watched her face as she listened to the song, and saw not just pain in her expression but anger as well. At least she was coming back to life. That was a good sign.

"What's wrong?" he asked quietly. "Can you tell me now?"

"Love is what's wrong," she said, with a frustrated

wave of her hand. "People like that guy who play love songs and pretend that love is the most wonderful thing of all, but it's just a crock of lies. Love creates nothing but problems. It's crap, that's what it is," she added loudly.

The guitar player shot her a pissed-off look, and J.T. quickly urged her farther down the street. "Could you be more specific, Christina? I don't think you and Maria just talked about love."

"We did talk about love. That's exactly what we talked about." She met his gaze for the first time. "Actually, I'm wrong. It wasn't love we were talking about. It was lust. You know what lust is, right?"

"I've got a pretty good idea," he said, almost afraid to speak. She was definitely on a roll now.

"Maria wanted to separate us, you know—you and me. It was deliberate on her part. She wanted to know who I was, my name, my age, my father's name. And you want to know why?" she challenged.

"I really do."

"Because I'm the spitting image of Isabella Benedetti—that's why." Christina paused, her eyes suddenly bright with tears. "She was my mother, J.T. Isabella and my father had an affair." Her voice broke. "She was my mother."

Her words shocked him to the core. He didn't know what he'd been expecting, but it certainly hadn't been that. "Are you sure?"

"Yes. That's why Maria fainted when she saw me," Christina replied. "It was as if she were looking at a ghost. Once her head cleared and she figured out I wasn't a phantom, there was only one other conclusion she could come to—that I was Isabella's daughter."

He blew out an amazed breath. "That's a hell of a secret."

"You can say that again."

"So Isabella was married to Vittorio—"

"When she slept with my father," Christina finished bitterly. "That's right, J.T. I'm the daughter of a thief and an adulteress. Maybe I could put that on the résumé for my next job, whatever that is, since I doubt anyone in the art world will ever hire me again. Who could blame them? I have such an incredible pedigree."

He frowned. "Okay, slow down. Back up. How did they even meet each other?"

Christina turned and looked out at the river. "Maria said they met in the library. My father swept Isabella off her feet. It was a summer thing. Apparently Isabella wasn't happy with her husband, so she and my father had an affair. Then my dad went back to the States and Isabella discovered she was pregnant. I have no idea how I came to grow up with my father instead of her—I assume she didn't want me. I guess that part of the story that my father told me was true. My mother didn't want me."

J.T. moved in behind her, slipping his arms around her waist. "You don't know that," he murmured.

"I know enough. My father is a liar and a cheat. He has no morals. My mother is—was—apparently the same way. And look at me. . . ." She turned in his arms to face him. "I've spent my whole life covering up and protecting my father. Why? Why did I do that? How could I be so blind? The evidence was right there in front of me. He's a . . . jerk."

J.T. let out a sigh, knowing there was probably nothing he could say that would make her feel better, but he found himself wanting to try. "Your father loved you. You told me about the great times you had—that it was just the two of you. He wasn't lying and cheating the whole time, Christina."

"Yes, he was. He was stealing when I was a little girl. He called them games. He said we were playing, but I know now that I was probably just his cover story. No one would ever suspect a man and his little daughter of being thieves."

It disturbed him to hear the disillusionment in her voice. Christina wasn't a cynic. She wasn't hard and bitter. She was passionate, romantic, generous, and hopeful. Since he'd first met her she'd never given up believing that somehow everything would work out. That she'd find a way to make it right. But now she was completely defeated. She'd lost her spirit. She'd lost herself. He rubbed her shoulders. Her muscles were so tight he could feel the hard knots.

"I should turn myself in," Christina said. "Call it quits. If they find my father and arrest him, whatever, I don't care."

"Of course you care. And you're not guilty of anything."

"Aren't I? I knew there was something wrong with the diamond, and I didn't do anything to stop Barclay's from trying to sell it. I knew my father was in town, and I hid it from everyone, including you."

"Okay, knock it off. I know you're hurt and furious, and you want to blow everything and everyone off, but I'm not going to let you throw your life away just like that."

"I'm tired," she said, with a dispirited shake of her

head. "I don't know where my father is. I don't know how to find him. It's probably too late anyway."

"We have to try. Evan is still out there, and he'll use you to get to your father whether you think your father will come running to your aid or not. We have to finish this. We can't stop now. Come on, babe, we're a team. Don't quit on me."

She gazed into his eyes. "You can go on without me. You can do it by yourself."

A week ago he would have agreed with her. In fact, a week ago he would have preferred to be on his own. But somewhere along the way things had changed. He couldn't let her go, not now, anyway. "We're in this together," he said firmly. "We're partners. Where I go, you go. Got it?"

"I don't know," she murmured.

"Sure you do."

"You're a stubborn man, you know that?" she said with annoyance.

"I've been called worse."

"Don't you worry that we're too involved, that there's a conflict of interest?" she asked, her gaze locking with his. "I know you're already in hot water because of me. It's only going to get worse the longer we stay together."

She was absolutely right. Even if he brought in Evan, even if he got the diamond back and cleared Christina's name, there would be a price to pay, but it was too late anyway. Whatever happened with his job, he could handle it—as long as he stopped Evan. That was the most important thing of all.

"I'll worry about that later," he told her. "Let's get

some food. I think we'll both feel better after we eat.
You wanted to see some of Florence. Here's your
chance. We'll get ourselves an authentic Florentine
dinner and regroup. What do you say?"

"I don't know."

"Come on. I know you must be hungry."

"I guess—a little."

He kissed the frown off her mouth. "Trust me,
Christina. At least about dinner."

"I do. I do trust you," she said, meeting his gaze.
"You're the only one I trust. Don't let me down."

"I won't," he said, knowing he would do everything
he could to keep that promise.

Christina hadn't thought she'd be able to eat a bite.
The tension of the day had put a knot in her throat the
size of a golf ball, but the festive atmosphere of the
restaurant helped her to relax. J.T. had outdone himself
with the ordering, and when the tagliolini in a delicate
creamy lemon sauce arrived, Christina's mouth began
to water and her stomach grumbled that it was about
time she ate something. The mixed fried vegetables
were equally delicious, and the Chianti slid down her
throat far too easily. The idea of getting too drunk to
think seemed appealing, but she'd never been much of
a drinker, and one glass of wine was already making
her head spin, which made her realize the last thing she
needed was more head spinning.

As she finished eating, she glanced over at J.T., noting the smile playing across his lips, the knowing
gleam in his eyes. "You're looking awfully satisfied
with yourself."

"I am satisfied," he replied.

"You were right about the food. I needed a good meal."

"That's not why I'm satisfied."

"Then what is making you smile?"

"You. You're back. And I'm very happy to see you." He leaned forward, resting his arms on the table. "You were like a zombie before. You almost got yourself killed, running into the street that way. You scared the crap out of me."

The worry in his brown eyes, the fact that he'd admitted he was scared, touched her deeply. "I'm sorry. I was in shock."

"I know. But next time run to me, not away from me."

"I haven't had anyone to run to in a long time. I'm not sure I know how to do that. And frankly, I'm a little surprised you'd suggest it. You don't seem the type to want anyone to cling to you."

"I want to keep you safe. It's my job," he added.

"Sure, your job, right. That's all it is, isn't it?" She searched his eyes, wishing she could read his expression better, but he was very good at hiding his feelings.

"Let's not do this," he said. "There's too much going on to get into . . ."

"Into us?" she queried when he didn't finish his sentence.

"Yeah," he said, lifting his glass to his lips. He took his time drinking the wine. He was probably hoping she'd change the subject.

"I'm not asking you for anything," she told him.

"I know."

"Okay, good." She played with her fork, frustrated

and restless with the conversation she wanted to have but couldn't because J.T. had thrown up a big wall. Not that talking about what was happening between them was going to help matters; it would probably just complicate everything. He was right about that.

She was a little afraid to know what he was thinking, because she was falling for him. And she was worried that he didn't feel the same way, that it was just an adrenaline-charged fling for him. To be fair, it had started out that way for her, too. Physical attraction, chemistry, danger—boom, they'd fallen into bed without deeper emotions, but now the deeper emotions were there, too, not to mention the chemistry, and despite her earlier venting about the damn stupidity of love, she suspected she was experiencing that very emotion.

"Do you want dessert?" J.T. asked casually, oblivious to her turbulent thoughts.

"No," she said shortly. "I'm done." She took her napkin and threw it on the table.

"Now you're mad," he said with a sigh. "I should have seen that coming. Whenever a woman wants to talk, it's never a good thing."

She frowned at him, not liking the cynical generalization. "Don't compare me to other women."

"Look, Christina, we're in the middle of a . . . a mess. It's not a good time to dissect what's going on between us."

"So you're happy to just have sex and not ask questions. Gee, I should have seen that coming," she said with sarcasm, repeating his earlier words.

"You're pissed off at your father. Don't take it out on me."

"This has nothing to do with my father."

"It has everything to do with your dad, and you know it. Why don't you figure out your feelings about him before you come after me?"

She wanted to argue that he was completely wrong, but in all honesty she couldn't. She was confused about her parents. She was tired of being in relationships that didn't quite make sense, that didn't follow the rules. She'd grown up with a man she couldn't really count on. And it scared her that she was falling in love with the same kind of man. Not that J.T. was a thief, but he was a loner, an agent, a guy who lived on the road. Did she really want that?

"I need more wine," she said with a sigh.

"No, you don't. You need to let things simmer. You don't have to answer everything tonight."

"This from the man who doesn't want to answer anything."

"You want an answer—I'll give you one," he said, meeting her gaze. "I like you. I like sleeping with you. I like making love to you. Do I have any idea where this going or where I want it to go? No. I'm lousy at relationships. Everyone I've ever loved has been disappointed in me. I've already failed at one marriage. I don't know if I want to try it again. I've never been a good loser."

She was so startled by his bluntness she wasn't quite sure how to react. "That was more than one answer," she said finally.

"Can we change the subject now?"

"I think that would be a good idea," she said, drawing a deep breath. She needed time to think about what he'd just said.

J.T. waved the waiter over and handed him his credit card.

While they were waiting for the bill, she said, "You never told me what happened with you and Vittorio. Did he know I was in the house? Did he ask you about me?"

"No, we didn't talk about you or Isabella. But Vittorio did tell me that the diamond is cursed and he sent it to you on purpose."

"Why? He wanted to curse me, too?"

"He thinks you have de Médici blood in you, and if you touched the stone it would take the curse away. Then you would sell it for him, and he'd get lots of curse-free cash. To hell with whoever bought the cursed stone. That wouldn't be his problem."

"Why would he think that I have de Médici blood? The Albertis are not descended from . . ." She paused. "Oh. I get it. He was talking about Isabella's bloodline, wasn't he?"

"Now that I know your relationship to Isabella, that makes sense," J.T. agreed.

"What else did he say about the curse?"

"Nothing. Just that Catherine de Médici put some hex on the stone."

"So Catherine de Médici is the key—where the diamond came from, maybe where it belongs," she mused. "That's it. That's the clue. My dad wants to give the diamond back to Catherine."

"And how would he do that? Hasn't she been dead for several hundred years? Is your father into grave digging?"

She frowned. "Not that I know of, but I'm not sure I could discount it. However, I think it's more likely that the stone belongs somewhere else or with some-one else. At least we can narrow our search to Cather-ine. Maybe I can find more information about the diamond in one of the libraries here. They could have old letters, texts. If the diamond came down through my mother's family, then that would explain why my father thinks Vittorio stole the diamond."

"Vittorio was married to your mother. That's hardly theft."

"True, but that wouldn't matter to my father if he believed the stone belonged somewhere else. You said Vittorio sent me the stone to get rid of the curse. That's why he picked Barclay's, and why the Kens-ingtons insisted that I wear it at the party," she said, putting more pieces of the puzzle together. "Vittorio had asked that it be displayed on a live model—on me. What did he think—that I had some magic power over the diamond?" Even as she asked the question, she remembered the strange, tingly sensation that had run through her body when the stone had touched her skin.

"I don't know. I also wonder how he could be cer-tain that you didn't know about your mother or the di-amond or the curse. Your father could have told you all of it at any time."

"You're right," she murmured. Had the men made some sort of pact? Her stomach turned over at the thought. What right had either of them to keep her from knowing the truth about her birth?

"And what about Vittorio's sons?" J.T. asked. "Why couldn't they get rid of the curse? They have Isabella's blood in their veins as well."

"Maybe it's a female thing; the diamond has to be passed down through the women."

J.T. raised an eyebrow at that. "Sounds like a lot of hocus-pocus to me. Do you really believe in curses?"

"I'm not a disbeliever," she prevaricated. "I've studied many legendary jewels. There have been unexplainable incidents. I keep an open mind. At any rate, we need to go back to the Benedetti house. I bet Maria knows more about the diamond, the curse, and my mother. She said she'd been with Isabella since she was a baby. And she's been with Vittorio ever since my mother died. If anyone knows the secrets in that house, it's Maria."

"We'll go tomorrow."

"Not tonight? I thought you were a man on a mission."

"A tired man," he admitted with a small smile. "And I'd like to take a few minutes to think, put together a plan of attack."

"You're right. It's been a long couple of days." She paused as music began to play and couples made their way to the nearby dance floor. The music was soft and inviting, romantic. She couldn't stop the impulsive question that sprang from her lips. "Would you like to dance?"

J.T. couldn't have looked more shocked if she'd asked him to jump off a cliff. "Dance?" he sputtered. "I don't know how to dance."

"It's not the tango. You put your arms around me and we sway a little."

"I'll step on your feet."

"I'll take the risk."

"You're sure you want to do this?"

"Yes, please." The look of discomfort on his face made her laugh. But she knew how to get him in the right frame of mind. She leaned forward and said quietly, "Just think of it as foreplay."

"Now you're talking. I will get credit for this later on, right?"

"Absolutely."

It turned out that he didn't want the credit, even though she was willing to give it to him. Making love to Christina was not something to be rushed. When they got back to the hotel, J.T. took his time undressing her, slowing down her hands when she reached for him with an eagerness that made him smile. He liked that she didn't play hard-to-get, that there weren't any games between them. He hadn't been able to give her the answers she wanted at the restaurant. He hadn't been able to tell her with words what she meant to him, but tonight he could show her.

He pulled her shirt over her head and undid the front clasp of her bra, slowly pulling it apart, taking a moment to savor the sight of her beautiful breasts. He skimmed the tips with his palms, feeling her shudder with pleasure. Then he ran his hands down her stomach. He unsnapped her jeans, slid down the zipper, and slipped his hands inside, his fingers tracing the shape of her buttocks as he helped her off with her pants. He loved the feel of her ass, so soft, so round, so perfect for his hands, for his body. He grabbed the strap of her thong underwear and sent the tiny scrap of material to the floor. Sliding his fingers into the nest of curls at her thighs, he explored the tender folds, loving the way she whispered his name and moved into him, rubbing her breasts against his chest, her hips into his rapidly hardening groin.

He kissed her on the mouth as he explored her with his fingers. Her tongue danced with his, demanding that he go deeper in every way. He could feel the tension growing in her body. He wanted to draw it out, to torture her—to make each moment count, each kiss, each caress. He increased the pressure with his fingers, at the same time dropping his mouth to her breast, encircling the nipple with his tongue, teasing and tugging until she came apart in his arms, crying out his name.

She reached for the hem of his shirt, ruthlessly tugging it over his head, her hands once again urgent, needy. This time he didn't try to stop her, didn't try to slow her down or prevent her from touching him, cupping him, stroking him.

He didn't know how they made it to the bed, how he had enough of a brain left to reach for a condom, or enough patience to let Christina roll it on to him as she pressed him back against the bed and straddled his legs, sinking down on him with a sigh of pure pleasure.

If he'd known a dance could lead to this, he would have started dancing a long time ago.

17

Christina was sitting on the bed, wearing only a robe, when J.T. came out of the bathroom the next morning with a short towel wrapped around his hips. The smattering of fine, dark hair on his chest was still damp from his shower. Beads of water clung to his face. He was a handsome man, and incredibly sexy. Christina couldn't keep the smile off her face as she thought about the night they'd shared. Her body felt deliciously tired, sore, satisfied.

"What's that grin for?" he asked, using another bath towel to dry his hair.

"Nothing." She got up and walked over to him, flicking a speck of shaving cream off his jaw. "You missed a spot."

His hand came around her neck, drawing her in for a lingering kiss. She wished she could take him back to bed, spend another few hours in his arms, forget about reality and the rest of the world. She gazed into his eyes and felt her breath catch at the intimate look he gave her. He knew exactly what she was thinking.

He knew how much she wanted him. It was scary to think how much of her heart she'd already put on the line. What would be left of her when this was over?

"Hey, hey," he said softly, his eyes filling with concern. "Let's go back to the smile."

"Sorry."

"What's wrong?"

"Nothing," she lied. "I was just thinking about . . . what we have to do today."

"It's going to be rough on you," he said. "Are you ready?"

"I don't think I could ever be ready, but there's no way around it. Now you'd better get dressed before I decide to make love to you again."

His eyes glittered. "You are an insatiable woman. I like it."

"It's all your fault." She gave the towel around his hips an impulsive tug, and couldn't resist taking a good look at him. The longer she looked the more aroused he got. "Oh, my," she said with a wistful sigh. "I wish we didn't have to leave."

"Do you seriously think I'm getting dressed now?" he challenged.

"We don't have time, J.T. We have things to do, places to be, people to see . . ." she said. "Unless . . ."

"Unless what?"

The rough, needy edge to his voice made her melt inside. He might not want her for the long run, but for now he was all hers.

"Christina," he prodded. "Unless what?"

"We skip the warm-up," she said huskily. "Go right to the main event."

"I can live with that." He hauled her up roughly against him, planting a fevered kiss on her lips before pushing her back onto the bed. His body immediately covered hers, his hands and his mouth eager, demanding. He tasted like mint. He smelled like musk. And when he slid into her body, Christina knew that everything else could wait.

All good things had to come to an end, Christina thought as J.T. paid off the taxi driver who had just dropped them off at the Benedettis' house. They were back to business now, dressed and ready to go. J.T. had on his game face. She was beginning to recognize the look of cold, hard purpose in his eyes that always appeared when his focus returned to Evan. For her, this journey to Italy had become all about her mother and her father, but J.T. was still on the lookout for his own personal nemesis, a man who was probably enjoying the fact that she and J.T. had gotten completely distracted by old family history. She frowned, realizing the truth of that. "We're playing into his hands, aren't we?" she asked.

J.T. gave her a curious look. "Whose hands?"

"Evan's. It just occurred to me that I haven't given him much thought in the past twenty-four hours."

"Don't worry; he's never far from my mind."

"Do you think he's here in Florence?" She couldn't help taking a quick look over her shoulder.

"I'm betting on it," J.T. said grimly. "He's biding his time, waiting for us to lead him to your father."

"I wish there were a way for us to avoid that."

"Let's take it step by step. We find your father; then we figure out a way to throw Evan off the scent."

"I'm a little surprised he hasn't contacted us."

"He doesn't want to show his cards yet, but he will. When he does, I'll be ready." He paused. "The question is, are you ready to face Maria again? Or is all this concern about Evan a stalling technique?"

She made a face at him, knowing he was right. "I am concerned about Evan, but I might have been stalling a little," she admitted.

J.T. smiled and rang the bell.

She drew in a breath and squared her shoulders. When Maria opened the door, Christina had to fight a split second's urge to run. If J.T. hadn't been standing behind her, his body a solid wall between her and the street, she might have taken off, but Maria was waving her inside, and J.T. had his hand on her back. She was going in, all the way in. There was no avoiding it now. She had to hear the truth, the whole truth, whatever it was.

"I thought you would return," Maria said, her expression wary.

"I need more information," Christina said. "Now that I've had time to think about everything, I have more questions, and you seem to be the one with all the answers."

"Come into the garden. I can't talk to you in the house. Signor Benedetti does not know that I told you about your mother." Her old eyes softened as she gazed at Christina. "You look so much like her, I still can't believe it."

Christina's lips tightened. She wasn't sure yet how she felt about the resemblance. It was too soon.

"I'd like to see the photograph," J.T. cut in. "I didn't get a chance yesterday."

They followed Maria into the living room. Christina was almost afraid to look at the picture again, fearful that it would make her mother feel more real, but she couldn't stop herself. Now when she gazed at Isabella she didn't just see the similarities between them; she also saw the differences—the stress in Isabella's eyes, as if she were pretending to smile, to convey the happy family feeling in the portrait. Christina glanced at the boys—her half brothers, she realized. They looked solemn, not one smile among them. And finally she turned to Vittorio. He was tall, proud, arrogant, with a mean glint in his eyes.

It was a family picture, but the people in the photograph almost appeared strangers to one another. Their pose was formal, forced.

Where would she have fit? Christina wondered. If Isabella had kept her, where would her daughter have been in the family picture?

"Well," J.T. said, interrupting her thoughts, "I can see why you flipped out yesterday. You look exactly like Isabella. The resemblance is uncanny."

"Yes, it is. I've seen enough," Christina said shortly, turning to Maria. "We need to talk now."

Maria nodded and led them back out to the courtyard where she and Christina had sat the day before. The sun was shining, and the patio was bathed in a warm light. They sat down at the table, and for a moment there was nothing but quiet. J.T. was obviously leaving it to her to speak first, but now that she was here Christina wasn't sure where to start.

Maria finally broke the silence. "I shouldn't have told you," she said, clasping her hands on top of the table, guilt evident in her black eyes. "Signor Benedetti will fire me when he finds out. I gave my sacred promise to him that I would never say a word. It was easier to keep the promise when you were in America, when I wasn't sitting across from you as I was yesterday, as I am now. I wish you had not come here."

"Part of me wishes that, too, but we can't go back; we can only go forward." Christina drew in a breath and continued. "I told you that the diamond Signor Benedetti sent to my auction house was stolen. I believe my father took it. He told me that the diamond didn't belong to Vittorio, and that it needs to be returned it to its rightful owner. My father is in a great deal of trouble. The police in San Francisco are looking for him, and for me, too, in fact. Can you help me find my father?"

Maria's eyes filled with confusion. "Perhaps my English is not so good. I don't understand what you mean when you say your father wants to put the diamond back."

"He believes the diamond belongs to someone other than Vittorio," Christina explained.

"If it belongs to anyone else, it belongs to you," Maria said.

Christina sat up straight, then exchanged a quick look with J.T., who appeared as surprised as she was by Maria's words. "What do you mean?"

"Your father didn't tell you the story of the diamond?"

"He didn't tell me anything," Christina said. "Can you fill in the blanks?"

Maria hesitated. "I don't know if it's my place."

"Please, this is so important to me. You have to tell

me what you know, especially if the diamond is supposed to belong to me. Don't I have a right to know its history?"

Maria let out a heavy sigh. "Yes, you have that right. And I will tell you, because I think it's what your mother would want me to do. Let me think for a moment. It has been many, many years since I heard the story." She fell silent, taking her time. The words came slowly. "The diamond has been passed down from mother to daughter for hundreds of years. Just before your grandmother died—her name was Angela—she told Isabella the story of the diamond."

"Go on," Christina encouraged, excited to hear the rest.

Maria gave her a sad smile. "Isabella had the same look on her face as you do now, as if something magical was about to enter her life. And that's exactly what would happen. She had never seen the yellow diamond before that night. It was tradition that the diamond be hidden away lest someone outside of the bloodline should try to take it, to steal its power. The stone would bring good luck and passionate love to those mothers and daughters who carried the blood of Catherine de Médici, but to anyone else it would bring tragedy and suffering."

"So the stone originally belonged to Catherine de Médici?" Christina asked.

"Yes. It is said that Catherine inherited the diamond from her mother, who died before Catherine was a year old. The nurse who took care of Catherine after her mother died told her that the diamond was her legacy from her mother and she must protect it always. No one else in the family could know she had it." Maria took a breath, then continued.

"When Catherine was eight years old, rebels attacked the Médici palace. Catherine was taken hostage and hidden away in various convents in and around the city, where she lived until she was fourteen years old. At one of these convents Catherine fell in love with a handsome young man. He was a painter, commissioned to paint a fresco on the wall of a chapel. He was so taken by Catherine that he painted her picture into the fresco. Sadly, they could not be together. A few weeks later Catherine was sent to Rome and married off to the future king of France."

Christina nodded, remembering the story of the Italian princess who grew up to be the queen of France. "What happened to the diamond?"

"Let me back up for a moment," Maria said. "Catherine had asked her friend Pietro, the painter, to help her find a place to hide the diamond, which he agreed to do. She was afraid that the diamond would be taken from her as part of her marriage dowry. She wanted to leave the diamond somewhere safe until she was older, until she had more control over her life. Unfortunately, before that could happen, Catherine left Florence. Her worst fears came true. Henry discovered the diamond, and to Catherine's shock and horror he gave it to his mistress. Catherine swore a curse on the stone and on Henry—that any man who took the stone from the woman to whom it belonged would suffer his worst fear and heartache until the diamond was returned to her. She said the diamond was her heart, because inside the stone—"

"There was a mineral inclusion of a heart," Christina finished. "That's what the report said. That's what I didn't see." She glanced over at J.T. and saw skepticism in his eyes. "You don't believe in the curse?"

"It's quite a tale," J.T. said. "What happened to Henry after he took Catherine's diamond? How was he cursed?"

"I know he couldn't get Catherine pregnant for ten years," Christina replied. She turned to Maria. "Was that part of the curse?"

"Some thought so, including Henry. He returned the diamond to Catherine and then she had ten children," Maria said. "Since then, over many years and many generations, other men have attempted to take the diamond from their loves, their wives, and they all suffered—including Vittorio."

"Good, let's bring it back to the present day," J.T. said approvingly. "What happened after Isabella got the diamond from her mother?"

"Isabella felt as if the diamond brought magic into her life," Maria continued. "She had been so unhappy with Vittorio. He cared more about his business, his money, and his reputation than about Isabella. Her life was cold and empty. Her only joy came from her children, but that wasn't enough to sustain her. When she received the diamond, she became obsessed with learning more about it. The diamond sent her to your father, Christina. That's how she met him, you know. She went to the library to find out more about the stone, and he offered to help her with the research."

That sounded just like her father. He wouldn't have been able to resist learning about a legendary diamond.

"Isabella fell in love with Marcus," Maria said. "I believe he was truly the one great passion of her life, and it was the diamond that brought them together, the magic of the stone."

Christina's stomach clenched at Maria's words. She wanted to believe her parents had shared something more real, more honest than a tawdry affair.

"So what happened?" J.T. asked. "Did Vittorio inherit the diamond after Isabella died?"

"He took it from her when he found out she was pregnant," Maria said. "He was furious. He was looking through her room for proof of her affair—letters, that kind of thing. That's when he found the stone, when he took it for his own. Vittorio told Isabella that she owed him for betraying him." Maria drew in a deep breath. "It was a horrible night. They fought so terribly. In my head I can still hear him yelling at her, and my sweet Isabella sobbing as if her heart had been ripped in two. In the end Vittorio sent her away to live in the country until she had the baby. Then he had a nurse take the child to America, to your father."

Christina felt a rush of emotion, knowing now that she was that baby. "Isabella didn't choose to send me away?"

"Oh, no. She cried for days after you were gone. She only got to hold you the one time. She wanted to fight for you, but she was too weak. It was a difficult pregnancy. She had no strength left to battle Vittorio."

"I don't understand why my father took me in without trying to come back here and get Isabella, too," Christina said. "Didn't he wonder why she'd sent him her baby?"

"There was a letter that went with you. Isabella was forced to write it, denouncing anything she had ever felt for your father and asking him never to tell you the truth of your birth. She said that she was ashamed of herself for betraying her husband and her other children. I don't know how your father felt about the letter, but by the time he came here to see her, it was too late."

"What happened to her?" Christina asked, needing to know the rest. "How did she die?"

"Isabella never recovered from the pregnancy," Maria said, her old eyes sad as she gazed at Christina. "She never recovered from losing you. She got weaker and weaker. Influenza struck. She couldn't fight it. Not even for her boys. She loved her boys, too. But Vittorio wouldn't let her see them. He kept them here in the city and made her stay in the country. He said he didn't want them to get sick. Without her children she had no heart left. She had been banished from her life. She was so alone, so filled with grief. I think she just gave up." Maria paused, her lips trembling as she said, "Vittorio buried her eight months after you were born."

Christina blinked back a sudden well of tears and drew in a shaky breath. "So if my father hadn't waited so long to see Isabella, he might have saved her life."

"I don't know if anyone could have saved her," Maria said. "I know I tried. I told her over and over again that she had to get well so that she could see you again, see her boys. She would perk up for a while, but then lose faith. She had always been a fragile girl, weak, thin, kind, soft like a little hummingbird. That's how I think of Isabella. She was always happy here in her garden, rarely anywhere else, except perhaps the library, where she met your father."

"If she hadn't inherited the diamond, they never would have met," Christina murmured. "It brought her the wrong kind of love."

"It was wrong because she was married," Maria said. "But Isabella was happy that summer. Perhaps that was all she was meant to have."

"And what about Vittorio?" J.T. asked. "What curse has he suffered since he took the diamond?"

"Many tragedies. Some years ago he was injured in a riding accident, and it was many months before he could walk. He still suffers a limp. Later he lost a great deal of money and his business holdings suffered. Six months ago his son Frances was killed in a car accident. Four months ago Vittorio was diagnosed with cancer."

"All things that could have just happened," J.T. said pragmatically, "curse or no curse."

"Vittorio said the same thing, but in his heart he started to wonder and to believe that his only chance of beating the cancer was to get rid of the diamond. I told Vittorio he should give you the diamond before it killed him."

"You told him to give it to me?" Christina echoed.

"You are Isabella's daughter. It was the right thing to do."

"But you know that he didn't give it to me. He simply sent it to my auction house and asked me to wear it. Apparently he thought that alone would relieve the curse."

Maria nodded. "I didn't understand his intention

until after he had sent the entire collection to San Francisco."

"He didn't want me to have the diamond," Christina said. "He just wanted me to save him from the curse and then sell the stone for him. He ends up curse-free with millions of dollars in his pocket. Sounds like quite the plan," she said bitterly, feeling a surge of anger toward the man who had quite possibly changed the entire course of her life. "I want to see him. I want to speak to Vittorio."

Maria immediately shook her head, fear flashing through her eyes. "No, you can't. He's ill. I can't allow you to upset him. He would be so angry that I told you. I am an old woman. I can't find another job, another place to live. My daughter works here, too. I only told you the story because I loved your mother so much, and I know she would have wanted you to understand the truth of your birth. She would have wanted me to tell you about her."

Christina could see the difficult position Maria was in, but still . . . "Maria. Vittorio practically killed my mother, and he kept me from her. I was her child. I had a right to be with her, to know her. He played God. No one has the right to do that."

"Your father did the same thing," she argued.

"Well, I want to talk to him, too." Christina glanced over at J.T. "What do you think?"

"That you should speak to Vittorio," he said, meeting her gaze. "But don't implicate Maria. Your father could have told you all of this. Vittorio doesn't need to know where your information came from."

"Yes, my father could have told me," she realized.

Why hadn't he? Why all the secrecy? Was it really a matter of his respecting her mother's wishes? Why wouldn't he have questioned the letter? Surely, if he knew Isabella was unhappy enough to have an affair, he would have suspected the note had been written under duress?

"Vittorio cannot tell you any more about the diamond," Maria argued. "I have told you everything."

"I need to see him." Christina thought about what she'd just said and realized it wasn't completely true. "Actually, I need him to see me—the child he made his wife give away."

Maria met her gaze, and there was compassion in her eyes. "I understand."

"What about my . . . my half brothers?" Christina asked. "I know Stefano is sailing somewhere. What about Daniel?"

"He went to Rome several days ago. He won't be back until next week."

"Do they know about me?" Christina asked. "Will I be destroying their vision of their mother if I show up?"

"Probably. They don't know about you or about their mother's relationship with your father. The boys grew up to be like their father—cold, distant. They could have used their mother's touch."

"Well, since they're not here, I'll think about what I want to tell them later." She rose to her feet. "I want to see Vittorio now."

"Do you want me to come with you?" J.T. asked.

"I really do," she admitted. "I know it would probably be better for me to do it alone, but I could use your support. I don't think he'll be happy to see me."

J.T. got up and gave her a reassuring smile. "I'll be

right by your side. If you want me to kick his ass, just say the word."

"Thanks, but I just want to talk to him right now. I'll save the ass kicking for later." She turned to Maria. "Thank you—for everything. I know you took a risk. I appreciate it so much."

The older woman nodded as she stood up. "I will take you to see Vittorio."

Christina's nerves tightened as they walked upstairs. She wanted to see Vittorio, and yet she was afraid. After hearing what he had done to her mother, Vittorio had grown to monstrous proportions in her mind. What would she say to him? Would she able to say anything at all? Or would he intimidate her as he had intimidated her mother?

She was still uncertain when J.T. paused in the hall outside Vittorio's room.

"Let me make this easier on you, Maria," he said. "Try to stop me from going in. You understand?"

"Yes."

J.T. pushed open the door to Vittorio's bedroom, saying, "Don't try to stop me. I want to see him now."

"Please, signore, you cannot go in there," Maria begged.

Christina followed J.T. into the large bedroom. Vittorio sat in an armchair, reading a newspaper. The paper fell from his hand when he saw her. His gaze narrowed and his thick brows drew together in one tight line. The blood drained from his face as recognition set in.

"I think it's time we met," Christina said, finding her voice and her courage. She walked over to him, stopping just a few feet from his chair. It helped that he was sitting. She felt bigger, stronger. "I'm Christina Alberti—your wife's daughter. Remember me?"

Vittorio didn't reply. He simply stared at her, his gaze as cold as ice. He shifted in his chair, reached for a cane resting against the table, and slowly rose. Standing, he towered above her by a good foot, and despite the fact that his illness had robbed him of his vigor, he was still a man who commanded respect simply by the way he held his head. He looked at her for so long she found herself willing him to say something—anything. The silence was killing her.

"What do you want?" he asked finally.

She had to think for a moment. What did she want from this man?

"Why did you do it?" she asked. "Why did you rip me out of the arms of my mother and send me away?"

"Because you weren't mine." His gaze was direct, his words unapologetic. "You were a bastard child, the symbol of her betrayal."

His words cut her to the quick, but she wouldn't give him the satisfaction of seeing her pain. "You killed her, didn't you? You destroyed her with your cold, heartless act."

"She destroyed me and my family," he said, fury steeling his voice. "She was the sinner, not I. Now leave my house."

"In a second. I'm not finished yet. You sent me the diamond to curse me, didn't you? It wasn't that you thought I could get rid of the curse. You wanted to brand me with it."

"It did not matter to me either way," he said with a

shrug. "Until your father stole it. If it takes my last breath, I will make sure he is thrown into jail. He robbed me of Isabella. He will not run away with that diamond. Now that I know he has it, I will send every police officer in Florence to search for him."

Goose bumps shivered over Christina's skin. Vittorio was a powerful man in Florence. He could probably back up his threat. But she still had one card left to play. "If you do that, I will tell everyone the truth about you, my mother, my father, and myself."

"I could have you thrown into jail as well," Vittorio countered. "The police in San Francisco believe you and your father worked together. I had a long talk with them this morning." He glanced over at J.T. "I believe you're wanted as well."

"J.T. didn't have anything to do with the theft of the diamond," Christina said quickly. "And neither did I. But if you want to have me arrested, fine. I can still tell my story, and I will tell it. In fact, if I'm in jail, I'll get even more press. By the time I'm finished, everyone in Florence will know the true story of my mother and my father and you. Or . . ." She paused deliberately, giving her threat a chance to sink in. "Or my father can return the diamond and you can drop the charges."

"You dare to blackmail me?" he asked incredulously. "Do you know who I am?"

"I know exactly who you are and what you have to protect."

He stared back at her, measuring the sincerity of her words. She didn't flinch, didn't look away. Her mother might not have been able to stand up to Vittorio, but Christina could, and she would.

"You have two days to get me the diamond," Vittorio said slowly.

She turned and left the room without replying, but she was shaking when she reached the hallway. She let out a breath of relief as J.T. pulled the door shut behind him.

He smiled at her. "You all right?"

"I'm not sure. I don't know where that all came from. I just couldn't stand there and let him threaten me and my father."

"I think you did your mother proud."

"Yeah, well, there's only one small problem. We have to get the diamond back in the next two days."

"Then that's what we'll do," he said confidently.

"Yes," she agreed, "because my father has a lot to answer for as well. I want to ask him the same questions I asked Vittorio. Neither of them had a right to keep me from my mother."

"No, they didn't. But I have to admit I can't see you growing up in this cold, dark house," J.T. said as they made their way down the stairs. "It doesn't suit you."

"I don't think it suited my mother either. She didn't belong here."

"She came willingly," J.T. reminded her.

"It sounded like her parents didn't give her much choice. But I know what you're getting at. She was married. She did have an affair. She wasn't honorable. Apparently she was in love. Maybe the diamond is cursed."

"Well, curse or not, we still need to find it in the next two days."

"I think we should check the house where my father stays when he's here in Florence. Maria can give us the address. Maybe he'll even be there. Although that would probably be too easy."

"Definitely too easy. But let's make that our next stop. If the house is in your family name, it would be a good place for Evan to target as well."

At the mention of Evan, she glanced at J.T. and saw new shadows of worry in his eyes. "It bothers you a little that he hasn't shown his face again, doesn't it?"

"Yes. I've gotten used to his frequent taunts. The silence is unnerving."

"No news is supposed to be good news, isn't it?"

"Not where Evan is concerned."

"We'll find him. Or he'll find us."

"Yeah, that's what I'm concerned about," J.T. said grimly. "You're very distracted, Christina. You need to keep your mind now on your father and Evan. The stuff with your mother you'll have to sort out later. I know that's a lot to ask, but it's important."

"I know. I understand. Believe me, there is nothing I want more than to find both Evan and my father and put all this behind us."

18

Evan watched the jeweler study the diamond under his gem scope. Giorgio was the best in the business, according to the Florence underground network of thieves. Italy might not be the States, but Evan knew how to work the underground in any country. The right amount of money, the appropriate threat, and any information could be had.

"Well?" he prodded impatiently.

"It is a brilliant copy," the man said slowly. He lifted his shrewd gaze to meet Evan's. "Perfection, but still a copy. You already knew that."

"Yes. And you're the man who made it."

Georgio shrugged his shoulders, but he looked at the stone as if he'd given birth to it. The pride of ownership was clearly evident in his eyes. "I am just a simple jeweler. This would require the work of an artist, a master of his craft."

"I don't need the artist," Evan said. "I need the man who hired him. Marcus Alberti. I'm betting you can help me find him."

"That information could be costly," Georgio replied.

"Not sharing it could be even costlier," Evan returned. "The real diamond is missing. A lot of people are looking for it. Some of them will eventually end up here. Some of those people will have badges, arrest warrants."

"It is not a crime to copy a jewel," the man returned.

Evan took out his wallet and laid several bills on the counter. The man's eyes lit up. Greed was such a beautiful thing.

"He has a house in the hills, but I don't think he's there," the man said.

"He's not. I've already been there. I want you to give him a message from me."

"I don't know where he is."

"You'd better find him then," Evan said purposefully.

"Signore, please, I am not involved in anything."

"You copied the diamond. That means you're involved." Evan made a quick movement, taking the jeweler by surprise as he grabbed him by the neck and pushed him up against the wall. Georgio's eyes bulged in fear. "Tell Marcus if he wants to see his daughter alive, he should meet me tonight at St. Anne's, the bell tower. I'll be waiting."

Georgio gasped as Evan let go of his throat. "What if I can't find him?"

"Then I'll be back here to see you. The thing about people like you, Georgio, who work in the back alleys, who take money from thieves, is that no one cares when you disappear. No one cares if you end up dead."

Georgio swallowed hard. "I will try to locate him."

"You do that." Evan adjusted his coat and walked out of the door with a jaunty smile.

J.T. was eager to find Marcus's house. After leaving the Benedettis', they'd rented a car, picked up a map, and were on their way to the farmhouse where Marcus stayed when he was in town. Now that Christina had dealt with the issues involving her mother, J.T. hoped they could concentrate on finding her father. He had to admit he was proud of how she had handled herself with Vittorio. She had faced down that ruthless old man and not even flinched. Yesterday she had been knocked off her feet, but today she was on fire. He'd never known a woman who could roll with the punches the way Christina did. She had a core of steel underneath that beautiful softness.

Christina consulted the map as he drove out of the city. When they left the busy streets behind, he relaxed and pushed his foot down hard on the gas pedal. Despite his efforts, the car still labored through the foothills. "I think we could walk faster," he grumbled, casting a quick look at Christina.

She simply smiled. "We'll get there. I feel like we're on the right track now."

"It's just not the *fast* track."

"I know. You've been very patient, letting me come to terms with my mother and the relationship between my father and the Benedettis. I appreciate it more than I can say. At least we know more about the diamond and the curse."

"We just need to find your father, or figure out where he has taken the diamond." J.T. thought about everything they had learned. "According to Maria's story, you're the one who should have the diamond after your mother. Is your father just holding it for you? Stashing it somewhere until enough time has passed?"

She shook her head. "I don't think so. He told me he was worried about the curse affecting me. It's possible that he knows more about the stone now than Maria knew when she heard the story. I'm sure he's researched the diamond all the way back to Catherine de Médici, and perhaps before that. Many large diamonds were originally part of religious and historical pieces such as crosses, swords, and crowns . . ." She paused. "He must have had a sketch that allowed him to have the diamond copied. There could even be another story we haven't heard yet."

"Great, just what we need, another story," he said dryly.

"A little too much history for you?" she asked, flashing him a smile.

"I'm more interested in the people who are living now than those who have been dead for several hundred years."

"I think you're on the wrong case then."

"No, I'm on the right case," he said, glancing over at her, "because Evan wants the diamond. And I want Evan. That's all that matters to me."

He saw a shadow flit through her eyes and regretted his choice of words.

"I understand," she said.

"Christina—I didn't mean it that way."

"I know what you meant. I know that putting Evan away is the most important thing to you."

"It is important," he conceded, "but—"

"I think we should try to trace the painter and his descendants," she interrupted, changing the subject. "He might provide a clue. And I would like to find out if the fresco he painted with Catherine's picture in it still exists somewhere. Maybe the information will be at my father's house. He couldn't have everything on him. He had to leave his research somewhere, and it wasn't at his house in San Francisco."

"Christina—" J.T. began, still feeling that he needed to say something, but not sure exactly what.

"Let's concentrate on what we need to do next, J.T. Okay? I can't handle anything more personal right now."

He glanced over at her, but she had turned her gaze on the passing scenery and all he could see was her profile. He didn't know why he wasn't happy about the fact that she was giving him an out of what would be a complicated conversation. For some odd reason it disturbed him that she didn't want to talk about it, that he couldn't read what was going on in her head.

"This place is beautiful," Christina murmured, gesturing toward the rolling green hills. "It feels so far away from San Francisco and Barclay's. I wonder what Alexis and Jeremy think now? I wonder if there's a warrant out for my arrest, maybe extradition papers? I don't even know how that works."

"Don't worry about it," J.T. advised. "You didn't steal the diamond, and there's no proof that you did. At worst you could be considered an accomplice, but your father is the main suspect. Once we find him, we'll be able to clear your name."

"But not his," she said, turning back to him. "I don't

want to put my father in jail, J.T., and I feel that every step I'm taking is heading right to that end. I hope you'll give me a chance to convince him to give the diamond back to Vittorio."

"Even if he does give it back, he still stole it. That's a crime."

"Well, there has to be a way around it. You can help me think of a way, can't you?" she asked with a plea in her eyes. "You're a smart guy. You know the law."

"Let's find him first; then we'll worry about how to keep him out of jail."

"You're right. I do know down deep that at some point he has to pay for what he's done. I can't go on living as I was, pretending not to see him for who he is, worrying about when he'll show up next, what he's doing, what new trouble might be coming into my life. I'm tired of his secrets and his lies. I can't go back to that, no matter what happens." She paused. "I'm just afraid. It's hard to let go completely. He's all I have."

"It seems to me you're acquiring more family by the minute."

"I don't think I can tell Vittorio's sons," she added, giving him a questioning look. "Can I? Would it be fair to them?"

"I can't answer that, Christina."

"If they don't know about me, if they think their mother was loyal to their father throughout their marriage, what right do I have to take that away from them? It would just hurt them. There's nothing to gain."

"Half brothers; that's what you have to gain," he reminded her. "More family."

"The cost could be huge. They could hate me. They could hate their mother, my father. It could get even messier. I'll have to think about it." She glanced down at the map. "That's the turnoff."

J.T. turned right on to a narrow, roughly paved road that wound through an olive grove and a line of cypress trees, ending in front of an ill-kept two-story stone cottage. The grass needed weeding, and an empty fountain with crumbling masonry stood in the front yard.

Christina was out of the car the second he turned off the engine. He followed her up to the solid front door of the house, appreciating her eagerness, but also wary of what they might find.

"I rang the bell," she said. "It doesn't look like anyone is here. No cars around. I don't see a garage."

She was right. There weren't even any other houses close by. It was quiet on this hillside, save for the song of a few nearby birds. The city of Florence was off to the left. He could see the tops of some of the tallest churches and buildings. In the city there was a hectic, busy atmosphere, but here on this hill it was peaceful. He wondered how long it would last. They certainly hadn't had much quiet the last few days.

"Let's try some windows." He moved systematically around the house, finding one of the back windows unlocked. With a few jolts he managed to push it open. He helped Christina through the opening and then went back to the front of the house. She opened the door for him a moment later.

J.T. walked into the living room, noting the exposed wood beams in the ceiling, the terra-cotta floors, and the large rock fireplace. The furniture was old but appeared comfortable, with big pillows on the sofas and chairs. There were colorful throw rugs on the floor, newspapers on the coffee table, and even a used coffee mug. He picked it up and saw a trace of liquid still in the bottom. "Someone was here not long ago."

"Probably Dad." Christina paused in front of some photographs on top of the mantel. "These are my grandparents and my father when he was a child. They died before I was born, long before my dad met Isabella. And this must be my great-grandfather," she added, pointing to a photo of a dark-haired man with a pencil-thin mustache. "There's so much of my family history in this house. I guess I know now why my father never brought me here. It was too close to the Benedettis'."

"And he didn't want you to find this." J.T. picked up a framed photograph on a side table. He held it against his chest, not sure Christina was ready for it.

"It's them, isn't it?" she asked. "Together."

He nodded and slowly turned the picture around.

She stepped closer. Her hand shook as she took the picture from him. She stared down at the photo of her mother and father, arms around each other, smiling for the camera. She wondered who had taken the shot. It would mean that someone else had known about them—probably Maria. "They look happy," she murmured, blinking back tears.

J.T. smiled and shook his head. "The romantic in you is back. What happened to the girl who was all fired up about her mother being an adulteress and her father a liar and a cheat?"

"Every daughter wants to know her parents cared about each other. I can still see the big picture. I can," she added defensively.

"Good. Why don't you check the upstairs bedrooms? I'll look around down here. We need to pick up the pace. Time is passing."

"I got it. Back to work."

As Christina climbed the stairs, J.T moved down the hall, stepping into a downstairs bedroom. It was obviously a guest room, containing nothing but a bed, a dresser, and a side table with a lamp on it. A thin layer of dust covered the floor and the furniture. It didn't appear as if anyone had been there in a while. Next up was a bathroom, then a small kitchen that led into the backyard. He opened the cupboards and the refrigerator, not surprised to see some food items. Marcus had been living here, maybe as recently as this morning. They were getting close, but not close enough.

Another door was located on the other side of the refrigerator. Opening it, he saw stairs leading down into a dark basement, where he could make out the shadow of a washer and dryer. There could be papers down there, but the room felt cold and damp. Still, he should check it out. Who knew where Marcus would hide information?

He had one foot on the top stair when he heard Christina come into the kitchen. "Did you find anything?" he asked, searching for a light switch.

"You," a man said.

J.T. whirled around just as Evan swung a shovel at his head. He fended off the first blow with his hand, smashing his fist into Evan's face. He felt a jolt of satisfaction when he saw the blood gush from Evan's nose. But his satisfaction was short-lived as Evan brought the shovel back around and, with a grunt of anger, nailed J.T. on the side of the head.

Stars spun before his eyes. He felt his legs crumple as a searing pain shot from his temple to the back of his skull. He had to stay on his feet. He had to protect Christina. He tried to grab the stair railing, but missed and tumbled down the stairs, feeling the force of each painful step. He tried to call out, to warn Christina, but the blinding pain in his head sent him screaming toward a tunnel of darkness.

Christina was on her own. God help her.

One large bedroom connected to a bath on the second floor. The queen-sized bed was unmade, the blankets tangled. Had her father spent the night here? Christina wondered, her senses overcome by the faint lingering scent of the spicy cologne she always associated with her dad. She moved into the adjacent bathroom. A wet towel hung on the rack. Soap, shaving lotion, a razor, and the cologne were on the countertop, more evidence that her father had been here. Where was he now? And was he coming back soon? She wondered if they should wait here for him to return. But what if he didn't? What if he had moved on again?

Back in the bedroom, she moved over to a desk next to the window. Papers, as well as several books, were spread across the top. Her heart quickened as she read the title on the first old text, *A Portrait of Catherine de Médici.* Her father had been reading about Catherine! His research must have something to do with the diamond.

Several pages in the book had been folded over. Christina flipped through them until she got to the ones that had been marked. She skimmed through the text on the first page, which discussed Catherine's dowry. There was no mention of the yellow. On the next page she found more information about Catherine's obsession with astrology, Nostradamus, fortune-telling, and poisons. She read with morbid fascination about how Catherine was believed to have had two hundred cabinets filled with poisons and those cabinets had, in fact, been buried with her.

Catherine obviously had a dark side. And Christina had the same blood running through her veins. That was an eerie thought. Had the loss of the diamond changed Catherine, turned her from a passionate, romantic young girl into a hard-edged, bitter, and ambitious queen who cursed those who betrayed her? Her husband had certainly shamed her by continuing his blatant affair with Diane de Poitiers.

As much as Christina wanted to linger on the history books, she moved on. There were loose papers on the desk, including several bills. It appeared from the dates that her father had been living here off and on for the past few months, maybe years. Or, at least, he had made this house his home base. She found receipts for dry cleaning and groceries, clothing and books.

Christina sat down in the chair and opened the top center drawer. She leafed through more papers, her gaze catching on a large art book in which she could see a yellowed piece of very thin paper stuck in the middle. She pulled out the parchment. It was a sketch of a painting. Her eye moved from the paper to the page of the book that was now open. The sketch was the same painting as the one in the book, but in color and finished.

Her heart skidded to a stop as she recognized a woman's face among the angels in the picture. It was Catherine—Catherine de Médici.

This had to be the painting that Catherine's love had done for her. Her gaze dropped to the caption. The fresco by Pietro Marcello was painted in the small chapel at St. Anne's Convent. Her pulse began to race as her eye picked out other details in the painting: the yellow diamond hanging around Catherine's neck, the heavy pendant nestled between her breasts. Pietro hadn't just painted Catherine; he'd painted the diamond. And her father had the picture.

The answer was suddenly so clear: The fresco was the key. Catherine had asked Pietro to help her protect the diamond. And the painting was a huge clue. Now they knew where the fresco was painted. They just had to find St. Anne's Convent.

Christina got to her feet as she heard footsteps coming up the stairs. J.T. was going to be so happy that they finally had a solid lead. She ran to the door to tell him. But the man standing in the hall was not J.T. This man had blond hair, blue eyes, a bloody nose, and the most evil smile she had ever seen.

Evan! It had to be Evan. And the blood on his face made her fear for J.T.

She opened her mouth to scream, but he covered her lips with a cloth, pressing it against her nose and mouth. It smelled vile. She gagged and coughed, struggling to get air. She hit, kicked, trying to get away, but her limbs were growing heavy, her brain fuzzy. She was suffocating. She pleaded with her eyes for him to let her go.

"Don't worry, Christina," she heard him say as her brain began to shut down. "You're not going to die—yet."

J.T. struggled to wake up. The pain in his head was relentless, as if someone were hammering against the front of his skull. He tried to move, and finally his hands touched something cold and hard. Cement, he realized. He was on a floor. Where? He couldn't think. He blinked and took a breath. Slowly his head began to clear. He opened his eyes all the way, squinting in the darkness. He could make out the shadow of stairs off to his left. A water heater was right next to him, a sink, a washer and a dryer. The basement. He was in the basement of the farmhouse.

For a moment he just lay there, trying to remember what had happened. He'd been in the kitchen, checking out the cupboards, thinking that Christina's father had been there recently— *Christina!* Where the hell was Christina?

He sat up, and crawled to his knees. He had to grab onto the bottom stair as a wave of dizziness almost sent him crashing down to the ground. He fought back—hard. He had to get up. He had to get to Christina before Evan did. He climbed up the first stair, then the second. Each movement was agony. It wasn't just his head that was hurting but his left wrist, his back, his knees. He'd hit everything hard on his way down the stairs. He was probably lucky he hadn't broken his neck.

Pausing on the third step, he put his hand to his scalp, feeling a huge bump. When he pulled his fingers away he could see blood. The reality of the situation sent him up the rest of the stairs. When he reached the top, he grabbed the doorknob with his right hand. It was locked. *Dammit!*

Turning around, he saw a pile of gardening equipment, shovels, picks, axes in one corner of the basement. He made his way back down the stairs as quickly as he could and grabbed an ax. When he returned to the top, he swung the ax at the door several times until the wood splintered. Finally he was able to reach inside, unlock the door, and let himself out.

He stumbled into the kitchen. The silence in the house was alarming. He ran down the hall and up the stairs, calling out Christina's name.

When he got to the bedroom, he saw immediately that it was empty. She was gone. Evan had Christina. He knew the truth deep down in his gut. And as further evidence, Christina's purse was still on the desk.

He grabbed her bag and looked out the window. He could see the road leading up to the house. His rental car was parked below. There were no other cars in sight, but he could see a lingering haze of dust in the air.

The rush of fear and anger that ran through his body was overwhelming and paralyzing. He had to find Christina. *Think,* he told himself. Where would Evan take her?

He glanced down at the desk. The open book called out to him. He stared at the page. At first it looked like any other art book, but then a dazzling splash of yellow took his eye to a diamond pendant worn by a young girl. Catherine. The fresco. His gaze moved down the page. St. Anne's Convent.

Marcus must have taken the diamond to the church. That must be where he thought the diamond belonged. Had Christina seen this page? Had Evan?

What did it matter? It was the only clue he had. He had to follow it. It shouldn't be too difficult to find the convent. Locating Evan would be another matter.

Jogging back down the stairs, J.T. ran out to the rental car, praying it wouldn't be too late. It wasn't just a diamond on the line now; it was Christina's life. He couldn't let anything happen to her. He'd already lost his father to Evan; he couldn't lose another person he loved.

He loved Christina. What a hell of a time to figure that out.

He hoped to God he would have a chance to tell her.

Christina felt sick. Her stomach was heaving, and some nauseating taste on her tongue made her want to throw up. She tried to move, then realized that her hands were tied behind her back. Her memory slowly returned. She'd been in the bedroom at the farmhouse. She'd found the book, the sketches. She'd heard J.T. coming up the stairs and she'd run to the door. But it hadn't been J.T.; it had been Evan. And he'd put something over her nose and mouth so she couldn't breathe.

Her eyes flew open and she blinked rapidly, trying to focus. Where was she? What was happening?

It took a moment for her brain to catch up. She was lying on her side on a cold cement floor. Her feet were tied at the ankles, her hands roped behind her back.

Painfully sticky tape was wound around her mouth to the back of her head. She couldn't move, couldn't speak, couldn't do anything but try to figure out where she was.

A cold wind blew through four open floor-to-ceiling arches, one on each wall. She was in a tower. A bell tower. Several iron bells were suspended above her head along with pulleys and ropes. About ten feet away was a door leading somewhere, probably down to the church below. Was she in a church in Florence? There was no writing on the walls and no people in the room. She didn't know how long she'd been unconscious; nor could she catch a glimpse of her wristwatch. Judging by the lengthening shadows and the darkening sky, she suspected it was almost dusk.

Why had Evan brought her here? And where was J.T.? What had Evan done with him?

Terror gripped her heart as she realized that Evan must have taken J.T. out. Otherwise he never would have been able to get up the stairs to kidnap her from the farmhouse.

Had Evan hurt J.T.? Had the long history between them and the hatred on both sides led to violence? Evan had probably killed David and Nicole, not to mention numerous other people over the years. There was no reason to think he wouldn't kill J.T., too, especially if J.T. was standing in the way of his getting the diamond.

She and J.T. shouldn't have split up, she realized, not even in the house. They should have stayed together. It was too late now.

A sudden movement behind her sent her gaze darting to the door. She prayed for J.T. to walk through. But it was Evan, tall, blond, blue eyed, exactly like the photograph J.T. had shown her the first time they'd met. He wore a navy blue suit with a white dress shirt open at the collar. There was no sign of Stefano in him now. He looked like an ordinary businessman, except for the wild gleam in his eyes and the shadow of beard along his jaw that gave him a weary, jaded appearance.

"Well, well, look who's awake," Evan said, squatting a few feet away from her.

She struggled into a half-sitting position. It made her feel only marginally better not to be lying at his feet.

"Relax, Christina, we have time. Get comfortable. Nothing will happen until dark," he told her.

She tried to swallow, but her mouth was too dry. She cleared her throat and motioned with her eyes and her head for him to take off the tape. If she could just take a deeper breath, she would feel better. Not to mention the fact that she could let out a scream and hopefully call someone to her rescue.

Evan smiled. "I don't think so. It's my turn to talk. You can listen." He paused, his gaze narrowing on her face. "You're probably wondering about your good friend J.T. Don't worry. He won't bother us. He's done."

Her heart stopped. It couldn't be true. J.T. could not be "done." He could not be—God, she couldn't let herself think for a second that J.T. was dead.

"This little party is just for the three of us," Evan continued. "You, me, and your dear old dad. That's right, your father, Marcus Alberti. You've wanted to get in touch with him, haven't you? Well, you'll get your chance when he brings me the diamond."

She shook her head.

Evan's gaze bored into hers. "You don't think your father will trade the diamond for his precious daughter? That would be most unfortunate. Then I would have no reason to keep you alive." Evan paused. "Your father was smarter than I thought. Nicole said he would make an easy mark. Lure him back to San Francisco, she told me. Set him up to take the fall—along with you. It made perfect sense. No one would ever suspect that I had stolen the diamond. It was a good plan. But somehow your father stole the diamond out from under me. In any other situation I would admire his cleverness, but not this time. I don't like to lose, Christina. In fact, I always win. I'm the best there ever was. You'll soon realize that."

His voice grew almost dreamy, as if he were lost in his own mind. He was reassuring himself as much as her. There was a chink in his armor, a little doubt, she realized. Her father had put that doubt there. He might be the first person in a long time to outsmart Evan. And Evan was not going to let her father get the better of him. But how could he be sure that her father would come? Had Evan found a way to contact her dad? If he had, he was definitely one step ahead—again.

It was because of her, she realized. She'd wasted too much time trying to figure out her relationship to Isabella instead of concentrating on finding her father. That distraction had put her and J.T. behind both Evan and Marcus. She'd been selfish, wanting to know about her past. And J.T. had let her. He'd listened

patiently to Maria's story. He'd supported her when it
had felt as if the world under her feet were shifting
sand. J.T. had done all that, knowing that they were
losing time in the chase. And she'd never said thank-
you. Never told him how she felt about him. She was
terrified that she wouldn't get that chance now—that it
was already too late.

Listening to Evan ramble on under his breath, she
saw the mental instability behind the good looks. J.T.
had told her that Evan had started out as a charming
con artist, able to sucker his victims with bright blue
eyes and an inviting smile, but over the years things
had begun to change. His cons had grown more serious, more violent. J.T. had believed that Evan was losing his grip on reality. She thought J.T. was probably
right.

Evan met her gaze, saw something in her eyes that
made him frown. "You think you know something," he
said. "Something about me."

She quickly gave a shake of her head, not wanting
to set him off.

"What did J.T. tell you? That I fleeced his father—
that I caused his death? His father was a loser, a gambler, a two-bit asshole. He wasn't even a challenge.
And you know what? J.T. hated him when he was
alive, used to bitch about his old man whenever he got
drunk. His daddy wanted him to be a big football
player and poor ol' J.T. just couldn't stand the pressure,
so he quit. He's a loser, too."

Evan smiled as he continued, "You think J.T. is
going to come riding up on his white horse and rescue
you, don't you? You believe he's your hero. You're

wrong. I'm the hero. I'm going to get the diamond and the girl." He stood up and leaned against the wall, looking down on her. "You'd like Jenny. She's sweet, kind, beautiful. And she's going to be mine. I will give her everything she deserves and more. She's the only one who ever knew the real me, the only one who truly appreciated my talents. When she sees that yellow diamond, she will know that I'm the man for her. She'll believe in me again. Everything will be perfect."

Evan was truly delusional. Christina tried to hang on to the hope that J.T. wasn't dead, just trapped somewhere, but Evan's words scared her. There was a sense of finality to his statements, as if he were closing a chapter in his life.

Evan walked over to one of the arches in the wall and gazed out, resting his hands on the waist-high railing. She could see the darkening sky beyond him. Night was falling. Where the hell were they? And where was everyone else?

"It won't be long now," Evan said. "Not long at all."

19

St. Anne's Convent was located an hour and a half away from Florence, in the heart of Tuscany, set on a remote hillside, far from any towns. Fortunately the church was known to the locals, one of whom had steered J.T. in the correct direction; otherwise he might have driven right by the thickly forested hillside.

He pulled into the courtyard in front of a large Gothic church complete with spires and a bell tower. To his right, a high cement wall ran a half mile down the hillside, hiding the convent buildings from view. As he got out of his car, he saw a sign placed near a path that led to a gate in the wall. It said ST. ANNE'S CONVENT AND SANITARIUM. That seemed appropriate for a madman. Evan had probably liked the idea of the chase ending in a place like this.

As J.T. moved across the courtyard, he saw another car parked under a grove of trees on the edge of the property, a flashy BMW with a convertible top, just the sort of car Evan enjoyed driving. J.T. jogged across the lot, ignoring the pain that stabbed at his head and other bruised body parts. He'd deal with his injuries later.

The car wasn't locked, so he opened the door to take a look around. In the backseat he saw a hoop earring, the kind Christina wore. His heart stopped. She was here. Evan had brought her here. Quietly shutting the door so as not to alert anyone to his presence, he headed for the church. He knew the fresco was supposed to be located in one of the rooms off the main chapel. Since the diamond was painted into the fresco, he was betting that it was some type of marker for a hiding place.

The church doors were open, which surprised him, since there didn't appear to be anyone around. Where were the nuns—the sisters of St. Anne's? It seemed awfully quiet, too quiet. He glanced down at his watch. It was six o'clock. Maybe everyone was at dinner, or perhaps this was one of those convents where they took a vow of silence. It didn't matter. It might be easier if no one was around, and certainly more logical for Evan to try to meet Marcus in a location where there wouldn't be any witnesses.

J.T. was certain that was what Evan intended. He'd kidnapped Christina for a reason—to make a deal with Marcus, the diamond for his daughter. He hoped to hell that Marcus wasn't going to act completely stupid and selfish and try to find a way to keep his diamond and his daughter. From what J.T. had heard of Marcus so far, it wasn't completely out of the realm of possibility. The man obviously had an ego and an arrogance that knew no bounds.

Entering the church, J.T. paused, getting his bearings.

He opened the double doors that led into the main part
of the building. A long line of empty pews met his gaze.
The altar was also empty. He strode down the center
aisle and through a door by the front of the church,
which led into a smaller chapel.

He caught his breath. There on the wall was the
painting. He stopped and stared, shocked that he had
actually found it, that it still existed. There was Catherine de Médici and her damned diamond.

J.T. walked over to the wall and ran his hand along
the surface, feeling lines and grooves beneath the
paint. He traced the diamond with his finger, pushed,
knocked, tapped to see if he heard a hollow ring. He
moved his hand lower, almost feeling like a jackass for
fondling the breasts of a woman in a painting, but his
instincts told him the fresco meant something. The
painter was supposed to help Catherine hide the diamond. What better place than in the painting itself?

He tried to remember what else Christina had told him
about the painting, about the curse. Something niggled at
the back of his brain. Catherine had called the diamond
her heart, because inside the stone was a rare flaw, a natural occurring mineral inclusion in the shape of a heart.
Bingo. He ran the tips of his fingers over Catherine's
heart and felt a small, inconspicuous knob. He pulled it,
and a small section of the wall opened up, revealing a
dark hole. Sticking his hand inside, he reached around,
hoping to feel the cold planes of a diamond. Nothing was
there. The hiding place was empty.

Fear rocketed through his body. Was he too late?
Had Evan and Marcus come and gone? Where was
Christina? What the hell had happened?

He closed the small door in the wall and looked around. Instinct told him that they couldn't be far. They had to be here somewhere. The car was still in the lot.

Christina shifted on the floor, trying to get her legs out in front of her so she could lean against the wall. Her muscles were cramping, and she was starting to panic at the thought of not being able to open her mouth. Evan was getting scarier by the moment. He kept walking around the small space, looking out each long window as if a different view would give him a different answer. He was getting impatient. She could feel the tension emanating from his body.

What would happen if her father didn't come? What would Evan do with her?

Evan turned to face her again. "He's late."

She wished she could answer him. She wished he would take the tape off her mouth so she could try to talk him out of whatever plan he had in mind.

"If he doesn't come, you're in a lot of trouble," Evan continued. "I won't have any use for you." He glanced back at the open archway. "It would be easy to fall," he mused. "Just that one little railing, not even waist-high. Someone could trip, stumble, go right over the side. It's a long way down to the courtyard."

Chills ran through her at his words. She wanted to pray. She was in a church tower, after all. Maybe God was listening. But what should she pray for? If her father came and handed over the diamond, Evan wouldn't need either of them. He might kill them both. If her father didn't come, at least he'd still be safe. But for how long? Evan wouldn't give up. He wanted that diamond, and he wouldn't stop until he got it.

The sound of footsteps drew her attention to the door.

Evan pulled a gun from his suit jacket.

The door flew open. J.T. entered the tower, gun drawn, eyes blazing. Christina couldn't believe it was him. She'd expected to see her father, but it was J.T. He was alive. *Thank God!* But he was hurt, she realized. One side of his face was swollen, purple, and the skin around his eye was turning black. She could see blood in his hair and on his shirt.

Evan moved closer to her, turning his gun to her head.

"Drop it," J.T. ordered, his gun aimed at Evan's heart.

"You drop it, or Christina dies," Evan returned.

"I'll kill you before you have a chance to pull the trigger."

"Are you sure you can beat me—that you won't miss the shot?" Evan drawled. "You're not a clutch player, J.T. Isn't that why you quit football—too many losses in the last two minutes of the fourth quarter? Too many missed passes? Are you willing to take that chance on Christina's life? This is my game. Don't let yourself think otherwise."

"Wrong. This is the end of your game. If you wanted me out of it, you should have killed me at the farmhouse." His gaze narrowed on Evan. "But you didn't. That was sloppy. Getting careless, Evan?"

"Not for a minute. It's more fun when you're in the chase, J.T. Don't you know that by now?"

"Drop the gun," J.T. repeated, his gaze determined.

Christina felt reassured by his demeanor. However, her hopes diminished when she looked at Evan and saw the same confidence in his expression.

Both men wanted to win, but that wasn't possible. Someone would lose. It couldn't be J.T.—not just for her sake, but for his sake as well. He had waited a long time to have Evan in his sights. He wanted payback for his father, justice, revenge. And she was in the way. She wished she could disappear, take herself out of this moment. She didn't want to be the reason J.T. lost Evan again, but she was caught. She couldn't move. She couldn't speak. She couldn't do anything to stop what was about to happen. She could only watch.

The two men exchanged a long, measuring look, as if they were each weighing their options. She knew J.T. was strong, courageous, and not at all the kind of man who would choke in a crisis. But Evan was clever, cunning, and far more reckless. Evan didn't have boundaries. J.T. did. Evan had nothing to lose; he was a criminal with no conscience. If he were caught, he could spend the rest of his life in jail. He would fight to the end.

"Let Christina go," J.T. said. "This is between us, Evan. It started with us, and it should end with us."

"We're nowhere near the end," Evan replied. "Not everyone is here yet."

"Her father isn't coming. He's downstairs. I told him to stay there," J.T. said, surprising Christina with his words. She wondered if he was telling the truth or bluffing. She certainly didn't have a good track record when it came to reading men and their lies.

"Oh, he'll come," Evan replied. "I have his daughter. There is nothing like the love between a father and his child. But you already knew that, didn't you, J.T.?"

Christina inwardly winced at the painful stab Evan had just taken at J.T., reminding him of the father he'd lost. Evan was certainly willing to play every card in his hand.

"Your father told me how disappointed you would be in him—after he lost all his money," Evan continued. "He said it would give you one more reason to hate him—the way he hated you. He said you were an ungrateful son of a bitch, not appreciating everything he had done for you."

"Do you really believe I care what you say or think?" J.T. challenged.

"Just passing the time."

"You'll have lots of time to pass in jail," J.T. returned. "You won't be getting out for a long, long time."

"You've said that before, but somehow it never works out that way. No one can catch me, J.T. I'm invincible."

Before J.T. could reply, more footsteps came pounding up the stairs.

"Stay out!" J.T. shouted. "Don't come in here. It's a trap. Call the police."

Evan shifted so close to Christina that his leg brushed against her arm, the barrel of the gun moving closer to her head.

The footsteps kept coming despite J.T.'s warning. A moment later her father entered the room. He was wearing black slacks, a gray button-down dress shirt,

and a confident, reassuring smile. Her heart skipped a
beat. He had come to rescue her. She didn't know why
she had ever doubted him. Of course he'd come. He
stopped just inside the door, his smile dimming as he
realized the trouble she was in. "Christina, my God!
Are you all right?" Marcus took a step forward.

"Not so fast," Evan warned. "Don't move or she
takes a bullet in the head, Pops."

Marcus stopped abruptly. "You don't have to hurt
her. I'm here. I have what you want." He glanced over
at J.T. "You couldn't stop this from happening? Aren't
you the FBI agent who's supposed to be protecting my
daughter?"

"Nice to meet you, too," J.T. snapped. "And you're
the reason your daughter has a gun to her head. You
have a hell of a lot to explain."

"He can explain later," Evan ordered. "Now hand
over the diamond, Alberti, or your daughter is dead."

"You think you're going to kill Christina and walk
away?" J.T. asked. "You're out of your fucking mind,
Evan. There's no way you're leaving here with the diamond. You shoot Christina, I'll shoot you."

"It could work that way," Evan admitted. "But you
can't watch me kill Christina. You won't take that
chance. I know you as well as you know yourself—
probably better."

Christina wondered if Evan was right. J.T. was an
honorable man, but he also wanted Evan so badly he
could taste it. She'd learned from her father that the
line between right and wrong could shift with desire.
Would it shift with J.T.'s desire for revenge and
payback? Or his desire for her?

J.T.'s hand was steady, his gun still fixed on Evan.
Evan was equally strong. Someone would have to
break first. Who would it be?

Marcus put up a hand. "There's no need for anyone
to shoot. I have the diamond. I'm prepared to hand it
over. No one needs to get hurt. Please."

Her father reached into his jacket pocket and pulled
out the diamond necklace. It glittered in the shadows.
Marcus looked at her, then at the jewel. She thought
she saw a flash of indecision in his eyes. Could he
really do it—could he put her first after all these years?

"Give it to him, Alberti," J.T. ordered. "You've
caused your daughter enough grief in her life. What are
you waiting for?"

"I am sorry, Christina," Marcus muttered. "I didn't
mean to involve you. I never thought you would come
to Italy." He fingered the diamond in his hand and then
lifted it to toss to Evan.

Christina watched the necklace leave her father's
hand. Everything moved in slow motion. The yellow
diamond streaked through the air. Evan's body tensed
as he raised his hand to catch it.

It was her moment, she realized. Evan was so close to
her, and all his attention was focused on the diamond. It
was possible that the gun pointing at her head would go
off, but it was a chance she had to take. She couldn't let
Evan win. She couldn't let anyone else get hurt. God
only knew what he would do once he had the diamond.

She threw her body as hard as she could at Evan's
knee. He stumbled and the gun discharged before it
flew across the floor. She waited for a searing pain that
didn't come.

J.T. tackled Evan. They struggled for the gun in J.T.'s hand.

Her father came to her aid, ripping the tape off her mouth. "I'm sorry," he muttered.

"Untie my hands," she said, keeping her gaze on J.T. and Evan as they battled for the gun. They shoved and pushed, ramming each other into the wall. They were evenly matched in size, height, and determination. They moved closer to one of the open arches in the tower, their struggle so intense neither one could see what was coming.

Christina screamed at J.T., "Watch out!"

"Get her out of here," J.T. yelled at Marcus. "Keep her safe."

"Help him," she told her dad. "I can do this."

"I have to get you away," Marcus said. Her father went to work on the rope binding her legs. Their hands clashed as she tried to help him with the knots. When she was free she jumped to her feet. She stumbled, her legs cramping from the position she'd been in. Her father tried to pull her out of the tower, but she couldn't go. She couldn't leave J.T. She had to find a way to help him. Evan's gun was on the floor where he'd dropped it. She scrambled to get it.

Her move distracted J.T. The second he turned his head, Evan wrestled the gun out of J.T.'s hand. He aimed it at Christina, his finger on the trigger, his eyes wild. "Stay back. I'll kill her."

Christina froze, seeing the truth in Evan's expression. His finger was already beginning to tighten.

"Get her out of here," J.T. told Marcus again.

"Christina, please," Marcus said, worry in his voice.

"Don't move," Evan ordered. His gun never wavering, he squatted down and picked up the diamond necklace from the ground and put it in his pocket. He had what he wanted. Now what?

Christina moved slightly, catching J.T.'s eye. His lips tightened. He gazed back at Evan and put up his hands. "You win. Take the diamond; go."

Christina couldn't believe what she was hearing. Evan also seemed surprised. His hand shook, a sign of indecision. That was all it took, one split second of hesitation.

J.T. launched his body against Evan's in a full-blown tackle. Evan stumbled backward, trying to grab on to the walls of the tower as his body slid toward an arched opening. When that didn't work, he threw his arms around J.T.'s neck, dragging him with him.

Christina watched in horror as Evan's body rammed into the single rail with so much force that he started to go over the side. His eyes bulged in fear. His arms tightened around J.T. Evan was going to take J.T. with him.

Christina threw her arms around J.T.'s legs. "Help me!" she yelled at her dad.

Marcus came up behind her and yanked Evan's arm off of J.T.'s neck. With nothing to anchor him, Evan fell backward over the railing, through the arch, into the night. It happened in slow motion, his arms and legs flailing, a blood-chilling scream filling the air, seeming to go on forever and ever.

Christina and Marcus pulled J.T. away from the opening. He bent over, hands on his knees as he struggled for breath.

"Are you all right?" she asked.

He straightened and opened his arms. She threw herself into his embrace, pressing her face against his chest, thrilled to hear the rapid pounding of his heart. He was okay. He was alive. *Thank God!*

Tears streamed down her face in blessed relief. She didn't want to let him go. She'd almost lost him. They'd almost lost each other.

"You scared the hell out of me," J.T. murmured as he pulled away. "Did he hurt you?" His worried eyes searched her face. "When I saw you tied up, with that tape over your mouth, I wanted to—"

She put her fingers against his lips. "Sh-sh. I'm okay." She reluctantly stepped back, glancing at her father. He was staring at her and J.T., probably wondering what was going on between his daughter and an FBI agent. "I guess I should introduce you."

"No need," J.T. said. "I'm the man who loves your daughter."

Marcus nodded. "I'm glad to hear it," he said with a slight smile.

Christina was thrilled to hear the words, but J.T. was already turning away.

"I need to check on Evan," he said grimly.

"We're three stories up. He couldn't have survived, could he?"

"I have to make sure." J.T. headed toward the door.

Christina and her father followed J.T. down a long, winding staircase that seemed to take them forever to descend. When they reached the ground they raced out to the courtyard. Evan's body lay in a crumpled heap on the cobblestones, one hand outstretched as if he had tried to break his fall.

When they moved closer, Christina gasped with alarm. Evan's bright blue eyes were open, staring straight back at them. Was he alive?

J.T. dropped down on one knee, gazing at Evan. "He's laughing at me, even in death," he said bitterly.

"Are you sure he's dead?" From the angle of his head, it appeared as if his neck had snapped, but there was something about those brilliant blue eyes staring up at them that made her spine tingle.

J.T. put a finger to the side of Evan's neck, searching for a pulse. "Nothing. He's dead." He paused for a long moment and then said, "I won, Evan. You lost. Game over." With one hand he reached over and pulled the lids down on Evan's eyes.

Christina blew out a breath of relief. J.T. had his justice. And Evan had died at his own hand. His greed had taken him over the edge of reality as well as the bell tower. She met J.T.'s gaze and saw conflicted emotions in his eyes. Then he pried Evan's fingers apart and retrieved the diamond necklace. That stone had caused a hell of a lot of trouble. He slipped it into his pocket and stood up.

Before she could say anything a group of three nuns came running across the courtyard, obviously having heard Evan's screams. Marcus intercepted them. They spoke in rapid Italian, hands gesturing, words flying. One of the nuns returned to the building, presumably to call the police, Christina thought. The other two dropped down on their knees beside Evan, one checking for his pulse, the other lowering her head and clasping her hands in prayer. Her father stood over them, watching, offering a longer explanation as to what had happened.

She wondered why her father wasn't trying to run, why he wasn't using the distraction to slip into the dark countryside. It would be easy for him to get away. But he wasn't even trying.

J.T. took her hand and led her a short distance away from the others. "We have just a few minutes before the police arrive." He put his arms around her and squeezed tight, pressing his face into her hair. She heard him take a long, deep breath; then he lifted his head. He touched her wet cheeks with his fingers, wiping away the remnants of her tears. "I was afraid Evan had hurt you," he murmured, "that he knew that hurting you would punish me more than anything he could do to me."

"He didn't touch me," she said softly, lacing her fingers together behind his neck. She needed to hold him for as long as she could.

"What happened? How did Evan get you out of the farmhouse?"

"He put some cloth over my face. It smelled vile. I couldn't breathe. It knocked me out. When I woke up, I was tied up and in the tower." She pressed onto her tiptoes and kissed him tenderly on the lips, needing more than just his touch. She needed to taste him to believe he was really all right. He kissed her back like he never wanted to stop. But they had to stop. They had to talk before the police came, before they had to explain everything that had happened.

"I was so scared, J.T.," she murmured.

"I know. I wish I'd gotten there sooner."

"Not scared for me—for you," she corrected. "I thought you were dead. Evan said you weren't coming. He acted as if he'd killed you."

"He knocked me out at the house and shoved me down the basement stairs."

"Oh, my God!"

He gave a dismissive shake of his head. "It was just a bump on the head, some bruises."

Observing his swollen face, she suspected he was downplaying his injuries, but at least he was still in one piece.

"It took me a while to get out of the basement," he continued. "Every minute that passed I thought of you."

"How did you know to come here?"

"I found the book and the sketch in the farmhouse. I figured the fresco had something to do with the diamond, and I took a shot that Evan might have brought you here. Thanks for leaving that book out."

"That wasn't deliberate. I had just found it when I heard someone coming down the hall. I thought it was you. I wanted to tell you that I finally had a clue, so I went running out of the room, straight into Evan. I recognized him from the picture you'd shown me. He wasn't in disguise anymore."

J.T. turned his head once more in Evan's direction, as if he still couldn't believe the man he had chased for so long was dead.

"You got your justice," she told him. "Evan Chadwick can't hurt anyone again."

"It hasn't sunk in yet." He gazed back to her, his hands moving to her arms, holding tight, as if he was afraid she'd run. "When I realized that Evan had kidnapped you, Christina, I was more terrified than I've ever been in my life." He paused, his fingers biting into her arms. "I love you. I want you to know that."

Her eyes blurred with tears. "I love you, too, J.T., and I was so afraid I wouldn't have a chance to tell you. We kept putting off talking about us, and then it was almost too late to talk. When I thought you were dead, I realized how much I had left unsaid. That I'd never told you I appreciated the help you've given me, the way you put your job on the line, the way you supported me when I found out about my mother, and the fact that you came racing to save my life tonight. I know you wanted to get Evan, but—"

"But I wanted to save you more," J.T. finished. "When we were up there in the tower, I had only one thought—to keep you alive. Evan was right when he said I wouldn't be able to watch him shoot you. There was no way I could let him do that. I was about to throw down my gun when your father pulled the diamond out of his pocket."

"He came through, too—in the end." She glanced back at her father and saw that he was watching them. "I thought he would have run by now, but he's still here."

"I thought he would run, too," J.T. admitted.

She met his gaze. "You were going to let him go, weren't you?"

"He is your father. And no matter what he's done, he loves you, and you love him."

She nodded. "I do. I'd better talk to him."

"Do it quick. The police will be here soon. I'll try to help him, Christina, but I can't make any promises. He did steal the diamond. We'll have to sort out who it really belongs to later."

"I understand. I'm not asking you for any more

favors. My dad has to face the music. I know that." She forced herself to let go of J.T. and walk over to her father. "Dad," she said, not knowing where to start.

Marcus opened his arms, and after a moment's hesitation she walked right into them. She cursed herself for being so weak. He'd lied to her, cheated. He'd stolen valuable objects over the years and put her life in danger. But he was still her father, still the man who had raised her all alone. It was so complicated. She loved him. She hated him. In the end he had come through for her.

She stepped back and gazed into his face. "How did you know where I was, Dad?"

"I received a message from Evan Chadwick. He told me to meet him here or he would hurt you."

"And you came."

He appeared surprised by the question. "Of course I came. You're my daughter. I love you."

"You lied to me. You kept things from me. I know everything, Dad. I went to the Benedetti house. I spoke to Maria. She told me about . . . about my mother."

He drew in a quick, sharp breath and then let it out. He slowly nodded. "I guess it was time."

"It was long past time. Why didn't you tell me? Why keep it a secret? Did you think I would go running to the Benedettis? I don't understand."

"I didn't want to hurt you. I wanted to protect you."

"No, there's more to it than that," she said with a skeptical shake of her head. "I know you, Dad. You're not that noble. I have to admit that up in the tower there was a part of me that wondered if you'd give up that diamond for me. I know how much you love historical pieces."

"Not more than I love you, Christina."

"If you loved me, you wouldn't have come to Barclay's and impersonated Howard Keaton and stolen the diamond from me. How could you do that? How could you look me in the eyes and lie?"

"It was necessary."

"No, it wasn't."

"Yes, it was," he said firmly. "And there's something you should know about the necklace—the one he has in his pocket," Marcus added, pointing to J.T.

"What?" she asked warily.

J.T. took a step forward, frowning at the turn in their conversation. "What's going on?"

"I had several copies made. Some were for practice," Marcus explained. "It took a while to get it exactly right. In the end, I kept the copies. I thought I might need them. A couple of months ago a woman contacted me, telling me about the diamond. She had no idea I knew more about it than she did."

"Was her name Nicole?" J.T. interjected.

"I believe it was. I met with her briefly. She said she and her partner had a plan to steal the diamond and thought I might want in on it. I told her I wasn't interested, that I would never bring trouble to you, Christina."

"Yet you did. And Nicole and Evan set you up as the scapegoat for their crime—you and me."

"I must admit I didn't see that coming. But the more I thought about that diamond, the more I realized this was my one chance to make things right. I also figured

that Nicole was planning to steal it anyway. I couldn't
let it end up in anyone else's hands. I had to make my
move first." Marcus paused. "In the tower I gave Evan
one of the copies I had made. I didn't think he would
be able to figure it out right away. I thought it would
buy us time."

Her jaw dropped in amazement. "And what if he
had figured it out?" she demanded. "My God! You
risked my life again. I can't believe it. I thought you
came to save me. But you wanted to have both me and
the diamond."

J.T. walked over to them and pulled the diamond out
of his pocket, his lips drawing into a tight line. "So
where is the real stone, Mr. Alberti?"

"It's where it belongs," Marcus said simply.

"It's not," J.T. said with a definitive shake of his
head. "If you're talking about the hiding place in the
fresco, I already checked. The diamond isn't there. I
bet Evan checked, too. That's why he took Christina
up to the bell tower. He knew you still had the real
stone."

"Where is the fresco?" Christina asked, distracted
by J.T.'s revelation.

"It's in the small chapel over there."

"The stone didn't belong in the fresco either," Marcus interrupted.

"Just stop it, Dad," Christina ordered. "Stop lying
and acting dramatic and telling half-truths. Maria told
me that if that diamond belonged to anyone, it belonged to me. I was the heir, so if you've stuck that
stone in some ancient cross or something, you'd better
have a good reason why."

Her father stared back at her for a long moment. "You're right, Christina. The diamond would belong to you if . . ."

"If what?"

"You need to come with me," Marcus said abruptly.

"Come where?"

"Into the convent," he said, taking her hand.

"If you're thinking of escaping, you can forget about that," J.T. told him.

"There's nowhere to go," Marcus said. "Except inside. You can come, too." He looked over at the nuns and said something in Italian. The older nun nodded and waved them toward the building.

"You know these people," Christina mused, realizing now that her father had been talking to the nuns as if they were more than acquaintances. "How do you know them?"

Marcus didn't answer her; he just kept walking.

They moved through another quiet courtyard and then into a building. It didn't look like a convent or an abbey. It appeared to be a hospital—a medical center, she realized. Her legs grew heavy with tension, and a terrifying panic ran through her body. Where on earth were they going? What could her father possibly have to show her in this hospital?

He stopped in front of a half-open door, then pushed it all the way open and waved her into the room. She hesitated. She couldn't handle any more surprises.

"You want the truth, Christina," Marcus said quietly. "It's in this room. The choice is yours."

Swallowing hard, she stepped over the threshold. There was a small lamp next to a bed. A woman sat in a chair facing the door. She had long brown hair that fell to her waist, and dark eyes that were so familiar. . . .

Christina's heart stopped. "Oh, my God," she whispered. "It's you."

20

Christina looked from the woman to her father. He walked over to the woman and put a hand on her shoulder. The woman didn't react in any way.

"This is Isabella," Marcus said gently. "Your mother."

She bit down on her lip. She'd never thought to hear those words—*your mother.* Her mother was dead. Her mother had left her. That was the story. Now her father wanted her to believe another story—that this woman sitting in this convent hospital in Tuscany was her mother. How could she be?

Christina started shaking her head. She couldn't move forward. She couldn't move back. Nor could she tear her eyes from the face that looked so much like her own.

Why wasn't Isabella saying anything to her?

In fact, her mother wasn't even looking at her. She was staring at the wall. She seemed completely oblivious to the fact that three people were standing in her room, two of whom she'd never seen before.

"What's wrong with her?" Christina whispered.

"She had a nervous breakdown. She lost her mind," Marcus said quietly, his eyes meeting hers. "After you were born, the depression set in. Then she got sick, a high fever. It ravaged her body. Her mind gave up. She's been like this ever since."

"For almost thirty years?" Christina asked in shock.

Marcus nodded. "Yes." He kissed Isabella softly on the cheek. She didn't even blink. Then Marcus gently pulled the top of her sweater to one side. Christina wondered what he was doing, and then she realized what her father had been trying to tell her. He had brought·the diamond back to its rightful owner. The necklace hung around Isabella's neck, the diamond glittering against her pale skin.

"It is hers," Marcus said, gazing back at Christina. "It was always meant to be hers—and then yours. Vittorio stole it from her when he found out about our affair. He took it to punish her. He knew how much it meant to her. Isabella was fascinated by the story of Catherine and her first love. It was all she talked about when we met. We learned the story together. We found the fresco, the secret hiding place . . . everything. Isabella said she would hide it away until she had a daughter or until one of her sons had a daughter. But everything went wrong," he said sadly. "Everything."

"Because the two of you didn't belong together," Christina said. "She was married. You should have left her alone."

"I tried. She was so unhappy, so fragile, so beautiful. I couldn't resist her. I was weak. But you know that about me, Christina. You know that I can't ever walk away from what I want."

She did know that. And still she loved him. What was wrong with her? Shaking her head, Christina turned her attention back to Isabella. "Why didn't you tell me she was alive and ill? Why did you make me believe that she had left me, when apparently she did everything she could to try to keep me?"

"I didn't want you to go looking for her. I didn't want you to be burdened with a mother who couldn't take care of you, who couldn't see you, hear you, touch you."

Were his motives pure—or was this just another rationalization?

"Will she ever get better?" she asked.

"The diamond was my last hope," Marcus answered. "She breathes. She eats when they feed her. She sleeps. But she doesn't speak. She doesn't live. She just exists. When I saw that the diamond was being sent to Barclay's, I knew I had to get it back for her. I thought its power might be able to help her. But it's been three days and nothing has changed."

She heard the hopelessness in his voice, the sorrow, and her heart softened in spite of her anger. Her father loved Isabella. That much was clear. But still . . .

"Why didn't you bring me to see her?" she asked. "Maybe that's what would have made the difference."

"I did bring you to see her," Marcus replied, shocking her once again. "Despite the phony funeral Vittorio set up, I knew she was alive. Maria had told me that Vittorio wanted the world, especially his sons, to believe she was dead. Maria tried to convince Vittorio that he was wrong, but he was determined to erase Isabella's existence. I was going to call him a liar myself, but then I saw Isabella, and I thought perhaps it would be easier for her to have no contact with him. But I did bring you, Christina, when you were about fifteen months old. We stayed for several days. I tried to put you in her arms, but she wouldn't hold you. She didn't respond at all. And you were scared. You started crying when you saw her. You wouldn't stop until we left the room. So I took you back home and I raised you myself. I kept in touch with Maria, who checked on her almost every day for the last thirty years. There was never a change in her condition." He glanced down at Isabella. "Her body is here, but her soul is somewhere else."

"Does Vittorio know she's here?"

"Of course. He pays the bills. He sent her to another institution at first, a cold, dark place. Maria finally convinced him to move her here. We knew the fresco was in the church, and we thought that since Isabella loved the story so much, it might help her to see the picture, to see the diamond, even if she couldn't hold it in her hand. The nuns took her in there all the time, but it didn't help. Nothing helps." Marcus let out a frustrated sigh. "I wouldn't have stolen the diamond from Barclay's if I'd had any other choice, Christina. Over the years I tried to get it from Vittorio, but he had it hidden away in a vault. I knew this was my one chance to get it back for Isabella. I had to take it. I disguised myself as Professor Keaton so I could switch the diamond at the party. I knew that Nicole and Evan wouldn't make their attempt until the day of the auction."

"Did you set the smoke bombs off, too?"

"No, that was Evan. It was convenient, though. It provided a good distraction."

"You knew Evan would steal the fake. Didn't you wonder what he'd do next?"

"It was a very good copy. As I said, the jeweler and I went through several tries before we got it almost perfect. I wasn't sure anyone would be able to tell the difference."

"But you left out the mineral inclusion of the heart," she said. "The noted flaw."

"I tried to put it in. It was never quite right, but it was close. You weren't sure. You told me so yourself."

"It was very good," she admitted. "You almost got away with everything—only you didn't."

"If I have to go to jail, I will," Marcus said. "But I had to try to bring your mother back to life one last time. The diamond belongs to her."

"I'm surprised Vittorio didn't send the police here," Christina murmured. "Didn't he know you'd bring the diamond here?"

"That would have meant revealing his lies," Marcus answered. "He wouldn't want anyone in Florence to know the truth. He probably thought he could steal it away later."

That made sense. Christina didn't know what else to say. She was so confused. She looked at J.T. "What should I do now?"

"Well," he said slowly, "maybe you should talk to your mother."

Christina turned back to Isabella, still not sure she could believe this woman was her mother. She moved a few steps closer to the chair. The woman's gaze

seemed fixed on the wall behind Christina. She didn't
seem to be aware of their conversation at all. "Can she
hear me?" she asked her father.

Marcus shrugged. "I don't know."

"I'm afraid I'll do something wrong."

"You can't make her worse," Marcus said.

Christina squatted in front of her mother, so they
were at eye level. She took a long moment to gather
her thoughts. This woman was her mother. She had to
be around sixty-two or -three. Yet, she looked younger
than that, as if she'd been frozen in time. In a way, that
was exactly what had happened.

What words could she say now that would cross the
decades of distance between them?

She covered Isabella's hand with her own.

"It's me, Christina," she said softly. "I'm your
daughter. I've come back to you. I'm . . . home."

Christina closed her eyes, overwhelmed by emotion.
And then she felt it—a small, tiny squeeze. Her eyes
flew open. Isabella still wasn't looking at her. Christina
gazed down at their hands and saw Isabella's finger
move. It tightened around Christina's finger, much the
way a mother would hold the finger of her baby.

"She knows you're here," Marcus said, jubilation in
his voice. "Her hand moved. I saw it."

"I felt it," Christina said, meeting her father's gaze.
"But is it enough?"

"It's enough for now," he whispered. "For now, it's
enough."

It was almost three o'clock in the morning, and
Christina still wasn't asleep. J.T. and her father had left

hours ago with the local police. She'd wanted to go along, but they'd both insisted that she stay behind. J.T. didn't want her to get caught up in her father's crimes, and Marcus had agreed that she should stay out of it. Fortunately, the sisters of St. Anne's had offered her a small room in the convent in which to sleep.

It was a simple, barren room—a single bed, a dresser with an old-fashioned washing bowl and pitcher, a lamp on the bedside table, a large cross over the door, and a Bible in the drawer. The nuns had been very kind to her, especially after learning that she was Isabella's daughter. It was clear they had a fondness for her mother, although she wasn't sure exactly why, since Isabella seemed incapable of expressing any emotion.

She'd had so many shocks where her mother was concerned, she didn't know how she felt about any of it, except that she was glad to finally know her mother's name and the reason why they'd never been together. It was so sad to think that Isabella had lived in a catatonic state for thirty years. Why? What kept her from returning to reality? Her father had hoped the diamond would bring her back to life, but so far it hadn't made a difference. There had been no change at all until tonight—when her mother's finger had curled around hers. Had it been on purpose? Had Isabella felt something—some long-ago connection between mother and child?

Or was Christina just hoping for a miracle—as her father had been?

She gazed toward the window, where the open curtain revealed a full moon and bright stars. Out here in the countryside there were no city lights to dim the stars. It felt so odd to be looking at the sky from inside a convent in Italy. Yet this was the same sky, the same moon, and the same stars that her mother had stared at every day of her life. For almost thirty years they'd been separated by emotional and physical distance, but tonight they were sleeping under the same roof. It felt odd and yet strangely comforting. She felt as if this place, this land, was where she was supposed to be. She'd always wanted roots. Her real roots were here in Italy. But her life was back in San Francisco.

And J.T. . . . well, his life was in LA with the FBI. He lived on the road, traveled from case to case. Although she wondered what he would do now that his nemesis was gone.

Was he feeling triumphant, victorious? She hadn't seen that on his face when he'd looked at Evan. Revenge usually turned out to be more sour than sweet. Evan was dead, but that fact didn't bring J.T.'s father back. It didn't change what had happened. Still, maybe J.T. could face the future with a lighter heart, a more carefree spirit. He deserved it after so many years of carrying the weight of his father's death on his shoulders.

A tap at the door sent her upright in bed, her heart immediately jumping into her throat. She knew the danger was over. Evan was dead. But it was the middle of the night, she was alone, and there had been far too many surprises already. She was thankful she hadn't bothered to change out of her clothes into the nightgown the nuns had offered her. Her instincts had told her to stay ready for anything.

The door slowly opened. She held her breath and then let it out in relief as J.T. slipped into the room. She put a hand to her heart. "You scared me."

"Sorry. I wasn't sure if you were asleep. I didn't want to wake you." He walked over to the bed and kissed her on the mouth, long and tender.

She scooted over on the bed so he could sit down. "What happened with my father? Is he in jail?"

"For tonight, but I think he'll be released in the morning."

"Why?"

"I spoke to Vittorio Benedetti. In fact, I woke him up. We had a little chat about you and your mother and the secrets he'd like to keep from his sons. They don't know their mother is alive and locked up in this convent."

"I had a feeling they didn't."

"He said he did it to protect them from a lifetime of sad and grieving visits with a mother who couldn't love them. That's why he held a public funeral all those years ago and buried an empty coffin, set up a false marker. He wanted it over."

"That's sick. He should have tried harder."

"At any rate, he's agreed to speak to Barclay's about dropping the charges against your father as long as he gets the diamond back. I have to warn you that he still might try to sell the diamond," J.T. added. "I know you think it belongs to your mother, but legally it's a lot more complicated than that. Maybe he'll have second thoughts when he thinks about it."

"Maybe I can convince him," she said.

He gave her a loving smile. "I bet you could. How are you holding up?"

"Okay. My pulse has finally returned to normal. I never imagined Isabella was alive. Although she's not really alive, is she?"

"I don't know, Christina."

"Me, either. What about you? How do you feel knowing that Evan is dead?"

"Like I'm about fifty pounds lighter."

"You got your justice."

"Yeah, I did. It's funny, though—in some ways I wish he had lived. I would have liked to see him in jail, behind bars, suffering the way he made other people suffer. On the other hand, now I know he's really not coming back. He can't escape. He can't cause any more trouble."

"So it's over."

"Yeah." Shadows filled his eyes. "I have to fly home tomorrow, to LA. I have to wrap up this case, talk to my boss, figure out how much trouble I'm in." He played with her hair. "Are you going back to San Francisco— or are you staying here?"

She took a deep breath. It was a question she'd been asking herself all night. "Staying here," she whispered, not sure what her decision would mean to J.T. or any future they might have together, but this choice was for her mother. "I have to learn more about Isabella. I have to try to connect with her. I can't leave without doing that."

"It's probably hopeless."

"I still have to try. I guess there's more of my father in me than I'd like to admit."

"Marcus isn't a bad guy. I don't know what he did in the past, but in this instance his heart was in the right place. He wanted to help the woman he loved. I can get behind that."

"Thank you for understanding his motives." Their eyes met for a long moment. There was so much she wanted to say, and yet so much she was afraid to say. "I know it's fast, J.T., but I do love you with all my heart. I don't know what you want from me, if anything, but—"

"I want you," he interrupted. "That's all I want."

"I don't know where I'm going to end up, what I will do with my life. I'm not sure I can return to Barclay's—even if they would take me back. I've spent so much of my life studying other people's history. Now I need to know more about my own history. I came to Italy to find my father, but I think I actually found myself."

He smiled. "Yeah, I think you did. I don't know what's in store for me either. I may retire from the FBI, if they haven't fired me already. The only thing I know for sure is that whatever we both end up doing—we should do it together. What do you think?"

"I think it sounds perfect. I don't care what you do with your life. It's your choice. You know that, right?" J.T. had already spent too much of his life trying to please the people he loved. She didn't want him to do the same for her.

"I do know that. I also know that you're an amazing woman."

"Tell me more," she said as they stretched out together on the narrow bed.

"You're strong, courageous, loveable, passionate. . . ."

"Keep going," she said lightly, smiling.

"Sexy, sweet, intriguing—"

She covered his mouth with her hand. "Okay, that's enough. You've earned a kiss."

"Hell, I'd better have earned more than a kiss."

"We're in a convent, J.T. We can't have . . . sex," she whispered.

He rolled her over on her back, pinning her beneath his body, cradling her face in his hands. "We're not going to have sex. We're going to make love."

"In that case," she said, "how can I say no?"

Epilogue

Three weeks later . . .

It was a beautiful, sunny day on the hillside above Florence. New flowers bloomed in the freshly weeded garden. A soothing stream of water trickled through the once-dry fountain. Hummingbirds pecked at the feeder Christina had set up in the yard.

As she stepped onto the porch, she let out a sigh of appreciation and satisfaction. She'd spent the past three weeks catching up on her past, learning about her relatives, going through the family albums, spending time with Maria, listening to stories about Isabella as a child. Most important, she'd spent time with her mother.

Isabella had made some progress. It was a miracle, the nuns proclaimed. Her father thought it was the diamond working its magic. Christina didn't know the answer, but yesterday when she'd visited her mother, Isabella had actually looked at her, and she'd lifted her hand and stroked her hair. She was coming back. How far back no one could say, but it was a start.

Christina had also spoken to Vittorio. She'd persuaded him that it was in his best interests to allow the diamond to remain with Isabella. He still didn't want his sons to know the truth about her mother or about Christina, so he'd agreed to trade the diamond for her silence. It was a bargain she was willing to make. Vittorio had also agreed not to press charges against her father. The Kensingtons and Barclay's had happily let the whole matter drop; they had other problems to deal with. Jeremy had been arrested for David's murder. And Alexis was coming to terms with the fact that not only was her husband a killer, but her cousin, Nicole, was the one who had orchestrated the plan to have Evan steal the diamond.

Nothing would be the same again at Barclay's, but Christina didn't care. That life seemed very far behind her now.

The sound of a car chugging up the narrow road to the house made her heart skip a beat. Every day she'd wondered if he'd come, if he'd forgotten about her, moved on with his life. She'd wanted to call him, but she'd stopped herself a dozen times. They'd each agreed to work out their own lives first. And then whatever happened . . . happened.

The rental car pulled up in front of the house. J.T. stepped out, wearing blue jeans and a leather jacket. He slipped the dark glasses off his eyes as he strode toward her. Her heart melted under the force of his smile, the promise in his eyes.

"Miss me?"

"More than I could ever say," she replied.

"I quit my job."

"So did I," she returned.

"How's your mother?"

"She looked at me yesterday—at me, not through me. There was something in her eyes. It might be my imagination, but I'm hopeful."

"That's what I like about you—you never lose hope. This place looks good, better than the last time I was here. Is your father around?"

"No, he's decided to move back to San Francisco for a while, give me some space." She swallowed hard, not sure what to say, but she knew she had to ask the question running through her head. "Are you staying?"

"I thought I would." He closed the space between them with a quick, impatient stride, his hands cupping her face, forcing her to look into his eyes. "Is that all right with you?"

"How long?" she whispered.

"How about forever?"

"I don't know if I'm going to stay here forever."

"That's fine with me. I don't care where you go, as long as I can go, too."

"That sounds romantic and completely impractical," she said, feeling tears creep into her eyes. "One of us has to work. Maybe both of us."

"So we'll work. We'll find jobs. We'll make a life somewhere. We don't have to decide today. In fact, I think we've both rushed into career decisions in the past. I played football for my father and moved into the FBI so I could catch Evan. You went into museums and an auction house to follow in your father's foot-steps. Why don't we take our time? Figure out what we really want?"

She felt a rush of pleasure at his words. The future could work itself out. Right now she was more interested in the present. "What are we going to do while we're taking our time?" she asked with a smile.

He grinned back at her. "I have a few ideas."

"I'll bet you do." She pressed her lips to his and murmured, "I love you, J.T."

"I love you back."

Don't miss the companion book to *Played*,
featuring Evan Chadwick and J.T. McIntyre

Taken
by Barbara Freethy

Available now

An excerpt follows . . .

"To my wife." Nick Granville gave Kayla Sheridan a dazzling smile as he raised his champagne glass to hers.

Kayla tapped her glass against his. As she looked into the gorgeous blue eyes of the man she had married, she felt a rush of pure joy. She could hardly believe she was married, but an hour ago she'd vowed to love this man above all others. He'd put a ring on her finger and a diamond necklace around her neck and he'd promised to stay forever, which was really all she'd ever wanted. A child of divorce, she'd split her time between two houses, two sets of parents, two cities, and she'd said more than her share of goodbyes. That was over now. She was Mrs. Nicholas Granville, and she would make her marriage stick.

The champagne tickled her throat. She felt almost dizzy with delight. "I can't believe how happy I am," she murmured. "My head is spinning."

"I like it when you're off balance," he said.

"I've been that way since the first second we met,"

she confessed. "Marrying you tonight is the most impulsive, reckless thing I have ever done in my life." She glanced down at the two-carat diamond ring on her finger. It was huge, dramatic, and wildly expensive. It wasn't the kind of ring she'd imagined wearing. She'd thought she'd have something set in an old-fashioned silver band, and in her wildest dreams the stone had never been this big; she was an incredibly lucky woman. And Nick was a very generous man. He'd been spoiling her rotten since their first date.

"You do impulsive well," Nick commented. "Better than I would have thought when we first met."

"Because you're a bad influence," she teased.

His grin broadened. "I've been told that before. Life is supposed to be fun. You are having fun, aren't you?"

"Absolutely. This day has been perfect. The chapel was lovely. The minister made a nice speech about love and marriage. I was afraid it would feel like a quickie wedding, but it didn't. And this hotel room—it's incredible." She waved her hand in the air as she glanced around their honeymoon suite. Nick had ordered in scented candles that bathed the room in a soft light, riotous colorful wildflowers on every table, rose petals lining a romantic path to the bedroom, and silver trays with chocolate-covered strawberries, her favorite dessert. She couldn't have asked for a more romantic setting in which to begin her new life. "You've made me so happy, Nick. You've given me exactly what I wanted."

He nodded. "I feel the same way." He leaned forward and kissed her softly on the mouth, a promise of what was to come. "I'm going to get some ice." He sent her a meaningful look. "I think we'll want some cold champagne . . . later."

A tingle of anticipation ran down her spine. "Don't be long."

He picked up the ice bucket and headed for the door. Once there, he paused and pulled out the antique pocket watch she'd given him as a wedding present a few minutes earlier. "Thanks again for this," he said. "It means a lot to me."

"My grandmother told me I should give it to the man I love. And that's you."

Kayla wanted him to say he loved her, too, but he simply smiled and gave her a little wave as he left the room. It didn't matter that he hadn't said the words. He'd married her. That was what was important. She'd spent most of her twenties with a commitment-phobic boyfriend who couldn't bring himself to pop the question. Nick had told her almost immediately that he intended to be her husband. She'd been swept away by his love and his confidence that they were perfect for each other. Now, only three weeks since that first date, she was his wife. She could hardly believe it. Three weeks! This was definitely the craziest thing she'd ever done.

Well, so what? She'd been responsible and cautious her entire life. She was almost thirty years old. It was about time she took a chance.

Too restless to sit, Kayla got up to look out the window. Their luxurious honeymoon suite was on the hotel's twenty-fifth floor and offered a spectacular view of Lake Tahoe and the surrounding Sierra Nevada mountains. She was only four hours from her home in the San Francisco Bay Area, but it felt like a million miles. Her entire life had changed during a simple wedding ceremony that had been witnessed by only two strangers. It was her one regret that neither her family nor Nick's had attended the wedding. But the past was behind her. Tonight was a new beginning.

Turning away from the window, she entered the bedroom. She took off her dress and slipped on a scarlet see-through silk teddy that left nothing to the imagination. Then she drew a brush through her long, thick, curly brown hair that fell past her shoulders and never seemed to do exactly what she wanted. Her best friend, Samantha, had told her that the messy, curly look was coming back in, so maybe for the first time in her life, Kayla's hair was actually in style.

A flash of insecurity made her wonder if the hot-red teddy was too much or if she should have gone with elegant white silk. But the sophisticated white lingerie she'd considered purchasing had reminded her of something her mother would wear, and she was definitely not her mother.

Smiling at that thought, Kayla couldn't help but be pleased by her reflection in the mirror. There was a sparkle in her brown eyes, a rosy glow in her cheeks. She looked like a woman in love. And that was exactly what she was. She'd made the right decision, she told herself again, trying to ignore the niggling little doubt that wouldn't seem to go away.

The quiet in the room made the voices in her head grow louder. She could hear her mother's shocked and disgusted words: *"Kayla, have you lost your mind? You can't marry a man you've known for three weeks.*

It's foolish. You'll regret this." And her friend Samantha had pleaded with her. *"Just wait until I get back
from London. You need to think, Kayla. How much do
you really know about this man?"*

She knew enough, Kayla told herself firmly. And
this marriage was between her and Nick, no one else.
Turning away from the mirror, she sprayed some per-
fume in the air and walked through it. Debating
whether or not she should wait for Nick in bed, she
tried out several sexy poses on the satiny duvet. She
felt completely ridiculous and chided herself for being
nervous. It wasn't as if they hadn't had sex. And it had
been good. It would be even better tonight because
they were married, they were in love, and they were
committed.

As she stood up, the suite seemed too quiet. She
wondered what was taking Nick so long. The ice machine was only a short distance from the room, and he
had left at least fifteen minutes ago. He must have decided to run downstairs and pick up another special
dessert or more champagne. She smiled at the thought.
Nick was so romantic. He always knew just how to
make her feel loved and cherished.

She walked into the living room and sat down on the
couch to wait. She flipped on the television and ran
through the channels. The minutes continued to tick
by. Glancing at her watch, she realized an hour had
passed. An uneasy feeling swept through her body. She
got up and paced. Within seconds the room grew too
small for her growing agitation. She had a terrible feeling something was wrong.

Returning to the bedroom, she slipped out of her

lingerie and dug through her suitcase for a pair of jeans and a T-shirt. All the while she kept hoping to hear Nick's footsteps or his voice.

Nothing. Silence.

She grabbed the key and left the suite, heading to the nearest ice machine. Nick wasn't there. She tried the other end of the hall, the next floor up, the next floor down. Her heart began to race. She checked the room again, then took the elevator down to the lobby, searching the casino, the shops, the restaurants and bars, and even the parking lot, where Nick's Porsche was parked right where they'd left it. She stopped by the phone bank in the lobby and called the room again. There was still no answer.

Kayla didn't know she was crying until an older woman stopped her by the elevator and asked her if everything was all right.

"My husband. I can't find my husband," she muttered.

The woman gave her a pitying smile. "Story of my life. He'll come back when he runs out of money, honey. They all do."

"He's not gambling. It's our wedding night. He went to get ice." Kayla entered the next elevator, leaving the woman and her disbelieving expression behind. She didn't care what that woman thought. Kayla knew Nick wouldn't gamble away their wedding night. He wouldn't do that to her. But when she returned to her room, it was as empty as when she'd left it.

She didn't know what to do. She sat back down to wait.

When the clock struck midnight, and Nick had been gone for almost five hours, Kayla called the front desk and told them her husband was missing. The hotel sent up George Benedict, an older man who worked for hotel security. After discussing her situation, he assured her they would look for Nick, but there was something in his expression that told her they wouldn't look too hard. It was obvious to Kayla that Mr. Benedict thought Nick was either downstairs gambling and had lost track of time or he had skipped out on her, plain and simple. Neither explanation made sense to her.

Kayla didn't sleep all night. In her mind she ran through a dozen possible scenarios of what could have happened to Nick. Maybe he'd been robbed, hit over the head, knocked unconscious. Maybe he was sitting in a hospital right now with amnesia, not knowing who he was. She hoped to God it wasn't worse than that. No news had to be good news, right?

Finally, she curled up in a chair by the window, watching the moon go down and the sun come up over the lake.

It was the longest night of her life.

A knock came at the door just before nine o'clock in the morning. She ran to open it, hoping she'd see Nick in the hallway, wearing a sheepish smile, offering some crazy explanation.

It wasn't Nick. It was the security guy from the night before, George Benedict. His expression was serious, his eyes somber.

Putting a hand to her suddenly racing heart, she said, "What's happened?"

He held up a black tuxedo jacket. A now limp and wilted red rose boutonniere hung from the lapel. "We found this in a men's room off the lobby. Is it your husband's jacket?"

"I . . . I think so. I don't understand. Where's Nick?"

"We don't know yet, but this was in the pocket." he held out his hand, a solid gold wedding band in his palm.

She took the ring from him, terrified when she read the simple inscription on the inside of the band, FOR-EVER LOVE, the same words that were engraved on her wedding ring. She couldn't breathe, couldn't speak.

This was Nick's ring, the one she'd slipped on his finger when she'd vowed to spend the rest of her life with him. "No," she breathed.

"I've seen it happen before," the older man said gently. "A hasty marriage in a casino chapel, second thoughts . . ."

She saw the pity in his eyes, and she couldn't accept it. "You're wrong. You have to be wrong. Nick loved me. He wanted to get married. It was his idea. His idea," she repeated desperately.

She closed her hand around the ring, her fingers tightening into a fist. Her husband had not run out on her . . . had he?